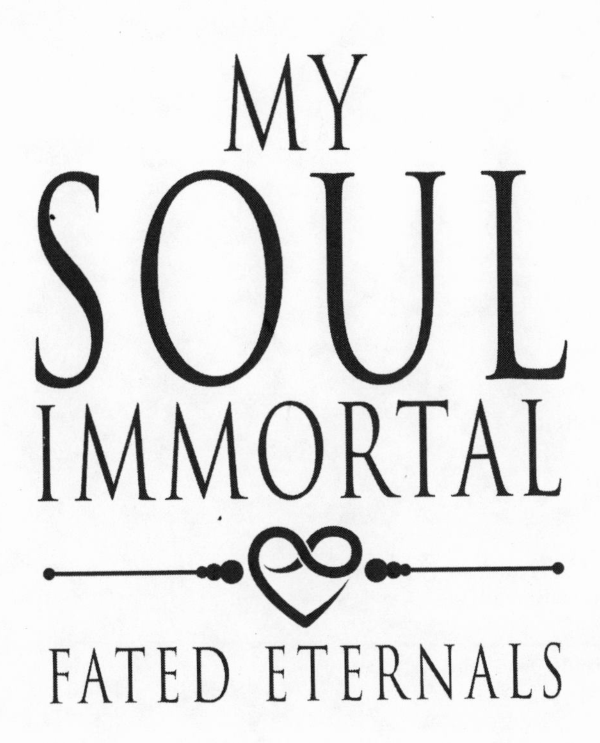

JEN PRINTY

My Soul Immortal
Fated Eternals: Book One
A Red Adept Publishing Book

Red Adept Publishing, LLC
104 Bugenfield Court
Garner, NC 27529
http://RedAdeptPublishing.com/

ISBN 13: 978-1-940215-25-9
ISBN 10: 1-940215-25-0

First Print Edition: February 2014

Cover and Formatting: Streetlight Graphics

For my father, Vern Howell, who smiled back.
I miss you more than words can say.

Death smiles at us all, but all a man can do is smile back.

Marcus Aurelius

PROLOGUE

I STARE AT THE DULL-BLACK BARREL of the 9mm pointed at my chest. My gaze shifts to my assailant's face. His eyes narrow, and his mouth thins for an instant before curving into a smirk.

My grip tightens on the cardboard handle, causing the beer bottles to clink together. There's no way this idiot is going to cost me my Prize Old Ale. It's the store's last six-pack, and who knows when I'll get more? To the ordinary Joe, this might seem like a foolish thing to be concerned about, especially at a time like this. But it's the good stuff, a taste of England, and the only enjoyment I have left.

I raise my free hand and keep my voice soft, as though coaxing a feral animal. "Let's calm down. You don't want to do something you'll regret."

The man's glare slides to the name embroidered above the left pocket of my navy-blue shirt, and he curses. "Jack, huh? Figures. Now you listen to me. I'm in charge here, kid. Remember that!" The weapon jerks to the rhythm of his words, and his eyes, although wild, are committed to finishing what he started. I recognize that look. This man cannot be reasoned with.

Usually, I'm the only customer in here at this godforsaken hour of the night. But tonight, Mae, the elderly lady who lives in the apartment above Irene's

Liquor, must have decided she required self-medication to soothe her nightmares again—a plight I sympathize with. I've carried her groceries upstairs enough times to know her fondness for Jameson and her propensity for using the spirits as a sleeping aid. Unfortunately, she came into the store at the same time the man pulled his gun. Luckily for her, he didn't shoot, but her thready, asthmatic gasp must've made him think she was about to scream for help. He smacked her across her temple as easily as flicking a light switch. And I, of course, unable to mind my own business, stepped in to defend her.

A low moan rises from Mae, now sprawled on the dirty linoleum floor, and drags my attention from the man. Her faded pink and yellow housecoat is spattered with drying blood. Crimson trickles from the gash on her temple. Her eyes are closed, but her chest rises and falls at a steady pace. Still breathing. But for how long? Anger builds deep in my chest, and on cue, the sensation of icy pins and needles shoots down my spine. I drag in a deep, ragged breath.

When my scowl meets his stare, the man squares his shoulders, his nostrils flare, and the gun wobbles. I brace myself in anticipation of the pain. Despite having never been shot before, I'm pretty sure this is going to sting like hell. I find myself wondering if a bullet speeding through my chest might grab *his* attention, and even though I shouldn't allow it to, a sense of hope sprouts.

I gesture at the elderly clerk cowering by the register, and he hunches out of sight. The gunman swings his weapon toward the counter. "Old man, are you deaf or stupid? Stand up!"

With his attention diverted, I set my beer out of harm's way on a shelf behind me. I take advantage of the would-be thief's distraction and lunge.

The gun swings back. A shot rings out. Another follows.

Each impact knocks every wisp of air from my lungs. I

stumble, clutching my abdomen, and struggle for a single breath. The pain feels like two red-hot pokers—blunt ones, at that—being shoved through my insides. The bullets speed through flesh and organs. Spasms quake throughout my body and slam me backward into the shelving. The shelf teeters then collapses, taking me down with it. Glass shatters, and the beer's sweet aroma rises from the shards.

I shove myself up from the wreckage. A mixture of surprise and confusion streaks across the gunman's face, wiping away his triumphant smile. Before he can act, I haul back my arm. A gratifying grunt spews out of him as my fist slams into his nose. Cartilage crunches, and he staggers backward, cupping his face with his hand. I wrench the gun from his loosening grip then smack the butt hard against his skull.

"You don't hit ladies," I say and glance down at the broken bottles at my feet. "And that was the last sixer of Prize, dammit!" I let my finger inch toward the trigger. I can't help but think how easy—perhaps even noble—it would be to rid the world of this scum. Instead, I rein in my instinct and lift the gun over my shoulder. With a restrained swing, I slam the gun against the man's temple.

The man slumps to his knees, disoriented. I walk around him, place the sole of my boot in the middle of his back, and apply pressure. With a rush of breath, he falls to the floor. After tucking the gun into my waistband, I pull his arms behind him and use the nylon twine from a nearby advertising banner to restrain them. He doesn't struggle; actually, he doesn't move at all while I loop the string around his wrists twice and yank it tight, finishing off the tether with a double-constrictor knot. Once his hands are secure, I fold his right leg behind his back and repeat the process then give the twine one last tug, surveying the restraint. All the while, the old clerk frantically blabbers the Lord's Prayer from behind the counter.

The gunman moans, and a silent sigh of relief steals through my lips. He'll have a whopper of a headache, but he'll live.

The heat of adrenaline that pumped through my veins slips away, leaving a sharp pain in my gut. I press my hand to my stomach, and a warm stickiness seeps around my fingers. I shake my head to clear the wooziness, and my eyes flick to the door. Hope withers when I don't see *him.*

"Another no show," I grumble. "Unreliable son of a—"

I stagger forward, my boots sliding in the remains of my beer. The shards of glass and ruddy brown liquid froth around my feet. Nothing worth salvaging. I huff in disgust. Losing the beer pisses me off, sure, but not as much as his failing to show. Again.

I kneel to examine Mae. The bleeding has stopped, and her breathing is strong and steady. She whimpers something incoherent.

"Shhh," I say, wiping a loose strand of white hair from her face.

"Is she okay? I've called 9-1-1. Should be here soon," the clerk says from behind me.

Dammit. I hobble to the register, slam the gun on the stained counter, and duck out of the store into the darkness.

The clerk calls after me. His astonished babble fades away with a swing of the door, only to be replaced by distant sirens.

Safety is five blocks away. Each step brings a new fire of radiating pain. Despite this, I keep a steady pace. The pangs dull my sight, narrowing it to a blurry tunnel, and I frequently melt into the shadows to listen to my surroundings. The slightest sound—the yap of a dog or the honk of a horn—makes me flinch.

At the second intersection, three people pass. A tall, black-haired man escorts his two female companions, a wiry arm around each, his hands low, just above the hems of their skimpy minidresses. I'm a sight to behold. My shirt is bathed in blood, and my jeans are stained with paths of dark scarlet. I lean against a building and pretend to vomit in an attempt to hide the gore. Without warning, the prickle—ancient and fresh, familiar and terrifying—stirs again and quickly blazes into an icy burn that surges up my neck. I've felt the sensation too many times to count—every time I hunger to take a life other than my own. I grit my teeth against the cold. My rigid fingers grasp at crumbling brick and mortar. Each helps me gulp back the craving.

The trio's steps quicken, and the man's baritone laughter echoes. They hustle out of sight, taking the wintry sensation with them. How haven't I realized how close to the surface my monstrous need lurks? I have to get my ass home.

Once I reach Seventy-Fourth Street, I slip into the alley behind a rundown apartment complex. The air is damp and cool. No light invades the confined space. I relax a bit when I catch sight of the gray building. *Hellhole, sweet hellhole.*

I scale the back of the apartment building one step at a time. The fire escape complains with moans and rasps, and so does my body. Every movement brings a new wave of pain, making me groan. I slide into my apartment through my unlocked bathroom window, yank the shade closed, and flick on the light.

I lean against the sink and breathe deeply. My hands grip the porcelain basin, and a young man no more than twenty looks back at me from the mirror. No external scars to remind me of what I've been through. My only blemish is the one I was born with—a sickle-shaped birthmark above my left eye. I see the same disheveled, sable hair of my youth, without an ounce of gray. My wide, square jaw and angular features have no wrinkles even though I'm nearly the ripe old age of one hundred seventy. The vacant blue eyes prove what I already know. I lost my heart a long time ago, buried it too deep. "Forever blessed. What a joke."

After splashing frigid water on my face, I strip off my blood-soaked shirt and hunch my back to examine my wounds in the mirror. The jagged holes have begun to heal—two entrances and one exit. I rub my hand along my spine, finding the skin hot to the touch. I press against the hard, pea-sized protrusion under the surface about a third of the way up my back, and I grimace. But I can't do anything about the bullet now. No time.

I wonder how long it'll be until the shooting makes the news. Any normal guy would be bleeding out in the gutter after taking two bullets to the abdomen. If I'm found healed and healthy, I'll become a sideshow freak and live out the rest of my existence Lord knows where.

I tug on a T-shirt and exchange my blood-splattered jeans for a clean pair, then I begin shoving my few belongings into a shabby black duffel.

"If he'd just shown up tonight, I wouldn't have to deal with this crap right now." I thrust another handful of dirty socks into the bag.

This isn't the first time Death has let me down. He's stood me up many times—stabbed through the heart and bleeding to death in a pool of my own blood, sitting on the rocky bottom of a lake until every breath left my body—the list goes on. Pain is as reliable as gravity, but Death never keeps his appointments. If he did, I would be enjoying the good life in paradise, with Lydia.

At the thought of her, the ever-present ache grows as if talons are ripping away pieces of my heart. Somehow, it keeps its endless rhythm. I know all too well that some wounds cannot heal. Instead, they remain open and raw. Having someone important torn away is bound to leave a hole. I gulp a deep breath, and anxiety winds into a ball in my stomach. Memories leak in behind my eyes, calling to me, but I groan and wrench my head to the side, ruthlessly shoving them back. I don't have time for an episode right now; I still have one task left to do. I stretch a yellowed map along the flaky gray walls and pin thumbtacks into each curled corner. No one will notice, let alone care about, the holes in the poorly treated drywall.

I step back and kiss the dart I swiped from a pub in York back in 1918 on the day my sister died and I decided to quit England for good. Since then, the old dart's become a talisman of sorts. "Where are we going this time, old friend?"

With a flick of my wrist, the dart glides through the air and sticks into the map with a thud. Just my luck. It landed in the damn Atlantic Ocean. Not caring where I end up, I pick the closest city. *Portland, Maine. Bloody marvelous.* Still muttering under my breath about the annoyances of moving, I roll up the map and thrust it into the black duffel. I zip the bag and sling the strap over my shoulder, almost forgetting my knapsack as I walk out of the apartment and into the graffiti-tagged hallway.

The staircase is empty, so I punt the duffel down each flight of stairs to rid myself of some of the frustration. It somersaults and rolls down the steps without objection. At the bottom, I fling the bag onto my shoulder. Taking in a deep breath, I open the door and slink into the night, being careful to look up and down the sidewalk. No police, no sirens, no nothing. On the dark, lonely street, I secure the knapsack to the backseat of my old Triumph Bonneville with a couple bungees. After I slip the strap of the duffel over my head and shoulder, I climb onto the bike. I wriggle around, trying to find the most comfortable position. Although no longer painful, my back is tender, and the bag's weight is a persistent reminder. I give up on comfort and turn the ignition. The motorcycle rumbles to life. I head out of Los Angeles and onto the open road.

CHAPTER ONE

Hours of steady rainfall leave the streets glistening with a silver sheen. People scurry past on the sidewalk as though trying to evade the drops, but there's no escape here. I've been in Portland, Maine, for weeks. Every day and every night, it rains, and I'm sick of it. My hatred for the rain is deep-seated. While Lydia lived, we both loved the gentle patter of a spring shower and the clatter of a late-autumn storm. Now the rain that dampens my clothes depresses my spirit. Too many memories cling to each stinging drop. But each moment remembered is of a century ago, and senility has yet to creep in to grant me a reprieve. The unrelenting spring weather seems to hear my inner complaints and take offense, because the rainfall intensifies.

"First a rat-infested hellhole, and now this dreary place." I glare up at the sky, hoping the elements can hear me. At least this particular dreary place has a bookshop, somewhere around here. I glance at the address I Sharpied onto my palm. I hope the help-wanted ad was current. The loss of Lydia may have transformed me from an upstanding member of society into a drifter, but a man's got to eat. Seems starvation can't do me in. Gravedigger and mechanic, bartender to tracklayer—the work or pay never mattered. I've squirreled away enough money to live completely off the radar for a while, in case my secret is discovered. But other than that, I've always been more concerned with obtaining a place in the hereafter than any monetary gain.

With the soaked hood of my sweatshirt up over my head, I slosh through puddles. Drops of rain pool like beads along the hood's rim. Maybe I need to come up with a better method of choosing my next home. This place reminds me too much of England. Old, yes. Merry, no. The bloody island has been the cause of many a foul mood of mine. I suppose I could leave and settle somewhere else. *Somewhere sunny*, I think, once more glaring skyward. But fleeing for this reason would feel like failure, as if my inability to forgive the past and move on with the present got the better of me yet again. Neither my pride nor stubbornness will stand for that. I'm staying.

For the thousandth time, I replay the incident that led me to this soggy city. I seem to have the innate ability of choosing the wrong thing at the wrong time, and allowing myself to be shot in the gut is the best example yet. I still have the little souvenir lodged in the muscle of my back to prove it. And after many attempts at Tug of War, I can't extract the blasted slug. *As if Death would take notice of me after all this time.* I laugh and shake my head. *Idiot.*

Deep in thought, I round the corner and collide with someone. My hapless victim is knocked to the ground, while I merely stagger backward. Her legs, arms, and knapsack become a tangled mess of flailing appendages.

"Sorry. You all right?" I extend my hand to help.

"I'm fine," she says from under a shapeless mound of yellow rain poncho among the puddles.

From the spirit of her tone, she seems unharmed. I probably bruised her ego, but little else. Relieved and amused, I suppress a laugh. "I need to pay better attention to where I'm going."

"Obviously," she mumbles, grabbing her knapsack.

Either unwilling or unable to see my hand, palm up, still waiting, she hops to her feet. From beneath the brim of her oversized hood, she surveys me. A pair of vivid emerald eyes burn into mine.

"Lydia?" I whisper. I stagger backward, angry at the delusion. Any memory connected to her reigns with perfect clarity. But must I be tormented every waking moment? My heart pounds in my ears, and without thought, I reach for her.

She flinches. Her reaction draws me back from a memory. My arm falls to my side, but my focus doesn't leave her eyes. She must be real. The desire to touch her surges again, and I need every bit of self-control to thrust my fists deep into my pockets.

Her guarded eyes narrow. She tucks an escaping golden strand into the confines of her hood. "Do I know you?"

I can't peel my gaze from those hypnotic eyes, and I stutter out a reply. "N-no, you remind me of someone. Forgive me."

Her attention drifts away and breaks my trance, allowing my eyes to fall to the sidewalk. I concentrate on the diagonal pattern of the red bricks, but the distraction doesn't help, and breathing has become impossible. My hands tremble in my pockets.

A car horn blatting jolts me back to a semblance of reality. When I look around, she's gone. The girl seems to have vanished into thin air, and I wonder again if Lydia's haunting me. I snort. *Sure, some guy points a gun to your chest, no problem. You beat the shit out of him. A girl looks at you, and you freeze up, lose the ability to speak, and think your long-lost love is visiting you from beyond the grave. What are you? Twelve?*

I thrust the incident out of my mind and trudge on down the sidewalk. I won't allow my stupidity to take over the day. *Sanity, remember sanity.* I repeat the mantra in my head.

Soon, I find the shop I've been looking for—a tiny dilapidated used bookstore with a faded sign that reads Rare Books. It's a grungy-looking place, and I can't tell if it's open or closed. The black-and-orange help-wanted sign stuck cock-eyed in the window suggests I'm right, so I try the door.

A tired buzzer whines, announcing my arrival. I remove my rain-soaked sweatshirt, straighten my clothes, and rake my fingers through my damp, tangled hair in an attempt to look presentable. With a deep breath, I swallow any lingering distress from the incident with the girl in the poncho. The musty smells of age-old paper and dust as well as a faint, sweet trace of pipe smoke fill my nostrils, and I find the scents comforting.

A balding man with horn-rimmed glasses sticks his head out from behind a row of bookshelves. The creases around his eyes fan out as he squints in my direction. "Hello. Can I help you?" he asks much more loudly than the distance demands. "You got here just in time. I was about to close up. It's been quiet 'round here today. Stupid rain."

"I'm here for the assistant clerk's position," I say, doubting that the weather can account for the lack of patrons.

"Oh, yes, yes." A wide grin creases the man's thin face and stretches wrinkles along his pale leathery cheeks. He studies me with kind eyes before beckoning me to follow. He meanders toward the back. Towering bookshelves overemphasize his spare stature.

In a small office space at the rear of the shop, the man pushes his glasses up the bridge of his nose and shuffles through a mess of papers strewn across a desk. It's quickly clear why he needs an assistant. The creased and coffee-stained application forms are at the bottom of the pile. He offers me the cleanest one, along with a pen.

The doorbell groans a distorted melody, announcing another arrival. The man excuses himself and lumbers to the front. From the sound of the resulting banter, the bookshop owner and his lady customer know each other well. She sounds like the kind of grandma who always has fresh cookies in her kitchen.

My attention swings back to the task at hand, and I scan through the tedious questions I've seen thousands of times before. When I've finished answering each question, I place the application and pen on the cluttered desk and step from the office to have a look around.

I wander down a cramped aisle. The floor is littered with novels of all shapes and sizes. The shelves bulge with random selections. A couple gems are hidden among the rabble, and my fingers run down the spine of a familiar leather-bound book. *Ancient Fairy Tales: Myths and Legends* is engraved in gilt across the rich-amber leather.

My hands quake. Memories delve deeper into a long-gone time. I can still smell the sweet floral fragrance of Lydia's hair. The haunting tingle of her touch runs up my arm, stealing my breath. I can see her eyes sparkle in the pale gaslight and the devilish grin that crosses her pink, full...

"Dammit all!" *Damn those eyes! Damn that phantom girl!* I clutch my tightened chest and lean against the bookshelf to steady myself. As the intense pain dissipates and returns to the standard hollow ache, a face full of concern peers down the aisle. Her sharp, youthful eyes don't correspond to the age that surrounds them. Her gray hair tied back into a sloppy ponytail and her dated outfit suggest she's stuck in a previous decade. She says something, but I can't hear through the ringing in my ears. "Sorry?"

"I said, are you all right?" the woman asks.

Ah, the new arrival. I force a grin. *Just talking to myself and clutching my chest. The usual.* "Yes, fine."

She looks skeptical. "You were in a lot of pain. Do you want me to call someone?"

"No. Heartburn." I pat my chest as I walk slowly down the narrow aisle. "Fine now. Too much curry for breakfast."

She hangs back, uncertain. "Are you sure? My late husband had a heart attack. You're young and all, but—"

"I'm fine," I say flatly. Hurt enters her eyes, and my regret surges. "Thank you, though," I add.

Her weathered lips produce a grin. "So, you're here for the clerk's position?"

I nod.

"That's good. Ed needs the help, whether he knows it or not."

"Ed?"

"Of course he didn't introduce himself," she mutters with a roll of her eyes. "Ed's the shop owner. And I'm Sally."

"Nice to meet you. Jack." I bow my head in greeting. I've carried the habit, which I can't seem to break, with me through the years. "Speaking of Ed, where did he go?"

"Oh, he's out back, getting a book I've been wanting forever." I sense a glimmer of excitement in her words. She pauses and blushes, then her voice falls to a whisper. "The shop is a bit rundown, I know, but Ed's got the best collection of antique books in the area, maybe the Northeast. If Ed can't find it, you can bet your life it doesn't exist."

"Here it is," Ed announces. He marches toward us, carrying the book as if it's a bar of gold.

After a euphoric Sally has left, Ed squints at me and asks, "When can you start?"

"But, you haven't even looked at my application yet, sir."

"I know. Ed Growley, by the way."

"Jack Hammond."

We shake hands, and Ed breaks into a crooked smile. "I'm a good judge of people. You're a normal enough guy. I can tell. Nothing like the kook I had working for me last month. Crazy hippie. Besides, Sally likes you. And don't tell her, because it will go straight to her head, but she's never wrong. The job's yours if you want it."

Ha! Normal? I almost laugh. "I can start tomorrow."

"Excellent! I have lots for you to do."

I smile, glancing around. *Nothing like stating the obvious.*

"Every summer, the shop runs a lecture series. It's a great way to bring in the tourists. The events aren't grand affairs, just a bit of coffee and snacks of some sort. Sally's an author, and her second book—or is it her third?" Ed stops and thinks, then shrugs. "Anywho, her next book is coming out in a few weeks, and we'll be hosting the book's launch as part of the series." He smiles proudly.

"Sounds good." I nod.

Before I leave, I drop the fairy-tale gem onto the counter. *Stupid. Idiotic. Self-defeating.* I should be avoiding the past, not bring a piece of nostalgia home with me. "I'll take this one."

"Ahhh, *Ancient Fairy Tales*. Good choice." He shoves the book in a plastic bag with Rare Books printed in burgundy across the front.

I groan internally at my impulsive act and dig my wallet out of my back pocket.

Out on the wet sidewalk, I make it three blocks before wetness tickles my cheek. I glower at the sky. It had previously hinted of relief but changes its mind and opens the floodgates. I throw the clouds the one-finger salute, hug the bag close to my chest, and dart into the nearest shop to escape the downpour. Shaking the droplets from my hair, I look around and find a coffeehouse.

Old Port Java is alive with conversation and laughter. The aroma of brewing coffee fills the air. I grab a cup of dark roast and a bagel then sit to wait out the deluge. At a table tucked away in the corner, I mull over the poncho girl. "An apparition or flashback. Or, hell, a psychotic episode." I chuckle without humor. The smallest trifle can spark a flashback: the scent of flowers—particularly roses—a familiar tune, a melodic laugh. But those eyes. No wonder the memories were so vivid and painful.

I wish I'd been more observant or been able to speak. All I remember is a strand of golden blond hair. And poncho girl's rich-green eyes were comparable to a precious emerald. Lydia's eyes. Over the years, I've had run-ins with eyes in all shades of green. There was that pair the color of moss in the Metro of East LA and a celadon set in New Orleans. Each time I was confronted, my stomach twinged or my limbs quivered. But nothing equaled this. Then again, never before were they her double.

That night in bed, I stare at the peeling, bubbled wallpaper that former tenants decided would look good on the bedroom ceiling. Interior designers, they were not. My one-bedroom apartment is furnished with an assemblage of mismatched seventies-style furniture, all probably found at yard sales. Despite the dull thudding of rap music through the wall behind my headboard, my mind is a hive of activity, swirling with impressions and theories about the young woman with the piercing eyes. Finally, close to three o'clock, sleep wins and claims me.

I open my eyes to a dream. Icy pellets of rain hit my face like a hail of bullets. I make my way back to the grove of elms. In the distance, Wind Rush House beckons to me. Even in the dimming light, the beauty of the rolling countryside can't overshadow the limestone estate's grandeur. My body is numb, but Dr. Edmunds's damning words roll through my head. *There's no more to be done.* I won't accept that she's dying. I can't, because her dying means I die, too. I cannot exist without her.

With a quick shake of my head, I blink away any betraying tears and step beneath the canopy of swaying branches, where I kept vigil for the past week. The wind pierces my thin shirt. With trembling hands, I tug my frock coat tight around my chest, and I draw closer to the trunk where I asked Lydia to be my bride. Despite the storm, I feel as if I can sense a terrible stillness cloaking the old Jacobean-style manor, then a candle appears in the upper-east window. It's Lady Ashford's signal telling me Lydia's alive. A relieved sigh breaks through my lips. I long to be with her and ache to comfort her, but Sir Robert will never invite me into the house again.

The sound of church bells resounds over the flurry of drumming rain. Then a lone owl screeches through the tall treetops. An omen. When I look at the window again, the light is gone, and the room is dark. I collapse against the unforgiving trunk. Nausea rolls over me, and I retch.

Chilled to the bone, I bolt upright in my bed, my heart pounding. My skin is drenched in sweat, and my breathing comes in labored bursts, fighting to keep pace with my heartbeats. *Breathe. Breathe. Breathe.* I close my eyes, but my relief is snatched away by a pair of emerald eyes gazing back at me. Maybe those sparkling orbs are tattooed under my eyelids. How else could I see them so clearly?

"And how many times am I going to be forced to relive that night?" I hiss between clamped teeth, trying to conquer the pain of the swelling ache.

I struggle into a pair of jeans and yank on the striped shirt I laid out the night before. I grab my damp hooded sweatshirt from the coat hook and trudge down the stairs into the morning drizzle.

CHAPTER TWO

BLUE.
Brown.
Blue.

Hazel.

Not one pair of eyes belongs to her.

The mist intensifies the salty scent in the air as the dampness persists. Unnerved by my new level of stupidity, I feel my frustration burn against the bleakness. If I were smart, I would be sitting in a warm coffee shop, sipping a cup of joe and gnawing on a poppy seed bagel. But I'm not. I'm here, leaning against a low brick wall that guards a collection of bedraggled petunias, on the street corner where I encountered that enigmatic girl one week ago. Obviously, age hasn't made me wiser, because my obsession grows by the day, fueled by a gravitational force even I don't understand. She's not Lydia; she can't be. I would be deceiving myself if I thought her eye color was due to anything more than ancestry or coincidence.

"Stupid. Stupid. Stupid..." I let my head fall back, and I stare at the clouded heavens, wondering if this pursuit has become more important than my own mental health. I grumble a string of curses behind my pursed lips when I silently confess the answer.

I've had two goals for over a hundred years—sanity and death. Psychologists would say those intentions lie in direct conflict with one another, but I'm fairly certain those doctors never handled a case like mine. For me, they're linked. One relies on the other. Nevertheless, as I know all too well, goals sometimes lead to bad choices. The worst thus far were my dealings with Richard Hake. I might have been born immortal, but it was Hake and my actions because of him that awakened my appetite to kill.

In the spring of 1864, I left the fresh air and open spaces of Lidcombe for the foggy, teeming streets of London. I was still dealing with the reality that Lydia was gone, and after several failed attempts at death, I still hadn't joined her. I tried to drown my sorrows in all the darkness London had to offer. As I struggled to hold on to the small amount of sanity I had left, I found the adrenaline rush of a Whitechapel fight house. The smell of sweat and blood permeated the room where men pummeled each other for money, thrills, and pride. My first fight left me with two dislocated ribs and a cut to my chin, but the next night, I returned. Strangely enough, the violence awoke something and helped me forget. Even though my release lasted only a moment, I welcomed the fleeting liberation. That was where Hake found me and spilled his golden words into my ear. Having heard his reputation on the crooked streets of the slums, I should have walked away right then, but he made a convincing argument I couldn't refuse.

"I can make you rich, loved, and happy," he promised. I didn't care about the money, and I knew love dwelled out of reach. But the happiness guarantee—that caught my attention. One year later, Hake lay dead, and I was on the run. To this day, I still feel the same wintry prickle along my spine, the same evocative rush that arose the night I killed him. Before his murder, I had known I was different and unable to die, but after that horrific event, I realized how dark I really am on the inside.

"What kind of monster does that make me?" I mutter to the petunias.

I have no idea. This question has preyed on me ever since I realized I was different, because if I discover what I am, I might know how to die. Every creature of myth and legend has a means of ending its torment. Vampires have their stakes. Werewolves, their silver. If the fables ring true, then logically I should have one, too. However, years have passed, and I'm no closer to the truth. And my confidence in finding an answer has waned.

I breathe deep, filling my lungs with the dank morning air. With a glance at my watch, I realize I have precisely four minutes until I'm due at work. No time for coffee. I huff in disgust and push away from the wall. On the way to the bookstore, I'm captivated by every flicker of gold, and my head swivels toward each fair-haired girl. *This is out of control,* I think then force my searching gaze to the sidewalk. Part of me still wonders whether the whole incident is a delusion. That would mean I've failed—and my sanity is gone—but I'm not ready to concede. Not yet.

I arrive with a minute to spare. Ed is slouched behind the counter, his glasses sliding down the bridge of his nose. He absentmindedly chews on the end of a pen while scowling at the newspaper.

"Hey, do you know what a four-letter word for a Glaswegian girl might be?" he asks without glancing up from the crossword.

"Lass."

"Ha. Right. Okay, try this one, kid. What are coffin flags called? Nine-letter word. Starts with a *B*."

Kid? I suppose it's better than Sport or Tiger. I suppress a sigh. "No idea. Sorry, Gramps."

Unimpressed, Ed shifts his eyes to me, and his heavy gray brows rise. "There's coffee in the back if you want some, kiddo. Hope you can handle it. I like it strong. Then again, maybe it will put some hair on that chest." He grins with self-satisfaction and returns to his paper.

In need of heat and caffeine, I chuckle and steer myself toward the office. As I drink, my icy hands cling to the warmth of the Styrofoam cup, and I realize that within a short time, Ed and I have fallen into an easy friendship of sorts. So strange. My life has been solitary for a century, not by choice, necessarily, but outliving everyone tends to ruin relationships.

"Which is the exact reason you should be avoiding the street corner and that girl, you idiot," I grumble then suck down the last dregs of coffee and chuck the cup in the trash. A consuming heat overtakes my irritation at letting my thoughts roam to her again.

The busy morning gives way to a slow afternoon, and I force my mind to concentrate on a new shipment of books. But every time I lower my guard, the little thought-stealer slips into my head.

Around four, Ed pops his head into the office, an apologetic grin strung along his lips. "I need to take off a little early. Can you close up?"

"Sure. Everything okay?"

"Sally called. The pipes under her sink are leaking. Don't know what she thinks I can do about it. Never been handy, but I probably should go over and give it the old college try."

A few minutes after he leaves, the buzzer whines. A dozen steps toward the front of the store, I run straight into a sight I hadn't expected. My breath hitches when I spy a slender woman gazing at the rows of books. Waves of gold cascade down her back. I slow as preservation fights for dominance. Struggling to suppress the conflict between my head and my heart, I force my feet to keep moving. My focus is transfixed by the swaying blond hair.

The woman turns and displays a set of deep-brown eyes, almost the color of chocolate. My lips surrender to the force of a disappointed exhale. I allowed hope to creep in, and my emotions paid the price. "How may I help you?" I ask, forcing a smile.

"I heard this was the best place for antique books."

I nod.

"I'm looking for an early edition of *Pride and Prejudice.* Please say you have one."

I want to roll my eyes, but I resist. The loss of Lydia has left me cynical, to be sure, but times haven't changed all that much. Every woman still longs for her very own Mr. Darcy. *He doesn't exist. He's fictional.* I'll never understand the attraction, but maybe that's because I've known his type in the flesh. He's never as appealing in person as he is on paper.

Chocolate eyes stare, waiting for an answer.

"Uh, yes, ma'am. We have a vast collection of Miss Austen this way." I berate myself for my new round of stupidity as I lead the way toward the rear aisle.

After the girl leaves, purchase in hand, I flip the sign to CLOSED. It's a little early, but my nerves are shot. "Maybe this is more than an episode. Maybe it's a whole psychotic break." I sigh. "I need a drink."

After locking up, I walk out the door and into the puddle-strewn sidewalk. Instead of taking my usual route past a small park, I take a sharp right, cutting through the park. A blustery, salty wind whips through cramped alleyways leading to the ocean, making me shiver. I slip my hands into my pockets and hunch my shoulders although the actions do little to defy the chill. Evening settles in around me, staining the rows of uninspired brick buildings with elongated shadows. Two miles of walking down a deserted side street dumps me in a part of the city I've never seen. The buildings here show more wear than the parts of the city to which I've grown accustomed. I stop, glancing around to get my bearings. A small lit sign grabs my attention. ROSIE'S, it reads, with a slanted martini glass painted across the *R.* "Perfect."

The bar's boisterous atmosphere deters my sour mood. Blues music twangs in the background. Glowing advertisements for the different beers they stock line the walls. A waitress hustles around the small circular tables, delivering drinks, plates, and pails of peanuts. I slip onto a beat-up stool at the far end of the bar and catch the bartender's attention. "Bottle of Prize."

"Sorry." She shakes her fiery hair at me.

Oh, look. A new layer of hell. "Whatever's on tap, then."

"ID?"

A man sitting on the stool next to mine chuckles.

I lob a dirty look in his direction as I dig my wallet from my jeans pocket, then I hand my forged ID to the redhead. She scrutinizes and flips the plastic over several times before returning it with a shrug and a smile.

Having my age questioned at every bar, pub, and restaurant began to grate on my nerves after a few decades. I often wondered why my body stopped aging when I was so young. Why twenty? Why not thirty, fifty, or even fifteen? I found the closest thing to an answer years earlier, sitting in the Detroit Metro Airport, waiting for a flight. I grabbed a newspaper to kill some time and found myself intrigued by an article about the medical fountain of youth. According to the article, a human body matures until age twenty. After that, erosion sets in. No eroding, no aging, it was as simple as that, but there, the article's help ended. The writer went on to discuss chromosomes, telomeres, and broken DNA, concluding that even if scientists discovered a genetic off-switch, living forever would still be impossible. Anybody who evaded old age would eventually succumb to cancer, disease, or illness. *If only I could be so lucky.*

When the bartender returns, she sets a frosty mug in front of me. I sip the icy froth and try to relax, but the muscles in my neck and shoulders remain tense. I realize as ridiculous as my wish is, I wanted the blonde to be Green Eyes, not just to prove who she's not, but to know who she is. *Fantastic. Nicknaming a delusion. Yeah, this is healthy.*

Before this girl, I'd settled into the remnants of a life—the scraps that fate left me—which wasn't easy by any means. But what else could I do? However, the leftovers don't seem to be enough anymore. Why? Because I want to be happy? No, that word's too strong. I want to not be broken anymore. *Bloody hell. What has seeing those eyes in the flesh done to me? I sound like such a pansy.* An irritated huff seeps between my lips. I swallow the last gulp of beer and then raise my glass to ask for another.

When the bartender returns, she glares at my neighbor and points at the prominent No Smoking sign hanging over her head. "Sir, you can't smoke in here."

The middle-aged man takes a long drag on his cigarette. He lets ribbons of smoke flow from his nostrils. An icy chill touches the base of my neck. Confused, I swat the sensation away.

"Those things will kill you anyway," she hisses.

His humorless laugh rumbles as he stamps out the butt in the peanut bowl. "I wish."

I half expect her to throw him out. Instead, she gives the man a disgusted look, removes the bowl, and walks away with a roll of her eyes. I notice a half-empty bottle of fifteen-year-old single-malt scotch in front of him. Definitely the reason for her understanding.

"Am I right, Jack?" A humorless smirk plays along his lips.

My gut twists, and despite the beer, my throat goes dry. Shifting my attention to the game on the beat-up TV behind the bar, I ignore him, but when he laughs again, my eyes meet his. He has a straight nose, a pointed chin, eyes the color of sapphires, and a jagged scar across his right cheekbone. Memories file through my mind, but I find nothing.

"I suppose you wouldn't remember me. It was a long time ago," he finally says.

I glower at the amber liquid in my mug, but my anxiety

rises, and sweat moistens my palms and beads along my brow. “You’re mistaken. I don’t know you.”

“A hundred bucks says you do.”

“Look. I’m not in the mood for games. Why don’t you just tell me what you want, and we’ll be done with it?”

“It’s just nice to chat with a peer now and again.”

“Peer?”

His smile begins rather subdued, then his mouth expands into a toothy grin. He glances over his shoulder as he rolls an unlit cigarette between his thumb and forefinger.

“You know what I am?” I ask as an uncontrollable hope builds.

The man ignores my question. His sapphire eyes fix on something at the back of the room. Annoyed, I follow his gaze and spot a young couple dancing in red-hued lighting. As the woman’s fingers sweep through her companion’s hair, their bodies sway together as one. The scene is irritating, I agree, but not unusual to the setting. I peer back at the sapphire-eyed man, but his focus has not changed. His intense interest in the young couple is odd if not bizarre. I hope I haven’t stepped into some lovers’ tiff. A moment or two later, the sultry melody ends and becomes a rhythmic throbbing. The couple step from the dance floor. Arms entwined, they head for the exit. I grimace when the young chap doesn’t hold the door for his dance partner. *Maybe chivalry is dead.* My attention swings back to the man.

He stands, and after a quick bow of his head, he starts for the door. “Another time.”

“What? No!” A frenzied need bubbles to the surface, causing me to grab for the sleeve of his blazer, but the material slips through my fingers like mercury. His wiry form glides out of the bar like the wind, following the couple into the night.

I jump to my feet and hurry past the counter toward the exit, but I’m hauled backward before I get very far. A vise-like grip holds me fast. The wide hand locked around my forearm belongs to a mountain of a man. Thick, graying hair, long and straggly, billows around his weathered face. He scowls at me as whiffs of alcohol swirl from him. "I got him for ya, Rosie."

"Leaving without paying? Not in my joint. You can pay for your rude friend, too," Rosie says, motioning toward the door with her head.

I toss the contents of my wallet onto the bar and hope it's enough.

"That'll do." Rosie nods to Mountain Man.

To my relief, he releases me.

"But don't come back!" Rosie yells.

I burst out the door onto the deserted street. The only loiterers are a row of cast-iron streetlamps sending smudged golden beams across the canvas of night. *Where could he have disappeared to so fast?* My pulse accelerates, and I pick a direction, sprinting down the one-way street in the direction of the wharfs, shooting frantic glances down each side street and alley. Still nothing. With a fluid motion, I head in the opposite direction, but the man is gone, taking his answers with him.

Anger and pain press in, and I walk toward Rosie's. I need a minute of peace, just a few moments to forget about Lydia, the girl, and my most recent failed attempt to discover what I am. And I know exactly how to achieve that level of release.

Mountain Man looks up from his bottle of Bud Light as I step in. Then he grins, showing off missing teeth. "Got a death wish, dumbass?"

I laugh. He has no idea.

"Didn't you hear Rosie? She said don't come back." He slides from the stool and towers over my six feet.

"Don't hurt him too bad, Tank," Rosie says from behind the bar. The other patrons' laughter follows in unison.

I snorted. "Tank? You've got to be kidding me. Who names their kid 'Tank'? Your mum wasn't a bright one, was she? Maybe she was in the tank when she had you, or is she built like a tank?" My goading is lame. Nevertheless, I need the fight to be a good one. No better way to secure that than to take a potshot at his mother.

Tank growls, and my smile widens.

"Not in here. Take it outside!" Rosie hisses.

I back out the door, and the mountain follows. "Come on," I say. "Bigger they are..."

A fist slams into my jaw. My ass hits the pavement, making my ears ring. *Oh yeah, the harder they hit.*

I stagger to my feet. I'm out of practice; that's for damn sure. I raise my fists and tuck in my elbows. *Time to return the favor.* I land a quick right hook on Mountain Man's chin, smearing his grin with his own blood.

Tank's massive head swings, but to my surprise, his stance doesn't budge. With a dirty shirtsleeve, he wipes blood from his split lip. I sense the ruse and pivot my shoulder just as his sucker punch flies toward my face. The blow grazes my forearm.

His other massive paw snags my collar. I would love to stagger away and create some space between us, but I can't. Tank's fist slams the lead slug still lodged in my back. Fiery ripples arc through me, and I twist in agony. Tank spins me free of his grip, and his uppercut thuds into my chin. Sparks fly across my vision. The world spins, then my palms and knees grate across cold asphalt.

Tank grabs my arm and drags me out of the road. Whiffs of vapor escape his muttering lips. He leans me against a lamppost and looks me straight in the eye. "Stay," he says. Then he returns to the bar.

I shove myself up. Back burning, jaw aching, I limp home with a shattered ego and bruised hide. At the apartment, I hold a bag of frozen peas to my swollen jaw and scour my mind for a memory of the sapphire-eyed man who might hold the key to what I am. After sifting through numerous images, I find nothing. His scar taunts me. Despite all the battering I've put my body through, I've never acquired one. The remnant of a jagged gash across his cheek hints he knows how to incur damage. Or he's a complete fraud. Nevertheless, the only lead I've had in decades slipped away. My grip tightens on the bag. *Pop!* Peas scatter all over the table and floor. I struggle out of the chair like a decrepit old man half my age. Muscles along my spine burn and cramp in objection to the smallest movement. I grit my teeth and work hard to disregard the flaring pain. I take in a long, deep breath, and the discomfort melts into tingling warmth. Miracle or curse, I'm healed again. Nothing of the fight remains; all the bruises faded into healthy skin. While sweeping up the peas, I curse the sapphire-eyed devil. Why do flashbacks flood in with such clarity, but helpful memories evade me? With my floor once again pea-free, I pitch the broom into the closet and slam the door.

Tired and drained, I slump onto the vinyl swivel chair of the lime-green dinette set. This encounter was the perfect reminder that I need to focus on things that will get me to Lydia, not on a green-eyed delusion that's doing me no good. I know I can't visit that street corner again.

CHAPTER THREE

WITH A SNAP OF MY wrist, the rolled-up newspaper smacks the coffee shop table, almost spilling my drink. The paper unfurls, and the front-page headline reads: DOUBLE HOMICIDE. SUSPECT UNKNOWN.

I sink into my chair. The couple from Rosie's Bar stare up at me from the printed page. The story that follows sends a chill straight through me.

> *Paul Lamonte, 23, of Portland, and Cindy Mears, 22, of Falmouth, were discovered at the parking garage at 182 Fore Street on Friday night, shortly before midnight. Portland Police Chief Daniel Richards said the victims had been shot to death in the late evening hours.*
>
> *Richards said drugs might have been involved, but there are no suspects.*
>
> *Lamonte and Mears were last seen leaving Tommy's Variety Store at 11:30 Friday evening. A man seen with the couple is wanted for questioning. He is described as 6'2" with short black hair and blue eyes. He was last seen wearing a black blazer, black*

shirt, and jeans. The only distinguishing feature is a scar across his right cheek. Anyone with information should call the Portland Police Department.

True, the sapphire-eyed man had been watching them, his expression focused like a predator zeroing in on the weakest member of the herd. Then he ran out after them. By themselves, these facts could lead to different conclusions, but the article suggested that he'd followed them. What bothers me even more is if the man was telling the truth, and we're cut from the same cloth, killing Hake might not have been a horrid misstep but a part of my nature. I've only killed once, but the almost-euphoric thrill that followed frightened me. After Hake's death, I vowed never to take another life again—except my own.

"And I let the bastard slip through my fingers." I heave a sigh and hang my head, knowing I would sell my soul for an answer. *That is, if I had one to offer.*

A wry smile tugs at my lips. I haven't considered the possibility for a long time, not since Hake's death. But now, with all the advances in technology at my fingertips, perhaps the time has come to revisit my old theory. Besides, diving into research might help with my new pursuit and keep me from chasing after the phantom girl.

The door flies open, interrupting my thoughts and stealing my gaze from the photos. The wind and the sound of drumming rain slip in behind a figure whose face and form are disguised by an oversized sunshine-yellow rain poncho. The color steals my breath and sends legions of tiny butterflies cascading into my stomach. Could this really be her? I hate to even hope.

My eyes follow the figure, who hustles behind the counter. I quash my anticipation. *Can't be,* I tell myself repeatedly.

"Sorry I'm late, Rachel. My alarm clock picked this morning to die." Her apologetic ramble holds a tint of annoyance.

Now not even doubt can persuade me. The late employee is Green Eyes. Unprepared for how to handle this situation, I return to the article. My heart rate accelerates. Sweat breaks out across my neck. *Okay, Sherlock, you wanted to find her. You got your wish. Now what?* Instead of stepping up to the counter and introducing myself like any normal gentleman, I eavesdrop on her conversation. I know it's rude, but I need to know about her, and at least for the moment, I've lost my nerve.

The girls' chitchat covers the inclement weather, then they babble on about Rachel's boyfriend. Laughter chimes through the shop, and my mind warps the sound into Lydia's bell-like laugh. *Delusions up to their old tricks again, no doubt.* Disapproval grows in my gut, but the craving to know more swells, regardless of my wishes. *Not Lydia*, I remind myself, but I can't help listening more closely.

Their chatter halts at the singsong tone of a cell phone.

"Speak of the devil. I have to take this. Get the apple muffins when the buzzer rings. Hey, baby. What's up?" Sticky-sweet and flirtatious, the words roll off Rachel's tongue. Her voice fades out as she walks into the back room.

All falls quiet except for the splash of dishwater and the tapping of rain on the windows. I concentrate on my paper, the tab on my coffee lid, and pretty much anything that doesn't remind me I'm losing my marbles—everything but Green Eyes and her distinctive laugh. The timer buzzes, drawing my attention toward a young woman taking the muffins out of the oven. Her wet hair is knotted into a tight bun. The dark-red apron tied around her waist emphasizes her slender figure.

The sweet aroma of baked apples and cinnamon fills the coffeehouse. Maybe I should grab some to take to work. A bag full of muffins will give me an excuse to catch a glimpse of Green Eyes, to prove she's not a figment of my imagination and save myself from dwelling on her later. Besides, Ed will be grouchy because of the rain, and the offering might soften him up a bit.

I haul in a deep, cleansing breath to calm my inflated anxiety. Then I toss the knapsack over my shoulder. After grabbing my recently acquired rain jacket, I head up to the front. The young woman's back is still to me when I reach the counter. I clear my throat.

She turns. The piercing stare of emerald-green eyes punctures my nonchalant exterior. The sight freezes my words on my tongue, and I take a step back. Same heart-shaped face. Same narrow nose. Same full lips. Her every feature is indistinguishable from Lydia's.

For a brief, solitary moment, I'm home. A warm, comfortable sensation sweeps me away. It takes every ounce of strength not to fold her into my arms and kiss her hello. Although the woman is identical, she's not Lydia. The puzzled expression on her face is evidence of that. The warm torment lingers before crumpling to an incessant ache.

Green Eyes bites her lower lip, swallows hard, and attempts a grin. "I remember you. You're the guy who doesn't look where he's going."

Still unable to utter words, I nod.

"I'm Leah. And you are?"

"Jack," I choke out.

Her breath catches.

Tremors begin in the tips of my fingers and hint at a pending flashback. *Escape! You need to escape! Escape!* The siren thrums, but my feet refuse to obey.

"Are you okay?" Leah asks.

I don't answer, and the awkward silence draws her attention to the floor.

Go! the siren bellows.

Rain runs down my face, icy and stinging. I'm on the sidewalk. I don't remember turning or running out the door. I don't recall anything except those eyes, that face, and the girl.

I stumble into a nearby alley and slump against a wall.

The snarl of pain that feels like a thousand needles jab my flesh, sending tremors through my body, and I collapse to the slick pavement, but the hard landing doesn't jar me out of shock. With my eyes closed, I let convulsive gasps rattle through me. Time loses meaning, and without my approval, my mind drifts into the past, to an afternoon filled with her laughter, spent under the elms. Back when the days were long, and the world was small.

When the haze releases, I'm lying on the bed in my apartment. *How did I end up here?* I hoist myself onto one elbow and look around. I'm in dry clothes. My rain-soaked ones are hanging in my closet. "Work. Crap!"

Ed picks up on the second ring.

"Hey, Ed. It's Jack. Sorry I didn't call sooner. I'm not going to make it in today."

"Flu, I know. Your friend stopped by. Take care of yourself and, hopefully, I'll see you Monday."

"Friend?"

"Yeah, some tall guy. I didn't catch his name. Then again, I don't think he offered it. I'd be careful of that home remedy of his, though." Ed chuckles. "Might put ya in the hospital."

"Thanks, Ed. Will do."

Curiosity forces me to my feet and makes me search the apartment. As I toss the place, I try to dislodge the paranoia that the sapphire-eyed devil was the one who got me home. In the refrigerator, a bottle of scotch and a carton of OJ bearing a Post-it note confirm my suspicion.

Two parts scotch. One part orange juice. We'll talk soon.

Before my mind reels again, I grab my iPod. A hard pulsing beat drives away the thoughts pounding in my head.

The day passes, and night settles in. My emotional exhaustion encourages me to sleep. The nightmares, however, don't.

Beads of cold sweat cling to my brow. In the darkness,

an image of Leah takes full possession of my thoughts. I hold the flooding emotions at bay and study her, starting with the eyes. The purity of the deep color in itself is extraordinary, except for one fleck of gold in her right eye. The vision widens to encompass her face. Her skin is creamy white, like ivory. The familiar aquiline nose leads down to full rose-pink lips.

I crawl out of bed and make my way to a small dresser tucked into the far corner of the room. The top drawer creaks open, and I grope through socks and underwear until I find the small square box. Silver moonbeams shine across the box's inlaid geometrical design. The passage of years has made the antique memento rough under my touch. I open the lid, and Lydia looks at me from the painted ivory. The tremors return and run up my arms. Fighting to ignore them, I steady my hand.

Staring at the miniature portrait, I know my impressions are right. Leah's face is Lydia's perfect replica, right down to the gold fleck. *Impossible.* The one thing I want more than death itself is buried deep in the ground in a land very far away. Without doubt, Lydia is dead. This is the one fact I'm sure of, and I have memories to prove it.

Ghostly echoes, familiar reminders of the past, call from the corners of my mind. My knees buckle. I cling to the oak dresser and shut my eyes. Pressure builds inside my skull. A gray light, beginning as tunnel vision, grows and blazes to life behind my eyelids. I instantly understand where my subconscious has dragged me. As if I've traveled through time, the scene plays out in the confines of my head. The genuineness is the worst part—the part that had once convinced me I was dying because I thought my life was flashing before my eyes. Now I bear reminiscences more stoically and count the seconds until the nostalgia ends.

I stand at the large double doors of Wind Rush House under a cloud-riddled sky. As powerless as a marionette to control its own strings, I play my part and remove my hat, rapping the lion-head knocker decorated with black, crepe, and white ribbons. The door creaks open, and the manor's housekeeper greets me. The bright expression she always wears is gone, leaving the folds around her mouth downcast.

In a hushed voice, Mrs. Mills begins, "The mistress will be grateful you came, Mr. Hammond. Sir Robert has gone for the day to make the preparations, and Mistress thought you'd want to see Miss Lydia one last time."

I nod and follow Mrs. Mills to the front parlor. The small room is wallpapered with a pattern that matches the curtains. The room is regally furnished—a lush cream-colored high-back sofa where Lydia and I read as children; an oval table with a green silk tablecloth on which we'd planned our future; the grandfather clock, which had been silenced at the time of her death; and the ornate mirror above the fireplace, now draped with black cloth. Our story from beginning to end sprawls out before me in this tiny room. A lump forms in my throat. *How did I think I could bear being here knowing she's not?* I slump against the mantel, unprepared for what's to come.

Mrs. Mills lingers. "Sir Robert was being unreasonable. And still is."

"He blames me?" The words tumble out.

No response follows. Her silence is all the acknowledgement I need.

"Do you know why she was out in that storm?" I ask.

She cocks her head, perplexed. "She was running to you."

"But why?"

"You don't know?"

Sucking in a sharp breath, I steel my emotions. "Know what?"

"After Master William's sudden death, Sir Robert wanted Miss Lydia to break off the engagement. Wind

Rush House, along with the entire estate, is entailed and will now pass to Sir Robert's nephew, a Granville Philips. Mind you, I don't listen to idle gossip, but according to the Harris' chambermaid, Frannie Harris has met him twice in London, and both times, he was extremely unpleasant, hardhearted, and selfish." She sighs. "Sir Robert said that Lydia would marry Philips. That it was beyond either of their choice now."

William had been like a brother to me and grew up in Wind Rush House as much as my own. He surely would have informed me of Lydia's new prospects, despite his father's wishes, had he still lived. But his death had triggered this terrible chain of events, and I had been shut out, like a veritable stranger.

She continues, "Miss Lydia said no, of course, that she'd rather throw away her position in society than marry any other."

I shift my gaze from her to the fire. "Sir Robert's right then."

"No. He's not," says Lady Ashford. She walks into the room, dressed in black bombazine. She straightens the onyx cameo pinned to her neckband. Her weak smile doesn't touch her eyes. "You came. After everything, I wasn't sure you would."

I bow. "Thank you for thinking of me at a time such as this."

"Jack, I believe we're past formalities. You were going to be my son. Come."

The scene shifts and warps, and I'm swept along like a leaf floating on a stream. I stand at Lydia's bedside. I choke back brewing panic. Seeing her with the lasting bloom gone from her cheeks, with no teasing smile on her lips, solidifies this hell as reality. In stark contrast to my building misery, Lydia looks peaceful, as if she's asleep and having a pleasant dream. For now, we live in separate worlds.

A single tear rolls down my cheek. I lean in and whisper a silent good-bye. When my lips press to her snow-white forehead, I cringe, finding her skin ice cold.

To my relief, the memory shrinks away, leaving me shuddering on the floor, disoriented and dizzy. The first moments after a flashback are like waking up after drowning in a sea of grief. The freezing wood floor against my cheek makes me wince, and I roll to my back. A haunting anger at what my actions caused swells. Lydia's death was my fault, at least in part. I had nothing and had no right to ask for her hand. Young and stupid, I didn't recognize my misstep until it was too late.

I tighten my hands into fists and grind my teeth into the soft tissue of my cheek. Soon, the metallic taste of blood fills my mouth, but it's necessary to trap the grief. Willing myself to stand, I use the dresser as a crutch and return the portrait to its home. With a shove, I shut the drawer and slump onto the corner of the bed. My gaze lingers on the dresser. The knots in my stomach twist and tighten. Well, that's the end of the search. No matter the reason for the likeness, I can't go near her again, not after an attack like that. Worst in years. She's a one-way ticket to Loonyville.

In my mind, a quiet voice begs, *Just another glimpse. To find out who she is.*

"Shut up."

But she stared back. Her reaction was bizarre.

"Shhhh, please," I whisper. I rub my temples, but the voice is relentless.

Who is she? Who is she? Who is she? it chants.

Even with renewed resolve, how long can I stay away from her? A month? A week? A day? "Leave." Yes, that would be the smart thing to do. I should find a sunny spot and never think of this cursed place again.

Who is she?

"I don't know!" I stand and storm to the closet to retrieve

the tattered map and rusty dart from my duffel. After pinning the map to the wall, I sink onto the corner of my bed, flipping the dart over and over in my hand. I should have left the first time I saw her. Hindsight is twenty-twenty. What was I thinking, staying? I don't belong here. I don't belong with her. The disembodied voice again pleads with me to stay. *When was the last time anyone actually noticed you? No one even knows you exist. But Green Eyes, she sees you.* I groan in defeat, slapping the dart onto my bedside table, and head for the bathroom.

Following a long shower to clear my head, I wipe the steam from the mirror to study my reflection, grumbling under my breath. An unrecognizable man looks back. His blue eyes no longer hold sadness, but possibility. I was fooling myself into believing nothing changed the instant I first saw her. Obviously, my belief is not even close to the truth. I'm a kingdom defeated, and I fear Leah has taken over.

"Damn girl! What hex has she cast over me?"

CHAPTER FOUR

OVER THE NEXT WEEK, I don't go into Old Port Java once. However, I do stray by the shop twice, technically not breaking the bargain I made with myself. The first time, the coffeehouse isn't open yet. I peer around the edge of the storefront window, darting out of sight anytime Leah glances in my general direction. Her golden hair falls around her shoulders, framing her face. I hold my breath. She twists her flowing locks up into a clip, revealing the graceful nape of her neck. Now and again, she laughs at something Rachel says. She looks happy, which bothers me. Shouldn't I want her to be happy? I huff. *Selfish still.*

The second time I play Peeping Jack, I witness a patron harassing Leah. A businessman with impeccable hair leans over the counter as if he thinks he owns the world and says something that turns Leah's expression wary. She shakes her head and starts to walk away, but the man grabs her by the arm and yanks her toward him. A consuming anger scorches me, whipping through me like a fire through a parched field. I could try to tell myself my reaction to his behavior is only gentlemanly, but I already know my need to defend her goes far deeper than common courtesy. I'm about to burst into the shop when Rachel comes out from the back room and kicks the bastard out.

He needs to be taught some manners.

What happens next is involuntary, almost instinctive. I follow the man and shove him into a nearby alley. He stumbles into the darkness, regaining his balance against the side of a lofty, brick building. He glares at me and puffs out his chest, ready to defend his ruffled pride. I grab his shirt collar and twirl him, nearly ripping the seams. Then I slam him up against the adjacent wall. "If you ever go in that coffeehouse or talk to her again, I'll kill you. Do you understand me?"

"I don't know what you're talking about."

My grip tightens, I smack him harder into the wall, and his head collides with the bricks. "Don't lie. Talk to her again, even look at her, you're dead. Understand?"

"Let me go." The man tries to squirm from my grasp.

I clasp my hand around his throat. His heartbeat pulsates at a feverish rate under my claw-like fingers, and his skin reeks with the fresh smell of fear. "Scared?" I grin. "Not a word. Not a look."

"Okay, okay! I won't. I promise."

"If you do, I will kill you. I promise *you* that."

As an intense thrill builds within my chest, tickling the base of my neck with an icy prickle. I release the man, and he crumples to the pavement. I back away and turn to leave. My pace quickens when I think about doing something I might regret. Then I curse myself for letting things go so far.

After work, I recline against the stark-white counter of Portland Public Library, determined to adhere to my plan—bury my focus in the possibility of me being soulless to force my thoughts away from Leah, for my sanity's sake. This morning's little slip-up was stupid and couldn't be repeated. I'm no one to her, and I need to remember that.

A lady with cropped salt-and-pepper hair hustles behind the counter, steering a cart stacked with books. I lean farther over the counter and crane my neck, trying to catch her eye before my resolve wavers.

"Excuse me. Can you help me? I'm writing a paper about cultural beliefs regarding soulless humans," I lie then flash her a smile.

She raises one eyebrow. "Soulless humans? What on earth are they teaching you kids these days?" She takes a seat behind the closest computer and begins to type.

I snort. I'm older than most of the books in this place, for crying out loud. And I've probably read most of them at least once. With so much time on my hands, books are a safe pastime and a useful escape from the real world.

The librarian shakes her head. "Nothing. Sorry, dear. Have you tried Google?" She points to a long S-shaped table lined with computer screens looming at the opposite side of the room.

"Thank you," I say flatly. I eye the machines warily and trudge toward the table. I'm prejudiced; I'll admit it. I can't help it. Computers and I have never gotten along. I'm not a complete technophobe. I have a good relationship with my cell phone and iPod. Granted, it took a neighbor's nine-year-old grandson to teach me the simplest tasks. But in time, I've mastered them. On the other hand, these infernal machines seem to have a grudge against me. However, today, they've become a necessary evil.

As I approach, the row of darkened screens leers at me, seeming to sense my deficiencies. I suppose I could ask Ed for help with my Internet quest. But he would laugh his ass off, and I would undoubtedly become the butt of his jokes for days, if not weeks, to come. Besides, how would I explain my need for the search? Student research project won't cut it. No, best to keep the two worlds separate.

A teenager at the farthest end of the table abruptly stands. Grumbling something about being late and his mom killing him, he shoves a couple of beat-up textbooks into an equally beat-up knapsack and rushes off. To my unexpected good fortune, the boy leaves the Internet search engine up and running. I drop into his chair, contemplating how to begin.

After a few attempts, I manage to clear "War of 1812" from the search bar. Then I hunt and peck my way through a long, detailed description. I include every particular I can think of, hoping that being thorough will prevent the need for a repeat performance. I drum my fingers on the light oak tabletop while the machine thinks, giving no hints about its progress. After a wait that feels endless, a frowny face pops up, apologizing for the inconvenience because I crashed Google. I sigh. *Fan-freaking-tastic.*

"How's everything—what did you do, dear?" the librarian says from behind me.

"I touched it."

She chuckles under her breath then pauses for a long moment. "Scoot over. Let me see. Did you type a whole paragraph? With punctuation... and in proper English?"

I shrug.

"Well, that's the problem. Google likes searches short and to the point." She speaks slowly, pausing after each word. With a few quick keystrokes, she gets an entire page of results in seconds. "There we go. Think you'll be all right from here?"

I nod, trying hard not to grimace.

She smiles and walks away, her long paisley-printed skirt billowing behind her.

I slip back into my seat and scroll through the list. There isn't much, just a few gaming sites, a couple of movies, and an indie rock band I've never heard of. A site called Strange Religion catches my eye, and I click on it.

I wait impatiently for the site to load. Finally, when the screen is finished, I'm greeted by paintings of blood rituals and black magic—all creepy, even to me—and a list of quotes. One stands out:

> *Indeed the Rwandoya people believe the offspring of Shanko-Tuku (the god of death) exhibit a lack of empathy and remorse as well as shallow emotions*

and egocentricity. It is also true that the Rwandoya deem these descendants soulless and shun them within the tribe.

Rev. Abelard Neumann, missionary to the Rwandoya from 1873-1898

Not a single attribute fits. Sure, I lie, and I'm selfish, but doesn't everyone display those qualities from time to time? For a moment, I almost wish I was shallow. Indifference would make living forever a hell of a lot easier.

The rest of the site is an alphabetized roster of religions from the common to the obscure. A brief description follows each. First, I click on the Mayans. Aside from the expected human sacrifice to please the gods, I learn that the Mayans believed a person's soul could be severed from its body. I search the rest of the entry for anything that seems the least bit beneficial but find nothing.

After three hours of clicking links, I'm disheartened to discover that only the Rwandoya and Pioche-Sioni of Ecuador hold promise. The peace-loving Pioche-Sioni believed a soul detached from one's body as punishment for taking a life. The offender would exist between life and death, never knowing either. *Sounds familiar.*

A tap on my shoulder shoots me into the air. "Holy shii—oot," I say, turning to find the librarian standing behind me, her mouth open in surprise.

"Sorry if I scared you. I just wanted to let you know the library will be closing in ten minutes."

"Oh." I sigh. "Is there any way I can get this"—I wave both hands in front of the screen—"on paper?"

"I could help you e-mail yourself the link."

I give her a dry stare.

"Okay, paper it is." She leans over my shoulder and takes control of the mouse. "Which web pages do you need?"

"Pioche-Sioni and Rwandoya."

Back at the counter, I occupy myself with reading a flyer of Portland's upcoming events while the librarian staples the printed copies in order so I "don't get them confused." The gesture is kind-hearted, but I've clearly given her enough reason to deem me a moron. I thank her and toss the printouts in my knapsack before heading out the door and onto the busy street.

After a dinner consisting of burnt frozen pizza—I ought to be able to cook after all these years, but I can't—I sit at my small dining table and thumb through the pages. I skim a series of photos showing examples of tribal art—distorted faces sculpted into pottery and carved into wood and stone. Each portrayal of the afflicted soul was obviously a vision of the netherworld.

If I'm already in hell, can I reach heaven? I'm not optimistic. As a young child, I went to church every Sunday and listened to my father's sermons. What little I do remember doesn't paint a bright future for me. I would be viewed as one of the damned. Maybe I've dodged the fire and brimstone, but does this mean there's no paradise for me?

I read the same passages again and again, hoping to find something to ease my anxiety. My eyelids grow heavy, sounds fade away, and I surrender to sleep.

My heart gives three thuds then sputters once more before falling silent. In a deep corner of my consciousness, I know I must be dreaming. But this awareness doesn't quash the excitement I feel when I hear my mother call my name.

I open my eyes then blink with confusion. I'm standing in the middle of a small room with gold inlaid walls and high domed ceilings. Shafts of light pour in through arched stained-glass windows, filling the room with rainbows. I look down at myself. I'm dressed in a coal-black morning coat, matching trousers, and a crisply pressed lavender vest. A white rose is pinned to the lapel.

"Yes," I answer hesitantly. The door flies open.

"My handsome boy!" my mum says, stepping into the room. I look into her blue eyes, which are the color of a cloudless sky. We share this feature, along with the sable hair. I wrap my arms around her. She buries her round face in the crook of my neck. "My son," she whispers.

"You've waited far too long for your paradise, son. It does me good to have you here with us." My father's deep voice booms from the door. At the tender age of seven, I lost my father when Saint Peter called his name. However, in this moment, he looks healthy, happy, and robust. He bears none of the evidence of the violent death that I associate with the last time I saw my father.

"You look well. It's so good to see you."

"You, too, my boy. You, too. Eternity looks good on us both, I dare say." He chuckles as he puts his arms around me and folds me in. Comfortable and warm, I feel like a child again. As he steps away, he says, "It's time. You don't want to keep that bride of yours waiting any longer. She's grown a bit impatient."

"Bride?" I look down at my clothes again.

"Of course. What better way for you to begin your forever?" My mother straightens my hair then brushes away the moisture sparkling on her eyelashes.

She's right. No better way.

I follow my parents from the room. Beyond the gilded door, the rest of my family waits for me. Ruth and Henry are accompanied by my youngest brother Fredrick, who didn't live past his first birthday but is now a man. Greetings of kisses and embraces follow. Pure happiness envelops me.

With the welcomes complete, they usher me down a long, narrow hallway, where the walls and floor are all constructed of polished white stone. The high ceiling is vaulted, and tall arched windows, like the ones belonging in a grand cathedral, line one wall. An open doorway waits at the end of the hall. Vines of multicolored roses are twined around the columns guarding the entry. I step into the vibrant light. The smell of sweetgrass and honeysuckle meander on each breath of wind.

I blink, adjusting to the brightness, and I realize I'm in a garden. Everything transmits its own prismatic light, sending beams dancing off every surface. The awareness hits me. I'm free. Heaven is even more beautiful than anything my imagination could have produced. I look for her, scanning the sea of familiar faces. She's here somewhere. She must be. Instead of Lydia, I find William, her brother and my best mate. He died just two weeks before his sister. I've missed him. I've missed them all.

William smirks. "Finally. You took your time. Lydia was never known for her patience, and heaven hasn't changed that."

Same William.

"My sister will be happy you're here." He grabs my shoulders and spins me around.

The crowd blocks my view. I strain my neck trying to look around them, to catch just one glimpse. The sea parts, and Lydia walks toward me, wearing pale lavender and a crown of white roses. Her eyes spark with expectancy, and as she steps in front of me, a beaming smile stretches across her face.

"I've been waiting for you," she whispers.

"Sorry I'm late, love." I take her hands in mine.

"It's time for you to be happy, Jack." She kisses my cheek. "And time for you to let me go." Her voice drifts through the chilled air. Wisps of fog overtake us. Lydia vanishes into the mist. Again, I'm alone.

I open my eyes to the faint light of the streetlight casting its golden hues across the walls of my dingy little apartment. I feel sick, and my mind continues to whirl with what-ifs. I had simple desires when I was young. All I wanted was to grow old with the girl I loved. This still doesn't sound unattainable. Marriage. Children. Happiness.

How naïve I was.

With no desire to sleep, I stumble across the room to

the brown-and-golden plaid sofa. After the dream and the memories it provoked, peace won't find me anyhow. I find the remote shoved between the cushions. I channel surf, finding only infomercials and a couple of B-movies based on immortals, who all live much more interesting lives than I do, either saving the world or destroying it. Every hero gets the girl, and every villain gets to die. I envy them all.

My life sits before me like a two-bit sitcom. Half of last night's dinner lies in an open pizza box resting on top of the one from two nights ago. Empty beer bottles clutter the coffee table. Not one is Prize Old Ale, I note. And here I sit, slouched on the ugliest sofa I've ever laid eyes on, brooding at well past three in the morning. Pathetic. No wonder they don't base any of these movies on reality.

Lydia's dreamful words roll through my head. I huff and lean against the cushion. I let my mind relive memories, searching for those sapphire-blue eyes and trying to avoid emerald-green ones. What I should do is find the devil and pump him for information. That would be the smart—and sane—path to take. He implied he would return. But when? Tomorrow or one hundred years from tomorrow? What's *soon* to an immortal?

My stomach drops. The quiet voice deep within pleads, *Stay here.*

Eyes closed tight, I press my lips into a hard line. A pair of eyes gazes back at me, matching the voice in my head. Leah. I'm barely holding on to sanity. Anger surges, and with a sweep of my arm, the beer bottles clatter across the floor. I know I'm not good enough for her, yet I think of Leah more than ever. Why is she the spitting image of Lydia? Maybe some research into her family tree might help answer my question and, in turn, remove her from my thoughts. But that option requires knowing more about her—a last name, to start. I groan. I'll be returning to Old Port Java tomorrow. *Sanity be damned.*

The small voice in my head cheers.

"Shut the hell up," I grumble.

CHAPTER FIVE

THE NEXT MORNING, LEAH ISN'T at the coffeehouse. At first, I think she might be in the back room. That hope quickly crumbles when I overhear Rachel talking with a customer, complaining about being on her own today. I listen, but she provides no explanation of Leah's absence.

My chest tightens with disappointment, but the real panic doesn't set in until the following day, when Leah still doesn't show. The uncertainty drives my nervousness to new levels, which causes me to think about her more, which ratchets up my agitation. A vicious cycle.

To make matters worse, the voice in my head grows more persistent. I'm not sure what it wants me to do about the situation. At first, I'd assumed the voice was just my longing for Lydia manifesting in a new, torturous way. Now I'm not sure. The voice seems to come from somewhere outside me and is not quite my thoughts. Maybe I really am mad. Regardless of the source—longing, a lost mind, or even a warped voice of reason—I can't make Leah materialize, no matter how much I wish it.

By Friday, I'm a wreck. I attempt to let a hot morning shower chase away the tension before beginning another tedious day. I need to be at work at seven sharp—the same time the coffee shop opens. This means no Leah today. Closing my eyes, I immerse my face in the water's steady stream and wonder how I have allowed this place—correction—*this girl* to get to me like this.

I arrive at the bookstore to find Ed unorganized, as I expected. The store's summer lecture series starts today, beginning with Sally's talk on the language of flowers. Although I'd offered—practically begged, actually—to stay late the night before, hoping for anything to keep my mind off this all-consuming pursuit, Ed claimed he could handle the preparation alone. However, nothing has changed overnight. The floor needs sweeping. Chairs are forgotten, still stacked against the wall. Boxes of Sally's most recent book sit sealed in the corner, where I placed them yesterday afternoon. I sigh.

Ed doesn't glance up, too focused on his disorganized efforts at arranging the napkins in a decorative fashion to notice anything. Grumbling, I grab the broom from the closet and sweep, starting with the entryway.

After several minutes, Ed notices me. "Oh, good. You're here. I need you to go over to Old Port Java and pick up the refreshments."

I freeze, suppressing a small smile.

"I've ordered four dozen muffins and three canisters of coffee. Do you think that will be enough?"

My mind rifles through strategies. Will she even be at the coffeehouse? If she's not, I'll ask Rachel. Surely, a smile or two will coax Leah's whereabouts out of her.

"You'll need to take my car. Jack? Jack! Are you listening?" Ed shouts, rattling my thoughts.

"Yes, Old Port Java." I lean the broom against the counter.

Ed presses his car keys and cash into my hand. "Hurry, okay? There's still a lot to do."

"And why is that?" I smirk and shake my head.

"I know. I know. My wrong."

I squelch a chuckle. "It's *bad*, Ed. My bad."

"Yeah, yeah, yeah, that's what I meant. My bad. Now hurry, okay?"

"Sure thing."

In Ed's beat-up Subaru station wagon, I sit, frozen. The last time I attempted to speak to her, I looked like a complete idiot. I'll have to do better this time. *If she's there. She has to be.* My knuckles turn white as I grip the steering wheel and inhale deeply. *Quit over-thinking this. She's just a girl. Stop digging up the past and talk to her, dammit!* I turn the key, and the old car groans to a start. Seems as though neither one of us has much confidence in my ability to pull this off gracefully.

Outside the door of Old Port Java, I rub my sweaty palms against the rough fabric of my jeans and gulp in one long breath for boldness. After I rake my fingers through my disheveled hair, I check my reflection in the front window. I sigh. No use. The hair's a lost cause. Through the glass, I catch sight of her. Leah's here. The butterflies take flight, fluttering against the walls of my stomach. Unexpectedly, the sensation feels good, like living instead of existing.

I walk in, reminding myself why I'm doing this. *Sanity. That's all! Oh yeah, and don't forget the muffins.* Ed will have a conniption if I forget those.

Waiting in line, I watch Leah work behind the counter. Her lithe hands move pastries into small lined trays. She chews her lower lip when concentrating. Under my breath, I list ways to look relaxed.

"Shoulders slouched. Check. Arms hang at sides. Check. Breathe steady. Check."

If this weren't so pathetic, I would laugh at myself. By the end of my checklist, I'm calm and collected on the outside—the perfect spokesman for any deodorant commercial. Inside, I'm a muddled mess. *Keep cool. Stay tough. Focus.*

Finally, the lady in front of me, who couldn't decide

between Coastal Miles Blend or Sunshine Decaf, steps away. My turn has arrived.

"Hey, handsome," Rachel says with a glint in her eye.

I shift back a step. "I'm here to pick up an order for Rare Books. Muffins and coffee." I keep my tone all business.

Leah glances over. Her eyes widen before they return to her work. The ancient warmth in my chest flares, and I take another deep breath.

Rachel leans forward, resting her elbows on the countertop, accentuating her assets. "Oh sure, honey. I have everything you need."

I attempt to ignore her remark's lecherous connotation and take a step back. How can someone make picking up muffins sound so dirty?

Rachel rolls up onto her tiptoes and stretches her neck to peer out the window. "Is that you parked in the loading zone?"

I nod.

"Is the car open?" Rachel asks and gives me an alluring little smile.

Leah walks toward us, hands full, and shoots Rachel a disapproving glance. She kneels by Rachel's side to place the platters of fruit tarts into the display case, and her eyes snap to me. I realize I'm staring.

I catch a hint of a smile on her lips before I return my attention to Rachel and nod again. This is safer than speaking. Because of the heat in my chest and Leah being so close, my voice is undependable. Besides, I don't want to risk encouraging Rachel. I have a feeling she would consider "not interested" a pick-up line.

"Leah, can you grab the boxes and coffee in the back marked 'Rare Books' and put them in the white station wagon parked out front?" Rachel asks.

"Sure thing."

Leah walks around the counter, lugging the first load. Her eyes meet my gaze, and a suppressed hint of expectation dashes across her face.

Flurries of excitement, trepidation, and doubt mingle together and chip away at my calm mask. I quickly suck in lungfuls of air then clear my throat to assess my voice before I begin. "You don't have to do that. I can get them." My words come out rough but coherent.

"Yeah, I kind of do. It's my job, and my boss is watching. I don't want to get fired." Leah speaks with something like amazement in her voice and jerks her head in Rachel's direction. A bright smile stretches across her face.

I swallow hard and open the door.

"Thanks. So you work at Rare Books, huh?"

"Yes." I follow her out of the store like a lost puppy.

"I haven't been in for a month or so. A hippie guy worked there. Journey, I think his name was." She screws up her face as if she's tasted something unpleasant. Then she laughs. "Everything was 'right on, man,' and 'power to the people.'"

"I'm his replacement."

"Phew, that dude knew nothing about books. Hopefully, you do."

"I know enough." I grin, opening the car's rear door.

"So are you new to the area? Or just the store?"

"The area. Moved here from LA a few weeks ago." A sudden dryness takes up residence in my throat. While her back is turned, I rake my fingers through my hair again and then peer at my reflection in the car's grubby window. *What am I doing? Sanity, remember.*

"Wow, that's a trip. What brought you here?"

I shrug. "Just needed a change."

"Well, you got it." She laughs again. "It can be hard fitting into a new place. I remember when I moved here from Wiscasset. It's a small town about two hours up the coast," she adds, sliding the box into Ed's backseat. "Anyway, I was lucky. My brother already lived here, so I never felt alone. And Rachel and I became fast friends." Leah pauses and looks at the sidewalk. Seeming to find something about the red bricks captivating, she gnaws on her lower lip again. "So, there's a group of us going to a movie this weekend, if you'd like to meet some people."

"What movie?" I blurt, attempting to keep my voice nonchalant. My fingers find their way to my hair again.

She peers up. "*Death Will Come.* Have you heard of it?"

I chuckle with wry amusement and shake my head.

"Well, it's good. It's a cult classic and one of my favorites."

I think I catch a hint of pleading in her eyes. This is my hope and not reality, but the figment still causes my words to seize in my throat, leaving me stunned.

Disappointment flickers across her face. "I better get the next load before Rachel really does fire me." She laughs nervously.

I snap out of the stupor and walk to the door. Fingers tingling with the need to touch her, I yank the curved handle and hold the door for her. When Leah passes, her perfume—the faint aroma of jasmine and vanilla—lingers, and I inhale the scent. My gaze follows her. Unable to look away, I find myself mesmerized by the way she moves.

Inside, I lean against the counter while Rachel rings up the order, and I watch Leah through the large plate-glass window. Leah places the second load in the car and then glances my way. Again, I try to persuade myself that I need to get to know her for sanity's sake, but down deep, I know the truth. I'm hoping for more than just a few facts. I shouldn't start something I know I can never finish.

I've partially convinced myself to refuse the movie invitation when a man approaches Leah while she walks toward the coffeehouse door. Something about the way he smiles at her annoys me, making my jaw tense. With a jerk of his head, he tosses his shaggy blond hair out of his face then hugs her. Jealousy jabs me in the gut as she laughs. They talk for a moment before she heads back inside. Shaggy Hair runs ahead and opens the door, an irritating smile sweeping across his face.

"After you," he says.

"Gentlemen are everywhere today. What's gotten into you?" Leah asks.

Inhale. Exhale. Inhale. How did I not see this possibility? My hands clench into fists at my side. Of course, she has suitors. *Stupid!* Swells of nausea creep over me. My thoughts flitter around Leah and this man, who is wearing a cable-knit sweater that matches hers. They both sip cocoa while she laughs at his ridiculous jokes, and I bite the inside of my cheek to rein in my emotions.

Shaggy Hair laughs at something then smacks Leah's shoulder with a playful cuff. I growl under my breath. *What a putz.*

"Grady, this is Jack. Jack, my brother," Leah says as they draw closer to me.

An uncontrollable smile spreads across my face. I study Grady, looking for traces of his sister hidden in his features, but I find none at first. Unlike his sister, he has an open, honest face. The creases around his mouth reveal that he smiles often. His steel-gray eyes retain a sense of humor even when he isn't smiling. The expectation of happy endings is unmistakable in his expression. I find the same glint evident in Leah's eyes.

"I'm trying to talk Jack into going to the movies with us tomorrow night," Leah says.

Grady's scrutinizing eyes dart from me to his sister and back to me, then he extends his hand to give me a rough handshake. "You should come. The more, the merrier."

The words escape my lips before I can stop them. "I'd love to go," I say. *Way to stay tough, Jack. Oh yeah, you're a rock.*

A warm smile rolls across Leah's face. She swipes at an escaping strand of hair and tucks it behind her ear. "Great. We're meeting at the State Theatre tomorrow around seven."

"I'll be there." I glance at my watch. "Excuse me. I

better get back to the bookstore, or Ed's going to have a fit. Nice to meet you, Grady. Cheers, Leah. See you both tomorrow night."

I walk out the door, a stupid grin plastered across my face.

By some miracle, the store is ready by the time the first patron arrives. Despite the disorganized start, the morning's festivities go smoothly. Sally's love for Victorian floriography rings clear in her voice, and she certainly did her research. "The language of flowers was a way to convey feelings that the strict propriety of that age would never allow. Red roses meant true love, while a striped carnation spoke of refusal." She holds up the corresponding flowers. " Even numbers had meaning. A single bloom meant love at first sight..."

And fifteen, an apology. I prop one elbow on the counter and let my chin drop to my palm, and my mind drifts. I find myself smiling for no good reason. Whether or not it's wise, I think about Leah endlessly.

Around mid-afternoon, the doorbell buzzes, and Grady steps in. He flips his mop out of his eyes.

"Afternoon, Grady."

He studies me curiously then relaxes against the counter, leaning on one elbow. "You work here?"

I nod. "How can I help you?"

"I'm looking for a book called *Ancient Fairy Tales: Myths and Legends*. You guys are kinda my last hope."

A shockwave ripples through me, and I keep my mouth shut, because I'm not one hundred percent certain what might pour out if I open it.

Ed steps to my side. "No. Sorry. Sold our only copy a while back. I can probably find another one, but that'll take time, maybe a month or even two."

"Nuts. Today's my sister's birthday. Serves me right for procrastinating. She's been looking for it for a while." He grimaces.

My mouth falls open. I slam it shut. Out of all the books in the world, she wants that one.

"I probably could have the book for you in a few weeks. That will be the best I can promise," Ed says. He walks out from behind the register.

Their conversation rambles, but my awareness of my surroundings weaves in and out as my thoughts retreat into the reasons why Leah might want this book. The one possibility I've established as unfeasible races into my mind. *Don't even go there. She's not her!* I cast off the thought, but not a single one takes its place.

"Hey, Jack," Ed says, interrupting my jumbled thoughts. "I need you to write up an Internet order for *Ancient Fairy Tales,* by Jane MacLeary, then toss it on my desk so I don't forget."

I nod. *Thank God, Ed leaves the Internet searches to his own expertise instead of mine.* I chuckle.

The two men shake hands, and Ed heads for the back then calls over his shoulder, "I'll let you know when I track one down."

Grady leans back against the counter, his attention on Ed until he disappears from view. Then he turns to me, giving me the once-over again.

If Leah wants that book, then she'll have it. Besides, I can get the information I need from her brother. "Look. I have that book. I bought it, but I haven't even cracked it open. It's yours if you want it."

"Seriously?"

"Yeah."

His perpetual smile widens. "That would be wicked awesome. Leah's gonna freak. Thanks."

"Not a problem. I can't get it to you until after work, though."

"That's fine. Um, I hate to ask, but is there any way you could drop it off at my apartment? I'm attempting to cook Leah a birthday dinner, and I'm afraid I've bitten off a little more than I can chew. My apartment's close, just over on Pearl Street."

"Sure. I can swing by right after work. Around five thirty?"

"Perfect. It's really nice of you. Thanks again."

Before Grady leaves, he scribbles his address and phone number on the back of one of the store's business cards. With a grateful wave, he darts out the double doors into the rain.

I glance at his scrawl. *Last name is Winters, huh. That's a place to begin.*

CHAPTER SIX

At 5:36, I climb the front stairs of Grady's square, four-story apartment building, planning to drop off the book and then hit the library before closing time. I choose the yellow-lit button by G. Winters.

After a minute, maybe two, I ring the doorbell again.

"Hello?" a rushed voice answers.

"It's Jack from Rare Books. I have a delivery for Grady Winters."

A buzzer beckons me in. I take the stairs two at a time to the third floor. The door to 3A is cracked open, and a peculiar smell—a mixture of garlic and burnt tomatoes—drifts out into the hallway. The odor attacks my nose and stings my eyes. *Good thing he's giving her the book.* I bump the door open a bit more. "Grady?"

"I'm in the kitchen."

I follow the sound of clanging dishes down the narrow hallway. Family photos line the walls. Leah takes center stage, her life laid out across the slate-green. A little boy holds a sleeping baby in his arms. Graduations. Family outings. Camping. Fishing. Disney World. I notice her father is missing from most of them. *Probably taking the photos*, I surmise.

I can't help but chuckle at one with Leah and Grady

dressed as Beauty and the Beast for Halloween. Leah is all smiles and posing like a ballerina, holding her plastic jack-o'-lantern bucket above her head. Towhead ringlets cascade over her petite shoulders. She can't be more than five. Grady looks less than thrilled, his arms folded across his chest, a scowl creasing his brow.

Still smiling, I step to the kitchen door and set the book on the table.

Grady wipes his hands on a wadded dishtowel, picks up the book, and thumbs through the pages. "This is awesome. How much do I owe you?"

"No worries. Come by the bookstore next week, and we can settle up." My attention wanders along the counters, over heaps of dirty pots and pans. The kitchen looks like an EF5-tornado passed through. "You got your hands full. I'll see myself out."

"Hey, you should stay. I can't guarantee the quality of the grub, but I got plenty." He laughs.

Tempting. So tempting. "I don't want to intrude."

"Come on. I owe you, and Leah will want to thank you for this," he says and waves the book.

I'm about to agree when three quick knocks interrupt me.

"Oh, crap. She's only early when I need her to be late." Grady tosses me the book and rushes back to the stove.

"The man in 1B let me in. He was coming home with an armful of groceries, so I helped him upstairs. You better hide whatever you don't want me to see," Leah warns.

My heart pounds. I glance down, half expecting its pulsation to be visible through my shirt. *Nope.* I conceal the book behind my back as Leah walks in. Surprise floods her face.

"What are you doing here?" Her words rush out like a breeze, and she steps closer. Her blond hair is pinned up into a slipshod bun, leaving her graceful ivory neck exposed.

I flounder for words, and my voice cracks. "Just dropping off something for your brother." *Great. Smooth.*

"It's another book, isn't it?" Leah says with a huff as she looks around the kitchen. "Grady, you're leaving soon. How many books do you think you can store in my cramped little dorm room? You really need to take them to Mom's."

"Actually, Jack's delivering your birthday present. I was trying to talk him into staying for—crap!" Grady opens the oven, and smoke billows around him, swirling toward the ceiling. He removes a smoldering casserole dish and sets it on the stovetop.

The smoke alarm blares. After setting the book on the table, I rush to open the windows. The cool breeze is refreshing, relieving my burning eyes a little. I turn to see Leah waving a broom in front of the buzzing detector. Her blouse, which matches her eyes and hugs her form, inches upward. My eyes slide down her back, en route to... *Be a gentleman. Stick with the nape.* I study her for one more moment then tug my gaze away.

Disgruntled, Grady gapes at the briquette and pokes it with a fork. "I killed your birthday dinner."

A sly smile plays across her lips, as if she's fighting the urge to crack a joke.

"How about pizza?" Grady asks.

"Sounds great." Leah looks to me. "You'll stay, right?"

I nod. "Of course."

After Grady orders a large pie, he drops next to Leah on the sofa, the book tucked under one arm. Leah peeks around him, her eyes sparkling with excitement. A ridiculous grin breaks across Grady's face, and he clumsily hands Leah her gift. She glances over the yellowed pages with amazement, stops, and lets her finger trace over the vivid colors of an illustration. The painting depicts a fair-haired girl lying among a forest of green trees. A radiant golden butterfly hovers over her chest. The creature's large translucent wings cover her. A man in a midnight cloak kneels at her side, his face hidden by his hands.

"It's just like the one Gram had."

"It's not every day your little sister turns the ripe old age of eighteen. I wanted it to be special."

"It is. Read it to me?" She offers the book to her brother. A look I don't understand flickers across Leah's eyes.

"I can't very well deny the request of the birthday girl, can I?"

Their relationship reminds me of the one I had with my sister, Ruth. My secret bonded us; she was the only member of my family who knew I couldn't die.

"I haven't read to you since..." His voice falls silent, and his expression hardens, as if he's recalling a bad memory. "Which story would you like?"

"Olluna and the Golden Butterfly," she says.

I bite my tongue. This was Lydia's favorite story.

"Should've guessed." Grady chuckles and begins, his voice deepened to add drama.

The words flow verbatim through my head...

Long ago, in a cottage at the northern edge of the Black Woods, there lived two sisters. The older was named Olluna, and the younger, named Catia. The two sisters loved each other very much. Years past, Catia grew old, but Olluna never lost her bloom, not aging one day past her youth. Her hair stayed the soft gold color of the fields. Her bright eyes were the color of the sea. To Olluna's great sorrow, Catia became sick and soon died. But Olluna did not. Instead, she lived many years past her sister, always longing for the day she would be reunited with Catia.

On her one-hundredth birthday, Olluna decided to venture to a nearby town to buy herself some plum tarts, for they were her favorite, and she hadn't had one in a very long time. 'No one will know me after so many years,' she said while walking down the curvy country road toward the town's gate. Within the little walled city, life was busy and captivating. So different from the lonely life Olluna had grown accustomed to. Soon, she noticed a white-haired woman bent over from extreme age following her from shop to shop.

Finally, the old woman spoke, pointing her crooked finger at Olluna. "I know you. You are Olluna of the Black Woods."

Olluna shook her head.

"I may be old, and my eyesight weak, but I recognize you. You cannot fool me," the old woman said. "We played as young girls, and you came to my wedding. But how can it be that you have not aged? Unless you are a witch?"

The townspeople gathered around Olluna, whispering among themselves, and the old woman continued to chant, "Witch, witch, witch!" Believing that Olluna must indeed be a witch, the people picked up stones to do Olluna harm.

"Leave this place," they cried, "and never come back."

Fearing for her life, Olluna ran from the town, left her home, and took refuge in the Black Woods. As night fell over the forest, Olluna grew afraid. She had heard many stories, all frightening, about what lived within these borders. Shouts from the townspeople forced Olluna deeper and deeper into the woods. When she could walk no more, she curled up to sleep within the hollow trunk of an oak.

With the sun, Olluna woke. A beautiful forest, green and lush, stretched out around her. The sight gave her peace from her nighttime fears. Days blended into nights, and she drifted through the Black Woods, not knowing where to go or what to do. Artagan, the son of Death, clad in a black cloak given him by his father, saw Olluna and approached her.

Out of fear that the childhood stories were indeed true, Olluna collapsed to her knees and cried, "Oh, please, oh, please, do not eat me."

Artagan, surprised by the girl's reaction, removed his hood, revealing to her that he was no more than a man. His eyes were caring. His voice showed kindness. "You are in no danger from me. Are you lost, child?"

"No, sir. I've hidden in the Black Woods. Everyone in the town wants me dead. They think I'm a witch, for I am one hundred years old." With that, Olluna began to cry.

"Don't weep, my fair one. My name is Artagan. I am the son of Death, but I do not know your name and mean you no harm."

"If you are who you say, do you know when I will see my dear sister again? For I have lived a long life and wish to go to heaven and be with her."

But Artagan would not answer her question.

As the days passed, Artagan taught Olluna how to build a fire, where to find water, and which berries she could eat. Each night before she fell asleep, Olluna pleaded with Artagan to answer her question, but he refused.

Over time, Artagan fell more in love with Olluna. Every evening, he found it harder to deny Olluna her request, for he would have given her the sun and the moon if she had asked for them.

One night, Olluna grew angry. "If you care for me even a little, how can you be so cruel? Answer my pleas. Will I ever see my dear sister again?"

Artagan could no longer deny her, so he answered, "No, my fair one, you will never die. You will live forever, safe with me in the Black Woods, because there is no one else I love."

"I don't want to live forever," she cried, weeping in distress. "Leave me be."

Brokenhearted, Artagan left her alone in the forest. Late that night, men from the town who had tracked Olluna into the Black Woods found her. They chased her up into the mountains.

As she ran, Olluna cried out, "Artagan, where have you gone? Come save me, and I will love you forevermore."

But Artagan was far away and did not hear her pleas. The angry men chased Olluna to the edge of a great white bluff and surrounded her. They pushed Olluna from the cliff. She fell, but survived, leaving her body broken below. Though she could not die, with her tears, she begged for Death to come.

Artagan returned to where he had left Olluna. Finding her gone, he searched the entire forest. Near dawn, he found her at the foot of the cliff. Cradled in his arms, Olluna pleaded with him to let her die. Artagan loved her so much that he granted her request.

As Olluna lay dying, Artagan began to sing:

Golden wings will come to take thee
Eternal slumber closes round thee
Forever in Death's arms
My heart forevermore your keeping
My soul for you always weeping
Close your eyes, love, time for sleeping
Forever in Death's arms

With you, my love, I long to be
All eternity always with thee
Forever in Death's arms
My heart forevermore your keeping
My soul for you always be weeping
Close your eyes, love, time for sleeping
Forever in Death's arms

When the angels come to greet me
In the clouds with you I will be
Forever in Death's arms
My heart forevermore your keeping
My soul for you always be weeping
Close your eyes, love, time for sleeping
Together in Death's arms.

With the final word of his lullaby, a golden butterfly appeared and carried Olluna's soul to heaven. In anger and anguish at the loss of Olluna, Artagan in his cloak of death, hunted down the men who had pursued her. He found them celebrating in a pub and killed them all instantly. He then took revenge on the rest of the town that had cast Olluna out. All the men, women, and children fell dead in his presence. Not even one animal in the town was left alive.

Artagan never saw Olluna again, but his love for her never faded. And to this day, one might catch a glimpse of a black-cloaked man in the shadows, as he roams the world searching for a love he can never find.

Grady closes the book and sets it on the sofa next to Leah.

She's leaning forward, her hands clasped, a spellbound expression on her face. I wish could read her mind. She catches me watching her. And I'm the first to look away.

"That was one creepy-ass lullaby," Grady mutters. "I mean, who would sing that to a kid?"

"Older brothers who like to scare their little sisters before bed, is my guess," Leah says with a smirk.

Grady tries to look innocent. "I'd never do a thing like that."

Without warning, Leah tosses her arms around Grady's neck. "Thank you for my present. I love it."

"You're welcome, Lee-lee." He leans in to peck her on the top of the head. "Wouldn't have happened without Jack, here."

Again, an unexplainable expression flits across her face. "Thank you, Jack," she says then looks at the floor.

Over dinner, I turn the conversation to Leah, trying to learn all I can about her. "How do you like working at the coffeehouse?" I ask as I sip my Coke.

She shrugs. "It's a job. I work there to pay the bills. I'm an artist, or at least that's what I go to college for. I paint, mostly oils."

"Do you have a favorite subject?" I ask.

"Landscapes. Sometimes, I paint portraits, but they aren't good. I can't capture the eyes. Windows to the soul, you know." She pauses, and her careful gaze darts away.

Embarrassed or self-conscious?

"Her paintings are beautiful. Don't let her fool you," Grady says. "Although, she won't let me see her latest work." He flings her an irritated glance.

"I painted you once, not that long ago. You hated it." She rolls her eyes.

"Hey, I loved the painting. It was the process I hated."

"Here we go again," Leah says as Grady's attention shifts to me.

He huffs. "She made me sit in the same pose for hours. Leg cramps, arm cramps, whole body cramps, nothing mattered to her. There was no moving. Did I mention the lack of bathroom breaks?"

"You're such a baby. It's called a sacrifice for art," Leah teases.

A robust laugh escapes my lips. *Is that me? It doesn't sound like me.* I haven't laughed deep and pure like that, well, since Lydia. I glance at Leah, and the look that passes between us sends warmth pulsing through my veins. Neither of us pulls our eyes away. A flaming tingle stirs deep in my gut, and I imagine how soft and tender her lips would feel under mine.

Grady clears his throat. "Leah mentioned you moved here from LA."

I break the stare and nod.

He inhales through his teeth. "Some change. Trading in the big city lights for fresh air and pine trees." He chuckles.

"Yeah, I guess. My uncle died last year," I lie. "He was the last family I had. Needed to live somewhere new."

"What happened to your parents—sorry, that's prying," Leah says.

"I don't mind. My dad was a vicar of the C of E."

"C of E? What's that?" Leah asks.

"Church of England," Grady says.

I nod. "He died when I was seven. Heart attack. Eight years later, my mum, brother, and sister were killed in a car accident. My mother's brother took me in."

I've told this story before. The dates change, but the general falsities stay the same. I'm at least able to offer bits of truth mixed with lies. I did lose my father at age seven, but he didn't die of natural causes.

One afternoon, he went to town to buy a music box for Mother's birthday. I'd begged him for days to go. And on his way home, he was accosted and killed for the shillings in his pocket. My brother, Henry, and I found him face down in the dirt, the smashed music box by his side. His murder scarred us all, but I blamed myself. If I had not insisted he go buy the present that day, my father would have survived.

"We lost my dad at age ten. Not an easy thing, is it?" Leah smiles at me understandingly.

I shake my head.

"Okay, enough of the morbid stuff. This is supposed to be a party," Grady says. "Which part of England are you from?"

"The Cotswolds. Lidcombe." My truthfulness catches me off guard. Self-conscious, I let my stare drop to my plate, and I pick at the pizza crust with my fingers.

"What's it like there?" Leah asks, a faint hint of excitement in her voice. I look up to find her smiling.

"Lush rolling hills and farmland. My favorite time was spring with the blooming hawthorn and dog roses. White and red flowers everywhere. Stunning against the backdrop of golden limestone buildings." *Dammit. Stick to the script.* I look at my glass. Did she slip truth serum in my drink?

Grady looks at Leah, his forehead puckered. "Hey, the Cotswolds? Isn't that where you said our ancestors are from?"

"Yes," she says.

"She's been obsessed with Ancestors.com. It seems we're related to some dead, rich snob. Sir Robert Ashley." Grady twirls his finger in the air.

"Ashford," Leah corrects, sounding annoyed. "Besides, we're descendants through Robert's youngest daughter, Elisie, who was broke because she married for love." Grady rolls his eyes, but Leah ignores him and continues. "She had three sisters and one brother. Two of them died before they reached *your* ripe old age of twenty-four. So keep being annoying, and you might meet their fate." She grins at her brother and cuffs him across his chest.

A sudden wintriness strikes my core and traps my breath in my lungs. Well, there it is—the reason for the resemblance. The likeness followed the twists and turns through the tangled branches of the Ashford's family tree through Lydia's baby sister to Leah. Mystery solved. But does that explain away the other similarities? The laugh? The way she chews at her lip when she's thinking? Her sense of humor?

"Whatever. See, obsessed." Grady chuckles. "Anyway, I'm trying to talk her into visiting while I'm over there. I'm moving to York to teach history at the Redding Boarding School for Boys this summer. I went to the University of York for a couple of semesters and made some good contacts. I'm trying to talk Leah into visiting while I'm over there."

"You should. York is farther north than the Cotswolds, but within driving distance for a weekend excursion. Besides, York's enchanting. You'll believe you've stepped into that storybook." I point to her present.

"Have you ever been there?" Leah asks.

I nod, but I keep my mouth shut in case more truth attempts an escape.

"When I can go, you're taking me to the Cotswolds," she says, raising her chin slightly.

Grady rolls his eyes. "Sure, I guess."

Images of Leah strolling down the streets of my hometown drift through my head. The mental pictures send a warm shudder through my body.

Leah yawns and looks at the time. "This has been fun, but I need to call it a night. Work comes early tomorrow."

"Okay. Let me grab my coat, and I'll drive you."

"No need. I'm a big girl. I can walk myself," she insists.

"It's a little late for that, don't you think?" Grady lifts his eyebrows.

"I'll be fine." Her tone is forceful and brisk.

I peer at her. That same lightning from long ago surges again. Pure pleasure. Throughout that evening, I felt myself waking up from a long hibernation. Over time, I've shut away much of who I am. I don't want this new feeling to end. Not ever.

"I can walk with you if you'd like. That way, you can walk, and your brother's protective nature will be satisfied," I say.

"That would be perfect," Leah agrees. Then she snaps her attention to her brother. "There, does that satisfy you?"

"Thank you, Jack," Grady says and then looks at his sister. "Can I have a word with you before you leave?"

"Thanks for the pizza, Grady." I glance at Leah. "I'll meet you in the hallway when you're ready." After bowing, I leave the apartment. Leaning by the door, I can overhear their discussion and debate with myself whether I should move farther down the hall, but stay where I am.

"You do know him, right? I'm not sending you out the door with a serial killer?"

Not a serial one, at least.

"A serial killer? Really? That's the scenario you're going with?"

"I know. I know. I'm overreacting. And honestly, he seems like a good guy, but I'm sure that's what Jack the Ripper's victims thought right before he slashed them to pieces."

"Nice. So you're saying you invited a man you think is a homicidal maniac to my birthday party?"

A chilly hush hangs in the air.

"Exactly," says Leah. "He's fine. I know him from the coffee shop, anyway. He's a friend of Rachel's."

"You never mentioned that. And I'm not sure that fact helps your argument. From everything you've told me about her, Rachel sounds like she's *friends* with a lot of dirtbags," Grady says.

"Well, Jack's not like that."

Why is Leah lying to her brother to be alone with me? Grady has every right to be concerned.

Grady chuckles darkly. "Uh-huh. That's what they all want you to think."

"Tell you what. If I'm not home in a half hour, you can call the National Guard."

"Deal." Grady laughs.

Leah walks out into the hallway, passing me. The back of her hand skims my arm. The touch is undoubtedly an accident, but it ignites an old, dormant heat. *Just my body reacting to the physical contact it's been deprived of for years. That's it. Nothing else, nothing more.*

"Ready?"

"Yup." I smile, rubbing my forearm and savoring the dwindling sensation.

We walk through the shadowed streets, past dimly lit windows. The shops soon give way to apartment houses. We talk, but I'm just rambling, trying hard not to notice how much I like the way she looks in her tight-fitted jeans. *Eyes up!*

"So the movie we're seeing tomorrow night, what's it about?" I ask.

"Same old, same old. An undead creature attacks a small town, kills all the promiscuous teens and anyone who wanders off by themselves. That's rule number one in horror movies, never stray out alone. The monsters will slaughter you for sure." She grins. "Anyway, the effects are awesome. Great blood splatter." She attempts an evil grin, but her beautiful features can't master it. It comes across sexy.

"Sounds... interesting." I grimace. My possible future played out on the big screen. *Fantastic.*

She laughs at my reaction. "It won't be that painful. I promise."

"I'm sure." I grin. "So, where have you been the last few days? You weren't around."

"Why? Looking for me?"

Deny? Lie? Turn tail and run? I clear my throat. "Maybe."

She smiles as if pleased with herself. "Well, if you must know, I was sick. The flu's going around."

A haunting fear rises from my depths. Influenza stole Lydia from me. I swallow the reaction to draw her close and keep her safe, hoping I've hidden my instincts well. "But you're okay now, right?"

"Yes. I'm not contagious, if that's what you're worried about."

Leah walks along, drawing her hand along the uneven bricks of the nearby buildings and gnawing on her lower lip. "Do you think fate has a plan? Or do you think life's just random?"

"Geez, where'd that come from?"

Leah shrugs.

"Well, if it does, it hasn't shared it with me."

She scowls, seeming unsatisfied with my answer.

I search for the witty response that will bring a smile to her lips and break the uncomfortable silence that's fallen between us, but I come up empty.

Leah stops in front of a redbrick Queen Anne-style home. I scan the familiar romanticized architecture, including the sweeping steps. A decorative cast-iron fence leads to a carved-stone doorframe.

"This is me."

“Beautiful home.”

“It’s college housing. My room is more like a closet, but it’s better than living under Grady’s watchful eye twenty-four, seven.”

“Speaking of Grady. Don’t forget to call your brother to let him know you’re not lying in a ditch on the side of the road. We wouldn’t want him to call the National Guard.” I smirk.

She frowns. “You heard that? Sorry about him.”

“Don’t be. He’s right. You should be careful.” *Especially of me.*

She ignores my comment. “See you tomorrow night. State Theatre. Seven, sharp.”

“I remember.”

A craving nags at me. *One touch,* it whispers. My intense scrutiny doesn’t cause her look away, making the longing all the more difficult to resist. The need swells with the thought of her soft skin and lips. I shove my hands into my pockets. “Good night, Leah.”

As she walks away, I resist the need to follow her. Only my vision trails up the stairway after her, to caress her shapely form. Halfway up, she pauses for a second, but doesn’t turn around as I expect and hope. Instead, she bounds up the rest of the steps. I stand, staring at the closed door before heading for home.

Sleeping is impossible, but not because of nightmares or regrets, as it is most nights. This insomnia is brought on by the unfamiliar feeling of happiness—an emotion I barely remember. Maybe I should have stayed away from her, but I know I can’t now. Desire has crept through a crack in my resolve and opened a part of me that hasn’t seen the light of day in almost one hundred fifty years.

CHAPTER SEVEN

To my dismay, Ed calls early the next morning. I've just hopped out of the shower. Wrapped in only a towel, I stand in the middle of my living room. I drip all over the carpet while Ed prattles on about burnout and how Sally mentioned I had worked every day since he'd hired me. I argue, but Ed dismisses each attempt. By the end of our conversation, thanks to Sally's interference and Ed's generosity, I've earned myself a day off, whether I want it or not.

Since I don't have any plans, the day drags, and I find myself counting the hours until seven. I debate stopping by Old Port Java to see Leah, but that reeks of desperation. The last thing I want to do is scare her off. I'm completely out of my depth. Times have changed, and I've adjusted, but not in this area. Courtship in the nineteenth century was so different. There were rules to follow. While I despise the prejudices that accompanied them, I miss the manners and the courtesy. So instead of going to the coffeehouse, I spend the morning reading, or rather, trying to read. By noon, I give up and focus on forgotten chores. After I make my bed, I think of her. I think of her while I'm doing the week's worth of dishes and while I throw out the trash.

I carefully choose my clothes for the evening, settling

on dark-washed jeans and my blue-and-black striped button-down. Finally, close to six thirty, I roll my sleeves up to my forearms and tuck in my trailing shirttails before running a comb through my hair. I show more concern with my appearance tonight than usual. With summer hinting at its arrival, I leave my leather jacket hanging over a kitchen chair.

Hustling down the four flights of stairs, I skip every other step. The man who lives in the apartment across the hall clings to the banister on the second landing. As I barrel past him, I call out an apology but keep going. His grumbles follow me. The protest doesn't end until the front door swings shut behind me, leaving nothing but the city hum in the air. I catch myself whistling. Nothing can change my mood. Not tonight.

Winding through the streets with purposeful speed, I round the next corner, and the theater comes into view. Waiting patrons spill out the double doors and onto the crowded sidewalk. I weave through the swarm, eagerly scanning the faces for Leah's. When our eyes finally meet, Leah breaks into a wide, eager grin. On its own, my gaze dives to the hemline that just touches her knees.

Stop gaping at her like the village idiot. "Is everyone else inside already?" I ask, glancing around.

"No. Rachel and her boyfriend, Tom, decided to go clubbing, and Grady is home sick with some bug. So, it's just you and me."

I swallow hard as a flock of seagulls replaces the butterflies in my stomach. Catching sight of a pair of tickets in Leah's left hand, I grimace. I notice the other women around us have followed the same practice. *Rule change.* Back in my day, the game of courtship came with a different set of rules. Leah's simple gesture would have sparked gossip, and the scandal would have blackened the girl's fragile reputation for life. However, those days have long passed, and if I hope to have a chance in hell with this modern-day woman, I need to learn the new etiquette and fast.

"Ready?" Leah asks.

I look up to find the crowd filing into the theater. "Sure." I can't disguise the apprehension in my voice.

Leah laughs. "I told you. It's not going to be that bad."

I hurry ahead and grab the brass handle, holding open the tall bright-red door. Instinctively, I bow at the waist as she passes. Leah studies me before following the crowd. Inside, I try to convince Leah to let me buy the snacks. "You bought the tickets," I coax.

She shrugs and leans against the wall. "Fine. I'll wait here."

The shrug is a very non-committal gesture that implies a variety of meanings. That's probably the reason I use the gesture so often. In line at concessions, I find myself overanalyzing Leah's shrug. *Anger, indifference, annoyance?* I glance in her direction. To my shock, the sapphire-eyed devil is talking to Leah. A stab of sharp panic quickly turns into a frantic need to get to her. I elbow my way through the crowd. The mass of people keeps me away. I jostle against the throng, earning several complaints. I zero in on him as he removes a slender cigarette from a pack. He lights it and takes a long drag, never removing his focus from Leah. The smoke billows over his head as he exhales. She says something with a cool expression, causing him to chuckle and then walk away.

"What did he want?" I ask, trying to sound casual, but my voice cracks.

Leah's expression shows nothing but confusion.

"That man." I point to the door, but he's gone. *Again. Gone!* My mind spews curses, but I hold my tongue tight.

"Oh, him? Nothing. He asked what movie was playing, and I told him he couldn't smoke in here. Is everything okay?"

"Wait here. I'll be right back. Please." My tone is a bit

more composed. Still, I must look like a lunatic, but I can't let go of the fear that he's now targeting her. Of all the women here tonight, he chose to speak to Leah. That can't be a coincidence. If that sapphire-eyed devil is planning to hurt Leah in any way, I'll let loose my inner monster. It can have its way with him.

Outside, I catch a glimpse of him. The sidewalk is too congested for speed, so I swerve into the street. Brakes screech, and a horn blares. I pay them no attention. I weave around cars to get to the opposite sidewalk, where I launch into a run. He disappears into the shadows. My breath comes up too short, and I can't haul a full gulp of air into my starving lungs. Hands on my knees, I bend to catch my breath.

The first wave of hysteria dissipates, giving me one moment of clear thought before the next breaker crashes over me. My adrenaline spikes. Maybe he wanted me to leave and assumed I would follow. Maybe he doubled back.

I change direction. My pace accelerates as my feet thud against the bricks, urging me to go faster. Traveling those six blocks I came takes forever.

My eyes dart around the lobby. No Leah. Fear thrashes in my chest. I check the two screening rooms, where I earn a couple of choice words when I call her name. She's nowhere to be found. I charge for the ladies' room. The door swings open and out walks Leah.

She's okay. She's okay. The wintry tremors subside, replaced by a warm relief, and the rage subdues. I compose my expression then saunter to her side. "Sorry about that. Thought he was an old friend, but it wasn't him. Could've been his twin, though."

I half expect her to tell me I'm a nutcase and walk off, but she doesn't. "They say everyone has a *doppelgänger.* Are you ready? The movie's about to start."

I nod.

We find two seats in the back of the theater. The lights

fade. The monster reveals itself in the opening scene, slaughtering a young, horny couple in a spray of crimson. The beginning of the film holds my attention, but soon, I'm absorbed in thoughts of the couple from the bar two weeks ago. I remember how their eyes stared at me from the picture in the article.

Gentle warmth presses against my leg and drags me out of my grim, bitter thoughts. Electrifying heat races through me. The darkness emphasizes the attraction between us. I debate with myself then reach out and take her hand. A little smile touches her lips. Here in the dark, I make a pledge that nothing will ever harm Leah. No matter the cost.

Before I realize the movie is over, the lights slowly come back on.

"So, what did you think of the movie?" Raising her eyebrows dramatically, Leah tilts her head.

"Hum, it was good."

"Liar, you weren't even paying attention." She laughs.

Busted. "Of course I was."

"Okay then, what happened?"

I give her the generic description I heard on a TV ad last night.

She rolls her eyes. "You memorized that from the trailer."

I grin, throwing my hands in the air. "Okay, you caught me. I missed most of it."

A playful smile appears on Leah's face. "Why?"

Her smile makes me bold. "Because there was a beautiful woman sitting next to me. I'm sure not a man in the theater remembers what the movie was about because of you."

She laughs again. "Please. Is that the best pick-up line you got? It sounds like a line out of a Jane Austen novel. You need to work on your material, but don't ask Grady. His are even worse."

I shrug. "I've seen it work... in London." In college,

Lydia's brother was the master of sweet-talking the ladies. Of course, that was one hundred fifty-three—maybe fifty-four—years ago. Leah's right, I'm going to need new material.

Leah takes my hand and leads me out of the theater.

I smile. *Or maybe I won't.*

Out in the cool night air, we walk in silence for several blocks, until I break the quiet. "So you love horror movies. What else do you love?"

"Lots of things. But my all-time favorite is lobster ice cream. They make it for the tourists, but I can't get enough of the stuff."

I wrinkle my nose.

"Have you tried it?"

"No."

"Then don't judge. Maybe we can go to Lizzy's Ice Cream, and you can try it sometime." She smiles. "Well, here we are."

"I'd like to see you in if you don't mind."

Leah nods.

I shadow her into the building, through the lobby full of rowdy students enjoying their night of freedom.

A freckle-faced boy steps into our path. His bloodshot eyes snap to me and then returns to Leah. "Hey, I was waiting for you. This party is epic. You should come down later."

"No. I don't think so. Not tonight," she says.

"More like never. Come on, babe. You're breaking my heart here." The boy slurs his words and teeters. He reaches for Leah's hand but misses.

I imagine the exact sound his snapping neck would make, and a smile tugs at the corners of my lips. I stare down the inebriated boy. I'm able to tame the growl creeping up the back of my throat, but the lingering effects from the incident at the movie theater are still playing with my temper.

Freckle Face steps back, hands flying up as if to surrender.

With a shake of her head, Leah walks up the stairs, and I follow.

"Who's he?" I ask, looking over my shoulder to see the boy stagger into the crowd.

"Nathan. He's in the room across the hall."

"Nice guy."

"He's only a moron when he drinks. Nathan's harmless."

Uh-huh.

At her door, she fiddles with her keys. Halfway inside, Leah turns. "Thank you."

"Good night."

She gives me a penetrating look. My eyes retreat, and her door clicks closed.

Instead of heading back to the solitude of my apartment, I wander the moonlit streets. The air is crisp and clear, but thunder in the distance hints at an approaching storm. I can't help but see a connection. Despite the happiness Leah has ushered into my life, a heavy cloud of certainty in bruised shades of black and violet looms on the horizon. Heartbreak, abandonment, and loneliness are all certainties. Leah and I aren't the same. At some point, she will die. Even if I somehow gain her affections, she won't be mine for long. But that's the way life is supposed to be—living, breathing, loving, and dying. I'm the screw-up—the anomaly in the master plan. Still, I continue to walk straight toward her like a moth to a flame. My stride doesn't slow even a little, because somewhere deep inside, I've decided the moments with her are worth the unending feelings of loss after she's gone. My determination is undoubtedly ill-advised, but the course is set. I walk toward my apartment as the first raindrops begin to fall.

Late that night, the sapphire-eyed devil creeps into my dreams. He glowers from the deep recesses of my mind and laughs over Leah's crumpled corpse, jarring me awake. I kick at my stifling blankets. The thick layers fight against me, then I shove them to the floor.

I get up, yank on my jeans, and grab a T-shirt from the heap in the closet. The four walls are confining, pressing in around me, and I bolt for the door, pulling on the shirt.

After swinging by Leah's dorm and finding everything quiet, I begin my search for that devil, wandering from bar to bar. With his fondness for expensive scotch, the bars are as good a place as any to start. I know walking into one of the local establishments and finding him lounging at the counter, looking for other lives to screw with, is a long shot. But I have to try.

By closing time, all I've found is frustration. I walk down by the wharfs and drink in the calm, cool early morning air. The boats creak against their restraints as briny gusts rattle the rigging stretched along their masts. I perch on the edge of the weathered pier and dangle my legs.

Leah seems to lack the ability to identify danger, wanting to see the good in everything around her—even where it doesn't exist. Peril could walk right up to her and blow smoke in her face, and she would wish *him* a nice day. Lydia was the same. She saw the good in me, and look what it cost her.

As the night relinquishes control to the coming day, the fishing boats around me sputter and roar to life, shaking me from my dark thoughts. The boats exit the mouth of the harbor and press on toward the open sea. I wonder how I can possibly manage to keep Leah safe.

CHAPTER EIGHT

"THANKS FOR DOING THIS FOR me today," Ed says as he slides a stack of books onto the counter.

Yesterday, Ed requested a favor. He asks so little of me that I couldn't say no. So today, a sunny Saturday, I showed up to work in old jeans, ready to paint the storefront of Rare Books a bright, cheerful yellow—Sally's choice, for sure. I didn't have any plans anyway. Three words assassinated my schemes: Looming. Art. Assignment. I feel better knowing Leah's safely barricaded in her dorm room for a few days.

"No problem." I grab the paint cans and metal scraper Ed left by the door.

Outside, I climb the ladder and begin scraping away years of built-up layers of paint and grime. My motorcycle parked across the street seems to watch my slow progress and beg for an afternoon ride.

Unfortunately, the repetitive work leaves my mind free to wander. At first, I'm able to concentrate my thoughts on the flurry of paint flakes making speckled puddles along the sidewalk, but soon enough, my mind wanders back to Leah. I miss her more than I should.

Close to one o'clock in the afternoon, Leah's voice sings out from below. "Hey, just the guy I was looking for." Her face shines up at me, brighter than the early June sun.

“I was going to call you this afternoon, but I don’t have your number,” she continues. “I was hoping I could coax it out of your boss.”

“Were you?” I have no doubt Ed would’ve handed over the keys to the castle if she asked in that tone followed by that smile.

“What are you doing tomorrow? It’s supposed to be brutal. Record-breaking temperatures, according to the weatherman. A bunch of us are heading to the beach.”

“I’m supposed to paint.”

Disappointment replaces her smile.

“But I can get out of it.”

Her smile returns. “I’m not going until the afternoon because of that assignment.”

“Brilliant. I’ll paint in the morning and go in the afternoon.” *And keep an eye on you for the rest of the day.* The blue-eyed devil won’t get within a hundred yards of her, not if I have anything to say about it.

“Okay, I can give you a ride. I was thinking of leaving around two. Or will that be too early?” Leah studies my face while waiting for my answer.

I point at the glimmer of black across the street. “I got my own wheels. So maybe you can ride with me.”

“You’ve got a motorcycle! Oh my word, I love riding. My dad had a Harley. He adored that bike. Called it Babe.”

The thought of having Leah’s arms around me is more than I can resist. “If you’d like, I could take you on a short ride now. I was about to take my lunch break.”

“That would be awesome.” She sighs. “But I should get back and work on that stupid assignment.”

“A ride might clear your head.”

“Okay. Twist my arm.”

“I have to put this stuff away.” Glancing at my dusty clothes, I add, “And clean up a bit, and then we’re off. I’ll be quick. I promise.”

Leah insists on grabbing the paint cans as I carry the ladder into the alley behind the store.

"Thanks. I'll be ready in a few." As I take the cans in one hand, I hold the bookstore's back door open for her with the other.

"I'll meet you in the front. It's too nice a day to spend a moment inside that I don't have to."

I rush in, dropping the paint by the back door. I snatch a clean T-shirt out of my knapsack stuffed under Ed's desk and head for the bathroom. I wash the grime off my face, arms, and hands, and change in a minute flat. On my way back through the office, I grab an old jean jacket forgotten by a past employee. *Thank goodness Ed never throws anything away.* From the faint scent of weed and the peace patch sewn on the sleeve, I guess it was Journey's. But it'll have to do.

At the front of the store, Ed leans against the counter and peers out the window.

"I was going to take my lunch break. Would that be all right?"

"She's a cute girl." He jabs his finger to the window.

"Yeah, she's okay." I lie. She's so much more than *cute.* "I'll be back in about an hour."

Ed ignores me. "She. Is. A. Cute. Girl."

"Around two."

Ed rolls his eyes. "Take an extra-long lunch break."

"I can't. I want to get most of the scraping done this afternoon so I can take tomorrow afternoon off. If you don't mind, that is. It's supposed to be a hot one."

"How long has this place looked like this?" he asks. "Years," he says, answering his own question. "So if a pretty girl wants to spend time with you, take advantage of it. Someday, you'll look like this." Ed displays himself. I half expect him to twirl.

I laugh. "You're still a handsome dude. I won't be too long."

Ed huffs. "Romance is wasted on the young. If I were your age and a girl like that wanted to go on a ride with me, I wouldn't be back for hours. Work be damned."

I can't fight back the smirk. "Bye, Ed."

"Have some fun for me," he calls.

I grin back at him and head out the door. The heat from the afternoon sun blazes down.

Leah's waiting in the shade. "Wow, you were quick."

I smile, remove the helmet from the bike's side hook, and hold it out to her. "This is for you."

"Where's yours?"

I knock my knuckle on the top of my skull. "I don't need one. Hard head. And put this on, too," I say, holding out the jacket.

Leah begins to protest as she tugs on the helmet. "But it's gotta be close to ninety-five."

I rub the sheer fabric of her sleeve between my thumb and fingers. "If something happens, this won't be much protection."

She gives a defeated sigh and takes the jacket. She sniffs the sleeve and scrunches her nose. "It smells sickly sweet, like..." She pauses to think. "Like pot."

I mount the bike and start the engine. As the old Triumph rumbles to life, I tap the seat behind me. "The jacket isn't mine. I found it in the office. Probably Journey's. Wasn't he one of your favorites?" I grin.

Leah groans and rolls her eyes as she joins me—using my shoulder for support. She straddles the seat, and her legs press against mine. Her slender arms wrap around my waist. My heart quickens and feels as if it might lunge right out of my chest. Her breath warms the bare skin of my neck. As we begin to roll, Leah's arms tighten. I chuckle. Ed's right; an hour won't be long enough.

The road winds northward, hugging the coast. Between long stretches of sun-baked forest, small villages with tall, white steeples play peek-a-boo along the rocky shoreline. The wind ruffles my hair, giving me the sensation of flying. The road snakes right, then left. Every sharp corner earns me a squeal, and Leah's arms wrap tighter around my waist. Again, the woods begin to thin, and a town situated on a lazy flowing river unfolds before us. With shop-lined streets set against the backdrop of a spectacular view, it looks as though it's been plucked off a postcard.

I slow the bike to the curb. "This is a pretty little spot. Whatcha say we have a look around?"

Leah fidgets on the seat. "If you say so. This is Wiscasset. My unchanged and very boring hometown. My mom still lives down that way, in the house I grew up in." She points down a small side street.

"Let's go."

"I don't know if that's such a great idea."

"I'd love to see where you were raised." My small smile builds.

After a tense silence, Leah's posture sags. "Okay, won't *she* be surprised. Fourth house on the left." The nervous edge to her voice mixes with a touch of resignation.

Within minutes, we pull up in front of a small New England–style farmhouse dwarfed by the two primordial oaks flanking it. A porch wrapping the first story is lined with bold-red Adirondack chairs that stand out in contrast against crisp-white clapboards. From the mailbox post hangs a white sign with matching red lettering: MAINE WINTERS POTTERY.

"She's probably in her studio," Leah says, swinging her leg over the side, and removing the helmet.

"She's an artist, too?"

"Yup. Like mother, like daughter." Leah slips off the jacket and lays it over the seat. "I think it's safer if this stays here. My mom doesn't need to think I'm a pothead."

I smile and push off the bike.

Leah takes my hand without hesitation as she leads me through the deep shade toward the back of the house. We cross the rolling lawn to a small barn positioned on the river's edge. The glassy surface of the water reflects the building's weathered gray shingles.

The interior of the barn is cool compared to the mid-afternoon heat. The smell of earth mingles with pine. A petite woman with short strawberry-blond curls sits hunched over a potter's wheel. Her hands embrace and smooth a small spinning chunk of clay. Each touch changes the lump's form, and a shape begins to emerge. Around the room's perimeter are shelves stacked with brightly colored pots in different shapes and sizes.

Leah waits patiently for her mother while breezes blowing through the open door ruffle and play with her hair. Soon the wheel slows, and her mother leans back to examine her work.

"Mom."

She looks up, and a stunned smile flashes across her narrow face. "Lee-lee, what are you doing here? You didn't tell me you were coming. Or did I forget?"

"Nope. It's a surprise," Leah says.

As her mother steps toward us, her gray eyes flick to me, and Leah releases my hand.

"This is Jack. Jack, my mom, Marlee."

I bow.

"My, what manners." She grins at her daughter then returns the smile to me. "Nice to meet you, Jack."

"And you, Marlee," I say. "It's clear where your daughter gets her love of the arts. Your workmanship is impeccable."

"Thank you." Marlee grins and looks at her daughter. "Manners and taste. He's a keeper. I was just going to clean up and have lunch, or is it dinnertime? I never bother to keep track when I'm in the zone. Anyhow, hungry?" Without waiting for a reply, Marlee removes her apron, tosses it aside, and wipes her hands on a towel that was draped over her shoulder. She begins to hum as she heads out the door toward the house.

"You're loading it on a little thick, don't you think?" Leah murmurs.

"I want her to like me."

"No worries there. You got her eating out of your hand." Her smile looks a bit annoyed.

"Only one thing."

Leah stops and looks at me. "What?"

"Does she cook like your brother?" I whisper.

She laughs. "Thank goodness, no."

The interior of the quaint little farmhouse is not at all what I expected. One giant room takes up most of the first floor. Sunlight floods in through large windows that look out over the river, and each wall is painted a different color. Marlee disappears into the bathroom to clean up. "You should show Jack your sketches," she calls out before shutting the door.

I turn, giving Leah a hopeful grin.

"My mom's a bit of a hoarder. Upstairs is a sty." Her excuse seems half-hearted, as if she's trying to convince herself and me.

"I'm sure I've seen worse. Anyway, I'd love to see your artwork."

"No! Sorry, but no." She shifts away as an awkward silence follows.

Her refusal to open up and let me in is like a kick to the gut. *Hypocrite. Think what you're keeping from her.* In truth, we're practically strangers. I curse myself again for thinking we could ever be more. I realize Leah is studying me.

"Have you ever been to Wiscasset?" she asks in a whisper.

"Besides today, no. Never. Why?"

Leah doesn't answer. She stares out the window, blinking repeatedly while she gnaws on her lower lip as though she's trying to find courage.

"What is it?"

She shakes her head.

I'm about to press the matter when Marlee breezes through the room, heading to the kitchen. "Lee-lee, I could use a hand."

"Sure thing." Leah says, but the sound seems to get stuck in her throat. "I'll be right back." She smoothes her clothes nervously, and with a deep sigh, she leaves the room.

When the door swings shut, I hear Marlee mumble, but nothing clear leaks through the wooden door. Curiosity wins over manners. I walk silently to the doorway, where I begin to understand her apprehension.

"Well, he seems like a nice young man," says Marlee.

I'm amused, despite the tension still hanging in the air.

"Yup." Dishes clatter.

"So handsome and polite."

More clanging. "Don't go there, Mom."

"I'm just saying he's nice. What's wrong with that?"

Leah sighs. "You're right. Jack is a great guy, but we're only friends—"

Dropping my head, I close my eyes.

"Honestly, we haven't known each other that long. By the way, don't tell Grady that. You know how he can get."

Silence follows, giving me a chance to think. *Friends.* A twang of disappointment flitters in the pit of my stomach. I should be grateful she considers me a friend rather than a creepy stalker.

"You know, your father and I started out as friends."

"I know. I've heard the stories a thousand times. This would make it a thousand and one."

"Well then, if you're *only* friends, why do my comments bother you, hmm?" Marlee laughs. "Is it wrong for me to want you to find a nice man who will treat you like your father treated me?"

"End of discussion, Mom. What if he hears you? Now drop it. Please."

Silence blankets the kitchen, except for the occasional clinking dish.

I groan internally and return to my seat. I don't remember courtship being this baffling. But then again, I have been out of circulation for a long time.

Her mother is still grinning from ear to ear when she and Leah emerge from the kitchen. She sets a pot of steaming soup in the middle of the table and sits. Leah slides a stack of variegated bowls next to the pot. Her expression frozen in an annoyed frown, she slips into the chair nearest mine. I sit mindlessly at the small round table, pretending to be oblivious to the glares shot back and forth between mother and daughter. In my head, buzzing thoughts spin at a hundred miles per hour. Sure, Leah is friendly, welcoming even, but maybe that's part of her makeup and has nothing at all to do with me. Not liking where my assessments are leading, I shut them down.

Minus a cue, Marlee and Leah bow their heads, and I follow suit.

"Thank you, Lord, for this food. Bless it to our bodies. Amen," Marlee says, then looks up with a smile. "Now, let's eat." She ladles scoops of hot broth and vegetables into the bowls. "Oh, drat, I forgot the biscuits. Could you, Lee-lee? They're on the stove."

Leah gives her mother a wary look. "Sure." She stands, and instinctively, so do I.

Too busy gazing out the window, Marlee doesn't seem to notice my overly proper manners. Maybe she's just being polite or storing up material for another mother-daughter chat. Leah, on the other hand, does notice. She stares at me. I try to read her eyes but decipher only a swirling mess of emotion. She doesn't say a word before darting into the kitchen.

I hesitate before dropping back into my seat. When Leah returns, she avoids eye contact.

"I'm assuming that's your bike out front." Marlee nods to the window, blowing on her soup-filled spoon.

"Yup," I say.

"My husband loved to ride."

"Leah mentioned something about that."

"Is that a '69 Bonneville?"

My eyebrows rise. "Uh-huh."

"What's the '67 exhaust doing on it?"

"I had to replace the whole system a couple years back. It's all I could find at the time."

"Too bad. That will kill the resale value."

"That doesn't matter much to me. She's not going anywhere." I smile. "You know your bikes."

"My hubby made me a bit of a gearhead. It was his passion, and he unknowingly passed it on to me and the kids. Leah knows more than she lets on. She can change her own tires and oil. She insisted on it before she could drive."

Another similarity. In spite of Lydia's wealthy upbringing, she hated having things done for her. It was a trait that first attracted me to her.

Leah shrugs then grins as if she's up to no good. "Mom, I was just thinking. Did you get rid of that box of Dad's stuff in the attic?"

"It's still there. I know, I know. I should take it to Goodwill."

"Would you mind if I grab Dad's old helmet? Jack gave up his for me."

I shake my head. "Thank you, but I don't need..."

"Nonsense. You shouldn't be riding around with your head just asking to become a squashed melon." Marlee regards me with a motherly eye.

"Besides, if I have to wear one, so do you." Leah jumps to her feet then dashes up the stairs.

I sigh. No sense arguing now. I've been tag-teamed, and neither Leah nor her mother seem like the type to take no for an answer. I chuckle.

Without a word, Marlee heads into the kitchen. I grab the dishes and follow.

"Thank you, Mrs. Winters," I say, setting the bowl in the sink. "The soup was delicious."

"You're very welcome, but only if you call me Marlee. My mother-in-law was Mrs. Winters."

I smile then nod.

"She likes you, you know? You're the first *friend* she's dragged home. She's kept to herself ever since her bout with cancer." She pours the remaining soup into a container and pops on the lid.

My brow furrows. "Cancer?"

"Me and my big mouth." She slides the soup onto the top shelf of the refrigerator. "She doesn't like talking about it. Who can blame her?"

"How old was she?"

"Thirteen. It was a difficult time, as you can imagine. My husband had died a few years earlier, so it was just the three of us. Grady took it the hardest. Man of the house and all. It was his first year of college, but he came home every weekend to be with me and sit with Leah after her chemo treatments. It made him more protective than the average big brother."

"She seems healthy now."

"Oh, yes, she's cured. Funny thing is, somehow Lee-lee knew she'd be okay all along and kept trying to reassure us. I call it faith. Grady says it's a sixth sense. But who knows?"

"Mom?" Leah asks from the door, making us both jump. "Whatcha talking about?"

"Oh, nothing important. Jack and I are just getting to know one another. Right, Jack?"

I nod.

"Whatever she's saying, it's all lies. I'm perfect with no faults." Leah winks.

I gawk at the matte-black helmet in her hand. She rotates it, showing off the ridge of spikes down the middle and the tie-dyed skulls and crossbones decals on either side.

"It's interesting," I say.

"The stickers were my idea," Leah says.

"Your father was an understanding man, I see."

"Yeah, he had a quirky sense of humor. Straight as an arrow during the week, but a rebel on the weekends." She places the helmet on my head. "It fits."

Marlee chuckles.

"Fantastic. Maybe you should wear it, and I'll take mine back."

"Oh, no. I think it's perfect," Leah says with that mischievous grin.

The helmet's payback for Journey's jacket, I assume.

CHAPTER NINE

WE LOSE TRACK OF TIME sitting out by the river, skipping stones and roasting marshmallows. Throughout the evening, I ask her many times about why she wanted to know if I'd been to Wiscasset, but every time, she weaves and dodges, never giving me a straight answer.

Adding to my ever-growing list of stupid things to impress a girl, I wear the monstrosity that is her father's helmet all the way home. Luckily, it's well past ten when I return Leah to her dorm.

She fiddles with her keys. Again, she stalls. Once she enters and closes her door, I realize what a coward I've become. I take a moment to reach deep for boldness then knock on the door. Leah opens it, looking surprised.

"I wanted you to know I had a wonderful time." I take her hand, and in a nineteenth-century gesture of love, I kiss it.

Her breath catches softly, then she smiles.

"Until tomorrow."

"Good night, Jack," she says, closing her door.

The door across the hall cracks open, and Nathan looks out. I nod a hello, and the boy slams his door, almost smashing his fingers in the process.

After another fruitless search for the sapphire-eyed man, I crawl into bed around three in the morning. Exhausted, I slip easily into slumber, and again, I dream of Leah.

In my dream, she leads me through a field of flaxen grasses toward a lone elm. Tall and proud, the tree points straight to the sky. Under its canopy of leaves and branches, Leah stops. She cups my face in her small hands and stares into my eyes. "Who are you, Jack Hammond? And what are you hiding from me?"

I say nothing, but a need for Leah to know everything about me stirs within. Without my permission, scenes of my past burst to life around us, flickering like images from old home movies.

I want to yell for her to close her eyes or apologize for the fact that nothing but darkness resigns inside me now. But my mouth stays frozen shut. When the last image fades, Leah does something I never predicted. She smiles and then says, "See? You can't scare me away. I'm still here."

I wrap my arms around her waist and press her body against mine. Closing my eyes to savor the moment, I move in for a kiss. "Leah," I whisper.

An orange glow shines through my eyelids and invades my dream, waking me. The sun beams through my grungy east window, stretching warm streaks along my face. Streams of dust float and swirl through the rays. *Ah hell, only a dream.* I lie spread-eagle across my bed, wishing for just five more minutes in that paradise. Alas, I'm wide awake. I jolt up onto one elbow and glance out the window, squinting against the blinding brightness of the world. By some miraculous event, the meteorologist nailed today's forecast—bright sunshine.

After painting at Rare Books, I park in front of Leah's building at noon sharp. As my foot hits the curb, the door flies open, and Leah bounds out. A small backpack hangs over her shoulder, and her white jean jacket swings over her arm. Coral bathing suit straps peek out from the collar of her pale-yellow T-shirt. Her braided hair leaves her neck exposed.

"I finished. I finished. I finished," she chants as she hops down the stairs.

"Brilliant."

She fiddles with a stray lock of hair, twisting it around and around her finger, releasing it, then repeating the process again. "I have you to thank."

"Me?"

"Okay, maybe not you. I owe Bessy the thanks." A trace of humor appears across her lips then disappears.

Mesmerized, I step forward. The inner voice begs for a kiss. I resist, stride back, and lean against the motorcycle's smooth leather seat. "Who's Bessy?"

"The bike, silly."

"You named my bike Bessy?"

"Yup." The smile she's been restraining breaks through and expands across her beautiful face.

Leaning back, I cross my arms over my chest. "No way. You can't name a guy's bike something like Bessy. You'll get me beat up for sure. Rocky or Bud." *Or even Tank*. "But not Bessy." I mean to sound horrified, but the suppressed laugh that bubbles to the surface betrays me.

She blithely ignores my rejection of her naming choice. "A ride on Bessy made all the difference. After we got back last night, I stayed up late and finished."

"You could've gone to the beach this morning, then. You didn't have to wait for me." I hold the helmet out to her.

"I wanted to." She quickly slips the helmet over her head. No apprehension. No doubt.

Her response surprises me. *Just friends, my ass.* But is it possible Leah's developing real feelings for me? I grin and straddle the Triumph. With a turn of the key, the bike rumbles to life, and Leah climbs on. As before, when her arms tighten around my waist, my heart quickens into a frenzy.

Thank you, Bessy! I pull away from the curb.

As we head out of the city, the stifling heat surrenders to cool ocean breezes. Concrete buildings give way to sprawling fields and curvy roads with glimpses of the sea. Leah points. A crescent-shaped beach emerges through a grove of tall pines, stretching pale yellow along the shoreline. I drive into a dirt parking lot. Dust billows around us. I park alongside a row of cars lining a weathered split-rail fence.

We walk down the trail of wooden planks. The salty scent mixes with the sweet fragrance of the deep-pink sea roses that border the path. The dune grasses flutter and bend with the light gusts, submitting into waves of apple green. The beach is not as crowded as I would have thought. Just a handful of groups dot the sand.

When we reach Rachel, Grady, and others I don't know, Leah flops down onto one of the large multicolored blankets, leaving a spot open next to her, which Rachel takes. In front of me, a curly-haired boy crashes into a boy with fiery-red hair, causing me to step back. As Curly Head rams a guy's face into the sand and tears the Frisbee from his grasp, he says, "Oh, good. Now we have even numbers. What's your excuse now, Grady?"

"I said I'd play later, Tom. I'm finishing my lunch first." Grady looks at me, at Leah, then back to me. "Hey, Jack. Nice day, huh?" He grins.

"Yeah." I avoid eye contact. I can imagine the parade of questions marching through his head—*Why are you here with my sister? What are your intentions? When are you planning to snap and kill us all?* I grimace.

"You know what they call a day without sunshine? Night."

I shake my head and chuckle.

"Speaking of night, I called Leah yesterday. She was out late, for her anyway."

I nod, watching the heated game of tackle Frisbee.

"She's never out, even on Saturday nights."

"Oh," I say, still not looking at him.

"Bike ride, huh?"

I allow my eyes to stray in Grady's direction. "Yeah."

"Uh-huh." He looks at his sister again.

If I were a betting man, I would venture that the big-brother speech is on the horizon. I wheel around and look out across the sparkling ocean—out where blue meets blue—hoping the action buys me more time. I don't want to have the talk with an audience, if I can help it.

Thankfully, Grady drops the subject.

I remove my shirt and toss it onto an empty blanket. Closing my eyes, I enjoy the warmth. As I turn to Leah to comment on the gorgeous day, I freeze. All the girls' hungry eyes are trained on me. *Dammit.* Leah isn't looking, but her blush betrays her. Uncomfortable with the unwanted attention, I shuffle my feet in the sand. Tom mutters something about him needing to go to the gym, then smacks into my shoulder as he passes. He plops at Rachel's side, takes her hand, and glares at me.

Without a word, Leah gets up and walks past, heading down the crescent-shaped beach. I'm about to join her when I hear Grady behind me.

"Jack, can I have a minute?"

With a sigh, I take a seat on his beach towel. This time, Grady's eyes don't meet mine. Instead, he watches his sister walking down the beach alone.

"She'd kill me for doing this. There's been a lot of guys interested in my sister." He tilts his head toward the group of unfamiliar men standing by the ocean's edge, and he grimaces.

At least three of them have their eyes trained on Leah. My face flashes hot, and my hackles rise. They're looking at her like she's an edible treat created for their enjoyment.

Grady continues. "She's never given any of them the

time of day. Always too busy with school or some other excuse. Until you." He pauses. "Treat her right, okay? Or I'll kick your ass." He tosses the last bite of a bagel sandwich in his mouth, stands, and tackles Tom. The other guys hoot and holler. Grady can fight, that's for sure.

I jump up and jog after Leah. "Hey, Leah, wait up," I call.

She stops and turns, with a relieved expression.

"Do you mind if I walk with you?"

"No, of course not." She stoops and picks up another shard of color from its sandy bed.

I study the collection of lusterless glass in her open hand. There are shades of brown, green, white, and aqua. My fingertips trace the odd-shaped glass then skim her palm. Her skin is just how I'd imagined—soft like velvet.

"Beautiful," I whisper.

"You've never seen sea glass before?" she asks, a bit out of breath.

"No." I pause. "But I'm not talking about the glass."

"Oh." Her warm eyes study me. She bites her lower lip.

"Too cheesy?"

She shakes her head then she proceeds down the beach.

A piece of aqua catches my eye. I lift it from its dry sandy home and show it to Leah.

"See, this one isn't ready yet." She points at the shiny, sharp edges.

With a snap of my wrist, the glass sails and skips three times along the rippling surface before sinking into the ocean.

Her eyes dance as an impish smile appears on her lips. She tosses the shards and grabs my hand, hauling me toward the tumbling waves. I follow. The chilly water crashes onto our bodies, making my eyes widen, and I draw in a deep breath. Still, it's refreshing against the hot summery air.

"Life's too short. You have to enjoy the little things.

Doesn't that feel incredible?" she asks, amused by my reaction.

"It does."

She turns and squints into the bright sunshine. Her escaping blond strands play in the sea's gusts, twisting and whirling. Sea spray droplets glisten as they chase one another along her slender shoulders and down her delicate arms. Her coral two-piece swimsuit sets off her creamy, pale skin. The small of her back is a perfect ivory arch. I shut my eyes tight, grinding my upper teeth into my lower lip to fight the rush of emotion slamming into me.

Sexy as hell. She truly is going to drive me stark raving mad. I puff out a breath. When my eyes open again, I find Leah standing in front of me, studying me. I swallow hard.

"What does your tattoo say? It's French, right?" With her index finger, she followed the arched calligraphy along my chest to the left of my sternum. If I were mortal, I'd have a scar there—or be dead. Another missed opportunity.

Her touch sends thousands of shivers through me. I reach up and take her hand, entwining my fingers with hers.

"*Foi apporte la force.* It means, 'Faith brings strength.'"

"Beautiful words to live by," she mutters, still staring at the faded black cursive lettering.

"Yes." I tremble, and inside, I wince, remembering the feeling of the cold sharp steel of the bayonet piercing my chest, straight into my heart. As though it were yesterday, I can hear the artillery buzzing over my head.

It was 1914, and the Germans had invaded Arras, a small town in northern France that I'd called home for the past two years. Shouts and screams told me the invading army was drawing closer, and I ran through abandoned alleys, looking for an escape. I stumbled out of the cramped darkness into the sunlight and into a heart-wrenching scene.

A woman who owned a bakery two blocks from where I

lived lay sprawled on the street. Her vacant stare suggested she was dead. The sight wasn't uncommon that day. Her son, maybe twelve, stood over her, grasping a gun in trembling hands, readying to protect the slain woman. Her little girl huddled in a doorway, crying, and called for her mother. I heard the angry shouts—louder still. Time for fleeing was quickly running out.

With a gentle tone and encouraging words, I coaxed the pair to come with me. We crept down darkened alleyways, peering around corner after corner. Without warning, a German soldier stepped out of a back doorway of one of the abandoned homes, his arms filled with candlesticks and a teapot, which he was obviously looting. Silver clanked around his boots as he dropped the valuables. When his surprise quickly turned to hatred, he plunged his bayonet into my chest.

The little girl screamed, and I fell back onto the cobblestones with the bayonet still lodged in my chest. The ripping pain was intense. I gritted my teeth, removing the sharpened steel with a swift tug. Bayonet in hand, I stood.

Surprised, the solider grabbed the boy and placed a knife to his chest. "*Lassen Sie Ihre Waffe fallen!*"

I released the blade, and it clattered on the stone ground.

From the shadows, a shot rang out. The soldier fell forward, freeing the boy, but not before sinking his blade into the boy's gut.

The boy begged his sister to be brave, even as his blood pooled around us. "*Doux J*ésus*, sauvez ma soeur,*" he prayed. Touched by rage, I bit my tongue and kept my thoughts to myself. But it was clear, Sweet Jesus didn't care for any of us, including his sister. If he did, how could he take one so young and ignore another who was so old and longing for heaven?

The next words out of the boy's lips stuck with me. They were words to live by, or at least strive for, because despite it all, that boy's assurance never seemed to waver. He looked straight into his sister's tearful eyes and reminded her of what their mother taught them. "*Foi apporte la force*," he said over and over.

As the boy died in my arms, a tall, wiry man stepped out of a dark corner of the alley. He bandaged my wounds and muttered about going to hell for taking the life of a child. His eyes—sapphire blue—darted from side to side as he looked for danger.

A hand covering my trembling one summons me from the memory.

"Are you all right?" Her voice has an unexpected effect. The dulcet tone draws me out of the memory without lingering effects. The tremors recoil like snakes under the trance of a charmer's melody.

She fills my vision. A face full of concern without judgment looks into mine.

"I am."

"That's happened before. The trembling, I mean." It's not a question. She notices more than I give her credit for, yet she's still here.

I take a moment and drag breath in and out of my lungs. The sapphire devil had shown me kindness. If not for him, the little girl would have died, too. However, Death seems to follow this man wherever he goes.

The correlation between the flashback and the revelation has left me winded. I'm afraid that if I don't speak soon, maybe even say something clever, Leah might figure out what a complete nutcase I am. Unable to summon words, I nod, step out of the water, and sit on the sand. Stretching out my legs, I lean back on my elbows, trying to pretend what just happen isn't a big deal.

She sits next to me, curling her legs under her. "You were shaking the afternoon you ran into me, the first time you saw me. You looked like you'd been hit by a Mack truck. You said I reminded you of someone. Who was it?"

The question grips my lungs with an iron fist. *Think.* I look away, staring at the blanket of sand, the dune grasses, and the choppy waves—anywhere but Leah. She seems to be able to read me like a book, and I'm not sure what she might see in my face.

"You remind me of a girl I knew in England," I say.

"You loved her." This, too, is not a question.

I debate how to answer, but I'm too slow, and my silence seems to serve as a confirmation.

"I thought so," she says.

"She died a long time ago."

"Oh." Leah pauses, and I allow myself a look. She's staring off into the distance as though she's a million miles from here.

I wish I could read her mind. What must she be thinking? Freak? Crazy man? I grimace and let my gaze fall away.

After a moment of thought, she continues. "And the second time? In the coffee shop? Was that reaction for the same reason?"

"No, that was the flu," I lie. "You should be thankful I ran out when I did and didn't puke on you."

"Thanks for that. Rachel would've had me clean it up. She doesn't do messes." She laughs.

Leah dismisses my troubling behavior as if it's no more than an everyday ailment like a headache or the sniffles. First, she doesn't even recognize danger when its sapphire eyes are glaring straight into her face, and now this. The job of keeping her safe is going to be too big for one man. Maybe Leah had the right idea, even in jest. Maybe I do need the National Guard.

Deep in thought, Leah watches her toes wriggle in the sand. The quietude makes me nervous as I wonder what she's thinking.

"So, how was work yesterday?" I ask.

"It was almost uneventful."

"Almost?"

"There was this jerk a while back who didn't know what the word 'no' meant. Nothing happened, not really. Anyway, he came into the coffee shop again. Until he saw me, that is. Then he hurried out. Maybe he's embarrassed or something. Who knows? It's not like I did anything to scare him when he grabbed me."

A smile pulls ever so slightly at my lips. *Not as dumb as he looks.*

"You know something?"

"About what?" I ask, my eyes widening.

"You do. You know something. I can tell."

I look away.

"Tell me."

"He was rude to you," I say in a husky voice. Nervousness churns my stomach. I can't see her face through the curtain of her hair between us. I watch the frothy waves lap the sand. I said too much—more than I intended. My temper always gets the better of me. It's my worst trait.

"How do you know that?" she whispers.

I close my eyes as her voice summons the truth again. "The day that man grabbed you, I saw it. I was coming in to remove him when Rachel threw him out. I followed him, pushed him into an alley, and roughed him up a bit. That 'jerk,' as you properly called him, deserved far more than he got."

When I look at her, she's staring straight at me. I'm still fuming—the heat of remembered anger burns deeply—but the intensity doesn't frighten her as I expected. Instead, she reaches out to stroke the top of my hand with her fingertips, which are cool against my sunbaked skin. I suck in a deep breath.

"I can take care of myself," she says.

"I'm sorry if I overstepped my bonds."

"I've noticed something about you," Leah says as she pops to her feet before heading back toward the others.

"What?" I ask, uncertain that I want to know. There have been enough truths for one day. I push myself up from the sand.

"Along with your chivalrous nature and your cheesy pick-up lines, you have quite the manners," she says. "Opening doors, bowing, even standing when a woman gets up to leave. Your manners are like a character out of some nineteenth-century novel."

"Are they?" I changed my manner of speech with practice, ridding myself of the old-style pronunciations. Manners are a whole different beast. They're embedded. No matter how hard I try to break free, hints of them remain. Most people aren't observant enough to notice.

"Yes." She grins.

I shrug. "I'm a little old-fashioned, I guess."

"Yes, you are." She's looking at me as if I'm a puzzle she's trying to solve.

"It's ingrained. I don't think I could change if I tried. It's the way my mother raised me," I add, hoping she'll believe the oddity of my manners is a cultural difference.

Her forehead puckers; she's clearly not satisfied with my excuses. Lacking a response, she turns and runs to join Rachel and the other boys in a game of Frisbee.

My thoughts whirl. Immortality might have stolen paradise from me, but a twist of fate has given back at least a taste of it. Foolishly maybe, I yearn to open myself up to her and to have one person on this spinning ball who knows who I really am. And even if Leah's time on earth will be a brief moment compared to my lifetime, I want to share her life, which most people would take for granted. But that means I'll have to tell her the truth, and I'm frightened by the prospect. I've lied to her and hidden behind a normal mask. I groan. Lying is the least of what's wrong with me.

CHAPTER TEN

THE NEXT MORNING, I WALK into Old Port Java with a plan to ask Leah on a proper date and leave no room for doubt where my intentions lie. The plan is simple, but it's a starting point for a bigger, scarier scheme that requires me baring my soul.

Leah is too busy clearing and wiping down tables to notice my entrance. "Good morning, Green Eyes," I say, snatching trash from a neighboring table and tossing it into the white garbage bag at her side.

She stiffens then turns. A smile graces her face, but she quickly reins it in. "Hi." She grabs the bag and heads behind the counter. "What can I get you this morning?" Her tone is too brisk to be considered friendly.

I tilt my head. "Anything wrong?"

She washes her hands in a small sink hidden in the corner. "No. Just busy." Her eyes flit away.

The place is practically empty, except for two middle-aged women jabbering over their coffees at a back table. "I see."

"So, what do you want?" She locks eyes with me as if she's attempting to dissect my soul.

"Large dark roast. Please." I try not to squirm. "Are you sure nothing's the matter?"

She gives me a quick nod then pours my coffee. I stand dumbfounded, not sure if I should continue on the course I set this morning. "Three twenty," she says, placing my cup on the counter.

I nod, still dazed, and yank my wallet from my pocket. I take a deep breath as I hand her a five-dollar bill. "There's something I wanted to ask you." I gulp in more air. "I was hoping you might want to join me for dinner tonight." I recite my script perfectly, just like I did in the mirror this morning while shaving.

Gnawing on her bottom lip, Leah shifts from foot to foot then takes a step backward and squares her shoulders. Her eyes pool with moisture. "I can't. I have plans." Her voice is uncharacteristically timid.

Plans. The word hangs in the air. "Oh" is all I can muster.

Leah glances away, visibly uncomfortable. I want to ask if her plans are with Nathan or some other clown who is too naïve to understand how lucky he is. But I don't. I look at my coffee and keep my mouth shut. If I'm honest, any boy would be a better choice than an ageless man with a timeworn heart. They could give her the white-picket-fence dream I've seen on TV; I assume it's still a future most women of this day and age want.

When I look up, our eyes meet. Leah opens her mouth then closes it again.

"Maybe another time then," I say. "I should get to work."

"Yeah, of course. Your change." She holds out her hand.

I shake my head. "Keep it." I grab my coffee and move toward the door.

"Jack?"

I stop and look at her. "Yes?"

A pleading intensity blazes in her eyes. She sighs and looks away. "Have a good day."

I consider flipping the closed sign and spilling my guts, but the ladies look our way, leaning in to hear every word. *An audience. Grand.* I clench my jaw and fight the urge to tell Leah what I really am. "Thanks. You, too," I finally say. Forcing a weak smile, I walk out the door.

I stand outside, fighting against the rolling nausea. When push came to shove, I turned into a coward. Again. And no matter our words, I can't help feeling that Leah and I just said good-bye.

My phone buzzes in my pocket. "Hello?"

"Jack. It's Grady."

"Can't talk. Gonna be late for work." I sound like a half-dead zombie.

"Wait. Give me just a sec."

"What?"

"I know it's last minute, but I wanted to invite you to tonight's big shindig, if you don't have plans."

"Oh?" The smallest hope sprouts. I cling to it like a life raft in shark-infested waters.

"There's a student art reception tonight. Leah's one of the artists chosen to participate."

"I just saw her. She didn't say a thing about it." I look back though the coffeehouse window, watching Leah.

Chin propped on her hand, she offers a customer an emotionless expression while she waits for his order. She looks sad and lost.

"Bet she seemed a bit distant, huh?"

"Yeah."

"Typical," Grady says, but there's a shift in his cheery tone. "She's nervous about the show. Didn't know how to ask. I know she'd want you there."

"Are you sure?"

"One hundred percent."

"What time?"

"Starts at six thirty. Bayside Gallery."

"I'll be there."

"Perfect. See you tonight."

I arrive at work a few minutes late. I shoot Ed a greeting glance, then walk toward the back in silence, my head low.

"Everything okay?" Ed asks. His eyes are like hot irons on the back of my head.

"Yup," I say, retreating into the office. I toss my knapsack under the desk and let out a sigh. Ed pinpointed the problem—I have no idea if everything is all right. I'm a rookie. I could have done something stupid, screwed everything up with Leah, and have no idea. I consider the possibility that Ed might know something about the subject of women. I get the distinct feeling something is going on between Sally and him. Ed must have some skills in the modern dating arena, at least more than I do.

I march to the front. Ed is still in his usual spot behind the corner, reading the newspaper. "What do you know about women?" I blurt.

Ed raises one eyebrow. "Women? Ahhh, it's that young lady you went riding with the other day, isn't it? I knew you liked her."

I grimace. I'm usually so much better at hiding my emotions. Deep in my core, a siren blares. I don't like being an open book for everyone to read—except when I'm with Leah.

I realize Ed's still talking. "... and the way you've been acting this morning. Ha. It all adds up." He snickers. "My only advice is don't keep anything from her. Women know when you're not being honest. Lost my first wife that way. Bought a boat she didn't think we could afford, hid it at a buddy's house during the off season. Understand, the boat was a beauty." He closes his eyes and smiles. "Twenty-two-foot Grady-White. One-hundred-fifty-power Evinrude. All the bells and whistles." Ed looks at me. His pleasant expression fades to a more sober one. "Shouldn't have bought it, but, man, that baby was beautiful. 'Deal breaker,' she called it. Couldn't blame her. My mistake taught me to be honest to a fault. That's the reason I lost my second wife." He pats me on the back. "My advice: Don't screw up."

Feeling more helpless than I did when I arrived, I go back to worrying while I shelve Austen and the Brontë sisters.

Around noon, Sally stops in. She leans against the counter, watching me. "Are you all right?" she asks.

"Lady trouble," Ed chirps.

Sally rolls her eyes. "Oh, good Lord, what did he tell you? Never mind, I can imagine. Any way I can help?"

A resigned sigh breaks free from my lungs. "There's this girl."

"You got it bad," Ed says with a laugh.

"I haven't been completely honest with her. Past baggage."

Ed sucks in a breath through his teeth. "Strike one."

Sally ignores him, her sharp brown eyes still trained on me. "Girls aren't mind readers, dear. Do you want to tell her?"

"I don't know if I have a choice," I say.

"Well, then tell her." Sally gives me an encouraging smile.

"That's what I told him," Ed chimes in.

Sally shoots him a dirty look. "I'm sure, along with God knows what else. Look at him. Poor boy. He thinks he doesn't have a snowball's chance in hell."

He shrugs. "What he needs to do is man up and ask that girl out. She's a keeper." His attention turns back to me. "Three words for ya. Lou's Lobster Trap. Grab a couple of their famous subs..."

"No!" Sally says, horrified by the suggestion.

We both look at her, perplexed.

"Men," Sally grumbles. "Have you ever been to Lou's?"

I shake my head.

"The employees all wear lobster costumes for the tourists. In the kitchen, there's a fridge and a deep fryer. Not Maine cuisine at its finest."

"What's wrong with that?" Ed asks. "Not every restaurant can be five stars. Snap! Snap! You just got trapped. Best slogan ever."

"May thirteenth!" She points her pudgy finger at his chest.

"What about it?" he asks, his eyes wide.

"Our one-year anniversary! You took me to Lou's for a soggy fried-fish sub and potato chips," Sally says, then purses her lips and gives Ed a dry stare.

I shift from side to side, backing out of the line of fire. Sally's glare reminds me of my mother's the day she found out I was one of the boys responsible for cutting up horsehair and strewing it all over the dance floor at the spring social. The women were itching for hours, and we laughed for days, until my sister Ruth ratted us out. That little prank was the end of my summer fun.

"Coward," Ed whispers, looking at me from the corner of his eye.

The power of invisibility would come in handy right now. *Or teleportation.* I took on a towering mountain named Tank without a second thought, but I'm afraid of this five-foot-four-inch woman and that glare. At this moment, she looks far more dangerous than any Tank.

"I thought it would be romantic. That's where I took you for our first date," Ed defends himself.

"Exactly! And it wasn't!" Her attention turns back to me. "Tell her, Jack. And I'm sure everything will be fine."

As Sally turns to leave, an irked Ed calls out after her, "Hey, what about lunch? Our lunch!"

"Not today," she says and heads out the door.

Ed leans against the counter, arms propping up his chin, and looks over at me.

"Are you sure you two aren't married?" I ask.

"Nope, just sounds like it. We're dating."

"She's angry."

"Yup. She'll get over it. All joking aside, tell that girl the truth." Ed pats me on the shoulder then disappears into the back room, leaving me to my thoughts and the ominous lie hanging over my head.

Tell her. But how?

With Ruth, it had been simple. I was ten and fearless. I never got hurt and never got sick. My mum called me her healthy little colt. One afternoon, Ruth caught me climbing the old Douglas fir at the edge of the Edmunds' field, higher than Mother allowed. I'd been scolded about my adventurous nature too many times to count.

Ruth's concerned shouts made me scramble through the branches, faster and higher. She was two years older than I was and acted like my keeper. It made me want to push the boundaries. Every time she yelled, I climbed higher, until I was very close to the tree's top.

She screamed that she was getting Mother. I remember laughing and scrambling one branch higher. That was my folly. An earsplitting snap split through the air. I tried to grab the passing branches, but nothing stopped my fall. My only thought was *Ruth was right.* My back hit the ground with a deep thud and sent the air rushing out of my lungs. Blackness pressed in.

When my eyes did blink open, Ruth was by my side, crying. She said she thought I was dead. At first, so did I. Despite the pain and shock, my body had taken no lasting damage. A cut across my shoulder and a couple of bruises that healed and faded away in minutes was all I had to show for my fall.

Once the fact that I should've been dead sank in, we agreed never to tell a living soul about how different I was. However, Ruth was convinced that my affliction was a gift from God. But even then, I couldn't have disagreed more. It made me different. A freak. Damned. Even so, after that incident, Ruth and I were close, bonded by my secret.

I have to tell her tonight. I can't wait any longer. It's not fair to her. Once the reception's over, I'll spill all my secrets to her. A lump forms in the pit of my stomach. If she doesn't believe me, I'll show her somehow. I hope I won't have to resort to diving from a tree. There are plenty of secluded woods on the outskirts of the city, and it worked before. I'll do whatever I need to and pray to God it doesn't scare her away.

I arrive at the gallery late, which seems to be the theme of the day. A last-minute customer kept me talking about John Keats and his influence on the Romantic movement well past closing time, then he had the nerve to not buy the book I spent a half hour looking for because he was sure he could find it online for a couple bucks cheaper.

The gallery resides in a row of art-deco-style buildings respectfully renovated to pay homage to the era. Light radiates through floor-to-ceiling windows onto the street. The place is jam-packed with guests sipping wine and eating hors d'oeuvres. It's quickly evident I'm underdressed for the occasion. This isn't the "jeans and T-shirt" kind of crowd.

Nervous anticipation boils to the surface. I weave through the mass of people, catching glimpses of color and texture hanging on the walls, but I stay focused. I spot Leah. She's talking with an elderly couple at the back of the gallery. I press on through the crowd, working my way closer. Finally standing behind her, I wait for my turn. Soon, the man and his wife thank her for her time and move on to look at more paintings. Leah turns, and those beautiful eyes meet mine.

"It looks like the show's already a success," I say, raking my fingers nervously through my hair.

At first, she just stares at me. Her lips press into a hard line. It's obvious she doesn't want me here. Grady was wrong. "What are you doing here?" she finally asks.

"I'm sorry. Grady invited me. It looks like I shouldn't have listened to him. I'll leave." My voice sounds tired and weak.

"I wanted to invite you, but..." She takes a deep breath. In her eyes, I can see she's made a decision. "Will you come with me? There's something I need you to see."

I nod.

She takes my hand. Her skin is soft, but her fingers are ice cold. Tightening her grasp, she leads me back through the crowd to the opposite corner of the gallery then through a door with AUTHORIZED PERSONNEL printed across it in bold red letters. A quick glance tells me we're clearly in a storage area. The room is brightly lit. Framed artwork, all waiting for their debuts, lines the walls and covers the counters.

Leah stops. Moisture threatens to spill from her frightened eyes. As she turns from me, she says, "I had them take this down. I didn't expect you to come tonight, but if Grady had seen it..." She ends with a labored breath. "I wanted to tell you this morning, but I couldn't find the words. And those busybodies." She sighs then points.

I follow her gesture. Before me is a portrait of a man with sable hair and a pronounced square jaw. Light-blue eyes, the color of the summer sky, look back at me. He's dressed in a double-breasted brown frock coat with a cream waistcoat. A hint of a crisp white shirt peers out from behind a black ascot tied around his neck. All the details are there in each brushstroke, including the sickle-shaped birthmark over his left eye.

"I painted this last year," she says.

I run my trembling fingers along my identical blemish and stare at a portrait of myself—the me of decades ago. My breaths come rapid and deep, and the room tilts and spins. A surge of queasiness rolls over me. My mind argues with my eyes. Even though the proof is staring back at me, nothing makes sense. "How?"

"I don't know. I've dreamt of him since I was thirteen. Has Grady told you I had cancer?"

"Your mum did."

"I'm surprised. She hates talking about it." Leah takes a moment to find her words. "One night, there were complications with one of my chemo sessions. I almost died. This man came to me in a dream, told me to wait for him. I survived that night because of that dream, because of you. It is you, isn't it?"

I don't answer.

Eyes closed, she continues, "After that night, I dreamt of you often. In one dream, we were at a ball. You danced every dance with me. In another, we stood under trees. It was warm, summer, I think. You asked..." Her eyes snap open, and her gaze falls to the floor. She doesn't finish. She doesn't have to. I know this story's ending. I asked Lydia to marry me under the elms.

As my hands begin to tremble, I fold my arms and shove my hands in my armpits. *No flashbacks now, please.* Drawing in a long breath, I attempt to calm myself. I blink several times, but the painting's depiction doesn't change.

"Not all the dreams are pleasant. There's a reoccurring one that I don't understand. I hoped you would. I'm running in the pouring rain through a field, trying to find you, but I never do. When I wake, I always have trouble breathing. I don't know why."

"I need to get out of here," I blurt in a hoarse whisper. Darkness crowds in, and I wrestle against it, trying to stay in the present.

"I knew I shouldn't have told you. Maybe I really am—"

One of the gallery workers steps in, and Leah falls silent. Upon seeing us, she hustles out, keeping her eyes glued to the floor.

I can't tell Leah anything here. We have no privacy. Besides, the flashback that threatens harks back to the episodes I had directly after Lydia's death. I can't let everyone see me in all my freakish glory. Nothing says *nutcase* like a man crumpled over, shaking like a cat in a tumbling dryer.

"Can you leave now?" I'm able to force out.

Leah doesn't say a word, only shakes her head.

"When?"

"You don't have to come back. I know this all sounds crazy. I've heard it all before." Her voice is steely.

Does she think I'm showing her pity?

She turns and starts to walk away from me. *No!* My inner voice growls, and I manage to overpower the flashback, at least for the moment. Reaching out in desperation, I grab her shoulders and twirl her back toward me.

"Listen. I'm not leaving you. I need fresh air to clear my head. That's all. Then we can figure this out together. Okay?"

She nods. The tears well and start to trickle down her cheeks.

I wipe the droplets away with my fingers then lean in to kiss her, but she looks down, and my lips meet her forehead.

"When?" I ask.

"Nine."

"I'll be back then. Will you wait for me?"

"Yes, I'll wait."

With her reassurance, I rush from the storage room into the gallery. My eyes dart to the paintings around me. The artwork had faded into the background during my search for Leah. Snapshots of the past look back—my life with Lydia. In her vibrant palette, Leah has captured simple scenes. An afternoon under the elms. A silhouetted couple secluded in the shadows. A room filled with dancing couples in swirling colors of lavender, ruby, and royal blue. An aerial view of a man in the rain, looking skyward. And although his features are hidden by shadow, Leah captured my anguish perfectly.

My nerves stretch to their breaking point, threatening to shatter. The trembling travels from my hands to my arms. I need to get out of here. I shove my way toward the door, through the droning crowd. In my rush, I bump several of the guests. Irritated exclamations follow me. Apologizing, I keep moving for the exit and the solitude of the night.

Outside, the sea of blackness squeezes in around me. Dazed, I draw in air, filling my lungs in sharp breaths. I thought I had it all figured out. I didn't. The paintings are indisputable proof of that. And her words: *I dreamt of him since I was thirteen. Dreamt of you.* How is that possible? With shaky fingers, I rub my temples and begin to walk, fighting against each impending flashback. Strangely enough, the flashback retreats until nothing is left but a residue of a headache. I've never been able to control them before. The past has always reigned over me.

At the water's edge, I stop. My mind strives to find one logical scenario. I dive down one rabbit hole after another, but each serpentine path leads to the same conclusion, which I can't allow myself to believe. Life doesn't work that way, at least not *my* life. Happy endings are made for fairy tales and legends, not reality. My feet begin to move again, aimlessly.

As I resurface from the tangled thoughts, I find myself on a deserted street. A lone well-lit building stands amid the vacant lots lining both sides of the street. The fiery-red painted bricks stand out in contrast to the sparse, dark surroundings. A light over the old rustic door illuminates the gold lettering. Brian Ború Public House. The fresh air isn't helping. Maybe a beer will.

The pub is packed with regulars exchanging friendly banter. The ceiling is lined with aged wooden crossbeams, and the walls are the original brick and fieldstone. The pub feels as though it were transplanted from the motherland piece by piece.

I slip onto the stool. The bartender, whose tawny hair is formed into short spikes, comes by to place a small square napkin in front of me.

"Prize Old Ale," I say.

"ID?" His voice is smothered with a thick Irish brogue.

I grumble and dig my license out of my wallet then toss it on the counter.

The bartender studies it skeptically, shrugs, and hands it back. "Sorry. Just doing my job. We don't carry Prize. Can I get you something else?"

"Guinness." I heave a heavy sigh.

The sapphire-eyed devil's voice whispers in my ear, "Now that's funny. What are you? One hundred and seventy? And you're still getting carded. That's got to suck."

CHAPTER ELEVEN

COLD FLICKS THE SCRUFF OF my neck. I wheel around. The sapphire-eyed devil stands in front of me, looking at me down a long, straight nose. The suggestion of a smirk on his thin lips argues that he's amused.

"What the...?"

"Beer first, questions later. Life's uncertain." He gestures to the bartender and takes the stool next to mine. "Scotch. Oldest you got."

I glower at him. "I remember you. France. 1914."

"You owe me one Ben Franklin." He smiles but doesn't meet my glare.

"I want you to stay away from that girl. Stay away from Leah."

"And what if I don't? You'll do what? Kill me?" His eyes glide to mine, and the rich tone of his laughter sings over the chatter.

"Just like you killed them, if I could."

He studies me from under hooded brows. "Who?"

"The couple at the bar."

"I didn't touch them," he answers, curling his upper lip and spitting each word through clenched teeth.

"You were watching them, left when they did, and you were seen with them right before they died."

"So? She looked familiar. You know how that is. Leah Winters—she's familiar to you, right?" Sarcasm soaks his defensive tone.

My jaw tightens. "I said stay away from her," I hiss.

"Sure, sure. Don't get your knickers in a twist." He pauses. "I'm Artagan."

I snort. "Artagan? What, like the guy from the tale of Olluna?"

"Oh, you've heard it? Yes, one of my more dramatic moments." He smirks.

"You're suggesting you're the son of Death?" I eye him incredulously. He doesn't seem like the heartbroken sort.

"An honorary title, but yes." An amused smile extends across his face and serves only to anger me more.

"All right, enough with the bull—"

"Shhh. We have time. Lots of it, in fact." He chuckles, reaching for his scotch, but he halts, his hands still hanging in the air. A sleek brunette ambles to the bar. Dressed in a vivid red, the woman rests against the counter next to me and orders a drink. She cocks her head to the side and smiles. Then she laughs at the bartender's stupid joke.

Artagan leans around me, his eyes tracing every one of her curves before returning to her face. "You look stunning in crimson."

His lack of respect is unnerving. I realize I'll be lucky if I get a shred of information out of him, and my chest tightens. I've been scrounging for answers, and fate sent me this rude ass. I would laugh if I didn't find everything about him so unbelievably frustrating.

"May I buy you a drink?" Artagan adds, still ogling the woman, but he isn't looking at her eyes.

The bartender glares. "This one's on the house," he says, sliding a pink froufrou drink in front of her.

Artagan laughs. "Pink Lady. Interesting choice. I see you as more of a Dead Sexy or scotch fan." He raises his glass and grins wickedly.

First, the woman scowls, but then her fire-engine red lips form a grin, and she gives Artagan a flirty little wink. She scribbles her number on a napkin and tucks the paper into the breast pocket of his blazer.

As she slinks to her table, Artagan leans away from the counter. His stool balanced on two legs while he enjoys the view. *Nope, no heartbreak there.* He's still grinning when he brings his amber drink to his lips and is about to sip.

"Artagan, huh? The same son of a bitch who destroyed a whole village, including every child." My timing is perfect and gets the reaction I was aiming for.

Artagan slams his glass onto the counter, and the ice cubes clink against the sides. His eyes snap to me, then he shoots me a long, hard stare. White-hot fire seethes under the surface. "They all deserved it." He snarls. His resonant voice shows no sign of pity or remorse. "I thought you, above anyone else, would understand. What would you have done if it'd been your Lydia?"

My hand clenches involuntarily. *If influenza had been a village of people, what wouldn't I have done to avenge Lydia's death?* I inhale slowly, focusing. I can't let him distract me, not when I'm so close to getting answers. "Lydia died a long time ago, but if you're who you say you are, you know that."

"True. In part," he says.

I stare at him, unblinking. "Part?"

He smiles and gestures to an empty booth in the back corner. "May I suggest we move over there? It will allow us to talk more freely, away from prying ears."

I nod and stand, grabbing my bottle.

Once we're settled, I ask, "What do you mean 'in part'?"

"Patience. You've waited over one hundred years. A minute isn't going to kill you."

"How do you know my age?"

Artagan puts a finger to his lips. Then he takes three

long sips of his single-malt scotch, savoring each swallow.

My grip on my beer tightens with each second of silence. I'm wondering if the bottle or my self-restraint will break first.

"Ahhh, Macallan. The good stuff," he says. "Let's start at the beginning. I assume you know you're immortal."

"Yeah."

"Any theories why?"

"I don't have a soul?" I throw out my latest hypothesis with a shrug.

He bursts into laughter. "No, no, no, you're nothing like them."

"Then what? Am I a son of Death, too?" I ask, not amused.

"You might not be Death's son, but you're a relation. All immortals are. We don't die because Death doesn't claim his own. Welcome to the family, as dysfunctional as it is." He raises his glass as if to toast.

"A relative of Death?" My words trip over the clutter in my mind. The whole time I've been chasing *him*, hating *him*, and Death's part of me. "No!"

"Yes. The hereditary mutation shows up randomly through Death's family line. Sometimes sooner, sometimes later. The genetic change is infrequent, but when it occurs, the results are either immortal or soul immortal. Immortals are rare. Both the mother and father have to carry the gene. Soul immortals only have to inherit their abnormality from one parent, usually the mother, but not always. Even then, there's no rhyme or reason, none I can find, anyway. It's a crap shoot, just like life."

"Soul immortals?"

"Haven't you ever wondered why Leah is so much like Lydia? I don't mean physically. That's a fluke. Although, I've seen her, and the resemblance is uncanny."

"I know. I saw you talking to her at the movies." The habitual icy thrill of anger creeps into place, and I ball my hands into fists. I have to hold myself together; I'm too close to the truth.

A suggestion of pride teases his lips and eyes. "Did you?"

I glare at him.

Artagan puts up his hand. "Calm yourself. No harm, no foul. Soul immortals are different from us. For one thing, there are lots more of them. Moreover, our bodies are bound to earth, but their souls are bound to earth. That means they'll have a physical death, but at some point, their souls will return in a new body. Never the wiser. Lucky bastards. There will, of course, be differences from body to body, because of the new life experiences and all. But at the core, the essence of who they were will be the same."

"You're suggesting Leah and Lydia share the same soul?"

"Do you have a hearing impediment? I hate repeating myself." He swallows the last of his scotch and then studies me before shaking his head. "You don't believe you deserve any happiness, do you? Not deep down."

"Where'd that come from?" I grumble. "Besides, you don't know what I've done."

"Maybe. Maybe not. You worry about one life when I've killed a whole village."

I frown, questioning him silently.

"You're talking about Hake, right?"

"How do you know about him?"

Artagan rolls his eyes in annoyance and then points at his chest. "Son of Death, remember? Hake was a worthless street hood. Between the fighters he had killed and the prostitutes he beat beyond recognition, he had it coming. He died the way he chose to live. Brutally."

"There were more than Hake."

"More?" It's Artagan's turn to be confused.

I hold up three fingers.

"No. I'd know if that was truth."

"Hake. My father. Lydia." I fold each finger down as I say their names.

"You didn't kill your father or Lydia. You couldn't have saved them no matter what you did. It was their time."

"My actions caused their deaths."

"Yeah, asking the girl you love to marry you. What an arsehole you are."

I glare at him, but my mouth stays shut.

Artagan snorts. "And your father?"

"He was on an errand for me."

"So what? You were seven. You're gripping the past so tight you can't live. Or see how foolish you're being."

Death—or at the very least, his son—is giving *me* advice on living. I snort. "Thanks, Dr. Phil."

"Seems you're throwing yourself a pity party. The bombing in Cairo last week and the train wreck in California two days from now, they're your fault, too. Those two incidences alone will take a total of 243 lives." He mutters something under his breath. "Done?"

I glower at him. "Are you serious? I can't tell if you're lying or just crazy."

"Very serious. I am what I am, and I do what I have to."

"How can you just accept killing like you have no choice?"

He stares at me as if he has more to say, but instead of speaking, he takes a long sip of his scotch. "Do you want to talk about my crimes, or do you want to know about Leah?"

I sigh, keeping the rest of my thoughts to myself.

"Thought so. As I was saying, Leah's physical resemblance to Lydia is a twist of fate. Only the soul passes down the family line to the next descendent, a kind of inheritance. All except the eyes. They're called the windows to the soul for a reason. They'll always be the same."

I had dismissed the similarities as wishful thinking or family traits. Blocks away from here is a room filled with scenes of Lydia's past hanging on the walls. Those eyes aren't a likeness. They're the originals. "How do you know this?"

"The horse's mouth. After six hundred years, Death and I have had some heated discussions." He chuckles. "Leah's soul immortal, so she's kept the essence of who she once was, even though she doesn't remember her past life."

"But she does."

"What?" His eyes snap to me.

"Leah remembers moments, snapshots from the past."

"Not possible," Artagan says flatly. "A soul immortal gets the sense of déjà vu, but little else."

"Possible or not, she does remember those moments. She paints them."

Artagan's focus drifts. His thumb and forefinger stroke his stubbled chin. "Strange. So it truly has happened again," he whispers, still thinking.

"Again?"

"It's happened once before that I know of," says Artagan. "An immortal named Kemisi fell in love with a soul immortal man named Amun. They married and lived out the remainder of the man's natural life together. When his soul moved on to its next body, his memories of Kemisi were so strong that he searched her out. A complete abnormality. Unfortunately, war called, and the man died young. After the man's second death, Kemisi hoped his memories would bring him to her again. She waited, but he never returned. After years of searching for him, desperation forced her to ask for my help. I found him for her. She went to visit him. He didn't even recognize her—all his memories were lost. The man who houses that soul today lives in Duluth, Minnesota, with his wife and three children. Fate's a fickle bitch and rarely grants happy endings, so enjoy the time you're given." He smiles, but joviality doesn't touch his eyes.

After ordering another scotch, Artagan glances at his watch. "She was waiting for you, wasn't she?"

"What time is it?" I fumble for my cell phone.

"Almost ten after nine."

I jump to my feet. "I'm late. I have to go. She'll think I'm not coming."

A hint of jealousy flares in those sapphire eyes. "Enjoy your time, Jack. We'll see each other again, I'm sure."

I rush out into the night, thoughts swimming around my head in loops. I start to run. My heart accelerates into a steady thrum.

CHAPTER TWELVE

LEAH STANDS ALONE OUTSIDE THE gallery, her arms wrapped around her slender frame as if she's holding herself together. She tenses, and worry lines crease her forehead. Her eyes dash away every time they find me.

"Sorry I'm late," I say.

She gives me a quick nod and glance before looking away again. I catch a glimpse of her teeth biting into her lower lip before a thick curtain of golden hair slides between us, hiding her face from my view.

"We need to talk," she says, her voice cracking on the last word.

"Yes, we do." I smile, but I doubt she can see my expression through her shield of wavy strands.

"We should go to my place so we can have some privacy."

Puzzled by Leah's unexpected behavior, I'm slow to respond. I want to brush her hair from her eyes, scoop her into my arms, and tell her everything, but that would be the wrong move right now. Her reaction to my revelation could take so many forms. "That would be best," I say.

Leah swallows hard. She peers out from behind the curtain, studying me apprehensively. The lingering color drains from her face. Her reaction propels my feet forward, but she shies away, hiding behind her hair again. Then, almost in a trance, she turns and walks in the direction of her dorm.

I follow then quicken my pace to walk alongside her.

A block from her dormitory, Leah finally speaks again. “Grady said you wouldn’t come back. I convinced him to leave, telling him I needed some time to myself. This isn’t a conversation I wanted him to be part of in case you did.”

“Understandable.” I give her a sideward glance. “But I said I would.”

“Too much of a gentleman to leave a girl waiting.” She sniffs.

Is she crying? “Leah?”

I reach out and place my hand on the small of her back. She shrugs away. “Please, don’t.”

I restrain my hands at my sides.

“When you leave...” She sighs. “I don’t want this to be any harder than it already is.”

Pieces fall into place. A sense of relief rushes over me. The knots in my shoulders uncoil, taking the tension throughout my body with them. *She thinks I’m here to say good-bye.*

“Leah, I’m not—”

“Please, not here.”

Against instinct, I obey.

Leah’s small room is packed with two single beds and matching dressers pressed against opposite walls. The stark-white wall boasts a patchwork of brightly colored reproductions of Van Gogh, Gauguin, and Chagall. A square bedside table sits under the tall window, which offers a full view of the street. In the farthest corner is a bookcase made of four cinderblocks and two boards. Most of the books are Victorian or earlier with a few modern classics tossed in. Once the door is closed securely behind us, I can’t wait any longer. I step to her, winding my arms around her waist. At first, she attempts to yank away. I clasp her tightly with one hand, while the other catches her chin. I hold her face firmly until her gaze turns to me.

"I..." *How to start?* I stare into her confused eyes. I've waited so long, but I would wait an eternity for this moment. For her. It's worth every second of pain and heartache. No words I choose would ever be sufficient. *Maybe you're in a dream, a beautiful, but cruel hoax*, Doubt murmurs from my depths. I close my eyes, half expecting her to be gone when I reopen them. But she's still here. I smile.

Leah studies me, her chest heaving. Finally, she whispers, "You're not upset? You don't think I'm crazy, too?"

I chuckle when I hear my fears coming from her lips. "Of course I don't. You're the sanest of us all."

A hint of surprise spreads across her face, washing away her demeanor of nervous regret. "Are you sure?"

I pull her body to mine and press my mouth against hers. She pauses for a second before she wraps her arms around me. We kiss with our eyes open. Warmth explodes within me and crashes over me, awaking my spirit from a dark and cold slumber. Our lips dance together in a familiar way with growing intensity. I kiss along her arched neck, drawing in the scent of her sweet skin. She lets out a breathy moan.

"I've missed you," I whisper, brushing her velvety skin with my lips. Hauling in a deep breath, I pull away before I'm completely undone, and respectability flies out the window.

She leans her cheek against my chest. "Well, that was unexpected. I thought you were here to dump me."

I laugh and kiss the top of her head. Her hair smells like springtime and apples—a difference from her predecessor.

"No. I'm not going anywhere," I whisper. "By the way, I do remember. I remember every moment."

She draws away so she can see my face. "Every moment?"

I nod.

"Then you've dreamt about us more than I have. I just have pieces—a collage of a life together."

I take a sobering breath to prepare for what needs to

come next. "Because I lived it. Every beautiful, painful moment of it."

Leah asks nothing, but her eyes question each word I've said.

My stomach twists. "I am a little over one hundred and seventy years old. I was born on January second, 1841, in Lidcombe, England. My body hasn't aged beyond twenty, and I can't die."

She picks at her fingernails. Then swallowing hard, she shuts her eyes. The vise around my stomach squeezes.

"From what I know, I was born this way." I grin wryly, taking her hand and entwining my fingers with hers.

Leah's eyes open, flitting to the floor. "Then you and I are different."

"Yes."

She shifts away and crosses her arms. "What does that make me?"

"Maybe you should sit down first."

"I'm fine. What am I?" Her chin raises a fraction of an inch. Her eyes meet mine. Her determination betrays nothing.

"I think it would be best if you sit."

"Tell me!"

"Well, you're stubborn like her." I huff. "You're a soul immortal."

"What's that?" she rasps.

I explain everything to the best of my ability. I consider leaving out our connection to Death, but then I decide Leah has the right to know everything. However, when talking about her dreams, I choose to not to use Artagan's words—*strange* and *abnormal.* She thinks of herself as a freak already, and I know how that feels. I'm not going to corroborate the notion, because she's not. She's beautiful just the way she is.

Her legs wobble and struggle to hold up her slight frame. I fear she might faint, so I wrap my arm around her waist for support.

"I'm okay. Just give me a minute." She brings a shaky hand to her mouth then walks to the bed and sits down.

"Are you sure?"

Leah nods. "I always knew I was different." Her voice trails off, and she stares at the floor.

Afraid she might be going into shock, I grab the purple comforter from the foot of the bed and wrap it around her shoulders.

She looks up, a hint of a smile on her face. "Thanks. You think I'm going into shock or something, don't you?"

"Aren't you? I mean, it would be a normal reaction under the circumstances."

Her smile broadens. "You're right. I probably should be. How can I explain this?" She pauses. "I've wondered if I might be crazy for years. It made me second-guess what I knew here." She pats her chest. "Today, I found out I was right. You exist. My past life existed. It's... freeing."

I sit next to her and take her hand. "Yes, it is."

"I do have some questions, though."

"I'm sure. I'll do my best."

"Don't muddy the answers. Tell me straight, okay?"

I nod.

"So, someday I'll die, but you won't?"

The thought makes me flinch. "Yes."

"But my soul will stay on earth, waiting for another body, correct?"

"Yes." Another flinch.

Leah stares out the window. I wait, tracing circles on the back of her hand with my thumb. Her thoughtful expression remains unchanged.

When she speaks again, her voice remains steady. "So, I was Lydia, the girl from the story? And you're the man she loved?"

"Yes. And yes."

"So, I'm her?" she asks again, stiffly.

"Partly. But you have different life experiences than

she had. The eyes are the same, though." I reach up and brush strands of hair away from her eyes, so I can see her face. I don't want any shield or curtain between us now.

Leah leans her head against my shoulder. "Can you tell me about our past life? I don't remember much. Just bits here and pieces there."

"Of course." I tell her everything. How, at first, all she was to me was William's annoying little sister. How I saw her in a different light after returning home from school on holiday, then we fell in love. Being able to be my complete self with someone is amazing, but frightening as well. The instinct to hide what I am runs deep.

"You loved her so completely," she says, her voice curt.

I realize what my stories must sound like to Leah—less like reliving memories of a past together and more like hearing about my past with an ex. She isn't Lydia, and I need to remember that. Leah has her own set of memories, which don't include horse-drawn carriages, lavish ball gowns, or Victorian traditions.

"Yes, I loved Lydia Ashford, but a lot has happened to me since then. It changed me. I'm a far different man than I was then. The man sitting before you is in love with someone else."

The moisture in Leah's eyes rolls down her cheeks in narrow, steady streams. I move closer, wrapping my arms around her. She continues to cry. When the tears slow, she looks up at me. Her voice is raspy. "I was thinking the reason you wanted to be with me was because I looked like her."

"It's something so much more. The first time I saw you, it was like..." I pause. "I hadn't felt anything for so long. First, I was confused, of course. I thought you were Lydia's ghost sent to torment me. Then at your birthday celebration, I concluded the likeness was because of your ancestry, nothing more, but I was still drawn to you, not knowing it was because you began to heal me. Ever since

Lydia's death, I've been forced to relive memory after memory, never able to elude my past. The day at the beach when my mind drifted away from you—do you remember?"

She nods.

"I was having a memory. You had an effect on it, tamed my reaction. That has never happened before. Since then, all my past scars don't seem to matter anymore. But even before that, I knew I loved you, Leah Winters."

Her lips form a smile. She looks at me from under her feathery lashes and whispers, "Good, because I love you, too."

My throat seizes my breath. An uncontrollable smile stretches across my face. Waves of happiness roll over me as if I've returned home after a long journey. I never believed I would hear those words spoken to me again. I close my eyes, and my lips revisit hers. Her fingers play with the tiny hairs at the scruff of my neck, leaving a hot tingle in their wake. Leah's tongue traces the curvature of my lower lips before slipping into my month. My eyes snap open, and I give a short chuckle. "Times have definitely changed."

She looks up sheepishly.

"I'm not complaining." I haul in breaths to even the tempo of my heart.

Leah laughs and curls herself into my chest, cuddling in. "So in the coffee shop, you weren't sick, were you?"

"No." I grin.

"What were you thinking?"

"I thought you were repulsed."

"Repulsed by you?"

"You weren't?" I tease, moving her hair to her other shoulder and running my lips along the soft skin of her jawline.

"No. Repulsion wasn't what I felt." She grins. "You'd been haunting my dreams for years. It was the only place I was able to love you. Seeing you in the flesh was a bit... hmmm, overwhelming."

I laugh. "Overwhelmed?" I hadn't seen that reaction coming. I wonder what else I've gotten wrong. I sigh and lean my chin against the top of her head. "I'm glad we figured this out before I did something stupid, like showing you what I am the way my sister found out."

"Stupid?"

I cringe. I said too much. "Never mind."

"No, I want to know." She sits up straight.

I mutter curses under my breath.

"Tell me, please. I won't be mad, whatever it is. I promise."

Don't bet on it. Leah leans against my shoulder and begins to kiss up the side of my neck. I can feel my will caving. She doesn't play fair.

"Please," she whispers into my ear and then nibbles.

I moan softly. "Maybe you were sent to torment me." With a deep breath, I begin. "You see, I didn't know how to tell you I'm immortal without you thinking I was a complete nutcase. But after the cold shoulder at the coffee shop this morning—"

She winces. "I am sorry about that."

"No need. We've both been confused about what's been going on."

Leah nods.

"I was planning on telling you everything tonight, no matter what. It was time. If you didn't believe, I thought of a hike, but that seemed a bit extreme, so I decided against it."

"I'm not following."

"I thought of taking you to Bradbury Park. It's north of..."

"I know where Bradbury Park is. And?"

"At some point, I would have climbed a tree... and fallen. You'd see I wasn't dead. Then I could've told you what I was without you thinking I'm crazy." My words rush out in a rapid flow of air. "It worked before." I flash my best innocent smile.

Her jaw tightens. "Before?" she says, forcing patience into her voice. "Actually, I don't want to know any more. What's past is past. But you are going to promise me something. You will never think of doing anything like that again. I couldn't bear watching it, even if you can't die."

"Okay, I won't fall out of any more trees."

"Wait. Any *more* trees?" She gapes at me with disbelief.

I chuckle and kiss her lips. "Remember, love, you don't want to know."

Leah yawns, shaking her head. "You're right. I'm too tired to care anyway." She snuggles into my side. "Lots to absorb. And next week is gonna be a bear."

"Why?"

"Finals," she says with another yawn.

My stomach sinks. "Will you be going to live with your mom for the summer?"

"No. Plans changed after I saw you. Couldn't leave with you wandering around Portland, now could I? I'm staying at the dorms. More time to..." Her words give way to slow, steady breaths.

I lay on Leah's bed, my arms wrapped around her. I listen to her quiet even breathing and daydream of a future I wished for, but until today, never deemed possible.

CHAPTER THIRTEEN

A WEIGHT SHIFTS AGAINST MY CHEST. My eyelids flicker open to the morning sun blazing in through the window. I peer down at the golden tangles of hair. Leah is still molded into my side.

She stirs, and her face turns to mine. A smile spreads across her lips. "Good morning," she whispers.

"Good morning, yourself." I grin. "How did you sleep?"

"Wonderful. And you?"

"Never better. First dreamless sleep in, well, a very long time."

"Dreams aren't good?"

I look out the window, measuring my response, and decide to keep my answer simple. "They didn't used to be," I say, looking to her.

"Oh." Her stare darts away from mine.

"Did you dream?" I ask, just to get her attention.

"None of your business." She smiles. "Besides, I wouldn't want to make you blush."

I brush my finger along her jaw, smirking. "That good, huh?"

She wriggles off me and stands. "How about I make some breakfast?"

"Breakfast? There's no kitchen." I glance around, stopping at the perfectly made bed on the adjacent wall. "Do you have a roommate?"

"Yeah," Leah says, grabbing her towel and clothes from one of the dressers.

"What if she caught me here last night?"

Leah laughs. "Tina would've said, 'Good work.'"

I grimace.

"Don't worry. She doesn't stay here anymore. She moved in with her boyfriend two weeks ago. Says she's keeping the dorm room for her parents' benefit. If they knew she was shacked up, they'd kill her."

"Your roommate doesn't sound—"

"Stop right there. Remember, like you said last night, times have changed. You sound like Grady. I have one man in my life who thinks he knows best. I don't need two. So be nice. Now, I'm gonna shower then make breakfast, okay?" With a teasing scowl, she marches out into the hall.

Alone, I wander the small rectangular room. The crude bookshelf grabs my attention. I run my fingers over the worn spines of *Great Expectations*, *Wuthering Heights*, *Persuasion*, and Gaskell's *North and South*, all crammed in whichever way they fit. I pick up the book that tops the stack—*Jane Eyre*. One of my constant companions, my own tattered copy sits in my bottom dresser drawer even now. I thumb through the dog-eared pages, to Charlotte Brontë's closing words: "... his mind will be unclouded, his heart will be undaunted, his hope will be sure, his faith steadfast." I envy St. John's brand of faith but not his locked heart. No, I could never barricade my love from Leah—not now, not ever—even if that act meant gaining his level of assurance. She seems to have the power to exhume me from my past, and I love her more for her effort.

When Leah returns, she's dressed in an oversized Bruins T-shirt, and her wet hair is wound up into a sloppy bun. The shirt's hem barely touches her mid-thigh, showing off the long slender curve of her legs. My face flushes, and I drop my attention to the floor before being caught ogling.

She kneels to haul a plastic bin out from under the bed.

Rummaging through a collection of small appliances and kitchen utensils, she removes a frying pan and a battered camp burner with a frayed cord.

"You're going burn this place down with that thing."

"We college students have to be resourceful." She smiles and winks.

Soon, the room is filled with the savory aroma of coffee, eggs, and bacon. A knock draws Leah's attention toward the door.

"Expecting someone?" I ask.

"No." She bites her lower lip. "It's probably just Nathan or Max from across the hall, wondering if I made enough grub for them, too. Would you mind getting it?" she asks, flipping a second batch of bacon.

"My pleasure."

She must catch the glint in my eye, because she adds, "Be nice."

"I'll be a perfect gentleman. I promise."

A more frantic knock thumps the door. Maybe Nathan having the wrong impression wouldn't be such a terrible thing. I ruffle my hair then make quick work of the lock, and the door swings open to reveal a nervous Grady. *Shit!* He stares dumbfounded while seconds tick by.

"Where's Leah?" he finally asks.

"She's here," I say. "Everything all right?"

Grady jerks past me then stops dead. His eyes rove around the scene, and mine follow. It's seven thirty in the morning, his sister is wearing only a T-shirt, and I'm answering the door with bedhead. The scene doesn't look innocent—that's for sure.

"It's not what it looks like," I whisper.

His wary glare snaps to me, then he looks at Leah. His features soften. "You okay?"

"Of course I'm okay," Leah says.

"Can we talk?" he asks.

"All right. Let me finish. Then we can all sit down for breakfast and talk."

"Alone," he grumbles.

Leah scowls at him. "You're being rude."

"No worries," I say. "I need to get to work anyway."

She tosses me an apologetic glance. "Will I see you tonight?"

"Definitely," I say, sitting on her bed and slipping on my sneakers.

My response earns me another glare from Grady. Ignoring him, I walk over to Leah. She places her hands around my neck. I kiss her on the forehead. *No need to hurl Grady over the edge just yet.*

"See you tonight," I whisper.

When I arrive at work, the bookstore's windows are dark, and the door is locked. Ed might be the most disorganized man on the planet, but he's always at the store before me. I check my watch. 8:00.

Five minutes later, Ed hustles down the sidewalk in my direction, muttering. He looks more unkempt than usual. His shirt's untucked, and what hair he does have is sticking up in all directions. As he unlocks the door, his eyes stay riveted to the brass locks, and he doesn't acknowledge me at all.

"Everything okay, Ed?" I ask.

"Sally's still mad. She's never held a grudge like this," he says, more to himself than to me. "Tried apologizing. Didn't come out right. Actually, I think I just made her madder." He flicks on the lights and heads straight for the back without another word.

Ed's done so much for me. Besides being a great boss, he's a good friend. I want to repay his kindness somehow. By lunchtime, I have a plan—an apologetic ploy I saw work for my father. I might not be able to smooth things over with Grady just yet, but I certainly can coax forgiveness out of Sally. I pop my head into the storage room. Ed's sitting at his desk, staring at the ceiling, his feet propped up. He looks like a lost puppy.

"Ed. I'm going to grab some lunch."

"'Kay."

"Do you want something?"

"Nope."

I flip the sign to CLOSED on my way out.

The Village Florist is two blocks down. The scents inside blend to create a unique stinging-sweet fragrance all its own. The little shop is made smaller by the shelves crammed into it. Each is cluttered with decorative planters, gardening supplies, and random collections of all things Maine. Seafaring knickknacks are scattered among stuffed animals of seagulls, seals, and red lobsters. Even sea-glass jewelry is tourist ready.

A stout lady greets me from behind the long counter that stretches halfway across the store. "Good afternoon. How can I help you?" she asks, cheerily.

"I need fifteen red roses. Can they can be delivered today?"

"Is it in the area?"

"Yes."

"No problem. Just fill this out. I can make the bouquet now and have it delivered as soon as my driver gets back from lunch." She pushes an order form toward me and then steps to a cooler stuffed with colorful blossoms, some recognizable, some I've never seen before. She selects long-stemmed roses from a bucket in the front, looking each one over before placing it on the counter.

I fill in Sally's name and address. Now for the hard part: the message. *Hmmm. What should I say? I mean, what should Ed say?* I sigh and begin planning the words in my head.

My dearest Sally,

I am sorry for any pain I may have caused you.

I stop. *No, that's me, not Ed.* I need to keep the apology short and to the point. Ed's the no-frills type. Finally, when I think I have the right tone, I grab a pink slip of paper.

Dear Sally,
I'm sorry. Please forgive me.
Love, Ed

I read the note again. Definitely not the way I would apologize to the woman I love. Nevertheless, this isn't about me. My phrasing is as close to Ed's manners as I can impel myself to get. The "please" and "love" might be overdoing things just a bit. Still, both need to be said.

I return to the bookstore with two subs in hand and coax Ed into a bite or two.

The rest of the afternoon goes on in a routine fashion, except for the fact Ed is out of commission, staring aimlessly at the ceiling in the back room—until four o'clock, when Sally marches in. She gives me a little smile but doesn't slow her beeline for the office. I notice something different about her, but I can't put my finger on the change. Then it hits me. She's dyed her hair darker, to cover the gray.

Half an hour later, she emerges and leans against the counter. "Thanks for the flowers."

Dammit. "Flowers?"

"Don't even try it. Ed Growley isn't the type to send fifteen long-stemmed red roses from a florist. I'm lucky if he gives me carnations from the supermarket. The fifteen was a nice touch, by the way. You were listening to my lecture on Victorian floriography."

I didn't need reminding; I knew the language by heart. "You forgave him?"

"Yes. It was time. I love him too much to let something so silly get in the way."

"I'm glad. He was missing you," I say.

"I missed him, too."

"Like the hair, by the way."

"Oh, thanks. It's just out of a box." She gives the ends a flip.

Ed hurries out from the back room. "Hey, Jack? Can you close up? I want to take my girl out on the town tonight."

"Sure thing." I grin, watching Ed and Sally arm in arm.

The misunderstanding with Grady is not so easily mended. A week passes, and nothing changes. Grady is avoiding me like a plague, but every evening, he calls Leah, and every evening the two of them fight. Leah doesn't like to talk about Grady's disapproval. From the few details I've gathered, Grady doesn't believe I'm good enough for his sister, and Leah is tired of him butting into her business. Sally's words gnaw at me from the deep corners of my mind. *I love him too much to let something so silly get in the way.* I love Leah too much. But what to do? I can't make Grady accept me, and I'm not giving her up. We're at an impasse. The whole situation is a mess, and the separation has Leah frazzled. Her stress is hard to watch.

Despite all this, Leah and I spend as much time together as we can between work and school. Our free time is filled with motorcycle rides along the curving rocky shore, hand-in-hand walks through the city at twilight, and talking, loads of talking. She tells me how she visits her father's grave every May first, on the anniversary of the day he was buried. She loves the Golden Oldies, but fiercely dislikes the Beatles—we agree to disagree on the subject. Leah tells me she discovered her love of painting while she was sick in the hospital. I share stories about my childhood and family, but right or wrong, I avoid my past after Lydia. Although Leah has every right to know all, I'm not ready to confess my sins. Not yet. Not with Grady gunning for me.

"I can't believe the way he's acting. He had no right," Leah says and slams the clean dinner plates into my cupboard.

"Grady loves you."

She huffs. “Well, he has a strange way of showing it.”

“You’re his little sister, and, well, that’s not exactly the situation you want to catch her in.”

“It doesn’t have anything to do with that,” she mutters. “We weren’t doing anything.” She looks as if she’s about to say more, but she bites her lower lip instead.

“I know, but if I’d caught my sister in that situation, I wouldn’t have shown that kind of restraint.” I wash the last glass and hand it to Leah.

She rolls her eyes. “It was different then.”

I shrug. “Forgive your brother. He’ll warm up to the idea of me in time. You miss him, and it bothers me that I’m the cause of it.”

“You’re not. He is.”

“Please.” I urge.

“I’ll think about it. That’s all I can promise right now.”

“All right,” I say. “Soon, though.”

“But he’s so damn stubborn when he thinks he’s right. How am I going to convince him he’s being a complete idiot?”

“Give him time.”

“But he’s leaving for England in a little over a week. How is he gonna see how happy you make me from a zillion miles away?”

I entwine our fingers, squeezing her hand, and kiss the top of her head. “We’ll figure something out.”

She nods. But we have no other ideas, so the conversation ends.

Two days later, Leah calls me at work. Her strained voice triggers my concern.

“So, what’s going on?” I ask.

“First, promise me you’ll still come. It’s important to me.”

I groan. She just played the it’s-important-to-me card. *This is going to be a doozy.* “What are you up to?”

“Only a party.”

“All right. When?”

"Tonight."

"Hmm." The wheels in my head spin, trying to figure out where she's going before she takes me there.

"I'm just inviting a few friends, like Tom, Rachel..."

Ah, there it is. "Who else is on the guest list?"

Leah hesitates. "Grady."

"I realize you know your brother much better than I, but do you think this is a good idea?"

"I do." Belief and determination are clear in her voice. "Tom thinks Grady should just get over himself. Rachel's always been on our side."

"So you're planning an ambush?" I ask.

"An intervention."

I sigh, pinching the bridge of my nose. "Okay, I'm in. If it gets ugly, I'll leave."

"No."

"Only to defuse the situation," I say. "Then maybe Rachel and Tom will have more success."

Sounding reluctant, Leah agrees.

Although Leah's hopes are high, I have no expectation that this venture will go well. The closer dinnertime comes, the more I dread the approaching evening. In most of the scenarios I play out in my head, I end up being punched, and Leah ends up in tears. I find myself agreeing with Tom. Grady needs to get his head out of his own behind and see what he's doing to his sister. Furthermore, the tension between Leah and her brother has distracted me from much more important matters—Artagan and his preoccupation with my girlfriend. His motives seem more complex than he let on, and this fact worries me.

I head to Leah's dorm directly from work. She's uncharacteristically quiet. I can sense her nervous tension from across the room. I walk up to her and wrap my arms around her, but she pulls away, which is unexpected. I struggle to not be hurt by her chilly greeting.

"It's not you. I'm just a little stressed. This has to work."

"What do you want me to do?"

"Just sit."

Even though I recognize the bad timing, I share my concern that an ambush is only going to make Grady defensive. It's only a gut feeling, but my intuition is usually correct. Hell-bent on her plan, Leah doesn't want to hear any dissent. So I sit on her bed, watching her transform the room into party central while I do some scheming of my own. I glance at the clock. There are only twenty minutes until detonation, and I'm still sitting at point of impact. I stand. "I was thinking beer might help set the party mood."

"Tom's bringing some," she says without looking up as she dumps chips in plastic bowls.

Damn! "Oh, good. So you're sure he'll bring Grady's favorite, right?"

"I don't know." She looks at me. "Why?"

"It's just, we guys like our beer. And most of us are opinionated about which ones are the best. Unless you told Tom otherwise, he'll probably bring his own favorite. Do you know what that is?"

"Miller, I think."

I curl my lip and wrinkle my nose.

"Beer snob." She lets out a sigh. "But Grady will agree."

"I can handle it. I'll run and get some and be back before Grady gets here. What's his preference?"

"Geary's Pale Ale."

I peck her on the cheek then head out the door before giving Leah a chance to protest. Halfway down the staircase, I run into Tom and Rachel.

"Grady already whoop your ass and send you packing?" Tom asks then laughs.

I fake a smile. "No. Leah just needs me to run to the store."

"I got the alcohol." He holds up two six-packs of Miller Lite. "It's lite, but hey, this one's watching her figure," he says, glancing at Rachel. She scowls and cuffs him across the shoulder.

I grimace. "What's a party without beer?" *Cheap, tasteless beer, kind of like your manners.*

"Hell, yeah," Tom says, continuing up the steps with Rachel trailing close behind.

Outside, I take a seat on the front steps and wait. Before long, heavy footsteps hurry down the sidewalk. Grady, his hands tucked in his jeans pockets and his head hung low, is walking straight toward me. When he gets to the stairway, he looks up and jerks back.

"I knew it," he mutters.

"There's an ambush waiting for you upstairs. Leah is determined to make you approve of the idea of her and me together, but you and I both know either you can or you can't. I understand your apprehension. I just need to know what you want me to do. If you can't, I'll leave, and you can go upstairs to enjoy the party. If you can, we skip the ambush and go get a beer."

"You'd leave?"

I smirk. "Only for the evening. Like it or not, your sister loves me, and I love her."

Grady glowers at the sidewalk.

"What's it going to be?"

He stares at his feet and then looks me square in the eye. "Ambush, huh?"

"Oh, yeah. She went all out. The gang's all here."

Grady groans and heaves a long sigh. "Beer." He pauses. "How about the Dogfish? They're just a couple blocks down, and they have Geary's on tap."

I agree and follow.

By the third drink, Grady is patting me on the back and cracking stupid one-liners, more like the man I met all those weeks ago. The conversation bounces off a number of topics before landing solidly on me.

"There's one thing I need to know. Are you capable of hurting my sister?" he asks.

I flinch at the notion then take another swig of my

beer. His gaze is intense and probing. I get the feeling he's not talking about the incident in Leah's apartment. How much about me has Grady figured out? I play dumb, not wanting to open that can of worms. "No, of course not."

Grady turns to his drink, but his tone grows solemn. "The thing is, I've never seen Leah so happy. She's always seemed like she's been looking for something. As if she was waiting for something or someone to show up, so she could start living her life. After she met you, the waiting stopped. Do you believe in that fate crap?"

"Unlike Neo, I do." Fate seems to be the only reasonable explanation for what's happened.

"Me, too, I guess."

"You're a romantic! Does Leah know that?" I chuckle.

"No, and you better not tell her. I'll deny, deny, deny."

"Knowing Leah, she knows."

Grady nods and then peers at the clock behind the bar. "Speaking of my sister, she's going to be mad at both of us, you know?"

"Yes, I should give her a call." I slip my phone out of my pocket.

"One more beer first. For courage."

I agree and shove the phone away, postponing the inevitable. After another two beers, the time comes to accept the consequences. I retrieve my phone again and dial.

"Hello," Leah answers, her voice rushed.

I keep my tone light. "Hi, love."

"Jack! Where are you? I was worried."

"I'm fine. I had to try a plan of my own. I'm sorry I worried you."

"Tonight was a bust. Grady never showed. He completely blew me off—"

"Grady's here, with me."

"What do you mean, he's with you?"

"We're having a beer."

"Okay?" Her voice is thick with tension. "How's that going?"

"Fine, I think." I glance at Grady. "We're good?"

He shrugs and then gives a quick nod, taking another sip of beer.

"Grady agrees."

"Let me get this straight. You left without a word, talked my brother into getting a beer, and now everything's hunky-dory."

I'm not sure if this is heading toward praise or anger. Right now, her reaction seems to be leaning toward the latter. My explanation sounds so much worse when Leah says it than it did when the words were forming in my head.

"So it would seem," I say sheepishly.

The pause is long, leaving me fidgeting on my stool. "So the way into Grady's good graces is beer," she finally says. "Huh, why didn't I know that?"

"It's a guy thing."

She laughs. "Well, I'll thank you properly when you get here."

I smile and slip the phone into my pocket. "Phew, that went better than expected. Let's go see your sister."

Grady picks up a pint of Lobster Mash ice cream as a peace offering, and we walk to Leah's. At the door, Grady presents his gift in a flourish of pageantry and kneeling. All the stress has disappeared from her face, leaving her expression bright and content. Inside, she snatches three spoons sitting out on top of the dresser.

Grady scrutinizes the plastic ware. "Am I that predictable?"

Leah shrugs. "You screw up, you feel bad, you bring me ice cream. It's kinda our thing."

"I feel gypped," he says. "What do I get when you screw up?"

"On that rare occasion, an apology." She grins and hands out the spoons. "Now shut up and dig in before your admission of guilt melts."

Grady takes a step back, putting his hands in the air. "Have at. I've done my penance."

"Fine. More for me." She digs out a big spoonful of vanilla and pale-pink chunks. "Jack?"

I open my mouth, and a burst of salty and sweet greets my tongue. However, the chewy, crystalline texture of the lobster is the flavor's prominent downfall.

"What do you think?" Leah asks.

"Awful, right?" Grady chimes.

"Not bad."

"But not good," he mumbles with a smirk.

By the time Grady heads home, the fences are mended, and any harsh words between him and his sister forgotten. I'm not so sure he's completely sold on the idea of me as Leah's boyfriend, but we've made strides in the right direction. I relax, sprawled out on Leah's bed, pleased with myself and how the evening went.

"So what exactly did you tell him?" Leah asks, tracing kisses up my neck.

Heat surges, and I find my words through an amorous haze. "Same things I told you at first."

Leah props herself up on her elbow. "You lied to him?"

"Well, yeah. What did you think I was going to do? Tell him the truth?"

"I know. I know. He'd probably lock me away in a tower somewhere."

"I'd find ya." I kiss the tip of her nose and smile. "I can see his face now. Grady, there's been something I've been meaning to tell you." My voice drops a couple octaves into my best game-show-host impersonation. "I'm a hundred-and-seventy-year-old man who will live forever, and I'm in love with your sister."

Leah twists her face in pretend horror then laughs. "I still wish I could tell him." She repositions herself against me so that her head is resting against my chest.

"What bothers me most is, at some point, Grady's going to think he's right."

She squirms uncomfortably next to me. "What do you mean?"

"I'm not getting any older, appearance-wise anyway. I can only stay in one place for so long. Eventually, it will be easiest if Grady thinks I dumped you." I wince. "That way, when you visit alone, I'll be a touchy subject, and there won't be many questions."

"How long do we have here?"

"Seven years is usually the limit with no complications. After that, people get suspicious and start asking questions. I have to live on the fringes of society. What I am demands that of me. Can you imagine what would happen if my immortality went public? I'd be hunted down. They would attempt to figure it out, bottle it, and sell it for a million dollars a drop." I pause. "Unfortunately, loving me comes with a high price."

"I don't see it that way." She cranes her neck to brush her lips along my throat. "Maybe next time around will be easier. Maybe I'll be born into a family of witches or mystics who believe in immortality."

Next time? I close my eyes. "Leah—"

"I know what you're going to say. The story you told me about that woman, Kemisi, and her long-lost love, but I've been thinking if I've remembered once, why not again?"

I shake my head to banish the thought. "I can't think that way."

"Why not?"

I don't want to argue. Leah has a beautiful childlike faith, strengthened by discovering her dreams were real, but hope is still a four-letter word to me. "It's what life's taught me."

"So you don't believe there's the slightest possibility that I'll remember you again in my next life?"

My silence says everything I won't. Eventually, Leah will leave, this time forever. She sees life as a beautiful fairy tale. A belief I can't share.

"Do you really see the world so black and white? With no color?"

I open my eyes and look down at her. "You'll have to have faith enough for both of us."

"I hate the idea of Grady thinking badly of you."

"I understand. But you have to see why keeping him in the dark is for the best."

She sighs and nods halfheartedly.

Grady is leaving for England in a few days. Though Leah's eyes brim with tears, the firm set of her jaw and the small lift at the corner of her mouth tell me she meant it when she said she chose to stand by me. And my secret is safe with her—even from Grady.

CHAPTER FOURTEEN

"So what are you up to tonight?" I ask, flipping the store sign to CLOSED.

Ed grins and sticks one arm out, letting it hang in the air. The other rests on his stomach. He begins to sway, humming some old show tune. "I'm taking Sally ballroom dancing," he says.

I raise my eyebrows. "You dance?"

"Yes. I'm old, not dead." He huffs. "I'm taking her out for dinner, too."

"Lou's?" I swear I hear Ed growl as he glares at me. "Sorry. I couldn't help myself." I laugh.

"If you must know, I'm taking her to Fore Street."

"Impressive. You do know you'll have to wear a tie to go to that place?" I grab the broom and begin to sweep.

"Wow. You're full of smartass comments today. Nice to see you in a good mood, even if it's at my expense." He pauses. "I have to show you something, but only if you promise to behave yourself."

I stop mid-stroke, put my hand on my heart, and grin.

Ed rolls his eyes. He reaches under the counter and resurfaces with a small black velvet box. He opens the lid. A flicker of gold dances in the light. Tucked in white satin sits a diamond ring. From the patina and irregularity of the hand-cut gems, the ring is obviously antique and probably older than I am. The facets sparkle with crisp white flashes. "What do you think? Do you think Sally will like it?"

"It's beautiful. I'm sure she'll love it."

"I can't believe how nervous I am. This isn't my first rodeo, so to speak. I should have done this months ago. Life's too short to wait around when what you want is standing in front of you. Seize the day. That's my new motto." He snaps the lid shut and shoves the box in his pocket. "Wish me luck."

"You'll do great, gramps."

"Thanks, kid." Ed smiles.

On the way to work the next morning, I rush along. Somehow, I forgot to set my alarm, but luckily, the sun, which promises another beautiful day, woke me. In my dash to be on time, I'm actually on course to be early. My thoughts revolve around Ed. I wonder if he found his nerve. My pace quickens. My curiosity gets the better of me. I'll be able to guess her answer when I step through the door. Ed's face will tell the whole story in one glance.

As I round the corner, two figures step out of the doorway of Rare Books and walk down the sidewalk in the opposite direction. *Ed's opened the store early or—*

My thoughts freeze midstream. I recognize the tall, lean man smoking a cigarette. A petite woman with cropped dark hair prances to Artagan's side. I would have thought she was a young boy if not for her dark fitted suit that shows off womanly curves.

"Artagan," I call.

He looks over his shoulder, his grave expression etched into every crevice of his face. He turns and keeps walking. The pale woman turns her head. Her wintery-blue, deep-set eyes pierce right through me. Her smile makes my blood run frigid and sends me rushing into the bookstore.

All the lights are off. The store is uncommonly quiet without the hum of the prehistoric computer or the chatter of Ed talking to himself in the back. The smell of rust and salt permeates the air. I call out, but get no response. I look over the open drawer of the cash register—now empty—and my search settles on a pair of legs sticking out from behind the counter. Waves of panic roll over me, threatening to bring my breakfast up. My body goes taut and rigid, and each step takes effort. I stop short at the counter.

Ed lies crumpled on the floor in a pool of his own blood. Trembling, I drop to my knees. I prod his warm neck, desperate to find a pulse. Nothing. Uncontrollable gasps force my chest into irregular heaves. Ed's eyes stare straight at the ceiling, vacant, lifeless. I stand and stagger backward. Thoughts spin and thrash, trying to escape the reality lying before me. *He's dead... murdered.* The horror of this certainty threatens to plunge me into darkness. Every ounce of air is sucked from the room. Without warning, my legs fail me, and I stumble against a shelf. The tower teeters, spilling books at my feet, but my eyes stay glued to Ed's motionless legs. His blood pools, creeping its way around him. Rising acid sears my throat, shaking me from the shock and sending me tumbling out the door.

Outside, I lean against the cool brick wall and vomit then wipe my sleeve along my mouth. I want to wake up. This is just a horrible dream, right? This can't be happening. A strangled sound escapes my throat, as though an animal is dying inside me.

Ed. Not Ed.

Dazed, I scan the street, but Artagan is gone. I slump against the wall and sink to the ground in a stupor, my head cradled in my hands. The initial shock wears off. I slip the phone out of my pocket and dial 9-1-1.

"9-1-1. What's your emergency?" a woman asks in a monotone voice.

"My friend. He's... been murdered." A pain rips through my chest. I groan.

"Sir, are you hurt?"

"No, Ed. He's hurt." *By Artagan.* I wonder how much I really even know about him. He admitted to destroying an entire village without remorse. Then he had his reasons—revenge. Or was that an excuse?

"Sir, are you there? Sir!"

"Yes, I'm here."

"Your location? Where is it?"

"Rare Books. Exchange Street."

"The police are on their way. Is the offender still there?"

"No, he's gone." Anger surges. I grip my phone tighter, longing for my own retaliation. *But where did he go? Oh, God... no!* Fear shoots through me, freezing my breath in my throat. I hit the end button, cutting the operator off mid-sentence, and dial Leah's cell. I check my watch, trying to remember her schedule.

After three rings, she answers. "Hello?"

"Where are you?" I ask, with a mixture of urgency and helplessness in my tone.

"Jack, I can't talk. I'm running late," Leah says.

"Where are you? Answer me."

"I just left my place. What's wrong?"

"Good. I need you to trust me." My voice cracks.

"Is everything okay?"

The cop cars speed around the corner, lights flashing and sirens wailing.

"Listen to me and do exactly what I say. I need you to go to the dorm. Go upstairs. Don't talk to anyone. Lock the door and window, then text me and let me know you're safe. I'll meet you there as soon as I can."

"But work."

"When you get to your room, call Rachel. Make up some excuse."

"You're scaring me, Jack."

"Everything will be fine. Just do it!" I snap, my patience spent.

A silence hangs in the air. "Okay. I'm going now."

"I have to go. Remember, text me." I hang up.

The police are out of their cars before my phone hits the bottom of my pocket. I explain to an Officer Jenkins what I found when I arrived, leaving out the details of Artagan and his friend. The other officers buzz around like a well-oiled machine. They cordon off the bookstore with yellow tape and barricade the street to hold back the swelling crowd. The whole ordeal feels like an out-of-body experience. I check my phone. No texts. My eyes flit across the crowd at the edge of the barrier. I'm looking for Artagan, but I see Sally. She's frantically talking with one of officers, waving her hands and gesturing to the bookstore.

"Sir. That's Mr. Growley's girlfriend," I say, pointing at Sally.

Officer Jenkins beckons her to pass.

Sally hurries to me with fear and confusion in her eyes. "Jack, what's going on?"

"It's Ed." My body aches with the memory of what she will soon feel.

"Is it his heart?"

Officer Jenkins steps into the conversation. "No, ma'am. It looks like a robbery."

"Robbery?" Sally asks.

"We believe so. The register was left wide open. All the cash was gone," says the officer.

"He must be so upset. Where is he?" She takes a step toward the door.

I catch her arm.

"What's wrong? Is he hurt?" she asks. Her youthful eyes scan my face then widen. "Oh no, no. He can't be dead. He can't be. I would have—" Her words break into a sob.

I fold my arms around her quivering shoulders, noticing the gold band of an engagement ring wrapped around her finger. “I’m so sorry.”

“Excuse me, Mr. Hammond.”

I look up to find a short towheaded man dressed in an ill-fitting suit, studying me. “I’m Detective Samuels. I have a couple questions for you.”

I release Sally and step to her side.

The detective clears his throat and removes a pen and notebook from his breast pocket. “What did you see when you arrived? Anything out of the ordinary?”

“No. Not until I walked inside.” I pat my fingers against the phone’s silent bulge.

Samuels nods, scribbling down my every word. “What was different when you entered the shop?”

“The quiet.”

He thinks for a moment. “So there was no one else in the shop?”

“Like I told Officer Jenkins, no.” I shift my weight back and forth anxiously. “Just Ed.”

“Are you in a hurry? Do you have somewhere to be?” Samuels eyes me quizzically.

“It’s my girlfriend,” I say, keeping my voice composed. “I don’t want her to hear about this on the news.”

The detective’s posture relaxes. “Of course. Understandable. Just a couple more questions.”

I nod.

“Has anyone been hanging around the store?”

“No one I’d label suspicious, if that’s what you mean.”

“Do you know if Mr. Growley had any enemies? Anyone who’d wish to do him harm?”

“No!” Sally says.

“Sorry, ma’am. We have to ask.” Samuels studies his notes, flipping the pages. “Looks like we have everything we need for now. We’ll call you if we have additional questions. You’re free to go.”

I offer to walk Sally home, but she doesn't want to leave Ed. She says she knows he isn't with us any longer, but sometimes, feelings don't have anything to do with logic. And people have to do what their hearts deem right. I know all too well that she's right. I hate abandoning Sally, but Leah still hasn't texted.

I scoot around the barricade and dial Leah's cell first. I don't get an answer, so I call her dorm room. No answer. I burst into a full run. The five blocks and congested sidewalk rob me of moments I don't have to spare. The ticking minutes feel like a lifetime. As I approach Leah's building, I see Artagan's jet-black hair gleaming blue in the sunlight. He's sitting on her front steps, holding something pink, flipping it into the air over and over again. Leah's phone.

CHAPTER FIFTEEN

I SKID TO A STOP IN front of Artagan, my eyes transfixed on the phone while it rotates between his nimble fingers. Shivers of ice swarm down my back, and every muscle tenses, burning and tingling with the impulse to destroy Artagan. Without prompting from my brain, my arm swings.

Artagan catches my fist midflight. His sapphire eyes stare off into the distance, and he purses his lips.

In my head, the quiet voice returns. *Relax,* it says. My body rebels against the suggestion, and the icy burn spreads, slithering down each of my limbs. I jerk my fist out of his grip, debating whether to throw another punch or choke him out.

"I'm sorry about Ed." Artagan's voice is calm, almost casual. "If there was any way to stop..."

Ed. Dammit. The crazy, disorganized book-lover is dead. I can't help him anymore. But Leah... "What did you do to her?" I spit out.

His eyes shift to mine. "Her?"

"Leah. If you hurt her in any way—" My anger shuts down my speech, and I begin to tremble.

Artagan cocks his head to the side and narrows his eyes. "What are you going on about? Leah's fine. I saw her run upstairs about twenty minutes ago. In her hurry, she dropped this." He holds out the phone.

I snatch the cell from his hand and dial Leah's dorm room number. On the first ring, she answers. She's home, safe. Relief sweeps in but doesn't dissolve my burning tension and grief.

"Hi, beautiful." I clear my throat and attempt to win back my composure.

"What's going on?"

"I'll explain everything soon. I'll be there shortly. Stay put, okay?"

"All right." From the hardness in her voice, she's clearly irritated. "But—"

"Later, I promise. Love you." I close her phone with a snap. I stare at Artagan under heavy brows, while images of my dead friend parade through my head. A new wave of anger crashes over me. "Ed," I groan.

"I know you think I enjoy this. You're wrong. I don't." A frosty edge sharpens his tone, as if my pain wounded him. His fist lifts to meet his mouth, knuckles whitening against rigid muscles.

Artagan came to the wrong place if he expects my sympathy for his fate. My tightening jaw is my only response to this flimsy excuse.

"I didn't kill Ed. Some twenty-year-old junkie did that," he says.

I lean in so I'm an inch from his face. I stab my finger at his chest. "You were there. You had something to do with it."

"My job is death," he spits. "The unnatural ones. Time handles the rest."

I straighten. My mouth twists into a grimace. "So, people are no more than chess pieces to you?"

His eyes stray from mine. "We don't get our hands dirty, per se. We orchestrate death. From a distance, when possible. Nearby, when needed."

"We?" *Who's he going to blame now? Ed?* I growl.

"The Concilium Animarum. The council is made up of nine immortals. Seven of them are the actual sons and daughters of Death. One, the oldest of the Soulless, was invited because of his unique quality." He rolls his eyes. "And the last is yours truly. This job was thrust on me. My ancestor, Brennus, was a son of Death—a pureblood. Unlike me, an adopted son, he is a biological son of Death himself, and he was raised by Death from the age of two. Before that, he lived with his mother. Like all Death's children, he has a human mother. Despite his upbringing, Brennus's duties of taking human life weighed heavy on his heart. Unlike his other siblings, he was not made for such sorrow. Mind you, I knew nothing of Brennus or this world until he ended his life with the help of his cunning twin sisters. Before that, I was happy, living in a small village with my wife in the midst of the Blackmuir Wood, completely unaware of what I was. A soul immortal.

"You saw one of the twins today—Vita. She's the more brutal of the two. A purely sadistic creature. Let's just say she enjoys her job." Artagan's face flares with loathing. "It seems Vita plotted Brennus's death for years. From what I've been told, her hatred for him grew after he stood against her creation—the Plague. Back in the fourteenth century, she directed the Black Death toward Europe for fun because it would slaughter as many humans and soul immortals as possible. She believes they're both inferior beings. All the council does in their way—well, except me. They call the soul immortals the Ignorant. But Vita's hatred seems to run deeper than that. By the time Brennus convinced his siblings that Vita's motives were tainted, half the European population was wiped out." Artagan twists a gold ring with a black onyx stone around his pinky while he speaks.

"Vita never forgave Brennus for swaying the council against her. With help from her sister, she preyed upon

Brennus's weakness, his spirit, and his love of humanity. The twins systematically drove Brennus mad. Vita disguised her hatred of Brennus as pity, offering to help him find peace, but it was no more than revenge. In his fragile state, he accepted her help and, in turn, death. With his dying breath, he blessed, more like cursed, this legacy on me. Passing on one's position and power is a privilege reserved for council members. Because of that honor, I received Brennus's seat on the council and his duties. I became an honorary son of Death. Since then, Vita's been secretly hunting down Brennus's descendants, determined to kill off the whole family line. She's been effective." Artagan pauses, and his attention gravitates to the sidewalk. "I am truly sorry about your friend."

I examine Artagan, looking for spuriousness in his solemn expression, but I find his apology genuine.

"Ed wasn't my obligation. Vita received the assignment. I came anyway. She didn't appreciate my company, but I didn't give her any choice. My deal was too tempting. I knew you were close to him. As you can guess, Vita enjoys causing as much pain as she can to the person unfortunate enough to meet her at the time of their passing."

"So a sadistic loon is wandering Portland, killing whoever she feels like." I glance at Leah's window. *How quickly can I get her out of this place?*

Artagan chuckles. "If it's Leah you're worried about, she's fine. Vita's off on her next assignment in Africa. Swaziland, to be precise. She's long gone. I only stayed to reassure you that Ed had an easy death."

"An easy death? An easy death is when someone dies in his sleep at ninety years of age after living a full life. Ed died alone, crumpled on the floor, in a pool of his own blood." Images of Ed's lifeless body flood my mind.

"Ed died instantly. I promise you that. It wouldn't have been that way if Vita had been alone." His voice is authoritative, devoid of mercy and emotion.

My teeth clamp together in an audible snap. "He deserved better."

"Deserving has nothing to do with it. Most don't deserve it. Does a child deserve to die of cancer? Does a mother of three deserve to die in a car accident? Did a man deserve to be beaten to death for the shillings in his pocket? No. I hate it. If I could save them all, I would." Artagan's voice catches, and his chilled expression caves with regret.

His reaction to what he is breaks through my anger. I never suspected that an immortal who has brought death to so many could have a conscience or feel remorse. I slump onto the steps next to him, questions swirling through my head. *Brennus died. He was an immortal, and he died. And Olluna? Was that part of the fairy tale true? Maybe when the time comes—after Leah has died, of course—Vita would be willing to show me the door out of this life.* "Death for an immortal is possible?"

"Oh, yes, more than possible. I've thought about it, but I'm too attached to retribution to consider it. Or maybe I'm just chicken. I'm pretty sure I wouldn't be going up there anyway."

A smile breaks across my face. The longing for death in the foreseeable future vanished with finding Leah, but after her death, I never have to return to the life I had before her. No more pining for what could have been. No more flashbacks or searching for an escape as I had after Lydia's death.

Artagan glances at the clear sky. "Not after that village incident and all. Eternity on earth is a far better choice than an afterlife in Hades. Self-interest is a family trait. Death's perfected it."

"How can an immortal die?"

"Hemlock mixed with a touch of salt." His face contorts in suffering, as if he's on fire. I recognize the pain. Instantly, I believe Artagan has known the heartbreak of his fairy tale. His expression clears, but a hint of suffering lingers in his eyes. "Enough of that." He huffs, and his gaze drops to his feet.

When his eyes return to me, he's locked away his pain. He stands suddenly. "I'm sorry you had to find Ed like that. Vita had already planted the plan in the boy's mind when I came into the picture. There was no turning back then. I know the way he died must have reopened painful wounds. Sorry about that, too."

Then he's on the move, disappearing around a street corner.

Pressure builds in my head. My hands shake. I get to my feet, desperate for Leah's reassuring touch. This memory isn't one I wish to relive, not today. Stumbling to the top step, heaviness weighs me down, dragging me to my knees. I close my eyes, and I'm seven, a lifetime away, on a curvy dirt road on the outskirts of Lidcombe. I shuffle my feet, making clouds of fine powder behind me. The dusty earth grates under my leather soles. My brother walks several paces ahead, moving purposefully.

He stops abruptly, looking at me with exasperation. "Jack, keep up. No time for play."

I sigh and run to catch him. Mother sent us to fetch Father from town. Mrs. Piler, the schoolmaster, has been ill for weeks, and today, she took a turn for the worse. As vicar, my father is needed. Despite the nature of our mission, I cannot contain my excitement, and I bounce along at my brother's side.

Henry smirks and ruffles my hair. "I do hope you're not pinning your hopes on Old Vile Piler's death. Hasn't her switch taught you anything? She's too nasty to die."

I screw up my face, shake my head, then smile. "It's the gift for Mother. Father was buying it this afternoon."

"Ah, yes, the remarkable music box." He chuckles.

Another burst of anticipation charges through me, and I run ahead. Around the next bend, I catch sight of Father's gray speckled mare grazing in the Edmunds' field. I stop, and Henry halts at my side. "Look. Mags." I point and look up at my brother.

He stares into the distance, paying me no attention. His face is a ghostly white.

"Jack, stay here," Henry commands and runs toward a black mound lying in the middle of the road.

Instead of obeying, I follow him. Splintered wood litters the roadway. Sunlight glints off brass workings of a music box, strewn like rubbish in the dirt. I slow. Blood stains the ground. A pathway of crimson leads to a dark figure lying face down. My mouth goes dry, as parched as the dust covering my boots with a thin film.

Henry bends down. Grabbing the figure's arm, he twists the black heap over. My father's vacant eyes stare into mine. I scream, but no sound escapes.

The memory recedes. Trembling, I boost myself into a sitting position and slump against the iron ornate railing, finding my breath. With effort, I stand. The door swings open. A group of guys rush out in an explosion of laughter. The last boy catches the door for me. I look up to thank him, discovering Nathan smiling at me with mocking expression.

"Leah's gonna love this, dude. You're drunk."

I ignore him and stumble in though the open door. Outside Leah's room, I rest my forehead against the doorframe, regaining my composure before knocking.

"Hello," she says through the closed door.

"It's me."

The door flies open. "Jack Hammond! If you ever pull a stunt like—" Her angry expression morphs into concern. "Are you hurt?"

I look down to discover a brownish-red smear along my fingers and across my palms—Ed's blood. Still having trouble finding my words, I shake my head. She tugs me into her room, and I collapse into her arms, burying my face in her hair. "Ed died this morning."

"Oh my God! How?"

"He—" My mouth is dry. I clear my throat. "He was murdered. It was hard seeing him like that."

"You found him?"

I thrust away and rub my temples with my fingers, attempting to scour the images of Ed's lifeless body out of my head. It's useless. "Yes."

"Go sit on my bed. I'll be right back." Leah slips out into the hall, and I stagger to the bed, dropping to the soft mattress with a thump.

She quickly returns, a wet washcloth and towel in hand. She sits beside me and begins to scrub away the leftover gore from my hands. "What happened?" she asks, keeping her attention on the task.

"It looks like a robbery."

Leah's posture becomes rigid. "Looks like? You don't think it was?"

"The police are still investigating." Neither fact is a lie. Both details are one hundred percent true. Ed's death looked like a break-in gone wrong, and the cops are surely scrutinizing every clue, although I'm sure they'll never discover the truth.

Leah clearly trusts what I say wholeheartedly, which triggers my guilt. Needling me at the back of my mind is the obvious—Artagan is a carrier of Death. My only solace is his obvious hatred for what he does. He is a stark contrast to Vita, who seems to consider harvesting souls no more than swatting a mosquito. *Yes, Vita is a completely different beast.* How am I ever going to keep Leah safe from the monsters like her roaming the world?

The days that follow are a blur, one bleeding into another. I miss Ed, his sense of humor, his and quirky ways, but most of all, I wish he hadn't died alone. He must have been so frightened. The idea gnaws away at the pit of my stomach.

I watch Sally while helping her with the funeral arrangements. Each decision wears on her. My grief is merely a shadow compared to hers. Pale and forlorn, Sally's exterior claims she's as tough as nails, but her sharp brown eyes betray her. She's still wearing Ed's ring—a lost promise of a future cut short by a creature whose lineage I share.

The night before the funeral, Leah spends the night at my place.

"I feel so sad for Sally. I can't even imagine how she must feel," she says, crawling into bed next to me. "I mean, losing my dad was hard, but losing the one you're in love with—I'm sorry. I wasn't thinking. This must be dredging up some difficult memories for you."

"I'm focusing on counting my blessings. You're her now." I coil my arms around her, squeezing her tight, and kiss the top of her head.

Leah smiles. "We're lucky, if you think about it. How many couples are sure they'll have a second, third, and even fourth chance?"

"Let's not discuss this tonight."

She looks up at me and rolls her eyes, forcing patience into her voice. "Seriously, do you really think I'm going to forget you?"

Not willing to rehash this argument, I keep my mouth shut.

She stares straight into my eyes. "You're wrong, you know?"

"Please drop it," I say firmly. The anger and fear I've been hiding over the past days bubbles to the surface, and I find myself practically shouting. "I don't understand how you can believe we can beat the odds. It's a naïve view. It's not reality."

She yanks away and stands. Anger flickers in her eyes

like a green flame. "Listen to me. I know our odds. I'm not stupid. Our separation will be difficult, but it won't be the end, not as it is for Sally and Ed. I know it in my heart, and there's nothing you can say to convince me otherwise. The last time I checked, having hope wasn't a sin."

I take a deep breath and push the air out slowly, calming my emotions. "How can you be so sure?"

"Call it a gut feeling." She plops down on my bed next to me.

I suck another gulp of air. "I have to admit, I like your take of the future better."

"I'm not saying there aren't rough roads ahead. I'm just asking you to trust my view."

"I will," I lie and let the argument drop. What good is convincing her I'm right if the truth leaves her miserable? Leah will never know if she is. I will be the only one suffering in the end, and I'll handle that burden in my own way.

The next morning, I dress in the black suit Leah helped me pick out two days ago. After the third attempt at tying a half-Windsor, I chuck my tie into the sink. Dreading the day, I'm already wearing thin.

"Can I?" Leah says from the open bathroom door. "I used to have to tie Grady's all the time."

"Thank you." I hand her the strip of black silk. Leah lifts my collar then twists and turns the fabric a perfect knot. "You look handsome," she says, rolling up on her toes and pecking me on the cheek.

Hand in hand, we walk into the church at one o'clock. Having her here with me will keep all the old pain at bay, but these events have raised a new, unpleasant debate that I'm sure will revisit us again. I wish I could share Leah's hope, but I can't.

Like me, the old gray stone church is a piece of the past in the midst of the present. Towering redbrick buildings around it overpower the aged structure. The center steeple barely reaches its companions' top-story windows. Three black arched doors stand open to welcome the mourners. Small clusters of people stand near the altar. The hum for their chatter echoes off the bright-white walls.

Leah and I slide into a pew halfway toward the front. Ed's picture is sitting on a dark mahogany coffin. His smiling face looks back at me. Again, I wish I could have been with him in his final moments. I close my eyes and bow my head. Faces of all the people I've lost parade pass my eyelids. The weight of their loss feels like the weight of the world on my shoulders, and the ache is vivid today. Tears trail down my cheeks and drip onto my crisply pressed pants. Leah twines her arm around mine and leans her head on my shoulder. She whispers, "I love you, Jack. It's going to be okay."

"We here today to celebrate the life of Edwin Growley."

I look up to see that everyone has taken a seat. A tall, wispy priest talks about Ed as if they were long-lost friends, portraying him as a saint, even though anyone who really knew Ed could confirm he was not.

"Is there anyone who'd like to share a story about Edwin?" The priest smiles and waits.

A short man with a receding hairline stands and shuffles to the front. He straightens his glasses before he begins. "I'm Roy, Ed's younger brother. I'd like to start by saying my brother hated the name Edwin, and if he was here right now, he'd kick your ass for calling him that." Roy chuckles and glances at the priest then dabs his eyes with a wad of tissue. "Ed moved to Maine following a dream and opened the bookstore. I'll admit, I thought he was crazy, and maybe he was a bit. But he loved it here and always said this place felt like home. Thank you for always making my brother feel like he was a Mainer."

Next, a man as bald as an egg stands. "Ed used to tell me about Vietnam while I was cutting his hair. He never complained once, either, that bald guys don't know how to cut hair."

The mourners continue to stand, and the stories continue to flow. The church falls silent when Sally stands and makes her way to the front. When she trips on the first step of the platform, I begin to stand, but Ed's brother helps her to her feet. "I have a poem I wanted to read by W. H. Auden. He says it best, besides he was one of Ed's favorites. I can't remember the poem's name right now." Sally fiddles with her papers. "And it seems I didn't write it down. You'll have to forgive me." After clearing her throat, she begins. "'Stop all the clocks, Cut off the telephone.'"

I know this poem. I've lived it. In unison with Sally, I recite the dark, hollow rhythmic words in my head, focusing on the tempo to keep my mind occupied and stirring emotions at bay.

After the service, Sally goes to the coffin, places her hand on the lid, and stares at the framed picture of a smiling Ed.

Leah nudges me forward. "I'll be right here. She needs you."

I walk to Sally's side. Saying nothing, I place my hand on her shoulder. Sally reaches up and pats my hand. "Thank you."

I remember how my mother spent hours alone in a room with my father before she permitted the undertaker to bury him. "I can leave if you'd like to be alone with him," I say.

"No. Stay."

For a long time, we stand in silence with Ed, until with a weak smile, Sally gestures for Leah. "Let's give Jack a moment."

Leah extends her arm, and Sally's shaking hand loops around it. "I'll see you outside," Leah says, walking with Sally toward the door.

I notice how old Sally looks today—the stress of the last few days is evident on her face. Her rich brown hair has begun fading to a lusterless white.

I run my hand over the smooth mahogany. "Good-bye, Ed. Thank you for your friendship."

I turn to leave, brushing at a tear that threatens to escape. The tall arched double doors moan as I shove them open and step into the empty foyer. A movement catches my eye. A shadow—small and unthreatening—leans against the wall in the far corner.

"So, there's a riddle to solve. How do you know him?" a sweet voice sings from the shadows.

My eyebrows knit together as I step closer. All I can make out is a pair of frigid aqua eyes bearing down on me, then Vita walks into a shaft of light, an unreadable expression stretched across her face.

"Vita," I say.

Her mouth parts, then she grins. "He's told you more than I thought. Even more interesting," she says quietly. "It's really too bad Artagan didn't leave Ed and me alone. It would've been much more fun." She pauses and gives me a little wink. "Strike that. I would've had more fun. Ed, not so much."

My chest tightens. I clench my hands into fists. "I was taught never to hit a woman, but for you, I might make an exception." Vita laughs.

A low growl reverberates deep within me.

"You see, I knew from the start that Artagan must have his reasons for wanting Ed Growley's death to be pleasant. We can all be civil from time to time, no matter our motives, helping one another with assignments, and I couldn't complain. The trade was a good one, a swift death for coordinating a disease of my choosing in northern Swaziland. Hmm, I couldn't resist. Which I'm sure he knew. He's a clever one. I'll give him that. But not as smart as me."

I take a step toward her. "You killed Ed." My words are rigid. My voice is hoarse from fatigue and tears.

"We've established that already. Now keep up," she

says, unmoving. “You see, I was sitting on the bank of the Mbuluzi River, watching people drop like flies, and I started thinking. What if Artagan’s reasons revolved around you? And if that’s true, why?” All humor has vacated her face, leaving her expression stony and full of...

What? Hatred? Maybe.

As her eyes bore deeper into me, a pain stabs my skull like fiery daggers piercing my eye sockets. My stomach heaves.

“I know Artagan can be very persuasive, but so can I. Now answer my question. What are you to Artagan?”

I stumble, pitching forward. I fight the wooziness and keep my glare locked on Vita.

“Tell me!”

I remain silent. She clenches her jaw and bears her teeth. I cringe inside, readying myself for more pain.

A door creaks, followed by footsteps. The unexpected sounds distract Vita, then she slides into the shadows. “Not to worry. I’ll figure it out for myself,” she whispers. Then as quickly as she appeared, she’s gone. The pain dissipates.

The priest, looking concerned, walks out of the sanctuary. His long black robe swishes along the floor. “Are you all right, my son?”

I nod and step out into the garden to look for Leah and Sally.

Later that evening, I force myself to stay awake because the alternative is unbearable. Every time I even close my eyes, scenes of Ed’s death and Vita’s cruel smile materialize behind my lids. The night wears on, and my hallucinations grow more elaborate. Ed and Vita join forces with all the people I’ve loved and lost. Like an army of zombies, they hunt Leah down. By the time I get to her, Leah is aged and pale, staring at me with vacant eyes.

Two quick raps on the door cause me to jump and pull me from the newest horrors. I slowly stand. Each small movement is an achievement. I open the door and am surprised to find Artagan outside. His eyes dart around before he steps inside.

"Vita hasn't left. She's still here," he blurts in a deep husky voice.

"I know. I saw her today."

"Where?"

"Ed's funeral."

He groans. "It seems you've sparked an interest."

"Me?"

"Yes, you called out my name. She thinks she knows why." His eyes shift away in thought. "Always looking for a way..." he mumbles.

"So, why all the concern? What's this all about?" A thought hits me. "Wait. Is she after Leah?"

His sapphire eyes snap to me, a hint of amusement hidden in the blue. "No, not Leah. She's after you. You're one of my descendants. I've lost count of the greats, but I'm your distant grandfather. And I'm afraid Vita's on the verge of figuring that out."

My eyes widen, and his words roll over me. *Family?* Over the past weeks, everything I've wanted so long for—love and family—has been handed to me on a silver platter. The pessimist in me realizes that it's just more to lose, but I banish those thoughts and concentrate on positive ones.

"Are there others? Can I meet them?"

"No," he says solemnly. "Only you and I are left."

I sigh, glancing away.

"I can tell you all about them another time. For now, it would be best for you to take off until I can convince Vita she's wrong."

"But she's not wrong."

"True, but it's best if she doesn't know that."

"I'm not worried. I'm not that easy to be done away with. Believe me—I've tried."

"It's not only yourself that you should be concerned about."

My throat tightens. "Leah?"

Artagan nods.

My high crashes in around me. My eyes darken. Icy fingers trace up my spine. Hatred and terror clutch my spirit with viselike grips, both wrestling for control.

He continues, unfaltering. "Vita's MO has always been to strike at what her target idolizes most. She's skilled at figuring out the chinks in a person's armor. Death is singularly motivated, and it appears we are also. For Brennus, it was his love of humanity. For me, family. This is a tactic that would work easily on you." His eyebrows lift as if he's daring me to disagree. "Right now, Vita doesn't know about Leah. If she did, Leah would be dead. However, eventually, she will, so you need to leave and take Leah with you. She's not safe here, either."

I hesitate.

"Still don't trust me?" Annoyance grips Artagan's voice.

"No, I trust you. I'm just—if being with Leah has put her in danger, I'll never forgive myself."

"Everything will be fine. I'll trail Vita, but I'll need to know where you are. If she gets close, you'll need to know so you can move on."

"We'll start in York, England. Her brother's there. I can get Leah to visit him without suspicion."

"That'll work for the time being, but if Vita catches wind of Leah, you'll need a place with no connection to either one of you—past or present. Tickets will be delivered in the morning."

"But..."

"Get some sleep. You'll need to be at your best tomorrow. Leah will be safe tonight. I'll see to it." Then he's gone, out the door like a breath in the wind.

Thoughts whirl in my head. *Can I trust him? Do I have a choice?* I slip the phone from my pocket and dial, ignoring the international charges.

"Hi, Grady. It's Jack. I was wondering how you'd feel about a couple visitors?"

CHAPTER SIXTEEN

A FLIGHT ATTENDANT WALKS DOWN THE aisle, reminding passengers to buckle up for the landing. She takes my cup and gives me a polite grin. I whisper in Leah's ear. Her golden hair sways with my breath. "We're almost there. Are you awake, love?"

Her eyes flutter open, and she smiles. But to my disappointment, worry is still evident in her rich-green irises. She must know I'm keeping something from her. In truth, anxiety eclipses her every feature, from the deep creases of her forehead to the hard set of her lips, which never fully commit to a smile. Very un-Leah.

The realization of what I'm costing her tugs at my conscience. I never should have called out Artagan's name. So many emotions race through my veins that nailing one down is difficult. Regret. Vengeance. Fear. I made a conscious decision not to tell Leah the truth, believing her knowing would be worse. I already feel trapped in one of those nightmares, as though I've just crawled out of the deepest, darkest hole to find the exit locked tight. Then I wake, only to find that the bitter effects linger for hours. How can I justify dragging her into the darkness with me?

"Is everything okay?" She takes my hand. Small and cold, hers clutches mine.

"You're freezing." I frown and take her other hand, then rub them both. The gooseflesh of her arms is like an army of tiny soldiers all standing at attention.

"Maybe a little," she says with a reluctant sigh. Her lips press into a white slash, and she scrutinizes me.

Attempting to ignore her penetrating gaze, I release her hands and shrug out of my sweatshirt, which I wrap around her shoulders.

"You're avoiding my question, you know?" she says, her eyes never leaving my face. "You've been doing that for the last two days. What are you keeping from me?"

I shift away, readjusting the position of my knapsack. "Everything's fine." I pause, attempting to retain my lighthearted exterior. Lying to Leah is becoming increasingly difficult.

Leah pinches her lips together. Her eyes are still glued on mine. "I'm hoping Grady's overprotectiveness hasn't rubbed off on you. Against popular belief, I'm not a porcelain doll that can be smashed into a million pieces by the slightest bump."

"Nothing to worry about, except the possibility of lost luggage. We're on holiday... a first for me." I smile. "So, what do you have planned for us in jolly old England?" I let the back of my fingers skim the stack of travel guides piled in her lap.

The distraction works, and her enthusiasm bubbles over. She smiles—a real one this time. "Too much to name it all. Did you know the wall around York dates back to the fourteenth century?"

"Really?"

"Yup, and there are around sixty churches, museums, and historical buildings stuffed within that wall. It sounds like an amazing city with too much to see."

I nod.

"The school where Grady works is in here." She turns the booklet and flips through the pages. "Here it is.

'Redding Boarding School for Boys is one of the leading year-round boarding schools in England, educating two hundred pupils per year from ages eleven to eighteen. The school was founded by Sir Thomas Redding in 1838..." Leah tilts her body toward me then whispers, "You've been to York before, haven't you?"

I smirk. "Maybe."

"Why am I reading these things? I've got you." Leah shoves brochures in her carry-on and relaxes against my shoulder. Throughout the remainder of the flight, I fill her head with pictures of York, and for a shining, crystalline moment, my world is flawless.

Grady greets us with a wide, goofy grin at the baggage claim of Manchester Airport. He holds a small handwritten sign that bears our names. Giggling, Leah runs to him and throws her arms around his neck.

"I missed you so much!" she squeals.

Grady wraps his arms around her waist and whisks her feet off the floor. "I missed you, too, but I didn't expect you so soon. I know I'm an amazing brother and all, but I thought you'd be able to wait at least until Christmas," he teases, placing her back on solid ground. He glances at me with a hint of reservation clouding his eyes. Pulling one over on Grady is going to be as difficult as fooling his sister.

"Yeah, like I said on the phone, Leah missed you, and it seemed like as good a time as any for a visit, before her classes start up and all." I look at Leah, silently asking for backup.

I half expect her to fold her arms across her chest and stand shoulder to shoulder with her brother, demanding an explanation, but she doesn't. She nods, which seems to satisfy Grady's unfailing curiosity for the time being.

"Hey, sorry about Ed. He was one of the good guys," Grady says.

"Yes, he was." A dull ache swallows the pit of my stomach. Leah captures my hand with hers.

Grady eyes her, throwing his arm around her shoulder. "We can talk in the car. You two must be exhausted. We have a bit of a ride ahead of us, about an hour and half, so we should get going. Ready, Lee-lee?"

Leah glares. "Only Mom's allowed to call me that."

Grady chuckles then grabs Leah's suitcase before heading to the exit.

Lifting my duffel bag off the conveyor belt, I sling the strap over my shoulder and follow.

Leah leans to my ear. "If you ever call me Lee-lee, I will hurt you. You might not believe it, but I've got a killer right hook."

"I can't promise. You never know. I might slip."

She cuffs me across the shoulder, then scowls, looking fierce. I grin and follow her out the door. The old Leah's back.

In the parking lot, Leah climbs into the back of Grady's new Volkswagen so I can ride shotgun. Once we're on the road, I peer at Leah from the corner of my eyes as the hum of the engine coaxes her closer and closer to sleep while Grady rambles on about sports scores.

When Leah sighs softly, I know she's fallen asleep. So does Grady; he immediately changes the subject. "I was going to wait until we were alone, but now is as good a time as any. Why are you two really here?" Grady's eyes don't leave the road.

"Leah missed you," I say matter-of-factly.

"That crap might work on my sister, but not on me."

"It's the truth." I shrug.

"Truth? Ha. You haven't told me the truth since we met."

I'm silent. At a loss for words, I watch the passing lights flicker across his stony face. Time passes slowly and deliberately. When he speaks again, his voice is more controlled.

"I like being straightforward, and I expect people to be the same with me. I've noticed something about you and my sister. The two of you seem like you've known each other a long time. But you haven't, right?"

With a sideways glance, Grady evaluates the way I hold my arms across my chest, the tautness of my jaw.

I scrutinize him. His demeanor isn't angry, only weary. "No, we haven't."

"That's BS."

I freeze. I can feel my control slipping, so I focus on the blurry lights of the landscape.

He forces a laugh. "You should've known Leah would confide in me."

I look over at him. His smirk looks more like a grimace than a smile.

"When she was thirteen, she told me about her dreams—the strange ones about a long time ago. I chalked it up to a girl's overactive imagination and too much Emily Brontë. When Leah was older, she told me about the man in the dreams. I'll admit that it concerned me. I told her it was cute when she was a kid, but she needed to grow up. After that, she stopped talking about them completely. I convinced myself she'd grown out of them, but I never stopped worrying. For a long time, I think she was afraid I'd tell Mom, but I never told anyone. After Leah met you, everything changed, though. Her focus became you. Frankly, I was relieved. For the first time, she took interest in a real, flesh-and-blood man, and I encouraged her. When I found out she didn't invite you to her art reception, I thought she might be pulling away from reality again. So I stepped in. I got to the reception just when you ran out."

I shift nervously in my seat. The rough fabric of my jeans swishes against the upholstery. I glance at Leah—she's still sleeping.

Grady continues, "You were pale, like you'd seen a ghost. I rushed in to find Leah teary-eyed and dazed. She showed me the portrait, told me she'd painted it before your arrival. That's when I realized she thought you were the man from her dreams. To be honest, I understood your reaction. It was normal, and I didn't expect you to come back that night... or ever. What man in his right mind would? The girl you just started dating claims to have dreamt about you for a better part of her life. Talk about red flags." Grady clears his throat. "When I found you at Leah's the next morning, it scared the crap out of me. I couldn't figure out why you came back. I told Leah to stay away from you, that she didn't know anything about you. Well, you can guess how well that went over. So, I spied on the two of you."

I scowl at him with clenched teeth.

"A little stalker-like, I know," Grady admits without remorse.

"A little?" I say, unable to hide the insult in my voice.

"I was worried about my sister. She and my mom are the only family I have. As I was saying, I watched from a distance. Everything seemed normal. I told you before. You make Leah happy, so I decided to leave well enough alone, but I did notice something else. You act different. Your manners, your actions, they aren't from this time. We both know why. Don't we?" This isn't a question, but an accusation.

"Grady, I..."

"There's more," he says, his voice emotionless. "Soon after I got here, one of the professors asked me for a favor. I wanted to fit in, so I agreed. Newbie mistake." His laugh lacks its usual warmth and enthusiasm.

"I spent two whole weekends, morning to night, sorting tintypes and other old photographs Musheer bought from local estate auctions for his living history class. Boring beyond belief. In the pile of faces, I found this." Grady removes a thin, rectangular case from his pocket and tosses it into my lap. "Musheer said it dates from the early 1860s, and according to the elegant signature on the back, it's a picture of a Jack Hammond. To a Ruth Hammond."

In the dimming twilight, I study the decorative leather. With unsteady fingers, I flip open the two small brass clasps. From behind rippled glass, a monochrome image of me looks back. The photograph had been William's idea—a gift for our sister. We traveled thirty miles to Banbury to G. Herbert Photography to have them taken, and as far as I'm aware, it's one of only two photos of me in existence.

"Note the birthmark over the left eye. Same shape as yours. A bit of a coincidence, wouldn't you say? Explain."

I quickly piece together a story. The man is my great-great-grandfather. I'm his namesake. My grandmother always said I looked like him. *Believable enough, right? But what about the birthmark?* I'll cross that bridge when I get there. Of course, this will mean lying to him again. My guilt surges with thoughts of Leah's words. *"I just wish we didn't have to lie to Grady."*

Aw, dammit! Instead of playing it safe, I'm going to rip open that can of worms. I can hear the truthful words assembling on my head. Because I know if Grady can accept me for what I am, Leah can keep him fully in her life. He'll be the one person she'll never have to lie to, like Ruth was for me. And like an idiot, I have to try.

My eyes slide to him. "Do you really want to know?"

Grady nods once, but his eyes cling to the curves of the road, and he grimaces.

"I'm the son of John and Helen Hammond. I was born in Lidcombe, Gloucestershire, England on January second, 1841."

"1841?"

I hesitate. "Yes."

"What does that make you? A vampire? Or some zombie undead child of the damned?"

I chuckle darkly. *Damned? Definitely.* "Nope, just immortal."

His eyes narrow. "Immortal? How do you know? I mean, besides the not aging thing and all. How do you know you're not the next Methuselah, and when you reach nine hundred sixty-nine, you won't just drop dead?"

"I'm sure. I've tried quite a few times, unsuccessfully. My body's resistant to injury."

"What does that mean?"

"I heal quickly."

"How quick?"

I look back to make sure Leah's still sleeping. "It would be easier to show than explain, but you'd need to pull over."

Grady looks over to study me for an instant. The car wobbles over the uneven shoulder and slows to a stop.

I open my door, stop, and face Grady. "Do you get squeamish?"

He shifts in his seat. His hard-set jaw and rigid pose show his nervousness. "I don't think so," he whispers.

"Well then, come on."

CHAPTER SEVENTEEN

I SHUT MY CAR DOOR LIGHTLY, careful not to wake Leah. I open the hatchback and rifle through my duffel. I retrieve a slender pocketknife.

Grady's footfalls shadow mine into the nearby meadow. Neither of us speaks as we wade through the tall grass. I rotate the knife repeatedly in my hand in an attempt to settle my mounting nerves. When I'm about twenty feet from the car, I stop and stand in the light cast by the headlights. Grady steps to my side. Taking a deep breath, I flip open the knife, and before I can change my mind, I slide the blade along my arm, slicing open the tender skin from my wrist to my forearm. I grit my teeth. Blood pours out of the gash and runs down my arm, but then it slows to a trickle.

As the wound begins to heal, Grady's eyes widen, and he gasps. "You got to be freakin' kidding me!"

"Shhh. Leah," I say, squinting nervously into the headlights. All the moisture recedes from my mouth, leaving it as dry as a bone. I shift my weight from one foot to the other then turn back to Grady. His blank expression makes his thoughts impossible to read.

"How's your arm?" Grady whispers.

"Almost healed." I turn my arm over so the headlights illuminate the fading pink line.

The stillness returns.

"So you're like one hundred and seventy years old," he finally says, an airiness returning to his voice.

"I am."

"Can I ask you something?"

"Fire away."

"Why did Leah see you in her dreams?"

I take a moment to find my words. For some reason, this isn't where I envisioned the conversation going. "She didn't tell you?"

He shakes his head.

"You should ask her."

"You know."

I don't respond.

"But you're not going to tell me, are you?"

"No, I'm not. It's not my secret to tell."

He sighs. "Okay. You're right. I'll ask her myself."

"You're taking this all very well."

"Well, it's better than what my imagination brewed up. You don't suck blood, eat people's brains for dinner, or grow wolf ears during full moons, right?"

"Not that I know of."

"Compared to that stuff, you seem, well, normal."

I choke back a laugh. I never expected to be called normal after showing off my freak show ability. *A first time for everything.*

"So, you can't die. Cool."

"No, not cool. And I can die."

Grady snorts.

"With that talent, there's no way you can die. Well, maybe if you lose your head, but how often does that happen? It's not like we live in the sixteenth century."

"Not exactly," I say.

"How?" Leah asks from right behind me.

Grady and I jump like twin grasshoppers in the darkened meadow. "Hey, sleepyhead, how long you been awake?" he asks, his tense eyes shifting to me.

"Answer me. How?" she says.

"Hemlock with a pinch of salt."

"Seriously?" Grady sounds disappointed. "But that's so... boring."

A scowl planted on her face, Leah glares back and forth between the two of us and mutters.

"Well, it *is* boring, but it's not like he'll ever need to find out," Grady says. "I can't imagine a reason anyone in Jack's situation would choose to die anyway. Lucky bastard." He slugs me in the arm.

My brow furrows. My eyes meet Leah's then flit away. I can imagine. My plans are set—when Leah dies, so will I.

Grady's gaze shifts from Leah to me. A knowing look crosses his face.

The rest of the trip is uneventful. Grady babbles on about sports, while Leah rides in silence, lost in space. Finally, we arrive at Grady's small brick flat on Bartle Garth, close to the middle of town with a view of York Minster. Great Peter, the bell of the massive northwest tower, tolls the hour. Its clang reverberates off the building and rolls through the crooked streets, overpowering all other sound. I breathe deeply, taking in the smells of the modern city. Smoke and soot blended with the muddy river water of the Ouse have all vanished. Car exhaust and the homey fragrance of baking bread from a corner bakery have replaced it, commingling with the sweet scent of flowers from a garden along the westward wall of Grady's new digs.

Grady grabs Leah's suitcase from the hatchback. I sling my duffel over my shoulder and follow him and Leah up the two flights of stairs to his apartment. Grady's place is sleek and modern—a white box filled with black, glass, and polished chrome, decorated in the minimalist style. Leah freezes in the entryway, her mouth an adorable *O* of surprise.

Grady drops Leah's bag and smiles. "Don't say it. I know, not my style. The place came furnished."

"Yeah," she says, looking slowly around the room. "Understatement of the century. It's really... clean."

Grady's smile slips into a pinched expression. "Wow, glowing compliment."

"The place is just not what I expected." She glances toward the windows. "You've got a great view of the city."

"And an interesting choice of décor," I add, pointing to a painting hanging over the dining table—five dogs playing poker.

He grins at Leah. "That's all mine. Right, sis?"

She groans. "You still got that damn thing."

"Yeah. That's Americana at its best," Grady says, walking into his small galley-style kitchen. He opens the refrigerator and stoops to examine its contents. "Are you two hungry? There isn't much. Let's see... I could make grilled cheeses, or there's some leftover Chinese from last night."

"Chinese," Leah and I say in unison.

"Hey, my cooking has gotten better. I've been practicing," Grady grabs four white square boxes and tosses their contents in bowls before shoving our meager feast into the microwave. Leaning against the counter, he studies me. "So, 1841, huh? Did you meet Queen Victoria?"

I laugh. "No. We ran in different circles. After my father died, my family was poor, living off the generosity of others." I pause. "Where are your plates?"

Grady gestures to the upper-right cupboards. "The Crimean War. I'm teaching that conflict this semester. You would have been what? Thirteen, fourteen."

"Thirteen. Believe it or not, that was enlistment age back then, but I was too immersed in my studies to consider it." I grab three plates from the cupboard. "I wanted to be a teacher like you, not a soldier, and Sir Robert offered to pay for my education as long as I kept my grades up."

Grady out a little sigh. "Okay—" He drums his fingers along his lips, obviously thinking.

"Jack's not your private encyclopedia, Grady," Leah says, taking the dish out of my hands and walking to the table.

"Sure, sure," he says, not looking in her direction, keeping his gaze on me. "However, he is a walking, talking, living history museum."

Fantastic, here comes Dr. Grady and his mental probe. Why didn't I see this coming? History teacher, duh. I fake a laugh. "England was in a skirmish every other minute back then, at least that's how it felt. Do you remember much about the Afghanistan War? Or the Iraq War?"

He thinks for a minute then nods. "Point taken."

Over dinner, Grady's list of questions grows along with his eagerness to pump me for information. With a tensing stomach and dry mouth, I shrug and nod, giving bits of accurate information accompanied by a copious amount of lies. Leah grows quiet, focused on her pork-fried rice, picking at each grain.

"Sounds like you traveled around a lot," Grady says. "What countries have you lived in?"

"I trekked around England for a while. Around 1875, I left and headed to Ireland, then France and Spain. After my sister died, I went to the States."

His eyes brighten. "Ireland. How about the Famine of 1879? I know that famine is considered the smallest of the three, but were you there? What was it like?"

"I probably know less than you. I remember hunger and overcrowded slums, but that's the year I developed a fondness for whiskey." I chuckle with my lie. Actually, that was the year I attempted starvation. By the end of my little hunger strike, I looked like a walking skeleton. I passed out in the street and woke up in a neighbor's home. Mrs. O'Callaghan–a mother of seven and, for all intents and purposes, a drill sergeant–forced broth down my throat for weeks until she was satisfied with my *plumpness*. "Honestly, I wasn't paying much attention then."

Grady's face tightens, and he rubs the back of his neck. "So let me get this straight. You've lived through countless wars and some of the most life-changing inventions and events in human history, but you've pretty much lost the whole twentieth century and parts of the nineteenth—how does my friend James put that? Oh, yeah—you useless wanker." He chuckles, shaking his head.

"Grady! Geez!" Leah shoots her brother a harsh squint.

"What? I was joking," he says. "But as a side note, he's going to need to write down anniversaries and birthdays, 'cause he's got a piss-poor memory. I mean, I thought mine was bad—"

"I remember the Great Exhibition." I grin.

"You were there?" Grady's eyes widen.

"Yeah. I was ten. Sir Robert took William and allowed me to tag along. It seemed like the whole world was cramped into that ornate building of iron and glass." I look at Leah. "Artwork around every corner."

Her mouth slacks. "Really?"

I nod with a smile. "My favorite was *Richard the Lionheart* by Marochetti. The sculpture was so large, it had to be placed outside the Crystal Palace. Inside was filled with exotic people and inventions from all over the empire and the planet. The songs of colorful birds and the trumpets of elephants rang over the drone of the crowd. And the smell of flowers mixed with foreign spices. A pink glass fountain stood in the middle of it all. To me, it seemed like a hundred feet high, but Sir Robert claimed the structure was only thirty. The whole day was filled with one amazing sight after another."

He sucks in a quick breath. "Wow, now that must have been something to see." Grady drifts into his own world.

Leah gives me a sidelong glance. Her mouth opens then closes again, and she drops her attention to her plate.

"What's up," I whisper.

She shakes her head. "Not now."

Grady stands, seeming satisfied with his small taste of the past. "I don't know about you two, but I'm beat. I left a pillow and blanket on the sofa for you, Jack. Sis, how about I show you your room?"

Leah pecks me on the lips. "Night." She grabs her bag and follows Grady down a hall past the kitchen.

After putting the dishes in the sink, I sit on my makeshift bed, wondering if I've made the right decisions tonight. Grady seems to be taking all I've handed him in stride, but maybe that's just for show. Maybe when Leah said she felt she should tell her brother, her impulse was a pipe dream and not something she thought was a good idea. I try to sleep, still second-guessing myself.

Well past two o'clock, I'm wide awake, my feet hanging over the edge of the stone-hard sofa. I'd blame my sleeplessness on the different time zone or the uncomfortable accommodations, but I know neither is the case. I fluff my pillow for the hundredth time, roll to my side, tuck my arm under my head, and close my eyes, willing myself to sleep.

A door creaks open, then the patter of Leah's footsteps crosses the wooden floor. She pokes my bare shoulder a little harder than necessary. My eyes flick open.

Leah's face is so close that we're practically touching noses. She draws away, and I roll up onto my elbow. My brow creases.

"We need to talk," she whispers. "I know something's going on. Something you're keeping from me. We didn't come here because I missed Grady." She plunks down on the edge of the sofa.

"I'm not sure what you mean."

She shoots me a pinched expression and huffs out of exasperation. "Why are we here, Jack?"

"Well." I rub the back of my neck. "Because I thought you needed to see your brother. Whether you realize it or not, you missed him."

"That's a load of crock, and you know it!"

"You didn't miss Grady?" Pressing my lips into a fine line, I tilt my head, one brow arched.

"Of course I did, but that has nothing to do with the reason we're here." She throws her arms in the air. Her cheeks flush red. "You don't tell me you can die, and now this? You're confiding things to my brother that you're keeping from me. How do you think that makes me feel?"

She's right. I want to say I'm sorry and that I meant to tell her about the hemlock. With everything swirling out of control around us, I forgot. Finding a way to die was my focus for so long, but then when I find it... Leah really has changed everything. But I don't say any of that because my reasons would sound like excuses and lead the conversation to why we're really here.

"Everyone always thinks I can't handle things," she mutters in disgust.

"I know you can."

"No, you don't, or you'd tell me. And the last time I checked, having hope isn't a sin," she says, pulling farther away. I don't like the distance, but from her sweeping arm gestures and reddened face, I can tell Leah isn't ready for my apology. I look away.

"I can handle a lot more than anyone gives me credit for." Leah ticks them off on her fingers. "My dad's death. Cancer. Near-death experience. Weird dreams. Soul immortality. I've handled a lot, and look, still in one piece."

I stay quiet.

"You're not going to tell me, are you?" she says.

"Leah, I..."

She pushes off the sofa and storms out of the room. Moments later, I hear her bedroom door slam and then her crying.

I let my head fall into my open hands. I'm not sure I know what I'm doing anymore. I've been twisted into an impossible position. I'm damned no matter what, and the worst thing is: my actions put us here. If I had just kept my mouth shut—*No, what's done is done.* I need to tell Leah the truth. *But first...*

I stand, slide on my faded jeans, and tug on an old, holey Adidas T-shirt. After grabbing my phone off the coffee table, I dart to the door.

Grady eyes me from the hallway. His forehead puckers as his sandy brows pull together. "What the hell's going on! She's crying, and you're leaving?"

"Just for a bit. Need some fresh air. She doesn't want to see me right now."

He nods once and turns, heading toward Leah's room.

Out in the crisp night air, my fingers trace circles along my temples, fighting off an impending headache. Maybe keeping Leah in the dark isn't the same as keeping her safe. What good has lying done? Shielding her from the truth has brought her more distress than peace. However, before I tell her anything, I need to know what's going on with Vita.

I haven't heard from Artagan for almost a week, when he warned me to get away. I wonder why he hasn't called. Leah would say no news is good news. However, my thoughts fill with disturbing images, all revolving around Vita coming face-to-face with Leah, her sinister smile celebrating Leah's approaching death. I flip open my cell. No missed calls. No missed texts. If the mountain won't come to Muhammad, then Muhammad must go to the mountain. I dial his number.

It rings twice.

"Jack. What's up?" Artagan answers.

"I need an update. Any changes?"

"I've sent Vita on a wild-goose chase. Planted a couple clues in your apartment hinting that you're on your way to the land down under." He chuckles.

"Thanks. The farther the better. You should know, I'm telling Leah everything tonight."

He's silent for about three seconds then asks, "Do you think that's wise?"

"I don't know. The secret seems to be doing more harm than good. She knows I'm lying to her about something. Honestly, I'm not sure what else to do."

"If you think it's best. I'll call in a few days with an update, unless something changes, but I'm sure it won't. Between her day job and searching the whole of Australia, she'll be pretty occupied for a while," Artagan adds.

"All right." I hang up and shove the phone into my back pocket. Artagan seems to have Vita well in hand. Staring aimlessly, I inhale deeply through my nose to calm the queasy feeling in my stomach. In the gleam of a streetlight, a feathery plant with clusters of white blossoms catches my eye. *Hemlock.* I step toward the garden and pinch off a sprig of the lacy leaves. Rolling the stem between my forefinger and thumb, I survey the small, seemingly innocuous greenery. *So all this time, all I was looking for was you.* The solution to this new crisis stares back at me. Coerce a little salted hemlock down that vile throat of Vita, and Leah and I will be free. I smile, picking more and shoving the fern-like plant deep into my pocket, then I head back to the apartment.

Inside, I quietly rummage through the cabinets, pawing a menagerie of cooking utensils until I find a small box of plastic bags stashed in the far corner of a bottom drawer. I place the hemlock into one then sprinkle salt into the bag. The granular crystals fall over the leaves like snow. I seal the bag then slip the small packet of liberator into my pocket on my way to Leah's room. On the other side of her half-open door, I hear a soft murmur.

"Don't bother. Jack left. If it's any consolation, he looked like someone dug his heart out with a spoon. So why don't you just answer the question. Where did all those dreams come from?"

The room falls quiet.

"They're all memories," Leah finally says.

"All of them?"

"Yes."

"And Jack's memories line up with yours?" Grady asks tentatively.

Another round of silence.

I step into the doorway and bump the door open with my foot. "Yes, they do."

"Okay. But you're not like him." Grady's head bobs in my direction, but his eyes stay fixed on Leah. "That much, I'm sure of. Seems I was there the day you were born."

Leah purses her lips. She studies her brother while she nervously twists a stray thread of the comforter around and around her index finger.

"You're right. There are differences," I speak up, leaning against the doorframe. "It's more like we're opposite sides of the same coin. My body is earthbound, while Leah's soul is." I go on to explain the intricacies of what we are, laying out all the facts for Grady's examination.

"Wait. Wait. Wait," he says. His eyes swivel between Leah and me, finally landing on her face. "You were that rich dude, Sir Whatshisface's daughter? The girl you've been obsessing over."

"Sir Robert Ashford," she corrects. "And yes."

He turns his gaping expression to me. "You're the man the girl ran into the storm for."

I nod.

"This is making my brain hurt. I'm going to bed." Grady places his hand on my shoulder for a brief moment before stepping into the hall. A second later, a door shuts.

"He'll be all right," Leah says. "He just needs time."

"No doubt. He's had a lot to deal with." I stay at the threshold, waiting for an invitation.

"Please, come in," Leah says, almost in a whisper.

I enter and sit on the bed. "I realize I'm not being fair to you. You're right. I'm concealing information from you, and that needs to stop."

"Yes, it does."

I take her hand, entwining our fingers. "I left to call someone—Artagan. You might remember him from the theater the night we went to the movie."

She thinks for a second or two then nods. "The one you ran after because he reminded you of your friend?"

I stiffen. My eyes dart from her face to the floor and then to her face. "Well, yes, but that was a lie. I recognized him for other reasons. He helped me escape the enemy during the Great War, in France. I didn't make the connection until recently—at the beach."

I pause, taking a deep breath before I continue. "The day Ed died, I saw Artagan again. He wasn't alone. I thought he was looking for me, so I called out to him. It seems that innocent act has drawn me—and in turn, you—into some kind of feud, earning the attention of another immortal named Vita. I'm sorry for that."

"What does this have to do with you?"

"It's a long story, but Vita holds Artagan and his descendants accountable for things that happened long ago. She's intent on putting an end to his family line."

"So Artagan's your...?"

"He's my family." I can't help but smile.

Leah stands. "So, she's after you." A flurry of anger swirls behind her eyes. "Why would you keep this from me? I can help. That bitch's going to get to you over my dead body."

"That's what I'm afraid of." I squeeze her hand gently, leading her to the bed. "Artagan says Vita's tearing up the Outback, searching for me, so we're safe for now."

"Do you trust him?"

I mentally list everything he's done. I smile. "Surprisingly, yes. I believe he has my best interest at heart."

"Okay, I trust your judgment of him, but no more secrets, all right?" she says ruefully.

"Agreed. Just remember, it's been a long time since

I've been able to rely on someone. Be patient with me. I'm still learning."

"I have one more question. What happens to you if you die?"

I shrug. "Heaven, I guess." *Or hell.*

Silent, her gaze falls to the comforter.

"Don't worry, love. I'm not going anywhere. You're stuck with me." I let the back of my fingers brush along her cheek. "It's late. You should get some sleep."

I attempt to stand, but her hand holds fast.

"Were you planning on leaving?" she asks.

"I was."

"Please stay."

A smile takes full possession of my face. "My pleasure. Don't tell Grady, but his sofa isn't very comfortable. Hard as a brick."

She laughs, but the chime is deflated.

I rest against the headboard, my arms folded behind my head, my legs crossed. Leah snuggles up to me and curls herself against my chest. I wrap an arm around her and rub her back to soothe her to sleep.

CHAPTER EIGHTEEN

THE NEXT MORNING, I TRY not to wake her. Gently, I extricate myself from Leah's entwined arms. The bed wobbles as I stand, and Leah mumbles and rolls over. I freeze. Her tangled hair flops into her face. I stay still for another minute or two. Soon Leah begins to snore lightly. I grin and slink to the door.

I peer out into the dimly lit hall. Grady is nowhere to be seen. *Perfect.* I recoil at the thought of him catching me leaving his sister's room at this time in the morning. No need to revisit that scenario. Been there; done that.

"Where are you going?" Leah asks, a little annoyed.

I jump, turning around.

Leah peers at me from the comfort of her bed, her eyelids droopy with sleepiness.

"Do you want Grady to catch me leaving your room?" I ask.

She shrugs then shakes her head.

"Didn't think so." I return to kiss her before slipping out.

In the living room, I climb onto Grady's couch and yank the blanket over me. I shift about, finding a comfortable position among the pits and lumps. Just as I settle in, I hear a door open and Grady yawn. I close my eyes and snore lightly.

After listening to ten minutes of rummaging going on in the kitchen, I decide it's safe to wake up.

Grady's wearing plaid pajama pants and a Red Sox T-shirt. His hair sticks straight up like a rooster's comb. He looks at me sheepishly. "Did I wake you?"

"No worries." I add a stretch for effect.

"Sorry," he says, banging more pots and pans. This time, it's apparently intentional. A roguish grin spreads across his face.

"What are you doing anyway?"

He beams. "Cooking breakfast."

"So you're good? With Leah, I mean."

"Couldn't be better," he says, taking the eggs out of the refrigerator. "I was up until about three, when it hit me. Leah isn't crazy. Never was. What happened to her was normal for who she is. After that, I slept better than I have in years. A weight"—he cracks an egg and raises its empty shell halves over the frying pan—"has been lifted."

I smile and nod.

I'm sitting at Grady's small glass-top table, waiting patiently for his eggs to fry, when Leah emerges from her room, showered and dressed. When she sees Grady cooking in the kitchen, she wrinkles her nose. The worry in her eyes has vanished, and that realization brings a grin to my lips. She takes the seat next to me.

"Good morning," she says. "How'd you sleep?"

I feel the corners of my mouth twitch upward. "Never better. You?"

A muffled giggle escapes her lips. "Perfectly," she says.

"Grady insisted on making us breakfast this morning."

Her expression is a portrait of panic.

My callused hand slips into her soft, smooth one and gives a little squeeze. "Be brave, love," I tease.

"I heard that," Grady says. He sets two plates of burnt toast and greasy fried eggs in front of us.

Leah pokes at the inflated egg whites with her fork and

scrunches her eyes, wrinkling her nose again. "How did you get this consistency?"

Grady ignores her. "Charlotte has been teaching me how to cook. She said I've improved."

"Charlotte? Who's Charlotte?" Leah's eyes shoot to Grady's annoyed face.

"She's one of the teachers over at the school. Now try them and see what you think."

I chuckle, watching her poke at the eggs again, eyeing them skeptically as if they're toxic.

Grady waits, his arms crossed over his puffed-out chest.

She cuts off the tiniest piece, places the bit on her tongue, and chews. Swallowing, she chases the lump down with a large gulp of milk.

"Yum," Leah says unconvincingly. She puts down her fork and nibbles the dry toast.

Grady rolls his eyes and returns to the kitchen.

Taking a hesitant bite, I'm surprised. "These are bloody fantastic," I say, shoving another bite in my mouth. When my plate is empty, I eye Leah's. "If you're not going to eat those..."

"Have at." She picks up her toast and slides her laden plate toward me. She watches incredulously as I devour her eggs in three mouthfuls. "How can you like those? The sensation is more like a flavorless greasy mush than eggs."

"See, it's not my cooking. It's you," Grady says, returning with a bowl of steaming baked beans in one hand and a plate of sausages in the other. He places them on the table next to me and plops into a chair.

She shrugs halfheartedly and then takes another bite of toast. "Maybe. Tell me more about this Charlotte."

"I told you. She's a teacher," Grady says with a bit of apprehension hidden in his irritation. His eyes avoid Leah, and he scoops a pile of baked beans onto his plate.

Leah's eyes narrow. "Who's teaching you to make breakfast? How often does she come over to give you lessons? Oh, wait, I understand." Her face gleams with a wide grin. "Mom will be thrilled. And maybe having a girlfriend will keep your nose out of my business."

"Don't you dare tell Mom. She's a friend. That's all. Now eat your toast." Grady shoves a spoonful of baked beans in his mouth.

"Uh-huh. Mary Pinkus was just a friend, too, if I remember correctly. That is until I caught the two of you making out in the back of your car at the end of our driveway."

I laugh, stabbing a couple sausages with my fork.

Grady glares at Leah. "I was thinking you might want to meet some of my friends for dinner tonight, but not if you're going to act like this—"

The trilling ring of my phone interrupts Grady's lecture. The muscles along my shoulders and neck tense. I fish the phone out of my pocket and excuse myself, pushing away from the table.

I shut myself in Leah's room. "Artagan, what's going on?"

"Vita's on the move."

My mouth goes dry. "To where?"

"Venice."

A frosty burn overtakes me, extending from the base of my spine to my neck's apex. Slowly and deliberately, I pace the room, trying to keep my breathing even.

"Jack? You still there?"

"Yes." My words come out more like a growl than I intended. "That's a bit too close."

"Istanbul would be too close for you. Now listen. I debated whether I should call you or not, but I wanted you to know you can trust me. Her travels have nothing to do with you. A job popped up. One I'm also invited to, which is good. I can keep a close eye on her."

I tap the folded stash of hemlock in my pocket. My heartbeat speeds with the rush of adrenaline. "I could be on the next plane. I'd be there in a little over an hour. We could take care of that bitch once and for all."

Artagan laughs. "Believe me, I would love nothing more, but I can't help you with that. Rule number one. No slaughtering one's fellow council members."

"What? That's what you all do! Besides, according to the story, Vita murdered Brennus."

"No, Brennus committed suicide. Unfortunately, Vita's not the nothing-to-live-for, in-the-depths-of-despair type. Look, we can talk about this later. I have to go. I'll call you when this little assignment is finished." He hangs up.

Venice. Anger engulfs me, and fantasies of tearing Vita limb from limb then shoving hemlock down her gullet flash behind my eyes. The first might not kill her, but torturing her would make me feel better. In a pure wintery rage, my hand balls into a fist and slams into the nearest surface. A sharp bite cuts into the taut flesh of my knuckles. My vision skips from the lopsided hole in the wall to my bleeding hand, then to the shards of horsehair plaster littering the floor. I grab one of the socks from the top of Leah's suitcase and wrap it around my knuckles, slumping onto the edge of the bed.

The door creaks. Someone slips in from the hall. The footsteps are too light to be Grady's. I glance up to find Leah standing at the door, her expression a jumble of concern and anxiety. Her eyes trail from the fragments of shattered wall strewn across the hardwood floor to my improvised bandage. In three short steps, she's at my side, sitting on the bed next to me. Her hand grips my arm, attempting to pull it toward her.

Maybe I could hunt Vita myself. However, I would have to leave Leah behind, and Grady couldn't keep her safe from Vita. But if I stayed with her, could I do any better? I jerk my arm away and let my elbow rest on my knee. "It's fine," I say, my tone ragged.

"Let me see," Leah says firmly. This time, I don't resist, and she flips my hand over.

"Tell Grady I'm sorry about the hole in the wall." I

peer down. Blood has seeped through the fabric. "And the sock... I'm sorry about your sock."

She studies me apprehensively while gingerly unwrapping the sock.

Jagged gashes score my knuckles. Pieces of milk-white plaster stick out from the wound, but the bleeding has stopped.

She rummages through her makeup bag and finds some tweezers. "First, I'll remove these pieces of plaster. Then I'll see what first-aid supplies Grady has. We might be forced to use paper towel and duct tape." She attempts a grin.

As she removes each pointy sliver, her eyes widen. My skin begins knitting itself together. She puts on a brave face and continues to pick out the fragments.

"I heal quickly."

"I see that," she says nonchalantly, keeping her eyes hidden from my view behind her hair.

When all the remnants are removed, Leah sits as still as a stone, watching the remains of my wound vanish before her eyes.

"So, who was that on the phone?" she asks, trying to sound casual.

I'm quiet.

"You promised, you know. No more secrets." Leah's unyielding gaze trains on my face.

My shoulders tighten. "Vita's on the move. I won't let her near you."

Her attention returns to my hand. "It's you we need to worry about," she murmurs.

"Not true. The thought of the two of you meeting..." A shiver races through me. With a deep intake of air, I continue, "I was attempting to figure out a way to leave, but who would protect you?"

Leah's wide eyes snap to mine, moisture pooling along their rims. She blinks away the tears. Her jaw stiffens, and she lifts her chin. "You want to go after her?" she asks through clenched teeth.

"If it keeps you safe, of course. Sitting here waiting is driving me crazy. If I could trust that you'd be out of harm's way here with Grady, I'd hunt her down. Kill her myself..."

"Absolutely not! Heroic suicidal attempts might be romantic in novels, but not in real life. Are you insane?"

I wince.

"If something happened to you, there's no getting you back. You'd be gone forever. At least if it's me that dies, we have a chance of some kind of happily ever after."

"I don't want to get into this, not now." I close my eyes and pinch the bridge of my nose between my fingers. "Artagan said—"

"You know nothing about this man, but you're putting all your faith in him. I don't trust him!"

I huff. "I do. He's helping us. Give him a chance. He's the only family I have."

"Family." She scoffs. "Remember who he is, what he does."

"Artagan's different from the other members of the council. He lived a normal life before becoming what he is now."

Leah nods reluctantly. "Something about him frightens me," she whispers. "Please be careful."

I can see her soul through her eyes, and it's shrouded in fear. "I don't know what else to do," I say, the ice thawed from my voice.

Leah shifts to peer up into my face, and ever so gently, her fingertips caress the wrinkles along my brow. "It's going to be all right. I feel it."

The forever optimist. I open my mouth to criticize, then I stop short. In place of using spirited words, I put my arms around her and hold her tight. "It has to be. Losing you isn't an option."

Leah manages to persuade me to carry on with the evening's plans as normal. Over the ticking hours, my face becomes a composed mask. Attempting to fight the paranoia brewing inside of me, I smile and joke, but my tranquil nature is all a sham. Twilight comes, but Artagan's call does not.

I plod through the maze of crooked streets, a half step behind Grady and Leah. My nerves are raw. My eyes dart around, taking in every movement.

In stark contrast, Leah seems relaxed. Instead of concentrating on the turmoil orbiting around us, she's lost in the beauty that is York, babbling on about tapered streets and the medieval architecture. I want to shake her and yell at her that Death—or at least his daughter—is coming to greet her with a smile, but I keep my mouth shut. Besides, Grady's already noticing my surge of protectiveness.

At the next corner, we turn right into the Shambles. The overhangs of half-timbered storefronts, reaching out to one another over the divide, darken the cobblestone alleyway. The meager light that creeps into this cramped space leaves the alley gloomy. Dampness clings to the air. It's a scene right out of one of Leah's horror flicks. I half expect Vita to jump out from a dark corner.

Five blocks down, Grady slows to a stop. We're standing in front of the Golden Monk. The building looks as if it was crammed into the confined space as an afterthought. Not a lot has changed—the scenery is still more for locals than for the tourists. *I wonder if they want their old dart back.* I chuckle under my breath.

Laughter overflows from the open door. Footfalls approach us from behind. Leah turns, and a grin spreads across her face. I slide into her view, becoming a barricade. Two figures walk out of the darkness. My hand slips into my pocket and grips the bag. The plastic crinkles.

"Everything's okay," Leah whispers in my ear.

She tosses me a warm, reassuring smile. I reassert my calm mask.

Grady steps forward, greeting them warmly. Excitement surfaces in his voice, and he introduces the duo as James and Charlotte.

Charlotte is small, slender, and attractive. Her coffee-colored hair is cut at an angle around her oval face, and one side is tucked behind her ear. Her golden hazel eyes dance with sparks of mischief. From the goofy grin plastered across Grady's lips and the way he shuffles his feet back and forth nervously, Leah's instincts are correct. Grady likes Charlotte more than he lets on.

Next to Charlotte is her brother, James, a stocky guy closer to my apparent age. His expression suggests that he has the same disposition as his sister, although a bit more subdued. James smiles, and his eyes drift to Leah. His gaze lingers on her face a bit too long for casual friendliness. I stiffen, and my arm tightens around Leah's waist. When his eye meets mine, he looks away. *That's right, buddy. Move along.*

After the usual pleasantries, we move our conversation into the pub. Patrons crowd around the counter. The England fans sport red jerseys, while the Aussies wear gold—no commingling of colors. Every eye is glued to the TV hanging over the bar.

James leads the way through the crowd, finding an empty table next to the bar. As Grady sits, taking the seat next to Charlotte, the crowd erupts into shouts of victory and moans as Britain scores. "Honestly, I don't get it. This has got to be the stupidest sport on the planet," Grady says over the clamor.

A pin-dropping quiet settles over the pub. Angry eyes swing in our direction, all centered on Grady.

"Do you have a death wish?" I hiss just loud enough for Grady to hear.

"Don't. Diss. Cricket," Charlotte says, enunciating each word.

"Listen to the lady, ya bloody Yank," a redheaded man sitting at the end of the bar yells, slurring each word. "Or go back to that arse-slapping game you call football."

"Ah, that's not what I meant," Grady backpedals, panic on his face.

Charlotte glares at him, her seemingly fun-loving nature gone. "So that was meant to be a joke? You think we Brits are funny?"

I can't tell if Charlotte's toying with him or if she's serious. Either way, she has Grady on the ropes.

"Ahhh, no...?" Slack-jawed, Grady stares at Charlotte.

"Would you like a little help? You have no game," I say, leaning over to Grady's ear, and then I grin to lessen the insult.

"Just like cricket," Grady whispers.

"You're on your own," I grumble. I lean back, resting my arm along the rail of Leah's chair; I fake engrossment in the game. With each passing moment, displaying the image of perfect composure becomes more difficult.

"No one's ever listening until you make a mistake." Grady grins in Charlotte's direction. She laughs, and Grady's smile grows wider. "If you like one-liners, I'm full of them. Two wrongs are only a beginning. Or this one's my favorite—he who laughs lasts thinks slowest."

Charlotte laughs again, followed by her brother.

"See, I knew Charlotte was the smart one of her family."

His comment earns him a wink. *Huh, maybe Grady has game after all.*

The meals come, and the drinks flow. While Grady seems to have dug himself out of his trouble, I'm wading into my own. Every time I reach for the silent bulge stuffed in my shirt pocket, Leah shifts comfortably in her seat. Finally, I remove my cell and glare at the incoming-calls list. With a sigh, I place the phone on the table. Twelve hours, and still no call. Artagan must know something by now.

Minutes become an hour, then two. The conversation hops from light topic to light topic, but I pay little attention to the chatter.

My cell vibrates, scooting across the table toward the edge. I grab it just before it tumbles to the floor. Casting Leah a sideward glance, I stand and excuse myself then slip into the rowdy crowd and out into the night.

I flip open the phone. "Where is she? Where's Vita?"

"You don't have to worry about her." The solemn edge to Artagan's tone takes away any comfort the words should give.

"Why? What's going on? Has she lost interest?"

"You're fine. She's back in Australia. I'll send her to Canada or maybe Russia next. Enjoy your vacation. I've got a job to do," he says impudently.

"So, you're saying we're safe?"

"I don't recommend you heading back to Portland, but yes, you're safe. Now, I'm working."

Click.

"Hello?"

I get nothing but static. Artagan's gone.

I stare, unblinking, at the phone. Regardless of Artagan's unexpected behavior, relief washes over me. *Safe.* I turn to find Leah standing at the pub's entrance, an unreadable expression etched on her face. I close the gap between us and take her hand.

Her eyes shift away, staring at her shoes. "So what's the verdict?"

"Vita's no longer a concern. For now, anyway." I look up at the twinkling stars overhead to avoid meeting her searching eyes.

She steps in and rests her cheek against my chest, and I wind my arms around her. "That's good news. What's wrong, then?"

"Nothing to do with us. It's just Artagan was unfriendly."

"Has he been like that before?"

"No. Not like this, but he sounded in a hurry, like he was fitting me in between jobs."

She winces.

"I know, but it is what he is. I've just got to get used to the fact that my only family is a wielder of death." I chuckle coldly.

She rests her head on my chest. "Thank you."

I cock my head so I can look at her face. "For what?"

"For telling me."

I smile. "I'm doing pretty good, huh?"

"Very good." She kisses my chin.

"We should get back. Grady's already concerned about my behavior today. No need to give him more ammunition."

"I'll just tell him we had a fight," she says, snuggling her face into the crook of my neck.

I grimace. "What did I do this time?"

"Nothing. It was all me. I completely overreacted." She giggles. Her warm breath caresses my skin.

I can't help but laugh.

Inside, we reach the table just as Australia scores, tying the game. I groan while the handful of gold shirts bursts into excitement.

Grady stands, throwing both arms over his head. "Score!"

"What are you doing?" Charlotte whispers loudly.

"But they scored," he argues.

As I step behind Grady, I place my hands on his shoulders then force him back into the chair. "Wrong team, mate. That was Australia."

"How can you tell? They're all wearing white." Grady heaves a defeated sigh.

Charlotte grins. "Cor! I've a brilliant idea. There's a game at the York Cricket Club tomorrow night. James is playing. How about we all go? Surely, between Jack and me, we can teach you a thing or two."

Grady grimaces.

I speak up. “It sounds fun, but you’ll be on your own. Leah and I won’t be able to make it. I’m taking her to the Cotswolds tomorrow. She’s wanted to go for quite a while.”

Leah’s sparkling eyes snap to me. A new excitement pulses behind them. “We’re going to Lidcombe?”

CHAPTER NINETEEN

"ARE WE THERE YET?" LEAH asks, practically bouncing in the passenger seat. Grady generously loaned us his car because his work schedule demanded he stay in York. I cannot say I am disappointed—I love having Leah all to myself again.

"Not quite." I peer over at her from the corner of my eye and laugh. She's a bundle of excitement and nerves.

The woodlands dwindle into a patchwork of rolling countryside intermingled with twisting stone walls. When the road hooks to the left, I see them perched on a knoll fifty paces off the road—the pair of elms, aged, weathered, and twisted by the centuries.

"I know this place," Leah whispers, her eyes fixed on the elms.

A small grin plays along my lips. I stop the car on the gravel shoulder. Although this place has changed, she still recognizes it. "Wind Rush House is just over the next rise. Come. I'll show you." I give her knee a reassuring squeeze then climb from the car. After opening Leah's door, I take her hand and lead her toward the trees.

The breeze chases us up the hill, feathering grasses and carrying the aromas of earth and sunbaked evergreen from the nearby woodlands. Under the elms, shafts of light break through the green canopy. Interlaced branches sway with the breeze, revealing glimpses of the cloudless sky. Nestled in the hollow, the mellow gold of the mansion glints in the sunshine.

"It's the spot from my first dream, where you told me you'd find me and asked me to wait for you."

My smile fades into a tight line, and my eyes narrow. "That dream was here?"

"Yes. Except I was looking down on everything, like I was flying above it all." Above us, the birds flutter through the branches, singing their songs. "Like one of those birds," she adds.

"You never told me about that dream."

Leah shifts, keeping her gaze on the elms. "Another day, please?"

"All right. I'll wait until you're ready. The past can be difficult to talk about." I capture her fingers and lift her hand to my lips.

As Leah's eyes dart from the trees to Wind Rush House, emotions flit across her face. "I want to go inside," she blurts.

"I'm not sure we can. It's a private residence. I suppose we can ask, but..."

"There are tours. I read about them in one of the travel brochures."

"They still do that? Huh." I recall the summer William and I made sport of the tourist who came from London to see how the country folk lived. He left with frightening stories and colorful memories of the ghost of Wind Rush House. I hold out my hand. "Well, then, let's go."

Closer to the house's ivy-covered facade, I trace the lines of ornate windows and stone pilasters to a window of the upper east wing, where I linger. I brace myself, but nothing hints at rousing the flashbacks from their slumber. I smile. *Could I be free of them?*

My pace quickens. I tow Leah in the direction of the

house, eager to test this new freedom. I usher her through a large open door and into the grand entryway, where a statue of the Greek goddess Hera welcomes us from her post at the foot of the immense staircase. A mural of an assemblage of Grecian gods gazes down from the high ceiling. Leah gapes at the sheer beauty, taking in the grandeur.

"Like a museum, isn't it?" I give a low throaty chuckle.

She nods, speechless.

A petite brunette steps into the entryway. "Hello, everyone. Our little tour is about to start," she says in a high-pitched voice that bubbles over with enthusiasm. "First, I'd like to take this opportunity to welcome you to Wind Rush House."

The tour guide evidently loves her job. My shoulders slump, and I groan inwardly. Leah glances at me and giggles. She must guess how much this perky tour guide annoys me. I grin at her, trying to hide my grimace. Leah stifles another laugh, and I squeeze her hand.

"My name is Becky, and I will be your guide for this tour. This fine manor is the private home of Sir Samuel Philips and his family. He's graciously opened his home so others can share its beauty. Please stay with the group, and no flash photography. Now, if you would, follow me."

Lagging behind the others, Leah and I have little interest in the guide's monologue. I whisper details in Leah's ear as we follow the group through the maze of stately rooms into a long, narrow one that looks more as though it belongs at the Metropolitan Museum than a home.

"This is the sketch gallery," Becky announces.

Portraits still line the wood-paneled walls. From the gold-leaf columns around the windows to the intricate moldings and the ornate geometrical pattern of the ceiling—all the features are unique from the rest of the house. Leah's pace slows, and she studies each likeness.

I wait for her to catch up.

"I thought there'd be a painting of her here. I was so sure," she says.

"There was one. It was painted right before her nineteenth birthday."

Her eyes widen. "I remember. The artist wanted you to leave, insisting you'd be a distraction, but Lydia demanded you stay. The artist became annoyed because Lydia continued glancing at you throughout her sitting."

I nod. "The house is awakening more memories."

"Yes, I guess so."

"If it gets too much, we'll leave."

"I want to remember," she insists.

"All right." I point to a painting above us, hanging high on the dark-mahogany wall. "Do you recognize him?"

She looks up. Waves of strawberry-blond brushstrokes frame his long, narrow face. His features are soft, almost feminine. His solemn expression seems out of place because of the twinkle of a smile in his golden-brown eyes.

"It's William, Lydia's brother," she says in almost a whisper. "I was his favorite... Lydia, I mean."

Her words catch me off guard. I stare at her. My attention seems to make her uncomfortable, and she looks away.

"Yes. He was a good man," I finally say. I continue toward the rear of the immense gallery, in search of Lydia's portrait. Leah doesn't follow, instead deciding to stay with William.

I circle the gallery twice but don't find the portrait. *What happened to it?* I glance behind me to see if Leah has caught up to me yet. She's nowhere in sight. I scan the room, rushing past the familiar faces of Lydia's relatives, searching. No Leah. No anybody. I'm completely alone. Why wouldn't she let me know the tour was moving on? She would. Of course, she would—unless something, or someone, stopped her from calling out.

Vita! No, you're overreacting. With a gulp of air, I steady my emotions. I repeat Artagan's words in my head, willing myself to believe them. *We're safe. Vita's no longer a concern.*

"Excuse me."

My eyes flit to Becky's enthusiastic smile.

"The tour is in the music room now. This way," she says.

"The girl I came with, is she there?"

"Everyone's in the music room, sir. This way, please." The first hint of annoyance breaks through Becky's cheeriness.

I trail her down the hall. Leah isn't in the music room, so I slip away from the crowd. She's not in the foyer, the library, or the front parlor. I charge upstairs and run like a madman from room to room. When I pass the sketch gallery again, Leah's standing in front of William's portrait, in the same spot she was twenty minutes earlier, staring vacantly into space.

"Where have you been?" I say, dislodging the lump caught in my throat. "I've been looking all over for you."

"I think I had a flashback," she mumbles.

"Haven't you had one before?"

"No, only memories in dreams."

"What was it a flashback of?"

Leah hesitates.

"Tell me, please."

She looks around the room. "It was here in this room, I think. Was this the ballroom?"

Again caught off guard, I nod.

"I was standing in the midst of swirling dresses. Every lady was in an elegant gown, except me. I was in this same jeans and pink frilly blouse. I would've thought if I were going back in time, I'd at least get a dress."

Huh, that's different. In every flashback I've had, I was part of the action, not a bystander.

"Anyway, everyone was dancing. It was cool, kind of like being in the middle of a Jane Austen movie—a 4-D one."

"Wrong century."

She shrugs. "That's when I saw you, walking through

the crowd with William, laughing. By the way, you looked hot. The black dress coat, that white vest over the white pleated shirt. Hmmm... so sexy. Even in a flashback, you make my heart race."

I smirk and kiss her lightly on the head. "Good to know."

"When you walked by, your gaze reached past me. I knew you were looking for her. As stupid as it is, it bothered me."

My eyes narrow into slits. Odder still, this is different from any flashback I've known. Maybe it's because she's two people and one soul.

She reads my expression wrong. "I know. I know. That's why I said it was stupid. I looked for Lydia, too. She was younger than I expected—fifteen, maybe sixteen. She sat in a corner of the room next to an old lady dressed in black. Her governess. Miss Weeks. Lydia's eyes were trained on you."

She pauses and returns her attention to William's portrait, seeming to look at him for verification that she's remembering this past correctly. Satisfied, Leah continues, "I braced myself, expecting you to rush to her, but surprisingly, you didn't. Instead, you danced with a slender girl in a violet gown. That's when I realized this flashback was before you and Lydia were an item." Leah draws in a lungful of air. "Before you loved her, when she was only William's little sister. I hate it, but I've been jealous of her." Her eyes fall away from me.

"I did love her. *Did.* You have to know you've healed me like no one, nothing else could. It's you I love."

A radiant smile breaks across her face. "That's the silliest part—I know that in here," she says, pointing to her head. "But in my heart, your love for Lydia has intimidated me for a while."

I start to speak.

She puts her hand up. "Please, let me finish. This flashback was good for me. It helped me realize things.

When you danced with Margaret, it hurt Lydia. I wanted to take her hand and tell her it would be all right soon, but then I realized that would be a lie. She'd never have the life she wanted with you. She isn't yours anymore. I'm getting the life with you she only dreamt of and was promised. I'll have memories with you that no one else will. The thought gave me a strange mixture of emotions. Pity was there, but happiness, too. Does that make me a bad person?"

"No, of course not..."

The sound of footsteps hurrying down the hallway interrupts me. Becky rushes into the room, looking anxious. Relief sweeps over her face.

"Oh, this is where we lost you two. I'm sorry, but the tour is over." Becky looks past me and straight at Leah. Her eyes widen, and she stares. "Oh, my!" She takes a step away as her hand rises to her chest. "How didn't I see it before? Do you know if you're related to the Philips family?"

"Yes," Leah says with total confidence.

"Well, that would make sense. Your resemblance to the daughter of Sir Robert Ashford is uncanny. There's a portrait of her. Would you like to see?"

Leah nods and slips her hand into mine.

Becky beams. "Follow me."

She escorts us to the entryway and up the great staircase. I say nothing, but stay close, never letting go of Leah's hand.

Leah looks from side to side. Room after room stretches out from the central hallway. Drawing rooms and glimpses of lavish bedrooms lay beyond them. The last room at the end of the long hallway is a smaller bedchamber, no less luxurious than the rest of the home. It features a large bay window confined by green satin curtains. Lydia's bedroom.

For a few moments, I take in the scene. Nothing has changed. Hand-painted Chinese wallpaper of exotic birds and flowers covers the walls. A French writing desk and chair sit in the far corner next to an ornate fireplace. A vase of roses sits on the well-polished surface. Dominating the room is the Regency-period canopy bed with rich cream floral fabric spiraled down its embellished walnut posts.

I stay by the doorway. Leah walks into the room. Her fingers trace over the writing desk, and she makes her way to the window with a view of the pair of elm trees.

"Beautiful," Leah whispers.

"Over here, miss," Becky says, leading us to a painting of a young woman sitting in a high-backed chair by a window.

The sunlight plays along her golden curls. She's wearing her favorite lavender gown. One hand lies in her lap while the other touches a simple pendant necklace strung around her neck. The brushstrokes capture the gift I'd given Lydia in every detail, right down to the tiny glass tiles forming a bouquet of daisies. The brass necklace looks plain in contrast to the lace bertha neckline and silk fabric. My gaze follows the delicate chain up to Lydia's face, to her emerald eyes looking longingly out from the canvas.

I face Leah to gauge her reaction. She studies the portrait, then reaches up and runs her hand along her cheek to her chin, I suppose checking to see if each have the same gently rounded shape. They do. They're exactly the same. She leans forward, looking closer at the portrait. Her mouth falls slack, and then she whispers, "I've seen a necklace like that. My grandmother had one just like it. The pendant always reminded me of a Seurat pointillist painting. I used to wear it around her house when I played dress-up."

"I gave it to Lydia on her nineteenth birthday," I whisper.

As our eyes meet, I give her a knowing smile.

When we're finally alone out in the gardens, in a sea of white and purple hydrangeas, Leah speaks again. "I'm surprised by how much I look like her. Before today, I've never seen her. I've only looked through her eyes. I didn't expect it to be like looking into a mirror." The afternoon breeze snatches a wisp of her hair, flipping the end across her face.

I catch the strand and tuck her hair behind her ear. "Freaky... as you would say."

She nods.

"You do look like her, but like I've told you, there are differences. I want you to remember that."

"I know."

I cup her face in my hands, studying her expression. "I believe, Miss Winters, this is the spot where you kiss me this afternoon." I have many memories with Lydia in this garden, but I want to give Leah one she doesn't have to share, one that's all hers.

"Really? I'm not so sure." The twinkle returns to her eyes.

"I am." I step closer and bend in for a kiss, letting my lips brush slowly against hers, savoring the moment. I lean back and smile. "Now, are you ready to see Lidcombe?"

I drive through the town of my birth. Rich honey-colored homes line the quiet streets. Each door is painted with a vibrant color—fiery red, electric blue, and hunter green. Flowerpots hanging from the eaves brim with roses, dark-purple lobelia, and clusters of baby's breath. In the town's center, an old church stands proudly, its stone tower pointing to the heavens.

On the southern outskirts of the village is a storybook farmhouse. This humble two-story house with steep arched gables was once my home. Now this address is an inn. In front, stretching almost to the road, grows a garden of tall pink phlox where my mother spent her free moments. On the far lawn is the tall maple my father sat under while writing his sermons.

I park in the small paved lot and grab our bags. A crushed-granite pathway cuts through the garden and leads to a black lacquered door. Inside, the nostalgia ends. Walls have been deconstructed. Small rooms have been expanded into a large foyer to accommodate a long, dark wooden counter and a sitting area clustered with overstuffed armchairs. Although the changes sadden me, I know I shouldn't have expected my old, modest home to make it through the years unaffected.

We check in and deposit our bags in our room before heading out to explore on foot. An embellished stone wall guides us to a small country church, where I slow my stride and stop by the rough timber gate.

"This is where my father was a vicar. Would you like to go in?" I ask.

She nods.

The gravel path crunches under my feet. I lead the way toward the propped-open door. The gravestones around us catch Leah's attention. I step into the church's small foyer and realize Leah isn't behind me. The excitement drains from my system, leaving a dull nervousness in its wake. I know where she is.

I step out into the sun to find Leah making her way to the far left corner of the graveyard. I snake through the maze of headstones, reading the names of acquaintances, friends, and family. My fingers skim along the graves' weathered curves.

In front of an arched slab of marble with an intricate engraving of a weeping willow tree with its long branches hanging over an urn, Leah stops and stares at the name carved into the white stone—Lydia Ann Ashford.

As my arms envelop her, her head falls against my chest. "It feels weird being here. It's not that I didn't know this was all real, but standing here, looking at this grave of a woman whose life I have memories of is... surreal," she says.

"I can understand that. It's a normal reaction." My voice is more wary than I wish.

"How much are Lydia and I alike?"

At first, I'm quiet, weighing what I should say. I know she wants the truth. "She had your kind nature. When she cared about something or someone, she did it with all her heart, just like you. She saw the good in people." I run my fingers through her hair, and she tenses. Her expression is unreadable. "What are you thinking?"

She shakes her head. "It's stupid. Foolish insecurities, that's all." Her shoulders slump, and a short sigh puffs through her lips.

"There are similarities, but there are differences, as well," I say, glancing over to gauge her reaction. Her eyes brighten, and the tautness leaves her shoulders. I'm fairly certain I'm on the right track, so I continue. "Leah, you're not Lydia's clone."

She shoots me a pensive gaze. "So when you look at me, you don't see Lydia Ashford of Wind Rush House?"

"No, I see Leah Winters of Portland, Maine, strong with her own set of beliefs," I say with a smile.

Her expression lightens, filling her with an inner glow. "Honestly, I thought I'd already dealt with these insecurities when I found out Lydia and I shared two things—a love for you and one soul. But sometimes, the doubts creep in, latches on, and whispers, telling me you only care for me because I'm Lydia's carbon copy."

I look down at her, hugging her tightly. "Haven't you realized everything I love is right here? Lydia's and my story wasn't flawless. We had our problems, like everyone. We were both stubborn with fiery tempers. She'd fly off the handle without thought. It's probably what sent her into the field that fateful night. The fact is, you're much better suited for me than Lydia ever was. If those insecurities bubble to the surface again, please tell me, so I can chase them away."

"Deal." She pauses, arching her neck to look up at me. "So you're not blaming yourself anymore."

"I'm working on it."

We stand at the foot of Lydia's grave for a long while, listening to the birds sing. Her body presses against mine. My chin rests on the top of her head.

"Are you ready?"

She nods, but she abruptly stops. "No, wait. Is your family buried here?"

"Some of them." A somber tone clings to my words.

"Will you show me?"

I lead Leah to the other side of the graveyard. Three neglected headstones, much plainer than the other elaborately carved stones around them, stand in a line. Lichen grows in clusters across their faces, making their inscriptions barely visible. She kneels on the damp grass and scrapes at the crusty plant with her fingernails so the names are recognizable again.

"John F. Hammond," she reads. "Your father."

I nod.

"Fredrick Thomas Hammond. So young. Your brother?"

I nod again.

"And Helen Maria Hammond. She must be your mother."

I step past Leah and rub my hand on the top of the headstone. "Hello, Mum. You were right," I whisper.

My mother had such faith that I would find love again. The night before I left for London—a month to the day after Lydia's death—she came to my room, wishing me happiness and love. I'll never forget how her lips quivered when she smiled. The dark circles under her eyes told the whole story—she'd been silently suffering right along with me.

I turn to Leah. "She always knew I'd find you."

"Did she?"

"My mother believed I'd find love again. She wanted me to be happy. What every mother wants for their child, I suppose."

Silence surrounds me, and I say my private good-bye to my mother. I didn't have the privilege at the time of her death.

Finally, I turn to Leah. "Ready for the rest of your tour?"

Leah nods with a careful smile and then takes my hand, giving my fingers a little squeeze. Hand-in-hand, we travel down the main street, past the close-knit bundle of cottages built into the steep slope of the land. I point out the long black-and-white building—an anomaly among the golden color of the Cotswold stone.

"That used to be the blacksmith shop, and the small three-gabled home over there was once the schoolhouse where Mrs. Piler taught the three R's for over forty years. My parents had her, and so did I." Many things appear the same, but the paved roads, the cars, and the electric cables stretched from house to house all confirm that my little hometown has changed completely.

By the end of the afternoon, we relax on the green—a small park near the center of town. Leah retrieves her sketchbook from her knapsack. Stretched across the grass, leaning on my elbow, I watch her pencil skim across the page with fluid movements, capturing the details around us: the huddled cottages, the tall chimney, the steep gables lining the roofs, and the tiny attic windows peering out from the gold limestone bricks.

"She could never do that, you know," I say.

"Who couldn't do what?"

"Lydia could never draw, not even a stick figure. It wasn't from a lack of want or trying. She just never had the gift." Pleased with myself, I roll onto my back, fold my arms under my head, and watch the clouds racing into the western sky.

Too soon, the blue sky slips into a golden hue, and we return to the inn. We round the end of the rugged stone wall. A petite woman steps out from the far corner. I freeze. The gentle breeze catches the woman's short black hair.

"It can't be," I say under my breath. My mind twists and turns in so many directions all at once. *Has Artagan betrayed me? No, I don't believe that.* I shove Leah against the wall, out of the woman's sight.

"Jack!" Leah looks at me with wide eyes.

I press my body against Leah. "Shhh. Vita," I whisper in her ear.

Her chest heaves against mine.

"Stay here."

"Jack, no." Leah grabs my arm.

I gently pull out of her grip. "I need you to stay here. Please just do as I ask," I say and step out of the shadows into the revealing gleam of the streetlight, removing the hemlock concoction from my pocket.

CHAPTER TWENTY

I MOVE FORWARD, EACH STEP DELIBERATE and slow, while an icy grip encloses my spine. So close. I have strength and the element of surprise in my favor. After I restrain her, she'll have her last meal. I'm betting it won't take much because of her tiny frame. A cold smile pushes at my lips. Images of Vita's corpse float through my mind.

A handful of steps away, the woman looks in my direction. I stop short. Her dark eyes trace over the surrounding grounds, then she fumbles through her purse and pulls out a pair of glasses and a map. Not Vita.

A long, deep, audible breath passes my lips. Feeling disappointment intermingled with relief, I turn to find Leah standing behind me.

"I thought we agreed you were going to stay out of sight," I say, slipping the bag back into my pocket.

She raises one eyebrow. "No. You agreed. And what was that?" She points to my pocket.

"A safety measure. Do you think I'd come here with no backup plan?" My face flushes. "It's not her, but what if it had been?" I snap, sweeping my hand in the woman's direction.

Leah folds her arms over her chest. "You have to stop risking yourself for me."

Eyes closed, I continue. "I will do anything to keep you safe. One long life with you is all I'm asking. Fate owes me that much."

When I open my eyes, Leah is staring at me, her head tilted to the side, her lips pursed. With a heavy sigh, my anger drains. "We should leave. Now."

"Why? Nothing happened. It was just a woman you *thought* was this Vita character, but it wasn't." Her voice is steady and quiet.

"It could have been. Maybe coming here was a bad idea." An image from one of my nightmares revisits me. In my mind's eye, Vita and Leah face off in a disastrous, lopsided showdown. My heart rate accelerates.

"But Artagan said Vita is in Australia. You said you believed him."

I run my fingers through my hair. "I did. I do."

"Then what's the problem? We're as safe here as in York."

"I'm not sure York is our best bet, either. Maybe somewhere neither of us has been. Have you ever been to Dublin? Or Buenos Aires?" I scramble for words. "Cities are much easier to get lost in or escape from."

Leah cups my face in her hands. "Shhh. Calm down, Jack. You're overreacting. You blame yourself for everything. Lydia's death wasn't your fault. Whatever the future holds for me is not your responsibility. I know it sounds cliché, but whatever will be will be. I really believe that. And when I die, Jack—that's a when, not an if—it won't be your fault. You can't protect me from life." She takes a breath. Her expression begins to soften.

"Let's get you safe. Then we can talk."

"For right now, we're safe here. Remember, Artagan said Vita is far away from here." She speaks slowly. "Later on, if we need to, I'll go anywhere you want."

I nod, still trying to find air.

"Okay. Now let's go get some dinner. I'm starving."

I curl my arm around her waist and nuzzle my nose into her hair. "Thank you," I whisper. I kiss her cheek before we walk inside.

At our small table in the corner of the cramped dining room, we wait for our server. Whiffs of roasting meats, herbs, and baking bread float from the kitchen, and I have no doubt about why the inn's dining room is filled to capacity. A bearded waiter with a stout build and copper hair walks toward us. His rosy, freckled face is frozen in a perpetual smile. His pristine jet-black apron is tied around his bulging midsection.

"Hello, I'd like to welcome you to the Three Elms Inn. My name's Ian. I'll be your server for the evening. If you don't mind, I love to start by telling our guests a little about the house's history."

I flinch.

"Yes, please." Leah smiles up at him.

I grimace at her from under a furrowed brow.

"This old home was built in the sixteenth century and was the parsonage for many years, until it was turned into an inn in the early nineteen-thirties." The waiter continues to meander through the building's history, but as I expected, Leah seems to be stuck on the opening sentence. She stares at me and mouths, *Your house.*

Tongue in cheek, I nod.

After Ian leaves with our order, Leah leans in. "Why didn't you say anything? We could've stayed somewhere else."

"There is nowhere else. The Three Elms Inn is the only accommodation in the area. I didn't say anything because I didn't want you to worry about me... like you are right now."

"Are you okay? I never thought about what coming to this place would be like for you," she says, her eyes boring into mine.

"I'm fine. Stop worrying about me."

"You're always worrying about me," she grumbles under her breath.

"That's my job." I pause and grin, hoping this next bit of information will redirect the conversation. "By the way, you're sleeping in my old room."

It works, but not the way I hoped. My comment is followed by a long silence.

She turns to face me. "The other night at Grady's, I realized you've never told me what happened after Lydia. What your life was like after her."

"No, I haven't."

"Why?"

"Honestly, I've done many things I'm not proud of."

"Everyone has, Jack. Every human being on this planet wishes they could get a redo on something they've done."

"What regrets do you have? You don't smoke. You don't drink. It's a crime to stay out past ten on a school night. If there's a rule, you follow it."

"I stole once," she blurts out.

"Let me guess. A candy bar from a convenience store when you were ten."

A red bloom overtakes her cheeks, and she looks away.

"I'm right, aren't I?" I caress the blush with the back of my fingers.

"Shut up." She smirks. "And I was twelve."

Off by two whole years! I purse my lips, but my laugh breaks free.

"It's not funny. My best friend dared me. I couldn't say no, but I felt guilty about it for days. Never did eat it."

"This is what I'm saying. There's no way you could ever excuse the things I've done."

She crosses her arms. "Try me."

"Understand, back then, my behavior was often self-destructive. I was a mess, all alone in my self-made darkness. I cared very little for anything, and it showed."

She waits.

I look down and inhale long and deep. "It started one afternoon not long after I left Lidcombe. I filled my pockets with stones and jumped off Blackfriars Bridge into the Thames. In London, I knew my body would never be recognized. You see, if I was buried as an unknown transient, my family wouldn't be tarnished by my suicide."

She purses her lips and glances away.

"Do you want me to continue?"

"Yes."

"You see, I knew I was durable, but before then, I didn't know I couldn't die like anyone else. After several attempts, I tried new vices—drowning my misery in whiskey, opiates, and even a fight house. They didn't work, either, not for the long term, so I attempted to content myself with my predicament. Numbness became my best friend. I've bummed all over the world from one odd job to the next. Sailor, dockhand, auto mechanic—I've done just about everything, never settling in one place for too long in case someone realized I'm not getting any older.

"I showed up in Portland because of a flick of a dart, and then you stumbled into my life, washing over me like a tidal wave. At some points, it felt like you were going to haul me into the murky, grim depths, but you didn't." I reach for her hand and stroke it. "You saved me, you know?"

Leah's grown quiet, and I look at her from under my hooded brow. She's biting her lower lip, while a small smile dances along her lips. This isn't exactly the reaction I expected.

"You find this funny?"

"No, of course not. But I believe it was you who stumbled into me."

"True, very true." I laugh softly at the memory.

"Well, none of that's going to happen next time."

The stifling tension returns, clinging to the air around us. All the practice I've had hiding my true feelings pays off, and I manage to keep my tone light. "That's nothing we have to concern ourselves with tonight."

She ignores my dismissal. "I know you don't like talking about it, but this needs to be said. The next time we find each other, I don't want to find out you dove off the Empire State Building or any of that stupidity. We need a meeting place. Like the elms—"

If I believed she'd be there someday, I'd live under those damned elms. Feeling my temper rise, I grit my teeth. Emotionally drained and irritated by her optimism, I'm in no shape to rehash our old argument again tonight.

Studying her table setting, she continues, "I'm sorry. I know you don't believe even though I do."

Leah pauses. I'm aware she's editing, holding something back. "New topic. I was thinking where we might go next. If we can't go back to Portland or stay in York, we might as well enjoy the ride. Besides England, I've always wanted to see France. With the Louvre, the Eiffel Tower, Arch of Triumph, Paris alone is an artist's dream. I could sketch along the Seine in the very spot Monet was inspired." Her eyes shine with forced excitement. "What places are on your bucket list? Not many, I'm guessing."

"Rio de Janeiro, for one. The warmth would be nice for a change." I smile, but my voice is still chilly from the previous subject. "And actually, I've never been to Paris." I slip my hand into hers.

The end of the conversation leaves us to our own thoughts. I wish I could believe as she does. I wish I had that much confidence. *Faith brings strength.* The French boy's adage rings true. Leah is the strongest woman I've ever had the privilege to know.

When the waiter returns with our meals, he asks, "So are you enjoying our little town?"

"Yes, it's such a beautiful spot," Leah says.

"Did you get a tour of Wind Rush House?" the waiter asks.

"Yes." Leah says, enthusiasm leaking into her voice.

"It's a grand old house, isn't it, miss? I'd dare say it

boasts the most beautiful gardens in the county. There's a tragic love story that connects that manor with this humble home. They say Lydia Ashford still roams the manor's halls, looking for her Jack." The man recites the story of Lydia Ashford and her one true love perfectly, until... "Late one night, a week before their wedding, Lydia heard the rumor that her beloved Jack was unfaithful."

Leah's brows raise a fraction of an inch. I curse the man silently behind taut lips.

He leans forward, no doubt misinterpreting our tension as eagerness for his juicy tale. "They say she ran out into a storm, desperate to find him to prove the rumors false, but she never did. Instead, Lydia collapsed a mere quarter-mile from this house and died a week later, never knowing the truth."

"What do they say happened to Jack?" Leah asks. Her eyes flick to me for an instant and then to our waiter—the bloody fabulist.

"No one really knows. The story diverges there. One account says he died alone with a broken heart, while the other has him running off with Ashford's housekeeper, who was supposedly quite a beauty."

I almost spew my cola all over the white tablecloth. *Mrs. Mills? Seriously?* She had to be close to seventy at that time, and a beauty she was not. Leah gives me a severe stare.

"Excuse me, lady and gent. It looks like table three needs their check." The waiter wanders away, probably to screw with someone else's evening.

I look Leah straight in the eyes. "Listen. That's not what happened. There was never anyone else. Mrs. Mills was a very nice lady, but she and I never..."

Her smile returns. "I know, Jack. I remember." She laughs. "Gotcha."

I gape at her in surprise, a grin yanking up one corner of my mouth.

"See? I made you smile."

After dinner, I walk her to our room. "So, this was your bedroom?"

"Yes."

"Did you have many girls up here besides Mrs. Mills?" she teases.

"Tons, too many to name." I roll my eyes. "Of course not."

She scowls playfully. "Because that would have been improper," she says, imitating me.

I nod.

She glides her arms around my neck and rolls to her tiptoes then brushes her lips against mine. "How about that? What would that have been?"

"Scandalous." I chuckle, rough and deep. The backs of my fingers stroke her cheek. I savor the softness of her skin and lean in for another kiss.

A different kind of energy arises in this kiss, something more alive than before. My tongue skims the curve of her lower lip. Her breath comes in jagged gasps. She yanks my T-shirt over my head and tosses it to the floor. Her fingertips dance along my stomach. Electric currents run straight through me. A deep growl breaks from my throat. Her tongue pushes my lips apart, exploring the confines of my mouth. I twist my fingers into her hair to hold her close. We stumble backward. Something solid bumps against the back of my legs. We fall onto the bed. I break away, gasping for breath. Her lips burn a path along my collarbone to my jaw.

"See? I can break rules, too," she says, her hot breath against my neck.

My mind is invaded by images of us... together. With trembling hands, I grip Leah's shoulders and slip out of her grasp. "I think that's all a gentleman can take for one evening, love." I lift away from her and sit on the edge of the bed.

She sits up. "You know, sometimes you make me feel

like a villain in some fairy tale, trying to lure the innocent maiden out of her cottage with a shiny red apple."

"Me being the innocent maiden?"

Leah grins.

"Thanks," I huff.

"So what's this all about?"

I shrug.

"No, no. Don't close down on me now. I know you love me, and it's pretty obvious you want me as much as I want you. So what's the problem?"

"Of course I want you. And someday—" My face grows hot. Running my hand along the sweaty scruff of my neck, I glance away. "Look. I was raised with certain convictions that there are some things kept for marriage. I know the idea is old-fashioned, but although times have changed, I'm not sure I have."

"Marriage?" Her voice brightens. I look to find a Cheshire cat grin plastered across Leah's lips. "You want to marry me?" Her words tumble out. "I mean, I figured you did, but hearing the words out loud—*you* want to marry *me*."

"Yes." I smile. "More than I've wanted anything in this world, but I can't ask you properly until I buy a ring."

She laughs, her arms encircling my neck, and falls backward onto the bed. I tumble on top of her then kiss her softly. She catches my lower lip between her teeth. Again, my control wavers. A need to have our bodies fused together aches deep within me. I pull her closer. Our lips move together between gasps. My skin burns under every touch, stirring up levels of longing I've never allowed myself to feel.

"So." I clear my throat, trying to catch my breath. "Do you think I'm worth waiting for?" I ask, wagging my eyebrows.

Leah looks up and taps her fingers on her lips as if she's mulling over the question then grins with a spirited gleam. "Yes. But—"

"There's a *but*?"

She nods. "When you place an engagement ring on this finger"—she wiggles her left ring finger in the air—"we're renegotiating the no sex rule."

"Thanks for the warning. I'll make sure I have a chaperone with us at all times until the wedding to protect my virtue," I tease. "I'm sure Grady would be more than willing."

She furrows her brows and shoots me a wanton stare. "Don't you dare."

I chuckle. Sliding off the bed, I stand. Leah reaches for me and takes my hand. "Where do you think you're going?"

"I believe it's best if tonight I sleep on the floor." *Coward.*

Her face tightens. "You're kidding?"

I snatch the quilt from the foot of the bed.

"Jack, you're being silly. It's not the nineteenth century anymore."

"Agreed." I avoid her penetrating stare and unroll the bedding on the floor by the door. "If it was, a true gentleman would never set foot in a lady's bedchamber."

She heaves a heavy sigh. "If you feel that's necessary."

My eyes trace the open buttons of her blouse to the white lace of her bra playing peek-a-boo behind the lilac cotton. "I do." I swallow hard against the bone-deep need fighting to cloud my honorable intentions. "Sweet dreams," I say as I grab a pillow.

A glimpse of something like sadness flashes across her face. If I returned to comfort her, there would be no leaving her bed after that. I tug off my shirt and toss it to the floor. After lying down, I fold my arms behind my head, scrutinizing the tiny imperfections in the ceiling and attempting not to think about how warm Leah would feel in my arms. Soon the sound of her gentle, steady breathing fills the room. I close my eyes to find sleep, but my mind conjures behaviors well beyond the bounds of the propriety my mother would approve of. I thrust my thoughts in a different direction, giving in to my haunting fears again. *Vita's no longer a concern.* The words spin in lopsided orbits in my head.

That woman in Lidcombe wasn't Vita. But that doesn't conclusively mean that Artagan is right about her. What if he was wrong, and I endangered Leah by taking her on the grand tour of my early days? In all the what-ifs, one fact is clear—Vita needs to die. And I'm going to need Artagan's help to kill her. My biggest obstacle will be convincing Leah, but first, I need to talk to Artagan. I roll from bed and grab my phone then slip in to the hallway. Scrolling through the short list of incoming calls serves as a distraction. No new calls, as I expected, so I dial Artagan's number. His phone rings and rings, but no one answers, and then voice mail answers. Unsurprisingly, no message greets me, only a low, squawking beep.

"Artagan, it's Jack. Call me. There are some things we need to discuss."

I slide the phone into my pocket and step to the door. A noise like the sound of something falling and shattering in the background interrupts me. A shiver of alarm swamps my shoulders, tensing them. My hand frozen on the doorknob, I scan the hall. After another thud, I slowly and quietly steal down the dimly lit corridor. Murmurs of laughter and music float up from downstairs. The door at the end of the hall stands ajar. My mother's room. I nudge the door open with my foot. An overfed mouse scurries between my legs, followed by a gray-striped tabby. I twist to the side, stumbling against the doorframe.

Inside the room, a small circular table is lying on its side, a white porcelain vase smashed to pieces around it. *Damn cat.* I chuckle. My gaze falls on a hairline crack in the molding along the base of the wall near the shattered remains of the vase, and I recall a distant memory. My mother kept her valuables in a secret compartment behind the wall. I bend down, and with the help of my pocketknife,

I pry the short board loose. Lying in the narrow cubbyhole is a small collection of items—a pocket watch, a dark-patina wooden box, and a yellowed envelope.

I lift the antique pocket watch by its chain. The decorative gold disk swings and sways, playing with the lamplight while it dangles. Inside, I find the engraved message I remembered.

To my husband and our father,
John
With love,
Helen, Henry, Ruth, and Jack
3rd March 1847

It was our gift to my father on his last birthday. My mother saved every penny she could, and Henry worked odd jobs around the village so we could afford it. I set the watch aside and reach for the small box. The hinged lid squeaks open after years of neglect, revealing a gold band decorated with five rectangular-cut emeralds framed with pearls. The ring seems made for Leah; the gems are the exact color of her eyes.

With a deep breath, I reach for the letter. My mother had the knack of exhuming all my buried emotions with a few simple words. The old paper crinkles. I carefully unfold the delicate yellowing page. Scrolled in an elegant hand is written—

My Dearest Jack,
I am writing you this letter in hopes that someday you will find it, and these two items I long to give to you will be yours.

The pocket watch is for you, my son. It is the only thing I have left of your father's, and I want you to have it.

The ring was my mother's engagement ring. However, this is not for you, but for you to give to someone you love. Do not be vexed with me. My greatest wish is that you will allow yourself happiness and that someday you will realize Lydia's death was not of your doing. Dear child, seize that belief and hold it. May the Lord direct you.

I am afraid I am not long for this world, for my health is failing. The doctors fear I am stricken with consumption. I am at peace, for I know I will soon see your dear father and brother. I will be waiting patiently until we are all reunited in Heaven. Remember, I love you.

Your loving mother,
Helen Hammond

Tears spill from my eyes. Ruth had written to tell me that Mother had died, but nothing of the circumstances. I wonder if she suffered. I wish I could have come back and seen her one last time, but I was scared of her reaction. My mother was superstitious. What would she have made me out to be? If Ruth's and my intuitions were correct, to my mother, I would have been one of the condemned, doomed to hell, and knowing would have caused her nothing but pain.

After returning to our room, I lie back and examine the ring. My eyes close. My mother's words chime in my head... *Allow yourself happiness.* Ed's words trail in behind... *Seize the day.* They're right. It's time—time to heed their advice and enjoy each moment. That will require changes. I'll need to make amends with the bones rattling around in my closet, stop wrestling with the future, and start living for the present. All those things are easier said than done.

CHAPTER TWENTY-ONE

Back in York, I sit on a bench in King's Square, arms stretched along the weather-beaten back rail. A morning rain has given way to a bright afternoon sun, leaving behind scattered puddles and silvery streets. My eyes chase after Leah as she runs across Colliergate to the neighborhood café. Her ponytail bounces with her movement and exposes her neck. The blush color of her blouse sets off her creamy skin. She turns before entering the shop and gives me a little wink. The sight sends my heartbeat into uneven tempos.

Leah optimistically believes my letting her out of my reach is due to a good night's sleep and a new outlook. I wish that were the case, but it's not. Truth be known, my vantage point is much better from here. Vita won't be able to get within a hundred-foot radius of Leah without me knowing first. I can't chase away the suspicions that Leah and I are in a rigged game of chance. She and I are stuck in the middle of an elaborate spiderweb. We twist and turn while the eight-legged predator approaches. My new aspiration is going to take some work.

Seize the day. The words nudge the back of my mind again, and my hand dives into my pocket, feeling the band of gold and emeralds between my fingers. Despite my nagging concerns, I can wait no longer. *Today's the day.* My heart flutters with nervousness and excitement. After coffee, Leah believes we're heading to the York Art Museum to see an Impressionist exhibit—her favorite art movement. Little does she know that among the painted canvases of Monet, Renoir, and Cassatt, I will give her my ring and ask her to be my wife. *And tonight?* My stomach tightens, and I take a deep breath. *We'll see.* But I have no doubt that my convictions are no match for Leah's negotiation skills. That girl could sweet-talk me into doing anything. I smirk and laugh to myself.

I glance up and down the street then back to the café door as a couple emerges. Laughing, they walk down the sidewalk in the direction of Church Street. *I wish she'd hurry.* I rake my sweaty fingers through my hair. My self-restraint is wearing thin. I resist the urge to charge across the street and join her. If I did, she would be disappointed, and over the last few days, I've caused her enough distress. So here I stay.

As I wait, a quartet of musicians begins to play their melody. My foot taps impatiently with the rhythm of the folk music flowing from the nearby street corner. People soon gather, blocking my view. I move to a stone-block wall at the far end of the square to get a clear view of the little café and Leah.

Two coffees in hand, Leah steps into the street, peering to her left as she would at home. She doesn't see the Volvo heading down Colliergate straight at her, and the car isn't slowing down. Through the car's window, I catch sight of the driver yelling into the rearview mirror at the squabbling children in the backseat.

My heart stops mid-beat. "Leah!" I holler, but my voice is drowned out by the music and the laughter.

I burst into a run, screaming Leah's name over and over. My legs feel weighed down as if thousand-ton weights are chained to each ankle. I'm in the middle of one of my nightmares, but I can't escape into the morning light with a simple blink of my eyes.

The high-pitched screech of brakes and skidding tires silences every sound around us. Leah's face turns ashen, and her eyes widen when she sees her fate at the last possible second. She doesn't even have time to scream before the car slams into her and sends her tumbling.

The scene around us fades away to a vacant blur. I can hear the screams, the shouts, but garbled and muffled, they fade into the background as if I'm hearing everything from underwater. My eyes stay on Leah's motionless form. I stumble and fall to my hands and knees onto the pavement at her side. Her right arm and leg are twisted into unnatural positions. I press my ear to her chest, clinging to a sliver of hope. Her heartbeat is so weak that I can hardly hear a pulse.

"No... No, love! Please don't leave me. Open your eyes," I beg, sweeping her matted, bloody hair out of her face. Her eyes are shut. "Oh, please, no. Not now. Not yet. You're not leaving me!" I bellow, cupping her face in my hands. Desperate sobs erupt from my chest. I press myself against her; I bury my face in her hair. Then I'm being hauled away. I struggle against the hands, thrashing and clawing to get to Leah. A placid voice breaks through my chaotic thoughts.

"Calm down, son. We're trying to help her," a man says. My stance slackens, and the grip loosens. A bald, thickly built man kneels at Leah's side. After checking her vital signs, he tilts back her head and blows his breath into her mouth. Between puffs, the man calls to another. A woman hurries through the crowd, bends down near Leah, and with fisted hands, she begins compressing Leah's chest.

In the midst of the burgeoning chaos, Artagan's aloofness during our last conversation becomes clear. My last sliver of hope disintegrates, crushing my new resolve like a brittle, dead leaf. His curt manner hadn't stemmed from Vita's travels or his lack of concern. He knew we'd already lost and obviously didn't have the nerve to tell me. Darkness threatens to consume me, but I propel the nausea away and scan the sea of shocked, horrified faces clustered around us, looking for the real killer in the crowd—Vita. Artagan's words run through my head. *We don't get our hands dirty, per se. We orchestrate death.* I strangle the incipient growl in my throat. She's here. Somewhere. Waiting.

Leah's form draws my attention again. The woman doing chest compressions places two fingers against Leah's neck and looks at her partner, shaking her head.

"Don't tell the boy, but she's dead," she whispers.

My legs tremble, the sense of being smothered overtakes me. Moisture pools in my eyes. Quick gasps of air drag over my lips while understanding of the woman's words trickles in. Through the flurry of activity huddled around Leah, the same story is playing out all over again, one hundred and fifty years later. The scenario is different—the result is not.

Above the city, Great Peter strikes the hour. Between the hollow bongs of bronze against bronze, a siren wails in the distance, echoing the keening of my soul.

Gone. Leah is lost to me forever. Artagan's tale of Kemisi and her Amun haunts me from the depths. *He didn't even recognize her—all memories lost.* Memories—from my first glimpse of her vivid emerald eyes to our last kiss—stream before my closed eyes. I'll never forget them, but Leah will. Emptiness presses into my heart, followed immediately by a staggering pain. I grind my teeth into my cheek and clench my fists. Sorrow that clawed at me now rears up to devour me whole.

Hemlock, a sweet, feminine voice whispers through the anguish. The thought gives me my only sense of relief. I slip my hand into my pocket to touch the smooth plastic of my pathetic attempt at protection. What was once my weapon has now become my savior.

CHAPTER TWENTY-TWO

SLUMPED IN A STARK HOSPITAL-ROOM chair, teetering on the edge of darkness and lunacy, I listen to the relentless beep of machines. Every time I close my eyes to shut out reality and lose myself in the fantasy of a healthy, safe Leah, her dreamlike features mutate into unnatural shapes. Vita's face thrusts in, a smile rolled across her lips—the same fiendish grin she wore outside Rare Books and again at Ed's funeral. *I'm coming for her*, Vita's voice repeats in my head. My eyes spring open.

At my side, the actuality of these words is evident. Leah lies comatose and on the brink of death, her precious soul forced back into her battered body—just barely, and no doubt only temporarily—by the modern miracle that is the portable defibrillator. Should I thank the ambulance crew for drawing out my agony further, along with hers? A tube placed down her throat forces air in and out of her lungs. Wires poke out from under her hospital gown, connecting to machines monitoring her vitals. Her heart beats forty-eight times per minute. I know because I've counted every one. Nurses flow in and out of her room in a steady stream, but no one has told me anything. "Running tests" is their standard answer to every one of my questions, but in truth, I don't need to be told. Leah's future is clear—the tomorrows we hoped and planned for will never come. Leah and I are running out of time.

"God," I call out in desperation. "I know we haven't spoken in a long time, but I'll give you anything if you let her stay. Anything." I wait, but no response comes. *Course not.* I reach for her ice-cold hand. Her hand looks small and frail in mine. Under her strong exterior, she's always been fragile—each day, perishing a little, suffering from the mortal condition. I've always been aware of that aspect of Leah's future, but because of her fire for life, it was easily forgotten—until now. I see she's as delicate as the flower said to bloom once every hundred years deep in the forests of India and last only a day.

Grady barrels into the room, out of breath and wide-eyed. I turn my face to the window and swipe at my escaping tears with the back of my hand.

"What happened?" he demands.

"She crossed the street, didn't look where she was going. A car—" My voice weakens.

"Aw, hell." Moisture brims his eyes. "I was at Charlotte's and didn't get the message until... How is she?"

"They haven't told me much. Running tests."

"I should call Mom. But I don't know what to tell her."

I stare at tiny gray flecks in the white tiled floor. The door opens. I jerk my head up to find a thin doctor with wire-framed glasses perched on top of his balding head.

"Hello, gentlemen. My name is Dr. Jason Foster. I assume you're Ms. Winters's family?"

Grady speaks up. "Yes. I'm Grady Winters, Leah's brother, and this is Jack Hammond, her boyfriend."

"I wish I could bring you better news. Leah is in critical condition. The next twenty-four hours will tell us a lot. Understand, we're doing everything we can for her." The doctor tries to sound at ease, but tension clings to his every word.

"Can you tell me exactly what's wrong?" Grady asks.

I stop listening to the long list of damages after I hear multiple broken bones, collapsed lung, and possible brain injury. The part of the list I've heard is all my composure can handle. Instead, I focus on Leah's face, but I find no peace in her features. Each cut has been carefully stitched closed. A bruise covers her right side from temple to cheek, and her jaw is red and swollen.

"Can she hear us?" Grady's question captures my attention.

"Maybe. Try talking to her. It can't hurt," the doctor says then leaves.

I glare at the closing door. Heat rushes to my face. *No good news? No hope? How can this so-called doctor walk out of here and leave us with nothing?* A heaviness builds in the pit of my stomach. The truth is not the doctor's fault.

Grady gives a sigh and heaves himself out of the neighboring chair. "I'm gonna go call Mom and see if I can find her a flight."

I nod.

After Grady leaves, I sit on the bed next to Leah, being careful of the wires and tubes. "Leah? Can you hear me?" I kiss her pale gray cheek and wait. When no response comes, I realize I've still been holding on to the smallest shard of hope for a happy ending, like one in her fairy tales.

Idiot.

"I don't know how to keep my promise," I say. "I can't protect you from Death. I'm so sorry." If she can hear me, all I can give her now is peace. "I'll meet you under the elms, love. I'll be waiting for you at our spot."

A lie of mercy.

Finding Leah was a stroke of luck. That she looks like Lydia was luck. That I settled in Portland, Maine, and walked into her coffee shop was luck. That she remembered me at all was luck. In her next life, it will be as if I never existed. How can I wish for anything else? My selfish inability to let go has caused more heartache. I collapse back into the chair and close my eyes. Behind my lids, I'm trapped between the shadows of my yesterdays. Leah's touch, Leah's kiss, and Leah's laughter in my ears—each memory is akin to a blow to my chest. Finally, numbness takes pity on me, enveloping me. I don't fight against the bleak, dead feeling. Instead, I welcome the lack of sensation.

A week passes, maybe two, and I rarely leave my chair. I've lost all track of time. Daylight and darkness rotate past the window without my notice. Mechanical beeps count my moments, every one of them spent with Leah as I watch her grow weaker and weaker. I rarely speak. Food has no appeal. Neglect has given me a ragged beard, and I only change my clothes when Grady or Leah's mother brings me a clean set and insists upon it. In the dead of night, I crawl into bed beside her and lay my head on her chest to listen to the music of her heart. Its rhythm soothes me.

Late one afternoon after Marlee has left for the day, Grady paces the room then takes the seat next to mine. He clears his throat to get my attention. His forehead is creased with worry, and black circles sit beneath his eyes, which are tapered into slits.

I frown.

"I'm concerned about you. You don't sleep, you don't eat, and you never leave her room. Look at yourself. What is Leah going to think when she wakes up?"

"She's not waking up." My voice is dead even, as cold as ice.

Grady flinches but continues. "The doctors and nurses are getting anxious about your behavior."

"Tell them not to be. We both know starvation and insomnia can't hurt me. Focus on your sister. Everyone needs to focus on her."

"Hopelessness can. I'm watching despair eat away at you from the inside out. I know what you're planning."

"You don't know shit." I turn to Leah.

Grady grabs my arm, and I yank it away. He releases me, but I can feel his gaze burn into the side of my head.

"I don't understand you. When Leah does die, I'll never see her again, but you will." His voice cracks and strains against the words.

"She's wrong," I hiss, my focus barreling down on him. "Don't you see? She believes it, but she's wrong. She and I will never find each other again. Her remembering who I am, recalling our past was a fluke, a strange twist of fate. If I believed as she does, of course, I'd be saddened by her sudden departure, but my main concern would be for you and your mum. But Leah didn't know what she was talking about."

"I've doubted my sister before, but she's always right. Jack, have some faith."

"No! Faith won't do me any good here!"

Grady sounds too similar to his sister to do either of us any good. I leave the room, but I don't go far. Observers ogle me from the waiting area. Whispers flow from behind the nurses' station where I'm waiting. I fight the urge to growl at the onlookers.

When Grady finally leaves two hours later, I resume my vigil and collapse into the chair. Sometime around midnight, I doze off, coaxed into sleep by emotional fatigue and the electronic whir of the machines. The shriek of an alarm jolts me awake.

"Leah." I choke. In the staggering moments that follow, my heart feels paralyzed, frozen mid-beat. *Is it possible I'm dying with her?* A faint smile nudges my lips.

Medical personnel charge into the room, squeezing me out of the way. In an explosion of action, they fight to save her life once again. Pressed against the wall, I struggle for oxygen. Now that the time is here, how can I ever let her go? Movement in my peripheral vision beckons my attention. Artagan stands at the observation window, his eyes affixed on Leah. The sight takes me back to the evening he approached me at the bar, the night he glared at the couple in the very same way. The realization hurls me from the room. I claw at Artagan's shirt and shove him against the wall of the hallway.

Icy barbs stab down my spine. The freezing burn spreads, racing to the tips of my fingers and toes. I snarl between clenched teeth, "No! What are you doing?"

The unfeeling sapphire eyes snap to me. His words come out gruff and forceful. "My job."

"You can't have her!" I yell, driving my forearm hard against his throat.

A nurse scowls and steps from her station. "You two are going to have to keep the noise down." She wags her long finger in Artagan's face. "Or I'm going to be forced to have *both* of you removed."

I glower at the nurse but step away. Still trembling with anger, I place one hand on the pane of the observation window separating Leah from me. The never-ending alarm blares. Regardless of doctors and nurses all wrestling with Death to save her, whether Leah lives or dies isn't up to them. Artagan, the son of Death, holds all the cards.

I face him. "Please, first bring her back. Then we'll talk."

He looks away, rubbing his forefinger and thumb along his pointed, stubbly chin.

"I'm not above begging, if that's what you want."

A galloping rhythm of the machine takes off again, following the beating of her heart. I drag in a jagged breath. Artagan pulls his gaze from Leah to stare at me.

"Outside," he commands.

I nod.

As we leave, Artagan dramatically bows to the scowling nurse and smirks at her disapproval. His cavalier attitude stokes the fire of my temper. Somehow, I contain my hostility. I follow him to the elevator, through zigzagging sterile halls, and out into the dark. Out from under watchful eyes, anger explodes through the veneer of my control. My fist slams into Artagan's jaw, sending him sprawling to the ground.

"I'll do whatever I have to do to make sure you never go near her again!" I growl and rock onto the balls of my feet, poised for whatever Artagan might throw at me.

Artagan glares up at me, wiping away the blood trickling from his split lip. He pushes himself to his feet with a groan. Surprisingly he doesn't retaliate, and I relax. "Gathering Leah isn't my choice, Jack."

"Then whose choice is it? Wait. The decision lies with that damned council of yours, doesn't it?"

"Yes."

"Take me to them."

He looks me up and down and shakes his head. "That meeting will be quite entertaining. However, I'm not taking a man who resembles street scum to the council. Look at yourself. You've let yourself fall into wrack and ruin. And you don't smell much better. Go clean up first."

"Seriously? I couldn't care less."

"What's most important to you?"

I squint, unable to figure out what he's getting at, but I answer anyway. "Easy one. Leah."

"Just Leah?"

"Alive." I clarify.

Artagan smiles. "Thought so. So the real question is what is Leah's life worth to you?"

"Anything. Everything. Whatever the cost to give her a long, full life, I'll pay it."

He nods. "Your life, then?"

"Yes! Take it."

His smile grows wider. "Well, that gives you something to bargain with, doesn't it? You can't cheat Death, but that doesn't mean you can't buy him off. First, you need to clean up. You show up looking like this, and they might take offense. They think of themselves as royalty, at least some of them do, and you're going to need all the votes you can get."

"Votes?"

"We'll discuss the particulars later."

"What about Leah?"

"She's safe for now. I'm her gatherer, and no one else will touch her. It took some haggling, and I probably owe a million and one favors, but Thanatos, the head of the council, named me responsible for Leah's departure. So, I'll repeat myself. Go clean up."

"I need to see Leah before we go."

"All right. I'll wait here."

In Leah's room, only the beeping of the monitor remains. She looks better. A bit of color has returned to her cheeks, and she's breathing on her own. I sit next to her on the bed and take her hand. "I don't know if you can hear me, but if you can, remember I love you, and I'll think about you always." I lean in and press my lips gently to hers then whisper, "Good-bye, love." Summoning all the strength I can muster, I release her hand and walk out the door, knowing that one way or another, I'll never see Leah again.

CHAPTER TWENTY-THREE

THE APARTMENT IS QUIET. GRADY and his mum are fast asleep, exactly what I was hoping for. Paper and pen in hand, I sit at the dining table. When she's strong, Leah will need to know what I've done so that she can understand what she will consider a reckless act. I can't leave her always wondering. My absence will be hard enough without the uncertainty of where I've disappeared to. I stare at the blank paper. Despite all I need to say, after twenty minutes, all I've written is *Dearest Leah.* I lay down the pen. With a bit of time, maybe the right words will find me.

I grab clean clothes out of my duffel and slip into the bathroom. I turn on the shower and flip the knob to hot. Hunched in the spray, my head in my hands, I worry about how I'll convince a group of monarchical immortals to take me and spare Leah. No ideas come.

When the hot water expires, I halfway dress and open the bathroom door to release the steam, then I shave the weeks of growth from my face.

Artagan appears and leans against the doorframe.

I jump, causing the razor to nick my chin. "How did you get into the apartment?"

"Never you mind." His voice comes out in barely a

whisper. "What is that? The bump there." In the reflection, I see him point at my back.

"A bullet."

He snorts. "Nice."

The creak of a bed followed by heavy footfalls interrupts us. Artagan steps away and blends into the shadows. Without a sound, he's gone.

The door next to the bathroom opens. Grady steps into view, his eyes tired and wary. He cocks his head to the side, digesting the scene. His eyes then widen, and a flicker of hope darts across his face.

"Did she wake up?"

"No. Sorry I woke you. I was going to leave a note."

"A note? Why?" Grady gives me a sleepy squint.

"I think I might have a way to save Leah. I have to try."

"How? I'll come with you."

"No. This is something I have to do on my own," I say, keeping my voice easy. "Besides, I need you to tell Leah some things for me... when she wakes up."

He hesitates, and his brow creases. "You can tell her yourself when you get back."

In the mirror, I give Grady a long solemn look.

At first, he seems confused, but I see the full weight of my meaning sinking in as his expression falls. "Jack, no. Not like this. Leah wouldn't—"

"I refuse to live without her. Truth be told, I've always been a bit of a selfish bastard. If I wasn't, I would have walked away the first time I saw Leah."

Grady huffs. "Yeah, that would have helped, leaving her thinking she's nuts."

I continue, disregarding his comment, "We both know you'd give your life to save hers if you could." His silence acknowledges I'm right.

I set the razor down on the side of the basin and stare at the water dripping from the faucet into the soapy water. "When Leah wakes, tell her I'm sorry for the things I've done wrong and for the heartache I'm causing, but most of all, tell her I'm sorry for the life we can't share." I pause. *Faith brings strength.* What will Leah's life resemble with all hope stripped away? The notion of her future replicating my past makes me shudder. Spinning around, I face him. "No, forget what I said. Instead, tell her she's right. Tell her I will see her again in the next life. Promise me."

"First, you don't believe the two of you will ever find one another again. Secondly, she knows."

"Convince her."

Grady presses his knuckles against his pursed lips.

"Please try. I know the grief that lies ahead. Hope and faith will help her. She'll never know she's wrong, that we lied. When her next life comes, she'll have forgotten her past, won't even remember me." The ache in my chest flares with my words.

"How can you be so sure you'll never be together again?"

"It's happened before to an immortal named Kemisi. She's alone, and he's living his life happily with no memory of her. I can't live on knowing she's in this world, loving—I told you I was a selfish bastard."

Grady sighs. His rigid pose vanishes as his shoulders droop. "I'll find a way. I promise."

"Thank you. Take care of her for me."

He nods, and I offer him my hand. Instead of shaking it, he yanks me into an awkward one-armed hug, giving me three hard pats on the back.

He steps away without meeting my eyes. "Bye, Jack," he whispers then slips out of sight. I hear the click of his bedroom door shutting.

I lean against the sink, resting my forehead on the cold mirror. Moisture pools in my eyes. I look straight into the mirror, past my likeness, past the reflected room, directly into a pair of emerald-green eyes. In my magnificent delusion, she's whole and healthy, standing in front of me, behind a pane of glass. I cannot continue to exist while knowing that saving her is within my grasp.

"So sorry, love," I whisper. "There's no other way."

I tug my shirt over my head and walk into the living room. In the weak glow of a streetlight, Artagan reclines on the couch, looking at home as he thumbs through a magazine. What a difference those four short weeks have made—the happiest, scariest, and most painful of my life.

"Let's get out of here. I want to get this over with," I say.

Artagan stands and tosses the magazine on the couch. I shadow his steps out the door.

Within an hour, we're on a train. God only knows where we're heading. Somewhere northeast of York is all I can figure. The gray curtain of rain streaks in diagonal patterns across the glass, blurring the scenery beyond. A suggestion of pink bleeds into the eastern sky and hints at morning. Looking past the reflection of my drawn face, I see Leah's enraged expression staring back at me. Her emerald eyes spark wildly. I can even hear her words in my head. *Jack Hammond, don't you even think about sacrificing yourself. Turn around now and come back to me.*

I shake my head. *Too late to change my mind, love.* I exhale and glare out the window, trying to look beyond the furious likeness.

"Beer?" Artagan asks, interrupting my thoughts.

"Yes. Can you see if they carry Prize Old Ale?"

He nods, stands, and leaves. When he returns, he shoves a glass of amber liquid into my hand. "No Prize."

"Course not," I grumble.

"Thought you might need something harder anyway."

He's right, of course. I hold up the glass. "To what I've always wanted."

Artagan brings the glass to his lips but stops before he sips. "Leah."

"No. To Death."

Liar, says the voice in my head—her voice.

I gulp down the woody-tasting liquid in one swallow.

The burn ripples down my throat, followed shortly by a numbness leaching through my body. I roll my shoulders and crack my neck, hoping to loosen the tension stored in my muscles, but the tautness seems cemented in place.

"I grasp more of your situation than you might realize," Artagan says. "The legend you've heard about me isn't entirely accurate. After being handed down through the generations, the story has been shortened and modified. Portions are true. Olluna was an immortal who fled her village and died, but that's where the truth and the legend diverge."

I recall the fictional version of my story that Ian the waiter shared as gospel. *As truths and legends are wont to do.*

"Blackmuir Wood was a refuge for the Endless in 1406. That is what immortals were called in those days. The humans believed the woods to be haunted or some such rubbish, so they never entered. A small sanctuary for the immortals was established there. My family lived with them after my mother was accused of dabbling in witchcraft because of her ability to heal with herbs. If you know your history, you know it wasn't a splendid time to be accused of that particular crime. We were strangers, but the Endless took us in as if we were one of their own. The life was good, peaceful. After my parents' deaths, my brother left to seek a different life, but I stayed.

"Olluna wandered into the settlement one night. I remember how her hair gleamed like silver in the moonlight. She was the most enchanting creature I'd ever seen, skin like alabaster, eyes of sea-foam green. She stole my breath and heart in the same instant. I never believed in love at first sight before seeing her. Shortly after her arrival, Brennus died, and I became one of the Endless."

"That's right. You weren't always immortal," I whisper. The wheels in my head begin to spin.

"No. Thus, the reason I'm not carded at every pub I

walk into." He chuckles. "Frozen at age forty-two. It's you, the ones born immortal, who have it rough, always looking nineteen," he says, a suggestion of sarcasm hidden in his voice.

How did I forget the difference between my apparent age and Artagan's? Long ago, Artagan had been a soul immortal just as Leah is. Excitement builds in my gut. "So why won't this work for her? Why couldn't Leah become an immortal? You did."

Artagan dismisses the idea with a flip of his hand. "For two reasons. Number one, only council members can pass on their immortality. Do you know which one she's related to?"

"No, of course not, but you must."

"Members only know their own relations—a carefully guarded secret."

"But if I searched and found who it was..." I say, my voice elevated.

He's shaking his head before I can finish. "Through millennia of tangled family tree branches? Research of that vast scope could take months, even years. I'm sorry, but I can't give you that kind of time."

I bite the inside of my cheek, and a metallic taste fills my mouth. My hand rolls into a fist, and I hit the back of the seat in front of me. A man grunts, then shoots me an annoyed glare from between the backrests. I return the scowl, and he turns around.

Artagan lowers his voice to a hushed whisper. "Number two. Killing an immortal is damn near impossible. I've tried. So have you. Immortals as old as the council members aren't ancient by chance. They're cunning and suspicious of everyone." Artagan finishes his scotch with a long swig.

"Soon after, I took my inherited seat on the council. I chose to continue to live at the settlement. My new duties summoned me away often, but my time spent with Olluna kept me sane. Over the next months, I courted her. She loved the flowers that grew high in the mountains. I would pick them for her on my journeys home. Eventually, she came to love me, too, and I asked her to be my wife."

A burning ache flares in my chest. What I wouldn't give to be able to call Leah my wife, to have a future that included me on one knee, Leah saying yes, and a wedding. I shudder at the thought and reach for my glass then realize it's empty.

A steward walks down the narrow aisle, managing a refreshment cart. I raise my hand to catch the man's attention. He slows and looks down with a pleasant smile. "Yes, sir?"

"Scotch, please."

"How would like that, sir? On the rocks? With water—"

"Neat, and make it a double."

Artagan eyes me, impressed. "I'll have the same," he says.

I pay the man and send him on his way. I take several swallows of whiskey, letting the warmth numb some of my pain before I turn to Artagan. "What happened?"

"Olluna and I were married in the spring—her favorite season. By the end of year, we were expecting our first child. Those two years with Olluna first as my friend and then as my bride were the happiest time of my existence, until one afternoon, when an urgent message arrived from the council. The note was from Vita, calling an emergency gathering." His voice turns hard as he finishes.

I sneer. "How could you have trusted her?"

"You must understand—I didn't know Vita's nature then. She appeared to be indifferent, not evil. I didn't know Vita's hatred for Brennus had passed to me. She hid her true nature well, until she struck like the viper she is." He pauses. "Back then, we met in a castle ruin in northern Italy's Apennines. When I got to the council chamber, Vita wasn't there. No one was, except Thanatos. He was confused by my sudden arrival and told me no message had been sent. I traveled through shadow and was in Blackmuir Wood within moments, but I was already too late. The settlement had been destroyed. No one was left. I searched the forest for Olluna.

"I found her crumpled and bleeding at the bottom of the white cliffs. They'd thrown her down. Our baby lay dead in her arms, born too early. He was mortal. I buried our son, whom I named Lugus, at the bottom of the cliff and then carried Olluna up into the mountains to a cave I knew well. I cared for her, but her spirit was broken and couldn't be healed. She cried every night for our dead son. Sometimes, I'd catch her rocking an imaginary baby in her arms, singing to the emptiness. She died on the night of the first full moon, lying as an angel on our baby's grave."

His voice breaks off. He pinches the bridge of his nose, closes his eyes, and sits silently. I watch him, unable to tear my eyes from his still form. His expression tells of the turmoil raging inside. Artagan's pain is a harsh reminder. My plan has to work. I can't go back to a life without her. My manic energy spikes. I fidget in my seat, having a difficult time sitting still. I wish my sacrifice were over; I want Leah safe, and honestly, I'm not looking forward to the pain of dying. Taking another long swig, I let the alcohol settle my angst once again.

When Artagan begins again, his voice is strained, as if he's attempting to restrain a wild beast inside him. "She'd already eaten the hemlock. Following her death, I headed to where the men came from—a small town on the wood's edge." Blue flames of rage behind his eyes break free, and his stony facade crumbles away. A savage grin takes the place of his heartache. The look sends a shiver straight through me like an icy blade. "In the dead of night, I walked into the village. I took the children first, allowing them to meet the angels from their sleep. Their mothers needed to feel the pain of losing a child, just as my Olluna did. The women were next. With my fraudulent pleas to save themselves, I led them from the village and sent them running up to the top of the white bluffs. The men thought the women were possessed by demons and chased after them. But by the time the women reached the edge of the cliffs, I had complete control of their minds, and they followed my whispers to their deaths."

Artagan chuckles unsympathetically and takes a long sip of his drink. He bears no resemblance to the man he must have been before Death and tragedy sank their talons into him. Instead, a callous monster sits by my side.

I can't purge the pictures of dying children and tormented mothers from my head. "How can you be so cavalier? You killed children. None of them had a hand in Olluna's death."

"Walk a mile in my shoes, Jack, then judge me. Until then, you may keep your opinions to yourself."

I bite my tongue. *Play nice. Remember, you need him, not the other way around.* "I didn't mean to offend."

Artagan nods once. "When the time came to take the men, I stalked through the field. Back then, I sported the black cloak everywhere I went—the fashion. When the moon peeked out from behind the clouds, the night appeared as day, and a glint of silver caught my attention—a scythe, probably forgotten from the afternoon harvest. I lifted the long-handled blade, and the steel sang. I shifted the tool up and down in my hand, taking my time and testing its weight, and then I glared at them across the faint glow of the field.

"As I approached, most of the men charged. Brave, but foolish. They had no chance. I saved the man who led the horde against Olluna until last. I wanted him to see the pain and destruction his judgment caused."

I open my mouth to speak, but Artagan's glare stops me.

"The man huddled at the craggy edge as I approached, and then, like the coward he was, he jumped to meet the same fate as his wife. He didn't expect me at the bottom.

He wasn't dying until *I* said so. I let him beg before I sent his soul to hell. That day, I was the judge, jury, and executioner. In the end, every building was ash, just as they'd left my home."

The train begins to slow.

"This is us." Artagan stands.

CHAPTER TWENTY-FOUR

A COLD, BITING WIND HITS ME straight in the face when I step from the train. The raw air cuts me like a knife, causing my eyes to water. My breath pushes steam through the air. The conditions seem too wintery for summer—proof that we are at the earth's northern fringe. A sign over the door of the white-painted brick station swings from its hooks. Achnasheen. *Wherever the hell that is.*

My footsteps echo across the wooden beams of the platform, crunch along the gravel path, then thud down onto the uneven cobblestones. I trail Artagan past the whitewashed houses that blend into the overcast skies of the vast moorlands. Pairs of eyes peek through gaps in closed curtains, disappearing from view when I glance their way.

"Not a friendly place, is it?" I say.

Artagan shrugs. "They're frightened by us."

"Frightened? Why? Unless they know who you are?"

He nods, and his lips gather into a small smile as he spies my wide-eyed stare. "We have a longstanding covenant with them. The villagers here don't die by our hand in exchange for their silence. Only Time reigns here. In the last three hundred years, the understanding has never been broken, and not a single person born in Achnasheen has died before the age of one hundred and ten."

"So why are they scared?"

"We're still Death's council. No covenant can change that." He smirks. "I'll never forget the priest that kept spattering us with holy water like he expected us to burst into flames. Otmar finally had enough and grabbed the flask. By the end of the meeting, the agreement was forged, and we all had a good shower."

With a laugh, Artagan opens the wrought-iron gate that separates the town from the expansive moors. We trudge over the rough ground. A flock of black-faced sheep bleats their complaints of the trespass. The westward wind howls against us, but we continue to head toward the vacant skyline. The town soon disappears, and in the middle of this godforsaken place, Artagan sits on a rock emerging from the deep-purple heather.

"Have a seat," he says, pointing to the adjacent rock.

I look away. Completely aware of the pair of sapphire eyes staring me down, I focus on the nothingness around us. "No, I just want to keep moving and do what I came here to do."

"You need to know who you're dealing with. Sit." He takes out a box of cigarettes from his shirt pocket. He turns it over and taps the bottom of the box then offers me one of the slender cylinders that slide into view. When I refuse, he shrugs and lights a cigarette for himself. After taking a long drag, he releases the smoke slowly through his nostrils. Then he smiles.

I slump onto the jagged rock in defeat, letting my elbows rest on my knees.

"As I've told you, the council consists of nine members. Thanatos is the head of our little family and the oldest member. Rules and protocol are important to all of them. So keep your mouth shut and follow my lead. Your request will be brought to a vote. Understand, if the votes don't go your way, I'll be forced to take Leah. There won't be a thing I can do about it."

I glare at him. Molten anger hurtles through my veins, sending my hands into fists and forcing me to my feet.

"Relax. Sit. You're going to need to keep your temper in check if our plan is ever going to work." Slowly smoking his cigarette, he stares at me before continuing again. "Vita's vote is easy to predict, and her twin, Domitilla, will follow her lead. That will give you an easy three votes—Vita's, Domitilla's, and mine."

"Vita voting for my plan. Ironic."

He nods with a grin. "On the other hand, I'm sure Akio and Kemisi will vote no. Akio's love of immortality clouds every decision he makes. He won't understand why anyone would be willing to end the gift of eternal life."

"Gift." I snort.

"He won't know what to make of you. That's for damn sure." Artagan chuckles. "Kemisi, on the other hand, will be sympathetic, but because of her past, she'll vote no."

My eyes narrow. Artagan reads the question that must have been evident on my face before my mouth can form the words.

"Understanding and agreement are two very different things. I don't think Kemisi believes in love anymore. She'll be convinced you'd regret your decision. Furthermore, I'm certain she couldn't agree with me if I said the earth is round. I've burned a bridge or two. I don't think they can be mended."

"I'd never regret giving my life for Leah's. Besides, I'll be dead."

"It's best not to argue semantics with a woman, especially Kemisi." With a wry smile, he points to the scar on his face.

"She gave you that scar? How?"

"She didn't. The misunderstanding was with Kemisi, but the scar came from Death. He usually sides with his daughters," he says apathetically. Artagan stares out into the bleak surroundings.

"What are my odds?"

"Anything's possible. I wouldn't have brought you to the middle of nowhere if I didn't think it was a real possibility." Artagan takes another long drag on his cigarette. "However, the others will be difficult to predict. An immortal wanting to take the place of his mortal love in death hasn't come up before, as you might imagine." Expressionless, he folds his arms across his chest. "So you're sure about forfeiting your life for this girl?"

"Yes."

He stands. "All right. Let's get moving."

Over the next rise, a remnant of a once-magnificent building juts out of the horizon. Squinting into the wind, I study the ruins. Half the west wall has crumbled away, leaving the overcast sky in full view through the tall arched windows.

"There," he says, pointing in the rubble's direction.

"Is it an old castle?"

"Monastery," Artagan corrects.

As the ruins grow closer and closer, Artagan falls quiet. The last quarter of a mile, neither of us talks. His head hangs low, and he stares at the uneven ground. I welcome the silence, which gives me time to say my good-byes. I let the memories of Leah swirl in my head. Thousands of rainy days led me to her, and I would gladly suffer any pain just for one second with her. Regardless of the deep ache brewing in my chest, I remember everything and hope I can take each moment with me. The simplest details surge to the foreground—how her golden hair dances in the breeze, the way her hand felt in mine, and the sparkle in those emerald eyes.

Artagan clears his throat. "This way."

As we walk beneath the great stone archway, birds taking refuge in the crumbling crevasses fly off all at once, creating black silhouettes against the clouded sky. My feet trace Artagan's steps across the flat green lawn inside the perimeter of the rock walls. He ducks beneath a smaller archway guarding a stairwell that leads into the earth. We descend the stone steps, which are damp and slippery with moss. The cool underworld greets us, chilling me to the bone. The stairway curves and opens into a dimly lit room dug out of the dirt and rock. Torches line the earthen walls and cast flickering, elongated shadows along the cavern floor.

"Good. Some of them are here already," Artagan says, pointing at the lights.

As if on cue, a small figure saunters out of the darkness. Firelight dances strange patterns across her face and reveals the smile from my dream. Vita's hands remain tucked behind her back, and she flits to Artagan's side.

"I hope you're not up to your tricks again?" Vita's intense aqua eyes slide to me then shift to Artagan.

He snorts. "It's not all about you, Vita."

She squares her shoulders but keeps her hands hidden. "You're not going to take as long to gather Leah as you did Lydia, are you? Honestly, your soft heart for him is getting tiresome."

Artagan peers at me from the corner of his eye for a brief second before returning Vita's scowl.

Her lips bunch into a small *O*. "Doesn't he know?"

"I've heard enough from you." Artagan's tone is firm but still soft.

"You don't think Jack should know which one of us he should really hate?" she asks.

I stare Artagan down. He was the one who took Lydia, and I've trusted the same man to save Leah.

"Enough!" says Artagan.

"Fine. I almost forgot... I got you a little present, a peace offering of sorts. Aren't these your favorite?" She reveals a bouquet of deep indigo, almost-black flowers she was holding behind her back.

Artagan's facade doesn't crack, but sadness touches his eyes for an instant before they become steely again.

"Here." She thrusts the spray of blossoms toward him.

Artagan's jaw tenses. He turns his back on her, and Vita lets the black flowers cascade to the dirt floor. Quiet laughter echoes from the dark recesses. Vita's twin emerges from the shadows. Beautiful and alluring, she's the spitting image of her sister, except for the long hair that flows freely down the curve of her bare back. Her silk royal-blue dress hugs her elfin figure. She's a siren capable of seducing any man she wants—even into his own grave.

Vita crosses her arms and smirks. "I remember you—you and your Lydia. If I'd known you were coming, I would have brought daisies... or has that changed? The difference must be so hard to keep track of. First, your father, then Lydia, Ed, now Leah. Seems sorrow follows you wherever you go. Have you ever thought the problem might be you?"

The fury building in my gut explodes, forcing me to lunge forward.

Artagan catches my arm and brings me to his side. He whispers in my ear, "I understand your reaction, but under the circumstances, I don't think sending her arse over tit is the best course of action."

Artagan's icy tone sends the hairs on the back of my neck straight up. I nod then shrug free from his grasp.

"I'll leave you two alone. I'm sure you have so much to talk about."

Once she's gone, I step forward, stopping an inch from Artagan's deadpan stare. "You!"

His head falls, hiding his expression. "I am sorry."

"Was this your plan? To lure me away so Leah is easy pickings?" My words catch in my throat, and panic sets in.

"No, I'm not double-crossing you. Betrayal is not what's going on here. But as I've said, gathering souls isn't by choice."

"Your excuses sound very much like a cop-out." I need to keep him talking so I can think.

His icy stare snaps to me. "To refuse an assignment brings punishment. If I'd found any other option, believe me, I would've taken it gladly."

"What could be worse than this?" I gesture at the crypt surrounding us.

"Shadow Death. I'd be forced to drink a mixture of the juice of deadly nightshade and immortal blood. The combination turns an immortal into mere vapor, stripping your soul from your body. The ultimate pain for anyone."

I shrug. "Sounds like death."

"Shadow Death is far worse than your run-of-the-mill death." He pauses and takes a deep breath. "I'm sorry for any deception. Please believe me. Nevertheless, if I told you about my involvement in Lydia's passing, would you have trusted me enough to come?"

I glare.

"Remember why you're here. Leah."

The creak of the large wooden door interrupts us. Without a sound, six individuals walk into the room. Vita and her sister saunter behind them. Each pair of gleaming eyes rests on me. No matter what I think of Artagan, the kindness on his face stands out in stark contrast to the cold indifference on theirs.

"So, Artagan, who do we have here?" asks a tall man with olive skin as he studies Artagan's vacant expression.

"Good day, Thanatos." Artagan bows deeply.

"Who?" Thanatos's smoky topaz gaze stays glued to Artagan. Obviously, he has no patience for politeness.

Artagan smiles respectfully. "He's Jack Hammond, an immortal that requires an audience."

"Proof, Kemisi," Thanatos says flatly.

A woman with high cheekbones, amber eyes, and caramel-colored ringlets that extend down to her waist steps forward and removes an ornate golden dagger from her belt. Kemisi grabs my arm. I glare and pull away. Artagan whispers for me to hold still. I reluctantly present her my arm. She grips my wrist then places the chilled blade against my forearm. With a quick motion, she slices into the tender skin. I keep the pain from my face, not wanting to show weakness. Kemisi then counts to ten and bends my arm to display the healing wound to Thanatos.

"He's pure. An audience must be granted," says the flaxen-haired man at Thanatos's side. A tattoo of flames snakes up his neck and disappears under a closely trimmed beard.

"Very true, Otmar," Thanatos says, turning his attention to me. "Why do you want to speak to us?"

"Leah. Leah Nicole Winters," I say, disdain bathing my voice. Artagan clears his throat in warning. Taking a deep, cleansing breath, I restrain my hatred for these immortals and attempt to bury my fear.

Thanatos's face creases into a puzzled expression. "Leah Winters?"

Artagan steps to my side, placing his hand on my shoulder. "My latest job."

"Ah, yes." Thanatos's attention flashes to Vita then to me. "What about her?"

The callous tone of his voice sends renewed fear coursing through me. I glower at him as scenarios of the murders of each of the assembly members play out in my head. The fact that none of these acts would have the desired effect doesn't matter. They manifest on their own.

"Temper," Artagan whispers.

I ball my fists at my side and rein in my rage. "I want to save her."

"Impossible!" says a curt voice.

"Not impossible, Mosi, but unlikely," Thanatos corrects.

Hope first flickers then blazes with new urgency. I speak clearly and loudly. "If the proposal is unlikely, that means it's negotiable. Right?"

A burst of laughter rumbles through Thanatos, then he looks to Artagan. "He must be one of yours."

Artagan glances at me, a knowing grin slides across his lips, then he looks to Thanatos with a raised chin. "What would give you that idea?"

Thanatos snorts and faces me. "So what can we do for you, Jack?"

"I'm here to offer my life in exchange for Leah's." My voice peals above their mumbles so all can hear, even the brawny, heavily tattooed bull of a man leaning against the far wall. His face is hidden by shadow, but the others' displeasure is plain to see. Vita and Domitilla are smiling like sinister bookends.

A slender honey-skinned man with a long inky ponytail gasps and steps forward. "Your immortal life for a human?" he asks with disbelief.

"Jack, this is Akio," Artagan says.

Arms straight at his side, Akio bows, never losing eye contact with me. I dip my head in return.

"She's soul immortal," I correct. "Not that her status would make a difference to me."

Vita snorts. Domitilla whispers in her ear, and Vita laughs, shaking her head in agreement.

"You would truly sacrifice yourself and throw away your precious gift so easily for one of the Ignorant?" Akio asks.

What a heartless ass. I square my shoulders. "Yes, sir, I would for her. I love her."

Artagan bends to my ear. "Be polite, but don't waste your breath on him."

Akio scowls before returning to his place in the crowd.

"What if we agree and our decision gets out to the others? Any immortal unhappy with their life could show up on our doorstep, asking for help," Mosi says. "We don't have time for this kind of foolishness."

"Our brother makes a good point," Akio says. "Do we really want to open this door?"

My heart sinks. Another no, I'm betting.

"We take payment from mortals all the time to *forget* their names for a while," Otmar says, raising his voice. "Shit, half of Hollywood has a running tab with us. Why won't we consider a bargain with one of our own?"

Thanatos and Kemisi nod in agreement.

"You know as well as I their money helps buy the clothes on your back and the food in your belly, Otmar. Granting Jack's request serves us nothing," Mosi says.

Otmar heaves a sigh. "True, but does that imply we can't do something humane once in a while?"

"There should be a vote," Artagan says.

"Let it be known that Artagan has called for a vote. And I second that motion," says Otmar, his deep voice booming against the cavern walls.

Please, in the name of all that's holy, let my plan work.

CHAPTER TWENTY-FIVE

AS VITA STROLLS PAST, FOLLOWED by the rest of the council, her frosty gaze glints with anticipation. Artagan steps in line behind the others. He gestures for me to follow. I walk down the narrow corridor into another cavernous hollowed-out room, larger and brighter than the previous one. The stale, musty air is frigid and penetrates to the bone. Thin streams of water trickle down the uneven stone walls. In the middle sits a stone slab balanced by smaller blocks at each end. The makeshift table is encircled by nine ornate chairs. Each member takes a seat, and Artagan offers me his. I slide into place and rest my folded arms on the chunk of rough stone. Artagan stands behind me, one relaxed hand on my shoulder.

"Before the vote, I have more to say." Akio turns to me. "Most all of us have felt loss. Kemisi lost a husband. Otmar, two wives. My whole family died in a flood, and I'm sure Artagan has shared his tale with you. The pain will pass. I cannot stress this fact enough. Throwing your life, your immortal life, away on a whim is foolish." Every inflection of his voice carries indignation.

"We've loved each other for over one hundred and fifty years," I say. "I love her in the same way as you love immortality. I wouldn't call endless love a whim, sir."

Akio's eyebrows dip low. "I thought you said the girl was Ignorant," he says with distaste clear in his voice.

"She is. Not was."

With a jab in my ribs, Artagan growls under his breath.

"Sir," I add. Artagan is right. I need to control my anger. If I continue down this road, I will lose all control and possibly any chance to save Leah.

Akio shrugs.

Kemisi's focus skips to Artagan. "She remembers him?"

"Yes, she does," Artagan says.

"How do you know?" she asks.

"She told me," I say.

"Evidence," Akio demands, leaning forward on one elbow. "Not just mere words from a silly girl. The brain can be easily tricked into believing many things. Truth or falsehoods, the mind can't tell the difference."

I take two long breaths to steady my irritation. Artagan's hands weigh on my shoulders.

"There are paintings," Artagan says.

I freeze as my posture goes rigid. How does he know about the paintings? My hands stay folded on the table. I concentrate on my breathing, maintaining a steady rhythm. I try to appear calm on the outside, even though my insides are whirling apart. Splinters of ice stab into the scruff of my neck. I let my teeth sink deep into my cheek's fleshy tissue.

"Paintings?" Otmar interrupts my contemplation.

Artagan's voice invades my mind. *Tell him. The detail could gain us a vote.*

I look directly into Otmar's amethyst-flecked eyes. "Yes, she painted scenes from my past, our past."

Mosi rolls his eyes. "Trivial. You told her your memories. She painted them."

"Leah created them before she knew what I am, before I even arrived in Portland. Before she met me."

"So it's happened again." Otmar sits back in his large

chair, tapping his sizable fingers along the limestone surface, and looks at Kemisi, but her gaze has fallen to the floor.

"Again, yes," Artagan says.

"But why?" Kemisi asks. Her stunned stare reconnects with Artagan's.

"I'm working on that," Artagan says tenderly.

"The reason matters little in this case," a male voice says.

My focus is still on Kemisi, so I've missed who spoke. I turn in the voice's direction, toward the far end of the table. The bullish man's eyes—black as pitch and as empty as a bottomless well—drill into me. His vacant glare cuts straight through me. Artagan doesn't have to tell me who he is. He's an immortal with no soul. One glimpse into his eyes tells me he's capable of anything. The black emptiness ushers in a sense of desolation and fear I've never known. My breath is sucked away into the two black pits. I look away from him, not letting the soulless beast play with my resolve.

I take a deep mouthful of air then clear my throat. "I do have one request, if I may?"

Mosi's heavy brows lift over his chocolate eyes. "You're asking us for a favor? What right do you have to demand anything from us?"

"Let the boy speak," Thanatos says.

"Not a demand, sir, but my last gift to Leah. I'm sure my request will be trivial to you. All I ask for is a long life. That Leah is allowed to die of old age in the same way as the people of Achnasheen." I love her too much to bear the thought of one of these monsters coming for her after I'm gone. This act is a selfish one, I know. I console myself with the thought that my death won't be the same for Leah as Lydia's loss was for me. Leah is stronger than I ever was. Besides, I'm leaving her with the hope of our future reunion—my final lie.

Thanatos pauses. His brow puckers over his deep-set

eyes, and he stares. "We will see. Jack, I must ask you to leave." He raises his voice over the growing hiss of whispers and says, "It's time for the vote."

I push the chair away from the table. Its legs grate along the level rock floor. I rise, and Kemisi steps to my side then walks me into the dim hallway. Before closing the heavy wooden door, she gives me a faint smile. Maybe Kemisi will give me vote number four. The door shuts with a deep, booming thud, and I'm alone.

A groan escapes my lips. I lean against the damp craggy wall and thrust my hands into my pockets for warmth. Each moment seems like hours. If the votes fall my way, where am I heading? Heaven or hell? I count my sins, not liking my chances. The consequences that my decision will have on me make no difference. I would never retreat, no matter the price, because my decision is the right choice for Leah. I close my eyes, and emerald ones look back. I lose myself in them, allowing the memories to flood in and practically begging for them. In the midst of their haze, I hear a voice—her voice.

Jack!

I'm so sorry, love.

What are you doing? Don't. Please don't go, Leah begs.

I never meant to cause you harm. I'm so sorry. However, I'm going to keep my promise. For you, this will be for the best—a clean slate. Maybe you'll even fall in love with... I can't finish the thought. This is all in my head, yet her voice sounds so real. Her presence is just an illusion to get me by, and it probably means my sanity has finally given in to the madness.

Artagan clears his throat. My eyes snap open to find him scrutinizing my face, a perplexed expression etching his face.

"We're ready for you," he says. Nothing in his manner gives even the slightest hint about what Leah's and my fate will be. He ushers me in and returns to his seat. I take a short step forward and plant myself at his side.

Thanatos's deep voice fills the cavern. "Jack Hammond, immortal scion of Brennus, your request is hereby granted in full."

A concoction of emotions—triumph, relief, fear, and sadness—twists in my gut and washes over me like an incoming tide. Some of my body's responses, like the unease and fear, surprise me. Maybe the feelings are caused by facing the unknown—or by the finality. I find I'm having a hard time letting Leah go. My knees buckle. Artagan stands and offers me support. I refuse.

"The hemlock tea needs to be made. To brew the potion correctly, it will take a bit of time," Thanatos says.

"Tea?" I ask.

"What? Did you think we'd just shove a sprig of hemlock down your throat and chase it with salt?" Domitilla laughs. "A bit barbaric, don't you think?"

I stare.

"We found if we boil the hemlock, the poison is quicker and far less painful." Thanatos speaks pleasantly as if we're discussing the weather.

"Allow me to make the tea," says Vita. "Unless you'd like the honor, Artagan? Seems he's one of yours."

"No, I wouldn't," he spits through clenched teeth. "I might have voted yes, but not because I wish his death. But because I wish him peace."

Vita smiles and prances from the room.

Thanatos stands. "We'll reconvene for Jack's departure in one hour."

"Just enough time," says Mosi. "Anyone up for a quick game?"

Otmar glances at me with a touch of chagrin then stands. Stepping to Mosi's side, he grins down at him in a pose that perfectly depicts the battle of David versus the Philistine. "You're on, little man," he says.

The others file out after them, laughing and joking, except for Kemisi. She stops, turns, and surveys the scene before leaving Artagan alone with me. He stares at the empty space after she disappears, and I slump into a chair.

"I can leave if you'd like," Artagan offers. "But may I have a minute to explain what happened with Lydia in my own words?"

"All right, but first, you must promise to do me a favor."

"Whatever you need."

"This is Leah's," I say, setting my grandmother's ring on the rough stone table. "See that she gets this."

"Done." He slips the ring into the breast pocket of his blazer then gives his chest two quick taps.

I nod, studying my fists on the table.

"It's Akio who received the assignment of William's death. I discussed the possibility of holding off on its completion. 'What difference would a matter of a month make?' I asked. I could see the consequences of what the death of Lydia's brother would be. Akio's response was that I'd become too attached to what happened in your life, and he believed the experience would be good for me."

"Why did time difference matter?" I ask.

He looks at me with a glint in his eye. "Because if I'd gotten Akio to wait, Lydia wouldn't have died, and you would have been married. Instead, Lydia's gathering orders came the very night of William's death. And, of course, the job came to me. I was handpicked by Death himself as a lesson never to interfere again." He grits his teeth. "I planned to take Lydia in a different way, but I suppose that matters little now. When she ran out into the storm to find you, I had to act quickly. I feared if she'd gotten to you, the sight of her passing would have caused more pain."

I snort. "More pain?"

"If I'd let you witness her death or if you'd found her, wouldn't that have been more difficult? Am I wrong? You found your father. Wasn't that painful? Finding Olluna in the way I did haunts me to this day. She returns to my dreams often, begging for my help." He waits.

"If you were concerned about my pain, why did you allow me to see Leah smashed by a car?" I cringe at the memory. "Maybe you're as coldhearted as Vita now."

"Maybe." He purses his lips.

First Lydia, now Leah. Artagan had a hand in taking all I love from me. "Who took my father? Was that you, too?"

"No. That was Mosi. You were only seven. I'd never have used you like that. It wasn't necessary."

I square my shoulders. "Used?"

"The music box your father was buying for your mother. Mosi set the gift idea in your mind. He needed to have your father on that road at that moment."

"It wasn't my fault," I whisper.

He shakes his head and then exhales slowly as the wooden door groans open.

"Go away, Vita," Artagan says.

"I was just letting you know the tea is almost done. I'm letting the potion simmer a bit longer to make sure of its potency. We want to make sure it does the job. Don't we?"

I find no reason to restrain my words now. My lot has been decided. My gaze locks with her fierce eyes. "Yes, make sure the poison does its job. Because if there's the slightest chance I live, I'll make your death my life's ambition before leaving earth myself." *Because if I'm still alive, I'll have nothing left to lose.*

Artagan chuckles.

"He's been trying to kill me off for centuries," Vita says, pointing to Artagan. "You can see how successful his attempts have been. He finally gave up. No staying power, from what I've heard."

Artagan glares but offers no counter.

Thanatos steps into the room, making Vita jump. "Is the tea ready yet?"

"Yes."

"Then let's get this done," Thanatos says flatly.

Vita nods and withdraws from the room.

Thanatos glances at me. "The others will be here momentarily."

Emptiness swells in the pit of my stomach. I rub my hands along my jeans and stare Thanatos straight in eye. "I'm sure my actions make no sense to any of you. You look at my decision as me giving up immortality. This choice is my only reprieve from an eternity without her. It's quite selfish, really."

"I suppose it is," Thanatos says. "You're forcing her to live through the same pain you lived through. Some might call it revenge."

I sneer, tilting my head away. "They'd be wrong. I wish I'd found another way. I regret her pain. The thought of causing her grief gnaws at me like a cancer, but the bottom line is—Leah has to live. I made a promise to protect her, and I won't break my word."

"Not even for an Ignorant," says Thanatos, his eyes narrowed into slits.

"I told you—her title doesn't matter."

Thanatos nods. "You did. I'd like to meet this woman that causes such devotion."

"You won't. That's our deal."

"Yes, you're correct. I'll never meet her. None of us will. You have my word." Thanatos takes his seat at the head of the table. He leans back, staring at the uneven ceiling, his hands folded over his chest while his index fingers tap together.

Vita returns, carrying an iron kettle. Steam bellows from the spout. Domitilla follows her, bearing a golden chalice in her hands. *How very ceremonial.*

The others file in after them, each taking their seats. Otmar and Mosi are the last to arrive, with crimson smeared across both their faces. Otmar has multiple slashes down his right sleeve, but the blood that seeped from the wounds has already dried and begun to crack. Mosi's lips carry a smug grin.

"Tiger one, Otmar zero," Mosi whispers to Akio loudly enough for me to hear.

Thanatos shoots Mosi a meaningful glare and puts his finger to his lips. Domitilla places the gold cup on the table in front of me then sits. The gold glitters in the torchlight. A relief carving of skeletons encircles the cup's mouth.

Vita's lips form a coy smile, and she pours the tea into the chalice, causing steam to swirl into the air. She leans to my ear. "I've never seen an immortal die before. Brennus took the tea, but he drank it in private. It's all so exciting," she purrs, giving me a wink.

Thanatos gestures to the cup. "Drink, please."

I lift the chalice first with one, then both hands. The ornamental cup is heavier than I expected. My lips touch the cool metal, and I can't help but smile. The initial taste is metallic, but then a warm, salty sweetness washes away the tinny flavor. I'm surprised. I imagined the hemlock would be bitter. I gulp the liquid, disregarding the heat that scorches my throat.

I set the cup on the table and wait, but as the seconds tick by, I feel no difference, other than the fresh bloom of anxiety. I'm just about to complain that the poison isn't working when my vision blurs. I attempt to rub at my eyes with my palms, but my hands begin to quake uncontrollably.

"Vita, what have you done?" Kemisi demands.

Then I'm falling. The left side of my face slams against the rough stone floor, and I roll to my back. My body convulses. A frothy liquid dribbles from my mouth, running in warm paths down my face. I fight through my disorganized thoughts to spend my last moments with Leah, or at least my memory of her. I search for her face in the fog, but I only find her eyes, full of sorrow and worry.

Don't be mad, love.

But, Jack, I said no, she pleads.

"I love you," I whisper.

A screech echoes in my ears, causing my eyes to snap

open. Shadowy vapor hovers over me. The mass grows—doubling, then tripling, in size—taking a humanoid form. My heart races, nearly exploding. I attempt to crawl backward, but I'm frozen in place. I stifle a scream, gulping down breaths to stay quiet.

A pair of vermilion eyes materializes in front of me. No pupils. No irises. All red. They glower down at me. I'm held fast by an invisible specter. Burning pain slashes through my head while the beast rummages through my mind. Emotional torment accompanies every flip of a memory. Even my eyes can't escape the silent interrogation; the creature imprisons my gaze with an unbreakable stare.

Vita's laugh plays along the walls... or is it Artagan's? The swelling beat of my heart in my ears swallows every sound, covering voices and muffling sounds like a heavy wool blanket. As quickly as the pain comes, the sensation leaves. The eyes release me and turn to the council. The shadow lets out a primal howl—high pitched and deafening as if the gates of hell have opened to devour us all. I attempt to rise to my knees, but the room spins and sends me crashing to the floor. My limbs have gone numb.

Through the haze, I watch the shadow sail through the air and slam Vita to the ground. She sits, stunned, before retreating, crawling backward toward the door. Her eyes dart from side to side, desperately looking for an escape. The shadow beast faces her again. Vita screams—a name? Through the cotton in my ears, I concentrate on her muffled yells. "Serevo. I name Serevo," she says over and over. I can feel my lungs closing in, and my breaths become shallow and rapid. I'm losing my grasp on reality. It would be so easy to let myself fade into darkness, but I keep my eyes open, transfixed on Vita's horror-stricken face.

Vita is still calling the name when the Shadow lifts her high. It tosses her repeatedly. Each time, Vita whirls through the air, and each time, the creature catches her as if she's no more than a rag doll. She retches and fights, but with each throw, the beast tears bits of her physical form away from her wicked soul. Bursts of bloody mist swirl within the creature's black vaporous form. Pieces of flesh and bone turn to ash before hitting the floor. Soon, all that's left of Vita are long wisps of connecting fibers—a withered spiderweb. The small mesh writhes in the dark being's grip, trying to break free. Then those red eyes return to me. *This is it. This is the end. Good-bye, my love.* I close my eyes and think of Leah, then a final convulsion drags me into nothingness.

CHAPTER TWENTY-SIX

CONSCIOUSNESS USHERS ME OUT OF the numbness. My head throbs, and every one of my joints is on fire. Heaven shouldn't feel this way. Pain isn't supposed to be part of paradise. I blink, and my vision is blurry. Clarity fights against the jumbled thoughts swirling in my head. I concentrate on the first object that catches my attention—an unfocused orange splotch. *Flames*, I decide. Hell.

"Slowly, Jack, move slowly," says a familiar voice. Somewhere in the befuddled haze, dots connect. Artagan. My fate is worse than hell, a thousand times worse. I'm alive, and I've failed again. Leah isn't safe. She's going to die, if she hasn't already. Lydia... now Leah... I couldn't save either of them.

Unable to drag a full breath into my lungs, I attempt to sit up, but my muscles revolt and lock me down. Pain shoots throughout my entire body. The room spins like a top.

"Slow, I said," Artagan warns, his voice echoing and muffled.

"Leah." I choke. My throat is raw, as if I've swallowed a vat of acid. With as much effort as I can muster, I thrust myself to my elbows, but hands restrain me. I'm too weak to fight and fall to the cold unforgiving stone.

Artagan surveys the panic in my eyes and purses his lips before answering. “She’s safe. No one can hurt her anymore. Now stay down!”

I shake my head feverishly. “The bargain,” I rasp, my voice thin, lacking substance.

“Listen to me—Leah’s alive. No bargain needed. The debt’s paid—life for a life. Besides, the council’s embarrassed.” He smiles. “They won’t push the matter. Vita broke one of their precious rules. Now stop moving. Let your body purge the poison from your system.”

“Poison?” I ask.

“I can’t believe Vita did this. Well, maybe I can,” Kemisi says from across the room.

My vision is clearing, and I shift my gaze toward the velvet tone. Kemisi sits cross-legged in one of the chairs.

Artagan looks at her from under his black brows, one hand still holding me down. “I knew she would. I counted on it. To send one of my descendants to Shadow Death was more than she could resist.”

Kemisi huffs.

“What’s done is done,” Artagan says with a shrug, and a wide grin spreads across his face.

“What’s going on?” I ask.

“Revenge,” Kemisi says with a loud expulsion of air.

“I’ve tried numerous times to kill her. For the last seventy-five years, I’ve played nice, hoping an opportunity would present itself,” Artagan says, his eyes trained on me.

“Vita didn’t give you hemlock tea,” says Kemisi.

“Would someone like to explain to me why I’m still here?” I ask.

Artagan gives a quick chuckle. “Because despite being a martyr to your regrets, you’re not guilty of any crimes, Jack, at least none in the immortal world.”

“How did you know the punishment would reverse?” Kemisi asks.

“The knowledge came in so-called myth. If you haven’t

noticed, most myths and fairy tales are based on real-life events. In the cautionary tale, an immortal named Myron tried using a mixture of poisonous plants and his own blood to kill his friend Solon because Myron had a hard-on for Solon's wife."

Kemisi doesn't seem bothered by Artagan's choice of words. Maybe she's accustomed to his vulgarity.

The grin plastered across Artagan's face grows. "As expected, the tale didn't end well for Myron, but the theory sounded plausible."

"So, how did you know the poison would kill Vita instead of me? You tested your theory out on me. On Leah!" I grind my teeth, and my hands clench, then unclench, too weak to hold the tension very long.

Artagan rolls his eyes. "You were no one's guinea pig. I sought out Solon and his wife, Pelagia. The search took close to a century, but I found them—still together, by the way. They confirmed the story wasn't a fable and told me the plant Myron used."

"And Leah?" I ask.

"Is untouchable." A complacent tone clings to Artagan's rich baritone voice.

"Explain," I say, unconvinced.

"Leah is Vita's descendant."

Kemisi inhales.

My mind races, and I search his face for an explanation.

Artagan laughs. "Did you hear me, Jack?"

"Where's Vita now?" I ask.

"She's in Shadow Death—dead for all practical purposes. Her immortality was stripped from her and given to the next soul immortal in her line, a Miss Leah Winters."

He waits while I grapple with his words. When my mind, still slowed by the toxin, begins to make sense of what Artagan is saying, my battered heart gives an enlivened lurch.

"Leah is immortal now?" I ask.

Artagan puffs out his chest. “Am I forgiven?”

Fear sweeps over me. “Oh, dear God, doesn’t that mean she’s on the council? Like you because of Brennus?”

“No, Vita had a favorite protégé: Serevo. Brennus’s choices were slim—only one, and a soul immortal to boot. Most members of the council have immortal protégés to pass their seat to, along with their particular knowledge. But from what I understand, Brennus’s protégé had passed away by means of an *accident* shortly before Brennus’s suicide. Convenient. Since then, the punishment for even looking crossed-eyed at another’s protégé is hefty—belladonna. No one wants another mishap like me, if they can help it.” He chuckles darkly. “If Domitilla lets the vendetta die with her sister, she’ll have no problem from me.”

“Serevo? That’s the name Vita said over and over again.”

“Yes, her immortal sidekick. She’s been training him for years. He’s ready for the responsibility.”

“Do you think he’ll carry on with Vita’s plan of revenge?”

“No. I’m fairly certain he won’t.”

“How do you know?”

He waves his hand, dismissing my question.

I look away, letting my gaze wander along the uneven walls of the cavern then back to Artagan. “Seems too good to be true. You’re sure this isn’t a dream?”

The back of Artagan’s hand collides with my cheek.

“Artagan!” Kemisi shouts.

The blow makes my ears ring, and I manage to raise my hand as far as my chin. “Ugh! What was that for?”

“You’re not dreaming. If you were, that would’ve definitely woken you up. Besides, I owed you one.” He smirks, pointing to his lip, then looks me square in the eye. “I understand why you doubt. You have every reason to, but I know with one hundred percent certainty that Leah is living and immortal.”

I want to believe Leah is alive and that he’s telling the

truth. I wish I had that kind of faith in fate, or in people, but the possibility of happiness has been within my reach before, only to be snatched away.

Artagan must see the doubt in my eyes because he leans away, tapping his fingers against his lips, and his sigh is laced with frustration. Then a light flashes in his eyes. “Remember, she was mine to take. That craving is gone now. I can only think of two reasons why that would happen. One, she’s dead.”

I grit my teeth. “And the second?” I hiss.

“Her body is grounded to earth, like all immortals’.”

“And her soul?”

“Free to leave if her body were forced to release it. She’s no longer a soul immortal. She’s like us now. Like you.”

I observe Artagan for a long time, and I find nothing but sincerity in his eyes. No matter how much I know I should, I can’t doubt his words. An unencumbered smile breaks out across my face, and a sense of hope I’ve never known swells.

“I have to get to her,” I blurt and attempt to scramble to my feet, falling, then struggling again.

“Whoa. You can’t go anywhere, not just yet.” Artagan grabs my shoulder, pushing me down.

“You don’t understand. She’ll think I’m dead. Her brother was supposed to tell her good-bye for me. Grady knows what I was planning, and he’ll tell Leah.”

“Well, you’re not dead. She’ll have to wait a bit longer to get the happy news.”

“Wait, my phone.” I pat down my pockets. “Dammit! I left it at Grady’s.”

“Cell phones don’t work out here, and honestly, this might be the kind of news you want to tell in person.”

“How long?” I demand.

Artagan glances over at Kemisi. “What do you think?”

“Another hour, at least,” she answers with a touch of uncertainty in her voice.

"An hour! No way in hell," I say, trying to stand again and finding my legs are still made of jelly.

Kemisi frowns. "Men are always so restless. This isn't a choice, Jack. You physically aren't going to be able to walk before then. I might be wrong, but I don't think Artagan wants to give you a piggyback ride all the way to the station."

Artagan grimaces, showing off all his pearly white teeth.

Kemisi hops to her feet. "I'll go see if something might help to speed the process."

"Look in my books. Anything with dandelion root should help," Artagan says.

She nods then walks to the adjacent wall and straight through the shadow.

"I don't think I'll ever get used to that," I say, looking at Artagan. "So what the hell was that thing? The black mass?"

"They don't call this place the Valley of the Shadow of Death for no reason. Everything has a shadow, even Death. The creature was judging you. Did you see how it tore Vita limb from limb? Exquisite! Better than sex... almost." He laughs, rubbing his hands together. Artagan has fondness for the theatrical, to be sure. His growing excitement electrifies the air. "I can't believe that bitch is finally dead. Serevo is the newest member of the council, and Leah is the recipient of Vita's immortality. Everything's as I planned." He pauses, studying my face. "How are you feeling? You're not pasty white anymore. A bit more color in your cheeks now."

I push up into a sitting position but slump back to the hard earth. My head pounds, and again, the room spins. "I feel like I was hit by a Mack truck. What did Vita give me?"

"Belladonna mixed with three drops of immortal blood. The poisonous concoction summons the Immortal Judge—the Shadow of Death." His voice turns solemn, almost reverent. "The creature judges if an immortal's soul is culpable for a crime or not. One must be very careful. If the accused is found innocent, the judgment ricochets, returning to the accuser. When Vita brewed and presented the belladonna tea to you with full knowledge of what she was doing, she became your accuser."

"Not something most of us knew," Kemisi says, glaring at Artagan as she walks in with a mug of steaming liquid. "Otmar made tea for you. A blend of dandelion root, burdock, and milk thistle. Their properties should remove any toxins left in your body and help you recover faster."

I shrink back from the mug.

Artagan takes the tea and puts the cup to his lips, taking a large gulp. He counts to ten and then props up my head. The room seems to tilt and wobble.

"Drink," he says, putting the rim to my lips. "The tea's safe."

"Trust issues," Kemisi mutters.

"Blame me?" Artagan smirks.

Kemisi shrugs then strolls to her seat and curls into the chair like a cat.

I scrutinize Artagan, who still seems in good health.

"Drink," he says with a renewed grin. "Do you want to see Leah or not?"

I sip the hot liquid. Its sweetness makes my lips jump away from the cup. Artagan gives me another encouraging look. I drink again, taking a large gulp. The sweetness floods in, but a slightly bitter aftertaste follows, which calms my nerves. Warm needles prick my throat and trail the tea into my stomach. The sensation grows with every sip. Soon, I'm sitting without help and holding the mug on my own.

Finally, my limbs begin to move when and how they're told, and the room anchors itself into one place. I endeavor to stand. My muscles and joints are stiff, and I teeter then pitch forward. Artagan grabs my elbow to steady me.

"Let's go," I demand.

CHAPTER TWENTY-SEVEN

I STUMBLE FOR THE THIRD TIME, falling hard to my knees on the soggy green earth.

"I think we should stop, give you a bit of a break," Artagan says.

"Absolutely not. Leah's lying in a hospital bed miles away, mourning me, and you want to take it easy?"

"Have it your way." He yanks me up by my shirt collar.

Finally back in Achnasheen, I pace back and forth along the long platform. Artagan sits on a bench, one leg propped up on a knee, arms stretched along the backrest, watching me with an amused smile.

"Why don't you have a seat?" he says.

"Can't."

He puffs on his cigarette and then removes the box from his pocket. "Have one. They'll calm your nerves."

I concede and spend the next minute coughing, hacking up a lung or two. "Why do you smoke these things?" I manage between coughs.

Artagan guffaws then shrugs.

The train's headlight breaks through the mist before the train slows to a stop at the station.

The car Artagan selects is empty except for a dark-haired man sitting near the rear, reading a newspaper.

Artagan lets out a loud huff when he sees the other man. Muttered curses follow. Tucking the weekly under his arm, the man stands. I study him. *Ordinary bloke.* Typical height, maybe a couple of inches shorter than I am. Unassuming build. His untidy, slicked-back hair touches the collar of his long black trench coat. Nothing about his features sticks out, until he looks my way. His eyes are the color of garnet. I shiver against the cold that grows deep inside me and expands as rivers of ice dart through my veins. The man gives me a warm, welcoming smile for half a second then shifts his piercing gaze to Artagan. Then he passes us without a word and steps from the train onto the platform.

"Who was that?" I ask.

"The beast himself," Artagan says with a roll of his eyes. "Death."

I shoot him an incredulous look.

"What did you expect? A robe and scythe?"

"I don't know what I expected, just not something so... human. So ordinary."

Artagan laughs. "You haven't seen him in action. Hold your judgment till then." He pauses. Then with a wave, he says, "Forget about him. Now, how about that bullet?"

"What?"

"The bullet in your back. Let's get the damn thing out. Turn around." He digs into his pocket and returns with a Leatherman.

I swallow hard.

"Come on. It will be fine. I've had lots of practice. You won't feel a thing," he says, snapping the pliers hungrily.

"No thanks. I'll keep my little souvenir, if it's all the same to you." Turning my back to him, I look out the window.

"Suit yourself, but if I were you, I wouldn't want a weak spot." The heel of his hand rams the slug of lead. Fiery currents whip through me, making my eyes water. "See what I mean?"

A sigh breaks through my lips. “Fine.” I yank up my shirt and hunch my back.

His fingers search out the interloper and pull my skin taut. “So how did you get shot anyway?”

The burn of the first rip forces my teeth to clamp together. “Ugh. Playing hero in a liquor store in LA, a few months ago. Guess the bullet was the thing that sent me to Portland—damn, that hurts.”

“I’m almost done. Quit being such a sissy.”

I fight off the wave of nausea. Beads of sweat form along my forehead, and I bite my knuckle to keep from screaming. Finally, I feel the freeing of pressure followed by a gush of warmth running down my back.

“There,” Artagan says, sounding pleased. He holds a cloth to the wound. “Hold this there.”

I fumble blindly with the soft fabric—a handkerchief, I surmise—and press the cloth against the renewed injury.

Out of nowhere, Artagan is talking again, chatting away as if we’re midpoint in a conversation. “So, I found myself in Portland, Maine, for the first time last November. The case needed a personal touch. The target happened to be the director for the Bayside Gallery. While doing research, I stumbled across a painting by an up-and-coming local talent—a Leah Winters. The portrait was of a young man from Victorian times. Strangely enough, I recognized him. The director was kind enough to show me several other paintings by the same artist. You were the overwhelming theme.”

“The night you told me what I was, I told you about Leah. I told you about the paintings and that she remembered. You acted surprised, like you didn’t know.”

“I lied,” Artagan says nonchalantly. “Besides, I wasn’t one hundred percent sure my interpretation was accurate, until you told me. There could have been other explanations for the paintings.”

An irritated huff erupts through my lips.

"Never lied, huh?"

I glance at the window. "Touché."

Artagan laughs. "Leah's bio said she was a student at the Maine College of Art. Fancy my surprise when Lydia Ashford came strolling out of Advanced Figurative Painting. From the resemblance, I knew she was the twins' relation. After Lydia's death, Domitilla let the fact slip that Lydia was their descendant, not knowing the seemingly unimportant detail would end up biting Vita in the arse. I hoped someday to use the information, but I didn't know how until after Leah's name came to me for the gathering."

"So the phone call was true. Vita wasn't a threat any longer. You were."

Artagan nods.

Not attempting to hide my brewing anger, I ask, "Pawns still?"

"I had to keep you in the dark for the plan to have the slightest chance of working. What would you have done if I'd told you Leah was marked for death and yours truly was supposed to make that happen?"

My jaw stiffens. From the pit of my stomach, a snarl rises and bursts from my throat. I twist in my seat, wanting to hit something—anything. In truth, Artagan's jaw would satisfy nicely.

"Point proven. And you should know that if you strike me again, I'll return the favor."

"You're lucky I came to Portland at all."

Artagan snorts. "Luck. I had to get you out of that hellhole somehow." He drops the mangled slug into my lap.

I blink. "What?"

"I have a bit of a gift. Well, all descendants do. Most just don't know how to use the ability." Artagan smiles. His forefinger taps against his temple. "I had that punk shoot you. The voice in your head, sometimes that's me."

"You crazy son of a—you manipulated that boy. And me."

"'Manipulated' is a strong word. I simply influenced your inner decisions."

"That's manipulation," I grumble, not liking how often Artagan is pulling my strings.

He shrugs. "I couldn't make you do anything against your nature. And foolish me, I figured you might want to know the girl you loved was wandering around... alive."

He's right, of course, and he knows it. I would have done anything and risked everything for this outcome.

He reaches into the breast pocket of his blazer. "I believe you'll be needing this," Artagan says, presenting my grandmother's ring clasped between his thumb and two fingers.

I nod, taking Leah's ring, then slide the band onto my pinky. "Thanks."

Artagan sits quietly, gazing out the window, twisting his gold ring around his finger.

"Your ring, is it special?"

"No sentimental value, if that's what you mean. Just a trinket I picked up in Rome. It serves as a reminder that there's always a way out of any situation, even if the way means great sacrifice. You see, it's a poison ring." Artagan flips up the black onyx stone to reveal a small compartment with a small green pill tucked inside. "Having a mother who was an apothecary has its advantages. She taught me well. The pill's hemlock and salt, my backup plan," he says, snapping shut the small lid.

I grin then slide the plastic bag out my pocket and hold up my hemlock concoction.

Artagan lets out a laugh. "That's my boy." He returns his attention to the window, a grin still glued on his face.

After that, I have a considerable amount of alone time on my hands. Artagan's grown quiet again, seeming lost in his own thoughts. I watch the passing countryside through the streams of rain. I have so many things to think about. Because of Artagan and his insane plan, Leah is mine forever. I never have to say good-bye.

The train slows, and a gravelly voice over the loudspeaker

announces that we've arrived in York. I stand before the train comes to a complete stop. I elbow impatiently through the wall of bodies, Artagan following close behind.

Out in the fresh air of the rainy night, the crowd thins. I turn to Artagan and extend my hand. "Thank you for everything."

"You're very welcome. I'm sure we'll bump into each other again." He smiles. "I'll see to it."

I leave him standing by the station doors and begin to run. Artagan's laugh echoes down the narrow street then fades.

My feet beat against the pavement while my heart hammers in my chest, both longing to get to her. I run through the arched gate of the wall, past the homes, and then over the bridge into York Minster. The cathedral's lights gleam brightly, sending beautiful colors through the stained glass and into the darkness of the night sky. Organ music fills the air, mingling with the sound of the light pattering of rain, hitting the pavement.

So close.

Around the next corner, the hospital comes into view. I run through the front doors then race along the zigzagging corridors, leaving a trail of exasperated faces and shouts of disapproval. Ignoring the elevator, I take the stairs three at a time. After what seems like an eternity, I stand at Leah's hospital room door. The machines that kept her alive are gone. She is sitting on her bed, her face buried in her hands, her body trembling. At her side, Grady rubs her back and whispers. His eyes shift to the door. Doubt folds his brow and narrows his stare, but as his shock withdraws, his face relaxes. A murmur slips through his lips. "Leah. Look."

With red, puffy eyes, she looks up at me. Tears begin to fall freely down her flushed cheeks. She lurches forward, her arms outstretched. I close the distance between us in two long strides. I sit next to her on the bed. She stares at me as if she expects me to vanish in front of her eyes. I gently wind my arms around her shivering frame. She buries her wet face into the crook of my neck. Emotions crash over me when the reality of the situation finally takes hold. She's here. She's safe. We're free.

Grady stands. A smile passes between us as he slips from the room, closing the door behind him.

Driven by a need to see her emerald eyes, I push away, take her chin in my hand, and tug her face upward. I wipe away her tears with my fingertips. "Don't cry, love. Everything's going to be all right. Everything's all right," I whisper.

Leah studies every inch of my face. "I thought you were... you were... gone," she says between convulsive gasps.

"I'm here now." I press my lips against her forehead, savoring the sweetness of her skin.

"Why did you leave?"

"I had to. I wouldn't have, otherwise. You have to know that."

She glances away. "What were you planning to do?"

"Save you."

"Grady told me that much. But how?"

"I went to make a bargain with a group of immortals who handle these kinds of things."

"Bargain?"

"My life for yours. I'll never allow anyone to hurt you."

Anger lights her face. "How do you think I could live without you? Knowing you sacrificed everything for me."

"For me, hope has made all the difference. None of that matters now."

"Of course it matters."

I press my fingers to her soft pink lips. "Please listen. Haven't you wondered how you went from fighting for your life to arguing with me in just a few hours?" The corners of my mouth inch upward.

Confusion overtakes every aspect of her expression. "What's different?"

"You." My smile grows wider.

She wrinkles her forehead and bites her lower lip, obviously trying to wrap her head around a new reality. Then a light of understanding dawns on her face. "Wait a minute. You went to make a bargain. If you succeeded, you wouldn't be here. You'd be... be..." She runs her hands along the sides of my face. "Are you okay?"

"Everything's fine. And you, my love, have been granted a permanent reprieve. You're immortal now, like me."

Leah sits for a long while, hands folded in her lap, staring at the specks on her hospital gown. "So these immortals let you come back. Did you come to say good-bye?" She snuffles, and tears flow again.

"No, no more good-byes. We're both safe."

"Are you lying to me?" She looks up. "Please don't, not about this."

"I'm not, love. And I have lifetimes to prove I'm telling you the truth."

"Lifetimes?"

"Hundreds of thousands. You might get sick of me after that." I chuckle.

Leah smiles, scoots closer, and begins to trail kisses up my neck, leaving a warm tingling path in their wake. Fire ignites and courses through me when I press my mouth to hers. My need to be closer to her grows more intense with each kiss. I caress her neck down to the arch of her back, pulling her hard against me. Leah pushes me backward onto the bed. Our breathing becomes heavy and jagged. Her fingers tangle in my hair. A low moan breaks free through my lips.

"Leah," I whisper.

A clearing of a throat interrupts the moment. I glance to find a scowling nurse leaving in a huff. With a giggle, Leah slides off me.

I stay sprawled across her bed, trying to regain my breath. "Ah, Leah, you're going to be the death of me yet."

She swats at my shoulder.

"Ouch!" I rub my stinging skin and chuckle.

"Not funny, Jack. Besides, you're the perfect gentleman twenty-four, seven." She sits up and retreats to the corner of the bed.

I roll to my side. "Only on the outside, I assure you. So maybe a hospital room with an audience isn't the best place to test my resolve."

A hint of mischief twinkles in her deep-green eyes. She snatches a shiny red apple off a tray sitting untouched next to bed and tosses it into the air. After catching the fruit just before it hits me in the face, I look at her wide-eyed.

"Are you ready to stop holding on to the past and start living yet?" she asks.

"Probably not." I smirk. "Old habits die hard, but we can hope."

"Did Jack Hammond just say the *H* word again?" She winks and leans forward to kiss me lightly on the lips. As always, her touch releases a thousand maniacal butterflies. Desire stirs within me again. I take in a deep breath then stand. Holding my hands out, palms up, I invite her to join me. With bright eyes, she slips her hands into mine, and I help her to her feet. I release her and slide the ring off my pinky. Squaring my shoulders, I kneel in front of her.

"My heart is and always will be yours," I say, holding out the ring. "Leah Nicole Winters, I promise to love you endlessly. Will you do me the great honor of becoming my wife?"

A small gasp escapes her lips. She blinks to chase away her tears then smiles. Looking to the heavens, she shouts, "Yes!"

My chest lightens. Pure happiness consumes me. For once, the feeling is not intermingled with doubt, regret, or fear. I jump to my feet. She offers me her hand, and I slide my ring onto her finger.

"I've done the asking a bit out of order, though. I should've asked your brother first," I muse, staring at the new promise encircling her finger.

"Jack, you don't need to ask Grady. I'm a big girl." A smile breaks across her lips.

We lie cuddling on the bed, my arms entwined around her. In the complete quiet, I find solace in her breaths, her heartbeat, and the touch of her hand.

Leah rolls over, resting her chin on my chest. "You do realize I was right, don't you?"

"Right?"

She nods.

"About what?"

"I knew this life couldn't be the end of us."

I chuckle. Leah *is* right. Somehow, through all the twists and turns fate has thrown our way, Leah saw this end—this future.

"Yes, love, it will be forever." I flash a smile, and our lips touch.

Paradise.

EPILOGUE: ARTAGAN

THIS LIFE ISN'T AN EASY one, but occasionally, even fate tosses me a bone in the form of a good day. Now no matter what my actions cost me, I can die a happy man. *Ding-dong, the bitch is dead.*

Sitting on a creaky stool at the White Pony, elbows resting on the curved bar, enjoying my drink, I find myself peering into the shadows, half-expecting *his* arrival any moment. I glance around the pub, past empty mahogany tables lining matching walls.

Boy, do I know how to clear a room. Probably for the best. No mortal needs to see an immortal arse-whooping if Death discovers what I've done.

The patrons all vacated the premises soon after my arrival. Only two people in Achnasheen seem unafraid of me—the amiable old barman, Liam, and the priest, Father Croft. They're an odd pair.

Father Croft, I understand. He's a man of faith who isn't afraid of death in any form. However, I haven't quite figured out the barman yet, but I will. With enough time, I always decipher people's natures. Of course, I'm sitting here past closing time, smoking a cigarette, drinking expensive scotch that I have no intention of paying for. I look at the amber liquid, watching the ice cubes bobbing along the surface. The cell in my pocket buzzes again, cutting off my thoughts. *Bloody hell, can't a man drink his scotch in peace?* After I dropped Jack off in York, Thanatos called four times. But I didn't answer because I was planning to get shitfaced before facing the music. Peering at the number, I raise my eyebrows. *So soon?*

"Jack?"

"Sorry for bothering you so late. Leah's finally sleeping. I didn't want to leave her until she was. She shared one of her dreams with me tonight, which led me to a question only you can answer."

I shake my head. *Jack's worrying again, surprise, surprise.* "Fire away."

"Do soul immortals have memories when they're spirits?"

"A soul with a memory? No, not possible. The soul hibernates at the time of death, sleeps until the next body calls for it from the womb."

"This is Leah we're talking about. When has impossible mattered?" Jack mutters, as if he's talking to himself.

"What's this all about?"

Jack explains the dream Leah had years ago. "But the vision wasn't a dream. The event happened after Lydia died, that same night. When I called out to her and promised I'd see her again, I meant in paradise. Leah painted the scene, but I never put two and two together until tonight."

The wheels in my head begin to turn. *Perhaps this is the break I've been looking for.* "I think it's time for me to talk to this young lady of yours."

"They're discharging her tomorrow. We'll be returning to the States soon after."

"All right. I'll come to Portland, but I'll do some research first. Let's see what I can figure out."

"Thank you. By the way, you're going to tell me everything, no matter what's going on. Understand?"

"What? You don't trust me?"

"See you soon, Artagan." He hangs up.

I drop the phone into my blazer pocket and set my empty glass on the bar. "Hey, Liam, can I get my bill?" I ask, testing my theory.

Liam strokes the coarse white hairs of his beard with stubby fingers. "Why would you want one of those? I've never given you one before."

I switch to the straightforward approach. "Why haven't you? You're not scared of me, are you?"

He smiles, forcing the pronounced lines around his eyes to crinkle, then laughs. "People 'round here are fools. Why would I be scared of you? You can't touch me."

"True."

"Aye, besides, I've always felt I owed you somethin'. If the stories are true, you had a hand in the town's blessings. So I figure a scotch now and again is the least I can do." He tops off my glass with the last of the bottle.

"Good to hear, Liam." I pause. "To absolved sins." *And forgiveness.* I raise my glass to him then swallow the spirits in three gulps.

Outside the pub, under the blanket of the night sky, I call Thanatos. The phone rings once then sends me to voice mail. I snap the phone shut without leaving a message. He's either still at the ruins or out carousing in one of the neighboring towns. Women can never resist his Grecian looks and dark curly hair. *Lucky bastard.*

I step into the shadowed alley behind the pub and step out into the darkened arch at the ruins. After searching the catacombs, I find Thanatos deep in its belly, where dampness and cold reign, hidden away in his favorite smoking room. The only illumination in the room comes from the bright, crackling flames in the massive stone fireplace. Long, dark corners flank us. Thanatos is relaxing in an oversized red leather chair, puffing on a cigar. A half-empty bottle of red wine sits on a small table by his side.

"You should quit. I've heard those things will kill you," I say, slumping into the accompanying chair. I lean close to the roaring fire to rub my hands in its warmth and glance at Thanatos, gauging his mood.

"You're a funny guy." He pauses and takes a long draw on his cigar then blows billows of smoke in my direction. The wisps float, spiraling and swirling into my face. "But you need new material. After six hundred years, a joke tends to lose its potency."

I fake a cough and wave my hand to disperse the smoke.

"This was left for you." Thanatos sips his wine and slips a piece of folded paper across the table then gives me a knowing smile.

A twinge of nausea jabs my stomach. I grab the paper. Standing, I walk to the mantelpiece before opening the letter. One sentence inscribed in *his* embellished hand.

I want this to be the end of it.

I snort. "Death should tell that to Domitilla." I crumple the paper and toss the note into the fire, which devours the vellum, turning it to ash.

Thanatos sighs in frustration. "I'm sure Domitilla's irate, but then again, who could blame her?"

I glower at him. "I can. I might have been thrust into Vita's blood feud against my will, but I'm sure as hell going to finish it if I need to."

A chuckle erupts from deep within Thanatos's gut. "Always the rebellious one. No wonder you irritate dear old Dad so."

I square my shoulders and lift my chin, trying to hide the smirk. "Every family needs a black sheep."

"And you love your role." He shakes his head. His smoky topaz eyes narrow. "You didn't return all the way out here just to disturb my peaceful evening and be a pain in my ass."

"Being a pain in *your* ass was well worth my travels. Besides, you called me."

"That was hours ago. I figured you'd heard the news by now and were off doing hell knows what." He smiles ruefully. "Something reckless, no doubt."

"News?" I avert my gaze, removing the last cigarette from its box and lighting the slender roll in the blazing fire. I take a long drag and lean against the wall, watching. *What the hell is going on?* Maybe a decree for my punishment has come down from on high and is far worse than I'd anticipated. *Maybe death by hemlock.* I didn't kill her, though. I simply stepped through the same loophole Vita did all those years ago. *Hey, what the hell do I care?* Any punishment was worth the price of seeing Vita squirm and knowing she'd never squirm again. I attempt to hold a straight face, but I can't feign solemnness for long before cracking a smile.

"I went out on a limb for you, allowing you to take Leah, and this is how I'm repaid," Thanatos finally says.

"My apologies if my actions caused you trouble. We both know if Vita hadn't fallen prey to her own deeds, she eventually would have killed me. And you, for one, would have missed me."

"Maybe." A small grin pushes at his lips then vanishes. "But actions have consequences, justified or not."

"So what's the punishment going to be? Something beastly, to be sure." I shudder dramatically.

"No." He sighs. "You must look at this from Death's point of view. I don't want you heading off into the night half-cocked, not that I seem to have any control of you and your insolence."

My mouth goes dry. "What's this about?"

"For what it's worth, swear you won't do anything rash."

"Sure, fine, whatever."

He takes another long puff on his cigar and lets ribbons of smoke pass through his lips. "Despite her dying request, Serevo will not be Vita's successor. Father says he's handpicking the successor himself. There are several quality choices—Valentino, Loris, Dina." He avoids my stare.

And Leah. The hairs on the back of my neck stand.

"Father will be treating us all as if we're ill-behaved children for a while," he grumbles. "You and Vita should have put the feud to rest a long time ago before this got so out of hand. What Vita did happened ages ago and should have been forgotten by now."

I growl. An icy cold throb chases away any lingering good humor.

Thanatos scowls. "You prove my point. Your fondness for family interferes with your duties, and one of these days, it's going to get you into trouble you can't get out of. This boy isn't the child you lost. Guilt and affection are powerful emotions. They'll make you choose paths you wouldn't otherwise. Be careful, Artagan."

I grimace and drop my cigarette to the stone floor then stomp out the smoldering ember with the heel of my shoe. "Vita deserved what she got."

In a gush of air, the oxygen is dragged from my lungs. And I know exactly whom this precursor announces—Death. And he's pissed. One of my hands grips the mantel to steady myself while the other clings to my throat. Fighting for breath, I watch Death step out of the shadows from the far corner.

"I hate when my children squabble amongst themselves." Death speaks without inflection. His maroon eyes dart between us. The air rushes back into my lungs. Struggling to hide my heaving chest, I haul in deep breaths.

Thanatos stands and bows his head.

I don't follow suit, playing my role to a T. Instead, I lean against the stone wall. Slipping my hands into my pockets, I swirl my ring—my escape plan—around my pinky and wish I had just one more cigarette.

Death rubs his long fingers along his stubbled chin and studies me. "Artagan, I'm glad you're here."

I grimace and brace for my punishment.

"You'll be managing the majority of the training of our newest council member. But I want all my children to have a hand in the instruction." His eyes snap to Thanatos. "You make sure my request is followed."

"Of course," Thanatos says with a nod.

I keep my poker face in place, hoping for the best but preparing for the worst. "I'll get started. So who's the lucky victor? May I recommend Dina. She's easy on the eyes," I say, pushing myself upright.

Death cocks his head to the side, looking at me under hooded brows. "No," he says flatly. A deep emptiness overtakes my stomach, and I grow cold as the blood drains from my face. Death grins at me with his warm, welcoming smile, and all I can do is smile back when he speaks the name. "I've chosen Leah Winters."

ACKNOWLEDGMENTS

They say it takes a village to raise a child. The same can be said about a book. Without the help of my village, My Soul Immortal would never have seen the light of day:

To my family, Craig, Liz, and Nicole, for putting up with my crazy ramblings and scribblings. Thank you for your love and support.

To the Red Adept Publishing team, especially my editors, Kris and Stefanie, whoe tireless efforts made my story a stronger one, and because of it, made me a better writer.

To Sarah, who believed in this book even before I did. Where would I be without your red pen?

To Audrey, for being my stress reliever.

To my beta readers—Andre, Tracy, Beth, Peter, Terry, Megan, Heidi, Judester, Mysti, Onkwehonwe, Renea, and Allison—for all your support and advise.

To Amy Eye, for helping me get my manuscript into shape, and to the countless others who have stood by me.

Made in the USA
Charleston, SC
19 March 2014